Isabelle

Under Earth Book 1

Isabelle

Under Earth Book 1

Nicholas Konz

Nicholas Konz

Des Moines

Visit www.nicholaskonz.com
Email nick@nicholaskonz.com

To my amazing wife Andrea,
without your love and encouragement this book would not have been possible.

Central Under Earth
Crystal Lake
Granite Castle
The Brightstone
Entrance to the Ruined City
Brightstone Valley
Father Times Home
Forest of Forgetfulness
Gateway
Mushrooms
The Colorful Forest
Guardian Cavern
Faries Tree House
Bakkara Attack
Crystal River
N
W
E
S

Table of Contents

Chapter 1

Disappearance

It was a cold evening in early spring. Clouds covered the sky and a light snow was falling. A white dusting could be seen covering the ground and sidewalks, cars, and houses. A slight breeze caused the falling flakes to float and swirl through the air before they came to rest on the ground.

In the middle of a city, in an older part of town, stood a large, quiet neighborhood. It was one of the first built after the city was founded. The houses, which all varied in size and shape, stood close together like a tight knit community. This neighborhood seemed unique to anyone not used to its winding streets and many dead ends and cul-de-sacs, because the streets flowed around the houses and properties instead of the houses being built on the ridged structure of the roads. There was only one long winding road making its way through the whole neighborhood. All of the other roads either lead to dead ends and cul-de-sacs or started and stopped only to start up again a block or two later. Some of the roads started on the same street they ended on making a U shape or started on one street only to turn like an L and stop on a different one. The lawns around the homes also ran together so it was hard to tell where one stopped and another began.

All in all, the neighborhood was a nice, quiet place to live. It was much older than the suburbs surrounding it, but was well taken care of and had more character. The people living in the neighborhood liked it that way. One could tell the neighborhood was filled with people who loved dogs because it seemed like every other house had one or more. On nice days after work it wasn't uncommon to see people with their dogs out for a nice, peaceful evening walk.

There were many older or retired people living in the neighborhood and quite a few young families just starting out, but not many families in the middle. There were only a handful of teenagers living in the neighborhood who went to the high school just to the west. Most of these teenagers, however, lived on the outskirts of the neighborhood and hung out with friends in other parts of the city. Only two were seen on a regular basis walking through the neighborhood.

On this night, like many others, they were found walking down the sidewalk of a small street named Iola. A young woman with wavy brown hair waited at the end of the street as a young man with short brown hair approached. As they met they took each other's hand and started to stroll down Iola with worried expressions on their faces. They talked together as they made their way down the street and as they did, their expressions changed from worried to sad and tearful.

When they reached midway down the block they stopped walking and embraced tightly, oblivious to the rest of the world. The only thing moving besides the gentle snow falling was their fogged breath going out into the cold air.

Then suddenly, they separated and, with a few parting words, the young woman started running down the block. After a few long seconds, the young man started running after her. He caught up fast and was a few yards from her when he stumbled and fell. When he looked up the young woman was gone. Vanished! He scrambled to his feet and made it to the end of the block in a few quick strides only to see she was nowhere in sight. Since Iola formed an L, it only met up with the street it started on and the street it ended on. The young man was in the middle at the bend and he could see the end of the street in both directions. The young woman was gone, too quick to have made it off the block. The young man looked at the light snow covering the sidewalk and saw two sets of prints leading up the way he had just come and only one set which continued another yard or so until they stopped right beside a large, old tree, which rested right next to the sidewalk.

"Isabelle," cried the young man as he spun around in search of his friend. Then he stopped. Just a few yards away stood an old man with white hair, angled features, and shadowed eyes. Their gaze met and all of a sudden, the young man turned and ran off into the darkening night.

Jacob Cross awoke with a start! He was sitting in his bed, his covers thrown about as if he had been thrashing around like a mad man and he could feel a cold sweat covering his body. He'd been having the nightmare again. Jake lay back in his bed staring up at his bedroom ceiling trying to catch his breath. He felt like he had just run a mile at full speed and tried to calm himself and his racing thoughts. His mind was still in sharp focus on the dream and his emotions were rolling. After giving himself a few minutes to calm and let reality come crashing back, he sat up and swung his legs from the bed. He felt his adrenaline drain only to be replaced by the all too familiar dull ache in his chest.

In truth the nightmare wasn't a dream at all, at least, not the crux of it. Isabelle, his best friend for as long as he could remember, was gone, disappearing on that fateful night one month ago. Even though Jake knew he would probably never see Isabelle again, not a moment had passed in the last month when Jake hadn't hoped to see her reappear. He longed for Isabelle to be back and safe even though he had no clue where she might be or what had happened to her.

Since then, Jake had been having the nightmares about it almost every time he closed his eyes. At first, it was just the memory of what had happened that night. After the first few nights, however, the dream started to change. Instead of just reliving what had happened in a dream, the dreams started taking more control. The one he had just woken from was the strangest yet. It was as if he was looking at the account of what had happened from a third person's point of view. He had been floating over the neighborhood and come down to see Isabelle and himself from above on the dimly lit street where the disappearance had occurred.

Jake wondered why the dreams were changing. It could be because his mind had always been quite imaginative. He hoped this was the reason because the only other explanation was that his mind was starting to crack under the stress. It had been a month and still no one believed him. Well, that wasn't exactly true. His closest friends TJ, Eric, and Patrick believed him. The day after Isabelle disappeared, all three of them had come out to help him look for her. Eric had even convinced most of the football team to help as well. His little sister Alisha also believed him, but all of the adults in his life were in denial. He didn't know why and it made him frustrated just thinking about it.

He knew what he'd seen that night. He was there and yet, even his own parents couldn't believe him. They wanted to, of course, but everyone else had convinced them he couldn't be right. It was so confusing. It came down to the fact that Isabelle's parents were lying, they had to be. But the reason eluded Jake. He and Isabelle had been best friends for a long time and her parents had always liked Jake. So why now, out of the blue, would they choose to cover up and lie about something they knew to be false and make him look crazy in the process? Jake had even overheard his parents talking about sending him to a counselor! He didn't blame them really; it made sense from their point of view. It didn't mean he had to like it though.

Jake shrugged and stood, stretching. He looked at his clock, it read 6:00. It was Sunday morning and he knew his parents wouldn't be up for another 30 minutes at least, since they didn't have to be to church until nine. Jake walked slowly over to his closet to grab some fresh clothes and then went and hopped in the shower. As the hot water rushed over him, he let his thoughts roll around and came to the same conclusion he had come to every other time he thought about it. He had to talk to Isabelle's parents and find out what was really going on.

The problem was, they refused to talk to Jake. He had to try again though. After his shower, Jake quickly dressed and put on a light jacket. If he left now, he would have time to go to Isabelle's house and get back before his parents wondered where he was. Jake stepped out into another cool spring morning. He took a deep breath of the cool fresh air and watched his breath turn into a cloud of fog as he exhaled. He started walking down the sidewalk looking at the thin layer of frost still covering the ground, that would soon melt with the rising sun. The trees were in the early stages of blooming and Jake tried enjoying his walk even though his heart was heavy.

It didn't take long to walk to Isabelle's house and Jake stood for a minute on the sidewalk in front, looking at the house. He knew he was early, but he also knew Isabelle's parents were usually early risers and they had probably been up for an hour or more already. The house was large and very beautiful. In fact, it was one of the nicest houses in the old neighborhood. It was always well taken care of, though right now there were a few signs things had been lax as of late. There was a pile of newspapers just to the right of the door, which looked as if they hadn't been touched since delivery, and the mail box attached to the house was unusually full. The house was quiet this morning but Jake decided to go ahead and try anyway.

Jake strolled up the front walk, opened the glass storm door, and knocked twice not wanting to ring the bell in case Isabelle's little sister Rachel was still asleep. Jake stood there for a few moments before, out of the corner of his left eye, he saw movement. Jake turned his head, but, by the time he looked, all he saw was the curtain falling back into place. He hoped it meant they would come to the door, but didn't really expect it. After another minute of waiting, Jake knocked again, but nothing happened and no one came back to the window to look.

Jake waited, knowing they weren't going to answer, but not wanting to give up yet. After a few more minutes, he reluctantly turned and walked home, his heart heavier than it had been before. He was hanging up his coat in the front closet when his father came down the stairs in his pajamas, bathrobe, and slippers.

"Morning Jake, did you just come in from outside?"

"Yeah, I just felt like a short walk this morning." Jake assured, not meeting his dad's gaze, knowing he'd probably already guessed where Jake had been.

"I'm going to make some coffee before breakfast, do you want some?" his dad asked, trying to sound light and cheerful even though Jake could hear the subtle worry in his voice.

"No thanks, I think I'll just go up to my room for a little bit." Jake responded, heading up the stairs.

"Ok," replied his dad as he turned for the kitchen.

It was a busy Sunday and Jake was thankful for that because it didn't give him a lot of time to ruminate over his thoughts for long. After breakfast and church, Jake's family went out to eat for lunch and then went to help a family from church move. Though Jake didn't particularly like helping people move, it was good to have something physical to do and keep his mind busy. His closest friends, TJ, Patrick, and Eric, along with their families, were there as well and so the day went by quickly. His friends knew what weighed heavy on his heart, but since they were under the watchful eyes of their parents they kept things light and distracted Jake from his thoughts.

TJ told jokes to keep the afternoon going. Jake didn't know how TJ remembered all of the jokes, but he knew a ton of them. He had a knack for it. He would tell them in such a way that even jokes they had heard before made them laugh like the first time they heard them.

Eric lightened the mood just by being himself. He was a big guy and could pick up almost anything they were moving alone, but it was very humorous to watch him try to fit himself and the large items through the door at the same time. His large arms would inevitably get in his way and he would have to try a couple approaches before he was able to get through. He would usually get annoyed before he would ask for help.

TJ always took advantage of this. While Eric was stood back trying to figure out how to get a large box through, TJ walked through with a box and made a sarcastic comment about how easy it was to go through a door. Eric rolled his eyes and looked at the box again.

"It says clothes. I think I can make this work." With that Eric proceeded to carefully, but forcefully, shove the box through the door. "When in doubt, brute force usually works!" he laughed.

Patrick tried his hand at a few jokes while they worked. This was entertaining as well because Patrick was the opposite of TJ in this regard. He was very smart and could remember just as many jokes but didn't have the ability to tell them well. The jokes always came out kind of forced sounding and usually made the others laugh because they were so corny or terrible that one couldn't believe someone had dared to tell them. Jake thought that he had this problem because he was so analytical he missed the humor. After he tried this and failed, Patrick began describing a book he was reading about American history. This, he excelled at. Patrick could talk about a topic that would have put the others to sleep, but the way he described and explained things created a discussion that lasted for the rest of the afternoon.

After the move was done and Jake went home with his family he was feeling pretty good. It wasn't until later that evening that Jake's mind went back to brooding over those black thoughts.

Chapter 2

Heartbreak

Sunday evening was dark and cool. Jake Cross sat in his bedroom on a bench built into his window nook, which overlooked the street in front of his house, a tear rolling down his cheek. This was the way it had been every night for the last month. As he sat looking out his window at the yellow glow of the lonely street lights shining dimly into the dark night, Jake's thoughts raced.

A knock at his bedroom door brought him back to his senses. "Jake honey, are you okay?"

Jake reached up with his right hand and wiped away the tears drying on his cheek. "Yeah, I'm alright," he choked, though he knew he didn't sound convincing.

The door to his room opened and light from the hallway spilled into his dark room. His mom poked her head in. She was a youthful looking woman in her forties with brown hair and eyes. Jake had always known her to be strong, able to cope with just about anything, but tonight as she smiled he could see the worry behind her gaze.

"We're going to bed now, but if you need anything just come and wake us," she encouraged as she opened the door and crossed the room. She gave him a hug and smiled, "We love you," as a tear rolled down her cheek. "Try to get some sleep tonight, okay?"

He nodded and she walked out of the room and shut his door quietly, leaving him alone to stare out the window. It was then the loneliness crept in. He knew his dad and mom were just going to bed in their room down the hall and his sister was asleep in her room at the other end of the hall. He knew they loved him very much. He even knew he had a lot of friends from church and school who cared about him and he would see most of them tomorrow. But right now, alone in his room with the dim streetlight coming in through his window and the still night outside, Jacob Cross felt very alone.

Here, with only his thoughts to keep him company, Jake thought about Isabelle. For the last month she had been the only topic his mind would think about. It wasn't just that he had lost his best friend; it felt like he lost his future too. He loved Isabelle. From the time they met when they were just two kids playing on a playground until now he had always thought she was unlike any girl he'd ever met. As the years progressed and they got older, he decided eventually he would ask her to marry him. He couldn't imagine even considering anyone else. It was her. She was the only one, and now she was gone. His future was gone.

With nowhere else to go, his mind, like countless times before, took Jake back to the night Isabelle disappeared. Tomorrow would be one month and still no sign of her, no lead for the police to follow. Not that they were looking anyway, Isabelle's parents had seen to that!

Isabelle called him that evening a month ago sounding worried. She had asked Jake to meet her on Iola, one of their favorite places to meet. Iola was a neat little street buried deep inside their neighborhood. It was a quiet street with many retired people who lived there. Isabelle told Jake once that she liked walking down this particular street because it reminded her of a place pulled from a storybook. The houses were built close together, many of them with a small cottage feel. Most were small with beautiful landscaping and plant gardens. Some of the houses didn't even have lawns because they were filled with intricately placed plants and pathways through them, a tribute to the love of gardening.

Most of the houses were of varying styles, but Isabelle always thought any one of them could have been in a Disney story like *Sleeping Beauty* or *Snow White*. They were the type of houses that would look perfect standing alone in the middle of a forest clearing.

Jake hurried to meet her, throwing on a coat to ward off the cold air and few snowflakes falling to the ground. He was in such a rush that he forgot to grab his phone before he left. She was already there waiting for Jake when he arrived. She smiled, but Jake could tell she was sad. He took her hand and they slowly started to walk down the street. It was a quiet night with only the sound of a slight breeze to keep them company. Normally Jake would have enjoyed a night walk like this, but was too concerned about what was bothering Isabelle.

"What's wrong?" he asked breaking the silence of the night.

"We're moving," Isabelle whispered so quiet Jake almost didn't catch it.

"Moving?" Jake asked slowing to a stop about halfway down the street.

Isabelle turned to face him and he could see a tear starting to make its way down her cheek. She stood there with her brown wavy hair, hazel eyes, and green jacket. Her pretty face wrinkled with sorrow. Jake couldn't remember ever seeing her sad like this before, which only caused the knot forming in his stomach to tighten immeasurably.

"Why?" asked Jake with worry creeping into his voice.

It took a minute for Isabelle to answer, as she tried to calm herself, wiping away her tears. Then she let it all out like a dam breaking from too much water. "I don't know. My dad just told me about forty-minutes ago. When I got home from school my parents were hurrying around the house, packing bags with stuff like we were going on a trip. It was weird, so I asked my dad what they were doing. Without even looking up, he told me we were moving. I didn't believe him at first and just stood there for a minute watching them both running around packing. They looked scared. I asked him why and all he would say is we needed to. I asked him where we were moving and he just remarked, '*far away*,' like he wasn't even sure. He told me we would be leaving in the morning and I should go start packing anything I might need for a few days because anything left the movers would pack and bring to us in a week."

This new information hit Jake like a ton of bricks. He remembered he could barely breathe and felt like the wind had been knocked out of him. He looked at Isabelle and tears started running down her cheeks. Jake stepped close to her and she leaned into him, letting him hold her in a tight embrace. Her head rested on his shoulder and he felt her shake as she sobbed in his arms. He felt her warm tears wet his neck as she buried her face into it and cried.

Neither one said anything for a few minutes, both content to just hold each other. After a few more minutes, her sobs quieted and she pulled away, wiping her tears with the sleeve of her coat. "I wasn't supposed to tell anyone this, not even you! My dad stated it wasn't safe for me to let anyone know or tell anyone goodbye, but I couldn't bear not telling you. I was so angry I shouted at him to leave me alone and I ran to my room and slammed the door. They came up to make sure I was packing. I started throwing clothes into a suitcase and they left. That's when I called you and snuck out my window to meet you. I have to get back soon or they will realize I'm gone."

Jake remembered just standing there dumbstruck. He couldn't think of anything to say. The girl of his dreams and friend he had known for so long and had so many memories with gone. The young woman he wanted to spend the rest of his life with someday was leaving. It seemed unbelievable and yet, here she was standing in front of him telling him it was true.

"I don't believe it! This can't be happening. Why won't your parents tell you where you're going or even tell anyone you're moving? It just doesn't make sense."

Isabelle stepped back in and gave him another quick hug, her tears coming back anew. "I love you," she cried and then drew away. "Don't follow me home or my parents will know I came to talk to you. Wait an hour and then come over like you are just coming to visit. Maybe then my parents will be forced to tell us more. I've got to go. Come over in an hour," she sputtered again through the tears.

Jake watched as she turned and started running toward home. He remembered just standing there, rooted in place. Looking back, he should have run after her immediately and he might have prevented what came next, but he didn't. He couldn't think. He stood in indecision, unable to get his brain to work. Should he run after her? Should he go home and meet her later. The moment seemed like it was in slow motion. Then a thought crossed his mind. What if her parents changed their minds? What if whatever was making them run scared made them decide to leave tonight instead of in the morning. This might be the last time he saw her. He wasn't going to let that happen. She might be angry with him later and he might get her in trouble with her parents, but right now he needed to go after her.

Jake snapped out of it and started trying to catch up with her. He could see Isabelle nearing the bend in the road and could tell she must still be crying because she wasn't running as fast as she could and kept bringing her hands up to her face like she was wiping the tears away so she could see. He was having a little trouble seeing himself on account of the snowflakes hitting his eyes. It was starting to snow heavier. He was catching up surprisingly quick and was almost to the large bend where the street and sidewalk turned to give Iola its L shape. Suddenly, his foot caught on an uneven part of the sidewalk and Jake fell. He put his arms down to touch the ground and rolled to his left to lessen the impact of the fall. He scrambled back to his feet and whipped around to continue running, but stopped. He lost sight of Isabelle.

Jake remembered seeing her in the middle of the bend in the road right before he fell, but now he couldn't see her anywhere. He knew she couldn't have made it all the way down the block that quickly. Jake scanned the street again, but could only see the steadily falling snow . That was it! He looked down at the sidewalk covered in a dusting of snow. He could see both of their tracks coming up the sidewalk, but past him only one set continued. He followed Isabelle's tracks to the middle of the bend where they stopped right next to a large, old, dead-looking tree. He looked around again, but the tracks just stopped with no sign of Isabelle or where she had gone.

Jake remembered yelling her name and then he heard something behind him. He turned and saw the old man who lived in the brick house behind the large tree just standing a few feet away near the edge of the sidewalk. He stood there watching Jake with his dark eyes, white hair, and a shovel in his hand. Jake remembered in that moment he had felt terrified, sure the old man was responsible for Isabelle's disappearance, and his mind told him to do one thing. Run! Run get help!

Now, back in his room a month later, Jake's mind couldn't take any more remembering, any more loneliness, or any more pain. He got up from his seat in the window, stumbled over to his bed and crumpled into it crying. He buried his face into his pillow and cried himself to sleep.

Chapter 3

Iola

Jake awoke the next morning to bright sun shining through his window. He rolled out of bed still feeling drained like he hadn't slept much. He looked down and saw he was still wearing his clothes from the day before, now all twisted and wrinkled. Then he remembered he'd cried himself to sleep again. The sharp pain that had coursed through his chest last night was replaced this morning by a dull, empty ache.

His parents were busy getting ready for work and he heard his sister walking down the hall toward his room, the creaks in the old flooring getting louder as she neared. She knocked on his door.

"Come in," he invited, his voice still groggy.

The door opened and Alisha appeared with a big smile on her face. She stood looking at Jake with her blue eyes and straight blond hair shining in the sunlight coming through his window. She was 10, six years younger than Jake, but he always thought she seemed more mature than any kid he knew. Maybe it was her optimism or positive attitude toward life, or maybe it was her knack for encouraging people, Jake wasn't sure. The one thing he did know was she had been one of his best supports over the last month. They didn't always get along, but since Isabelle's disappearance, she had been able to encourage him more than anyone else.

His friends, parents, pastor, and even the counselor he had been seeing had all tried helping, but no one had the knack for it like his sister. She just always knew what to say.
He could tell, even now, she had something on her mind. She walked over and sat down beside him on his bed. She was holding one of her books full of mazes. Since she was

four or five she had always enjoyed solving mazes. Jake looked at the wall. "I feel like I'm trapped in one of your mazes, only this one has no way out."

"Don't worry Jake," she exclaimed in a cheerful voice. "I know it has been hard for you, but I think something is different today."

Jake turned and looked at his sister sitting beside him and wondered what she could mean. She turned to look at Jake and smiled. "I think things are going to change for the better today. Just listen to your heart and trust in the One who made you. If you do that I think you'll find your way out." With that, she winked, gave him a quick hug, and left.

Jake just sat there knowing she meant well, but not understanding what she implied. His family had attended church for as long as he could remember, but Jake still wasn't sure what he thought about it. He didn't mind going because his closest friends went as well. He knew all the Bible stories and all the right things to say, but wasn't sure they were anything more than just stories. Alisha, on the other hand, believed whole heartedly and everything she did revolved around her faith. Jake was truly proud of his sister. Even though he wasn't sure what he believed, he saw a faith in Alisha even most adults in his church didn't have. It made him long for that kind of faith too!

Jake knew his sister was telling him to trust God, but he didn't see how that was going to help. Isabelle had been gone for a month. Surely if God was there and He was going to help, He would have done so already. Even so, Jake whispered a quick prayer asking God to help him find out what happened to Isabelle and that she was safe. He figured it might not amount to anything, but it couldn't hurt anything either.

Jake shrugged it off and got up to get ready for school. He hopped into the shower and let the warm water wash away the worries from the night before. After brushing his teeth, he threw on a shirt and jeans, grabbed his bag with his school books, and ran downstairs for breakfast still thinking about what his sister had said. He was planning on asking her just what she had meant by following his heart until he pulled up in the kitchen and found a note from his mom.

Jake,

I had to take your sister in for a Dentist appointment this morning and your dad had to leave for an early meeting at work. Here is some breakfast for you and your lunch is in the fridge. Have a good day and we'll see you later. We love you! Mom…P.S. There's a note attached to your lunch bag. I found it stuck in the front door. One of your friends must have dropped it by last night. I didn't know what it meant, but figured you would.

Strange, his friends didn't usually leave him notes. Eric and Patrick usually called first and TJ would knock as a warning and then come right in like he owned the place. Jake walked over to the fridge and took out the paper bag with his lunch inside. On the front was a small, folded, white piece of paper. He opened it up and it read:

Jake, meet me at the tree after school. – T

The handwriting didn't look familiar. It must be from TJ, but Jake wasn't sure what he was talking about. TJ had been one of Jakes best friends since the fourth grade. They had done everything together from school, to sports, and even family vacations. They were practically brothers. That was why a note was weird. TJ would have just walked in the door if he'd come over, not leave a note. Jake made a mental note to ask TJ when he got to school.

Not being very hungry for breakfast, Jake put the cereal away and grabbed an apple before pulling on his jacket while running out the door. The first thing Jake noticed when he left his house was that he should have grabbed an umbrella. There was a light rain coming down and one look up at the dark storm clouds suggested it would probably start to rain harder any minute. That's strange, thought Jake as he walked down his street and took a left, it was sunny when he woke up. The storm must be moving quick because he couldn't see any trace of the sun, just low grey/black clouds. He kept walking, knowing his hard leather jacket would keep him mostly dry.

The second thing Jake noticed was that it was abnormally dark for this time of day. He knew it was because of the clouds, but it almost looked like dusk outside. Even the streetlights were fooled as they started to flicker on and gradually came to life. Jake turned right down the main road through his neighborhood, feeling the thick air around him. It was cool air, but felt very humid and there was a low fog starting to creep in.

Jake walked to school almost every day. He used to hate the fact his parents wouldn't drop him off, but after a couple of years he relished the time to walk and think. He used to pick Isabelle up about half way when she could talk her parents into letting her leave early and walk. The dull ache Jake had almost forgotten about came back and stuck in his chest.

As he continued down Kingman with its tall trees and many houses, Jake noticed it was abnormally quiet. Except for the rain and some deep rolling thunder, he couldn't hear anything but his own feet on the wet sidewalk. He didn't expect to see anyone walking because of the storm, but he hadn't even seen a car pass, which was unusual, because this was the main street through his neighborhood. The glow of the streetlights gave the dark morning an eerie look.

Suddenly Jake's heart sank. He was nearing the corner of Iola. Jake feared to go down that street now and usually just walked past looking the other way, continuing on to school. He stopped. Maybe it was the night he'd had last night or maybe it was the storm, but Jake suddenly felt scared. It was a raw fear unlike anything he'd felt before. Usually he avoided Iola because he was afraid of the memories the place would dredge up, but this time he was truly afraid. He could feel his heart quicken and the blood pulse through his head causing a slight dizziness as he walked. Jake couldn't place where this fear was coming from, but he knew he couldn't be late for school so he made himself continue on.

As he neared the corner of Kingman and Iola, Jake felt the fear constricting like a snake coiling around his chest. He stopped on the corner of Kingman and Iola and willed himself to go on and look straight ahead, but he couldn't. He was afraid to move but the fear was drawing him, no, compelling him to look down Iola. Jake turned his head and a shiver went down his spine.

Iola was dark. Much darker than Kingman or any other street he'd passed. Jake looked up and saw that none of the streetlights on Iola were on. That could be part of the reason for the darkness. Were they all burned out? Not likely. Even the small amount of light coming through the grey clouds dissipated before reaching this street. It looked almost like the air surrounding the street was absorbing the light keeping everything inside dark.

Jake could faintly see outlines of the houses nearest him on the street, but none of them had their lights on that he could tell. The urge to run away from this street was tearing at his senses and screaming through his mind like he was standing in front of a semi watching it bear down on him and yet, he was frozen in place. His heart was pulling him toward the unknown, toward the terrible darkness. Suddenly, Jake heard the words his sister had spoken just a short while ago…trust your heart! Jake wasn't sure this is what she had meant, but the longer he stood there, the more he was compelled to go down this street even though every ounce of reason he had screamed no! Iola. The place where it seemed the world as he knew it had ended.

Jake knew he would already be late for school now even if he ran. Pushing aside the consequences of being late or skipping school Jake took a step down Iola. He was now at the very spot where he'd left Iola, running for help the night Isabelle disappeared.

There was a low rumble of thunder from directly overhead causing Jake to jump. He walked slowly, scanning the street for anything out of the ordinary. After walking a few yards, he was surrounded by the darkness and he stopped. Looking back, Jake could see Kingman still glowing from the light of the street lamps, but none of it reached him now only about nine feet away. It was as if an invisible curtain was hung at the end of Iola, blocking the light from entering. Jake turned back to Iola, the sprinkle from the dark clouds above turning to a light rain. Still, that eerie silence continued.

Jake watched as the rain padded softly onto the plants and sidewalk, street and houses. The slight fog had condensed too and now rose to Jake's knees, making it hard to see the ground. He pressed on, looking from side to side at the dark houses on either side.

A cottage-style house to Jake's right stood silently, its old stone walls half overgrown with ivy. He strained to see any sign of life, but it remained quiet. He looked left across the street and saw a carpenter-style house with its grey stucco and red-tiled roof standing just as quiet, the old rocker on its covered porch was the only sign a person even lived there. Jake could only see a couple of houses on either side because of the darkness, so he walked slowly to see the new shapes coming out of the darkness. Jake couldn't make himself believe all of these people had coincidentally gone on vacation at the same time, leaving this street this deserted. Jake had walked this street enough at night to know, even if they were gone or asleep, the older folks who lived in these houses usually left some lights on at all times. The whole scene before him seemed surreal. His nerves were on edge.

After a couple of minutes of walking and carefully scanning each storybook house as they came into view, Jake saw the shape of the old log cabin-style house emerge from the darkness to his right. The long ranch-style house with its walls made of large round logs stood just as silently and lonely as every other house he'd passed. Seeing this house, Jake knew he was almost to the corner where Iola turned. Just past this house was the corner with the large old tree where the disappearance had occurred.

Jake didn't think the fear could get any worse, but it did. It wrapped itself tightly around him and his pulse continued to quicken, making his nerves raw and on edge. Before going on, Jake turned and looked over his shoulder toward Kingman. It was gone, or at least covered by the darkness. Jake couldn't even see a faint light from the streetlights he knew must be there only a block away. Everything was dark and Jake could still only see a couple of houses either way down the street.

Suddenly, out of nowhere, Jake heard music. He could feel the blood drain from his face and for a moment he thought his heart had stopped. It was a low mournful song and sent new chills down Jake's spine with each note. If he wasn't mistaken, Jake thought it was coming from somewhere near the corner. He pressed on, a slight breeze now starting to stir the trees and blowing the fog in swirls over the ground.

Nearing the corner, Jake could see the outline of the old tree starting to take shape out of the darkness. It looked even larger in this darkness with its massive trunk jutting into the air and its large branches reaching out. Behind the tree, the large old Tudor-style house where the white haired old man lived also came into view.

Jake felt a new chill as the water from his soaked brown hair started running down his neck and under his jacket, sending trickles down his back. His jeans were already wet and the cool air gave him a slight chill. It was raining steadily now and Jake wiped his face with his hands, trying to clear the rainwater running down his face. He stopped a few feet away from the tree, still looking around, trying to find the source of the music that was making his skin crawl with each passing second. It seemed like it was coming from everywhere and nowhere at the same time. Jake turned and glanced back the way he'd come and suddenly the music was directly behind him. Then it stopped! Jake spun back around and there, next to the sidewalk, in the exact same spot he'd been the night of Isabelle's disappearance, stood the old man with white hair.

Chapter 4

The Gateway

Jake just stood there in the darkness, staring at the old man, and feeling a chill from his now soaking clothes. The old man just stared back and Jake noticed an unusual instrument in his right hand. It was about the size of a flute or recorder, but was all twisted and misshapen. Could this have been the source of the noise? Jake found it hard to believe an instrument so small could make such a low and mournful sound, but the music had stopped just before he'd seen the old man.

Now, looking at the mysterious old man, Jake was just as sure as he ever had been that the old man knew more than he admitted. The night of the disappearance, when Jake had seen the old man, he couldn't understand how Isabelle had vanished. He remembered thinking the old man must have taken her, but dismissed the thought immediately, because, even the old man wouldn't have had time to catch and hide her in the couple of seconds Jake had fallen. The old man had just stood there staring, with his shovel in hand and a look of concern on his face.

So Jake had turned and fled, thinking the only explanation was that somehow he just hadn't seen Isabelle leave the block. Maybe when he'd tripped, he had fallen down and not gotten up as quickly as he thought. Whatever the reason, Jake thought his best chance of finding Isabelle was to go to her house and see if she had somehow returned home. But she hadn't. When he arrived at the Stevenson house and knocked on the door, Isabelle's father Jonathan answered. In between breaths of gasping for air Jake had managed to ask if Isabelle had returned. Jonathan immediately asked what Jake meant while her mother Sarah ran to check her room. When she returned and shook her head, Jonathan demanded to know what had happened. So Jake recounted their walk and, when he mentioned where they had been and how Isabelle had vanished, Jonathan just fell to his knees looking mortified. Sarah started to cry, collapsing onto the couch. Jake didn't know what to make of their reaction so he immediately grabbed their phone and called 911.

Just before the police arrived, Sarah knelt beside her husband and Jake overheard Jonathan tell her in a whisper, "We should have left sooner. It's too late; the police can't help us now. No one can." Then Jake watched, confused as they forced themselves to calm down, dry their tears, and started acting like nothing had happened.

Isabelle's parents took their youngest daughter Rachel, who had been sleeping in the large living room chair, up to bed. They then calmly asked Jake to step outside for a few minutes. Jake didn't understand why, but complied because they asked. About five minutes later they let him back in and he was astonished. Their home looked normal again. All of the items they had packed were now gone, put away, or hidden from view. He also noticed the Stevenson's look of desperation and brokenness at his news had been replaced with a look of concern for him.

Before the police arrived they started asking him if he was sure of what he had seen.

"Yes, of course I'm sure," Jake replied, indignant.

Mr. Stevenson looked at Jake and shook his head. "That's impossible Jake, Isabelle left this morning to stay with her cousin across the country. Jessica is very sick and Isabelle went to encourage her and help her mother take care of her while finishing her school year by being home schooled there. We let your school know this morning."

Jake couldn't believe what he was hearing. He knew he had just come from seeing Isabelle disappear and knew Mr. Stevenson was lying, but before he could respond, there was a knock on the door. Mr. Stevenson calmly went to the door and opened it, ushering in the police officer.

The officer took his hat off and put it under his arm. "Sorry to disturb you tonight sir, but we received a call from this address saying that there was a missing person."

Jake jumped in, "That was me officer, I called."

The officer turned to Jake and then looked back at Mr. Stevenson. "Is this your son?"

"No, he is a friend of our daughter's, but I think he is confused. Our daughter isn't missing." Mr. Stevenson replied sounding calm.

"That's a lie!" Jake yelled.

The officer turned to Jake and held up his hand. "Son, I will listen to you, but you need to calm down."

Jake reigned in his impulse to continue yelling. Once the officer saw that he was in control of himself again, he motioned for Jake to continue. Jake recounted what occurred earlier in the evening while the officer listened and took down a few notes.

"Okay, I think I have what I need for now," the officer stated, turning to Mr. Stevenson. "So if I understand this right, you don't believe your daughter is missing Mr. Stevenson?"

Jonathan Stevenson looked at Jake with a calm and pitying expression before replying to the officer. "I know she isn't missing officer. I know Jake, and he is usually a very kind and level-headed young man, but I don't understand what he is talking about."

Jake was about to object again, but the officer held up his hand and gave him a look of warning. "I have listened to your account son and now you will be quiet while I listen to Mr. Stevenson or I will escort you off the property. Please continue Mr. Stevenson."

Mr. Stevenson told the officer the same thing he had told Jake, but with even more detail. He sounded very convincing and even Mrs. Stevenson chimed in, sounding completely truthful. If Jake hadn't witnessed Isabelle's disappearance himself, he would have believed Mr. and Mrs. Stevenson's story also.

After he finished, Mr. Stevenson called his sister and put her on the phone with the officer. She must have corroborated the story because, when the officer hung up, he turned to Jake. "I'm sorry son, but your story doesn't add up. Do you have any witnesses?"

Jake just stood there stunned. He couldn't even think. None of this made any sense.

"Son, I'm going to have to ask you to leave. I don't know why you are telling this story, but you have no proof and no one can corroborate your story. I will call the school tomorrow to see if they can confirm that Mr. Stevenson did in fact tell them about Isabelle's leave of absence, but if they do, I will have no choice but to close the investigation."

Suddenly, Jake remembered! "The old man! The old man that lives on the corner of Iola behind the dead tree! He saw it too, or maybe he had something to do with it, I don't know, but you need to talk to him!"

The police officer looked very doubtful. "I'll go talk to him, but you need to go home now."

Jake wanted to object, but received another warning look from the officer. He left the Stevenson's home, furious. In hind sight, it only made him look less credible to the officer. He had run home and told his family, but the next day he learned that the old man told the police officer hadn't seen anything. The investigation was promptly closed and the officer had told Jake to stay away from the Stevenson's.

So, now Jake glared at the old man, sure he was involved in Isabelle's disappearance or the cover up. With that thought, an anger flared up inside Jake and he stepped toward the old man and was about to demand to know what he'd seen that night when the old man spoke.

"You're early," the old man spoke in a calm, even voice.

Jake was taken aback! Early? What was this crazy white-haired man talking about? Of all the things the man could have declared, this was completely unexpected. Jake felt his anger fade away and it was replaced by curiosity. He could never have anticipated that statement. "What do you mean I'm early?" Jake asked.

"Didn't you get my note?"

Jake thought for a second and then remembered the note in his pocket. He reached in and withdrew it. He opened it up and looked at it again. The rain had already gotten it wet and the writing was a bit blurred, but Jake could still read it well enough. "You're T?"

"My name is Tobias, and you had better come inside and dry off or you'll catch a cold. You don't want that with the long journey ahead of you." With that the old man turned and headed across his yard to the front steps of his large Tudor house with its tall sides and angled peaks.

Jake knew he shouldn't follow this guy, he didn't know anything about him. This whole morning had been strange and just kept getting worse. However, if he didn't follow him Jake might never get his questions answered. Jake knew he was taking a big risk and his parents would be furious if they knew what he was about to do, but he felt the same compulsion pulling him after this old man as he had to come down this dark, cursed street. If worse came to worst, Jake figured he could escape fairly easily. Even if he wasn't strong enough, he was fast enough to get away if the old man were to try something.

Jake knew it was foolish to follow this man, but his heart pulled him to go on. If there was even a small chance he knew something about Isabelle, Jake would find out. He looked up at the house, which stood as a dark shape in the storm. Jake could barely make out its stone front and brick sides. The old man had gone inside without looking back, apparently unconcerned whether or not Jake followed. He took a few steps toward the house and saw the door remained open. Jake made his decision and walked across the lawn, up the porch steps, and through the dark door into the house.

As soon as Jake stepped inside, his eyes started to water and he squinted. He hadn't been prepared for the light filling the room, since he had been in near pitch black once he started walking down Iola. He suddenly thought this was a trick so the old man could get a jump on him, so he frantically blinked and wiped his eyes with one hand while swinging his other arm outward defensively.

"It's okay," the old man's voice responded from across the room. "I didn't ask you to come in so I could harm you. Just wait a minute and let your eyes adjust."

Jake felt his heart rate calm and made himself relax. As his eyes adjusted, Jake started to see what the room he was in looked like. He stood on a small rug in the doorway of what appeared to be the old man's living room. Tobias stood near the opposite wall half facing Jake and half facing the large fireplace in the center of the wall. The fire was ablaze, creating most of the light in the room. Tobias stood behind one of two chairs that were angled in front of the fireplace so that people could sit in them and talk while they watched the fire. There was a medium-sized square table in between them.

To Jake's left was a staircase that went up a few steps to a landing and then turned to right to go upstairs. A polished cherry railing followed them up on one side with the outer wall of the house on the other. Underneath the stairs were book cases built into the wall and they extended from floor to the underside of the stairs, except at the other side of the room where the stairs ended and they reached the ceiling. There were two doors, one in each of the back corners of the room, leading to the kitchen and other rooms in the back of the house.

The fireplace, with its large intricately carved mantle, was centered between the doors on the back wall. More bookshelves were built into the wall on either side of the fireplace, framing it in. In the center of the room was a large red and green rug upon which sat a rectangular coffee table. Two chairs were on either side of the table and a couch sat behind it across from the fire place. The coffee table was littered with books and papers. The wall on the far right had two large windows that went from floor to ceiling and overlooked the side yard. Dark heavy curtains hung over them and down their sides, framing them in. In between the two windows was a small round table, which held the strange instrument the old man had been carrying.

The large front window looked much like the side windows going from floor to ceiling with the same dark curtains around it. It had a wooden framework inside it, making it appear to be made up of a hundred smaller windows.

Jake thought it was strange the curtains were open and yet he hadn't seen the light from outside. The old man couldn't have come in and lit a fire or even opened the curtains that quickly.

"It is not a normal storm raging outside keeping the light hidden. Please, come and sit for a few minutes, we have much to discuss."

Jake closed the door and crossed the room. He took his coat and backpack off, put them on the arm of the chair nearest him, and sat down, facing the fireplace and shivered, still a little unsure about this man.

"Please wait here while I get some tea. It will help warm you while you dry." With that the old man walked through the door behind Jake.

Strange, Jake thought as he sat near the fire. He should feel the heat from the fireplace, which was only a few feet away, and yet he sat there shivering just as cold as he was outside. Jake let his gaze wander to the bookshelf closest to the fireplace. Most of the books looked very old and worn. Some were so dust covered they looked as if they hadn't been read in ages. His gaze drifted over the spines seeing if there were any he could recognize.

There were many books on history and mythology. One large gold book was titled *Egypt: A Comprehensive Study of Its History and Beliefs*. Another book that caught Jakes eye read

The History of Ancient Greece with a book beside it simply titled *Greek Mythology*. Jake continued to look at the books until the old man returned. He noticed a few of the books even were in a foreign language with strange lettering and symbols on their covers.

When the old man came back in he was carrying a round platter with a small, loose leaf tea pot and two small mugs without handles. He set the platter on the table between the chairs and poured the tea into the mugs. He then took one and sat in the chair opposite Jake and took a sip out of it. "Please, have some tea," invited the old man gesturing to the other mug with his free hand, "it will help."

Jake had never really been a fan of tea, but if it would help with this chill, which was keeping him cold, he would try it. He reached out, took the mug, and had a small sip. The tea was pleasantly sweet, though Jake couldn't place its flavor, and as soon as it slid down his throat Jake could feel its warmth start to spread through him. As if the tea had broken a spell, he could now feel the warmth of the fire drying his skin and clothes. Energized by the tea, he continued to sip as the old man watched him. He even felt the sharp fear that had been nagging him since he'd set foot on Iola start to fade.

The old man finished his tea and set his mug down, folding his long skeleton like hands into his lap as his white hair shone in the light from the fire. "Why did you come?" the old man asked, looking intently at Jake.

Jake figured he may as well just get to the point. Besides, the tea had put him at ease and he figured if the old man had really wanted to harm him he would have done so already. "I think you saw something the night my friend disappeared, or at least know more than what you told the police."

"I'm afraid I only saw what you did."

"What do you mean?" asked Jake. He could feel himself becoming frustrated, but remembered he was the guest and he didn't want to be thrown out before he had the answers he'd come in for.

"On the night the young lady disappeared, the only thing I saw was the two of you running. I saw you trip and fall. Once you had regained your footing, I watched you run up and go past the tree and heard you call out your friend's name. It was only then I realized you were looking for someone. That is when you turned and saw me."

"I don't believe you!" Jake snapped, allowing the bitterness in his voice to convey his meaning.

"Ah," the old man replied, raising his bushy white eyebrows and pointing one long finger at Jake, "that is the reason I have asked you here today. I don't want to trick you and I have nothing to hide, but you must choose to believe in the information I give you or it will be meaningless and you will walk away even more frustrated than when you came."

"What do you mean?"

"I think I know how your friend disappeared."

Jake grabbed the arms of the chair he was sitting in with both hands, ready to spring up. "Why didn't you tell me this sooner? Why didn't you yell after me that night and keep me from running off so I could have found her right away?" Jake was almost yelling now, but he didn't care. He had been in anguish over what had happened to Isabelle and all the time this man had known something that could have helped! Guest or no guest, he was about to stand up and yell at Tobias, demanding he tell Jake what he needed to know when the old man put both hands up in a surrender motion. Jake stopped short.

"Jake, I know this must be upsetting for you, but I need you to remain calm and listen to me. I will tell you everything you need to know for now; but if you continue to get angry and interrupt me, I'll never get finished. Now please, sip your tea and let me continue."

Jake was still frustrated, but he thought Tobias was telling the truth and he knew it would take longer if he kept interrupting; so Jake took a moment to calm himself and sat back in the chair. "Okay, go ahead."

Tobias looked as if he was trying to figure out if Jake had calmed down and then continued. "Now, what I am about to tell you is going to sound foolish, but I need you to hear me out. I didn't tell this to you until now because I needed you to be desperate."

Jake's anger flared. "I have been desperate ever since Isabelle disappeared!" Jake yelled before he had the chance to stop himself.

The old man sighed and closed his eyes.

Jake realized his mistake and immediately let go of his anger. He had to hear what this man was going to say so he apologized. "I'm sorry; I didn't mean to lash out again. I promise I will listen without interrupting from this point on, you have my word."

Tobias looked up at Jake and then continued, "I know you felt desperate before, but you were not desperate enough to believe me. I knew the only way to get you to listen to the truth was by letting you try all the normal ways people react to this type of situation. Once you had found out the police couldn't help and you had nowhere else to turn, you would be more inclined to listen to me."

Jake raised his hand not wanting to interrupt but knowing he had to ask the question on his mind.

"It's okay, go ahead Jake."

"What do you mean normal?"

Tobias' right eyebrow shot up. "Does the darkness outside this house seem natural Jake? What about the chill that didn't seem to go away even next to the fire, or the unnatural fear that told you to run away from this street even though you were compelled to enter?"

Wow, thought Jake, how could this old man have possibly known all the things Jake had been thinking and feeling in the last few minutes?

"The reason the police can't help you is because your friend Isabelle disappeared through supernatural means."

This statement didn't shock Jake like he thought it should. Although he didn't necessarily buy it he couldn't deny it either. Maybe it was because of the wind storm this morning or maybe something else. Something he had tucked away in his memories he had forgotten about. Then, it hit him! Isabelle's father Jonathan had muttered something to this effect the night she disappeared. He hadn't mentioned anything supernatural, but Jake did remember him saying the police couldn't help and both of her parents acted like there was no hope even before the police had arrived.

"I believe you," Jake admitted, realizing he meant it.

Tobias smiled and leaned forward. "Good, now, there is a place few people alive today know about and even fewer have seen. I call it *Under Earth*, though what its rightful name is I don't know. It is a world deep beneath the surface of the earth, probably near its core. I believe this is where your friend Isabelle was taken and it is also the place you must go to find her."

"How do you know this?"

"Now is not the time for me to explain that. It would take too long and I believe you need to hurry or your opportunity to get there will be gone. Perhaps, if all goes well, I can tell you my story later."

"Okay, this does sound completely unbelievable to say the least, but I don't have any other answers; so, let's say I believe you, how would I get to this place?"

"I can help you find the passage, though the rest is up to you."

Jake sat for a few minutes in silence, finishing his tea and taking the time to think about what the white-haired man had stated. He had warmed back up and his clothes were mostly dry now.

Jake took one last sip of his tea and stood. "I'll have to talk to my parents and let them know first, and then you can show me how to get there."

"I'm afraid that's not possible," Tobias protested with concern in his gaze. "There isn't time. I have opened the gateway for you but, if you do not choose to take it now, I will allow it to close. The reason for this is simple. If you go talk to your parents, they will not believe you. Then you will not be allowed to come back and I may even get in trouble for telling you all of this. If that happens, your friend is most certainly lost for good. You must decide now whether or not to take the door because, if you decide not to take it, it will close and never again be open to you. The music you heard earlier came from the instrument on the stand near the windows. When I played the song it opened the passage between here and Under Earth. I am the gate keeper, but the rest is up to you. This is why I didn't tell all of this to you before. Had I let you know and opened the door before you were ready, you might have chosen not to believe me and your opportunity would be gone. Now that I have opened the door, however, if you choose to believe what I say is true and go through it you will be able to use the passage whenever you need without my assistance. Tell me Jake, are you a man of faith?"

The question seemed strange to Jake. "I go to church if that's what you mean."

"No, that's not what I'm talking about. There are people who attend their church, synagogue, or mosque, but that's where it stops. Then there are the people who show their faith not by their religion, but by the actions and decisions they make. It is this type of faith I believe you will need to finish this journey you are on. You need to be not only willing to believe the things I have told you are true, but act on them as well. This is the difference between belief and faith."

"I don't understand, I thought you were helping me find Isabelle, what does faith have to do with it?"

"More than you realize right now."

"For that matter, why can't you just take me to her and help me get her back?"

The old man frowned; "I'm sorry Jake, but as I told you before, I can't go with you and I don't have the time to explain why. I can tell you that I believe Isabelle is in Under Earth, but I don't know where. The reason I left the note for you and opened the passage is because I believe you are the only one who can help her and now is the time to do so. I know you probably have a lot of questions going through your mind right now, but I don't know anything more that will help you. It is up to you to find the answers. So, what is your decision?"

Tobias was right, Jake's head was buzzing with questions. This was a lot to process and Jake still didn't have any answers, only more questions. This sounded like a tall tale, but if it was his only chance to find Isabelle he would take it. "Show me."

"Grab your jacket," the old man beckoned, getting up from his chair. "Oh, one more thing. How far are you willing to go to rescue your friend?"

"As far as it takes," Jake replied, picking up his still damp leather jacket off the arm of the chair.

"Make sure you remember that Jake. The darkness and fear will come back more than once on your journey. I have felt it before as well and I know this, if you aren't fully committed to your cause the fear will drive you away from it. Prepare yourself so that you don't give in to it."

Jake just looked at the old man, unsure of what to say.

Tobias didn't wait for a response. He turned and walked to the door. "Follow me."

Jake pulled on his jacket and backpack, following the old man out the door. As soon as Jake stepped outside, the darkness returned. He looked back at the doorway he had just come through and only saw darkness. Even though the door to the house was still open, none of the light from inside the house just a few feet away could be seen from the outside. Whatever doubts Jake had about the darkness being supernatural were washed away in that moment. What had he gotten himself into? And just like that, the fear returned.

Jake turned and saw the old man had crossed the yard and stood near the large old tree by the sidewalk. Jake took a deep breath and let it out, trying to push away the fear unsuccessfully. The storm had intensified since he had entered the house. It was pouring rain and the thunder was loud, cracking and rumbling across the sky. Jake started across the yard, instantly getting drenched again. He looked up and saw the lightning flash in the sky, but none of the light could penetrate below the trees, leaving Iola just as black as it had been before.

Jake reached the old man. "Where's the door?" he shouted above the noise of the rain and thunder.

The old man pointed at the tree and then turned back to Jake. "Jake, one more thing. The tea I made for you helps with the cold. It can be made by crushing the blue mushrooms found in Under Earth. If you find yourself not being able to warm up, make the tea and drink it. Now hurry, or it will be too late and the passage will close!"

Jake turned toward the tree. It was the answer. That was why Isabelle had disappeared right in front of it. Jake walked around it now, straining to see anything unusual. Everything appeared normal. Wait! There in front of him was a large knot with a hole in it. He could have sworn it wasn't there a second ago. A chill went from Jake's head down his back. He tentatively reached out to touch the knot. It was cold and slimy.

Jake was now certain he didn't want to do this. All of his senses were screaming through his mind, telling him to run away and never return. The fear had returned with a vengeance and filled him until it was coming out of his skin.

Even though he was wet from the rain Jake could feel himself start to sweat. He didn't want to do this. Then, Jake thought of Isabelle and, without letting himself think another second, he shoved his hand into the hole! The darkness around him was complete. He could no longer hear the storm, feel the rain, or see anything other than black. The only thing he felt was the air rushing past him as he was falling and then he knew no more.

Tobias had watched as Jake walked around the tree. He saw the boy reach out and the next sight that greeted his eyes was a black vortex coming out of the hole Jake had his hand in. It covered Jake with spinning blackness and, in less than a second, it shot back into the tree leaving no trace Jake was ever there. And just like that, the darkness dissipated and the storm waned. The boy's journey had begun. Tobias gave the tree one last look and then turned and went back into his house.

Chapter 5

The Guardians

"Hey, slow down flash!"

Jake smiled as he turned to look at Isabelle a few steps behind him. He knew she was right, but for fun wouldn't dare admit it. He stifled a small laugh. "Well someone has to get going or we'll never get anywhere slow poke," he quipped grinning.

She gave him a mock frown and then a playful shove. "Jerk," she bantered as her frown gave way to a smile.

Jake held his hand out for Isabelle to take, knowing it would force him to slow down but not really minding. She reached out and took it, her smile deepening. They started to walk again and Jake felt electricity jump from her hand to his, traveling up his arm and hitting his heart, making it beat faster. It was the feeling that, at this moment, there was no other person he would rather be holding hands with and knowing she was special. In these moments he felt like he would do anything just to see her smile or hear her infectious laugh.

They walked a few blocks down the sidewalk they were on. Every now and again Isabelle would point to a house that caught her interest or a tree she liked. He loved it! They had been friends for a long time before they had started dating, yet she was still constantly surprising him. He felt he learned something new about her every time they were together.

They stopped at Sandy's Malt Shop and bought ice cream cones. Jake preferred chocolate whereas Isabelle always loved a good strawberry cone. They started walking again toward the old park with its large oak trees. Jake felt completely at ease as they continued down the street. It was a quiet Saturday afternoon. There were not many people around as they entered the park. A light breeze came up every now and then rustling the leaves in the trees and the sunlight filtered down between the branches, casting its golden rays here and there. The birds filled the air with their songs and flitted about between the trees.

Both of them finished their ice cream and then Isabelle chose a large tree near the side of the hill in the park where they could sit in the grass and enjoy the cool shade on this warm sunny afternoon. Jake had always thought whoever named Haven Park had done an excellent job. It was an old park in the neighborhood and took up a couple of blocks. It didn't have all the new jungle gyms and other play equipment many of the more modern parks had.

One corner had an old swing set, merry-go-round, and teeter-totters. All of them were worn with age but kept up with new chains, seats, and the occasional paint job layered over the last one that was flaking away from years of weather. Next to that, was a small basketball court and a single tennis court. The other end had a more open area where people could play Frisbee, soccer, or just run around and have fun. Down the middle of the park was a grassy area lined by old oak trees on both sides. The grassy area in the middle of the trees was recessed, making it look like a small valley with hills rising on either side.

Much of the park was covered by the shade of the large oaks with only little spots all around where the sunlight peeked through the leaf canopy. It was a nice, shady old park, which is why the name fit. It was old and comfortable.

They sat there for a long time, just the two of them. They watched the birds flutter around in the trees while the squirrels chased each other and the rabbits hopped around, foraging. It seemed magical. Jake couldn't remember feeling this relaxed and at ease for a long time. Then, ever so slowly, the feeling faded. The trees started to become a little less clear and the cool breeze stopped. Everything became darker and he couldn't feel Isabelle by his side anymore. Gradually, he started to feel very stiff and cool instead of warm and comfortable.

As the memory of Isabelle left, Jake could feel he was laying on his back on a flat hard surface. He must have been dreaming, because he could still feel the emotions of the memory in his chest. Suddenly, his walk to school, the storm, his meeting with Tobias, and putting his hand into the tree came flying through his mind. Now, all the doubt to whether he had been dreaming or not left.

Jake's eyes flipped open, or at least he thought he had opened them, but nothing changed. All he saw was black. Jake blinked. He could feel his eyelids moving but could still only see black. Just to be sure Jake squeezed his eyes shut tightly and then opened them. He knew his eyes were open but nothing but blackness stared back. Was he blind! Jake's pulse started to quicken. How long had he been like this? Would he be able to see soon? Had Tobias done something? Was this what had happened to Isabelle?

Jake took a few deep breaths to steady himself. He had to stay calm and think this through. When he had walked to the tree with Tobias, the old man had stayed a little way away and let Jake approach the tree alone. Jake remembered observing the tree and walking around it, finding that strange knot, which appeared out of nowhere, and then reaching out to touch it. Then his mind went blank. No wait, not blank. He remembered the brief sensation of falling through the darkness.

Okay, so he had fallen down somewhere; but if he had landed on his back like he was laying now, he should be hurt. Jake tested his right arm. It was a little stiff like he had been laying in this position for a while but it didn't hurt. He brushed his hands along the surface he was laying on. It was hard, cool, and dusty. It didn't feel like rock or wood, but like hard packed dirt.

Jake lifted his head slightly and then put it back down. Aside from the same stiff feeling he felt fine. Jake almost sat up when he realized he could see something above him. It seemed that maybe his eyes were adjusting to the darkness. Either that or his mind was playing tricks with his eyes because he had been in the dark so long. Jake continued to stare up, now sure he was seeing something. As his eyes continued to adjust, Jake slowly made out a rock ceiling and walls around him.

Curious and slightly relieved he wasn't blind, Jake sat up. From what he could tell, he was in a small cave-like room with rock walls and ceiling and a hard dirt floor. There was a dull, blue light just barely enough to enable Jake to see. It was coming in through an opening in the wall across from where Jake was now sitting on the floor. It was about the right shape and size for a doorway. He didn't see any other openings. Jake looked up again to make sure he wouldn't hit his head and stood, his muscles groaning in protest. As he stretched his muscles, Jake took a look around him. The room or cave he was in wasn't very big. The ceiling was about three feet above him and, if he had to guess, it looked like the walls were about six feet from him when he was in the center of the room.

Jake looked one last time around the small, round cavern and then figured he'd better see what was beyond the doorway. He hoped it lead out; he didn't want to be trapped in here. He wasn't really claustrophobic, but the thought of not finding a way out gave him the chills. Either that or his clothes were still damp, causing him to shiver. So, at least he knew he couldn't have been out for too long. The cave was dry, so his clothes must still be damp from the rain before he touched the tree. He took a step toward the doorway and then stopped. What was that? He was looking just to the left of the doorway inside the room where something small lay on the floor.

Jake had first assumed it was a rock when he had looked around the room; but now, being a little closer, the dull, blue light revealed the small thing was covered in fur. Not knowing what it was, he took a few cautious steps toward it. Now Jake could see it better. It was a rabbit curled into a ball. It appeared to be sleeping. Jake had never seen a rabbit sleeping, at least not a wild rabbit. As he watched a few more seconds, the rabbit's ear started to twitch. Then slowly, as if waking from a deep stupor, the rabbit slowly lifted his head and sniffed the air. After a few seconds in that position, Jake watched as the rabbit's eyes opened. Either the rabbit hadn't seen Jake or it couldn't see because it was suffering from the same temporary blindness Jake had.

Jake waved his arm as a test to see if the rabbit would run. The rabbit still appeared to be blind, but his ears snapped in Jake's direction and the rabbit tensed. Then suddenly, the rabbit looked directly at Jake and then took off running around the walls of the small cavern. It ran so fast it didn't see the doorway the first time around and shot straight past it.

On its second time around, the rabbit stopped and looked toward Jake who hadn't moved except to turn and watch the rabbit. Then, as Jake watched, the rabbit shot straight toward the doorway and out of the room it went. Jake thought it must have been hiding right by the tree when he was transported through the gateway. Well, he might as well get going too, there was nothing more in this cavern and now, after seeing the rabbit run around, Jake felt even more trapped than before. He wanted to find his way out too. Jake took the few remaining steps to the doorway and went through.

Once through the opening, Jake found he was in a small and narrow tunnel. It was made out of the same rock as the room. It must lead somewhere, Jake thought, and felt a little relieved at the prospect of finding a way out. He slowly continued walking down the hallway, noticing that the ceiling lowered in some areas and then rose back up. Had he been much taller he would have to have ducked. He could still see faintly in the dull, blue light, but still not very well, so he put his hands on both of the walls to be sure he wouldn't miss any opening he might have to explore and to catch himself if he tripped. As he made his way forward he felt himself walking downhill, first slightly, and then gradually more of an incline.

Just as Jake began wondering how long he would be in this tunnel, he spotted what he thought was a curve to the right in the tunnel ahead. The blue light became brighter just past the turn. Jake quickened his steps as much as he was willing in this darkness and cautiously rounded the turn. He walked around the curve in the tunnel and found it was getting brighter with each step. About 20-feet ahead of him he spotted another opening the same size as the tunnel. The blue light was strongest coming through the opening. Jake could see fairly easy now and walked quickly to the opening where the floor leveled somewhat.

When Jake emerged from the tunnel, the first sight that held his gaze was the source of all the blue light he was able to see by. Mushrooms! Glowing blue mushrooms! It was an amazing sight that Jake had never seen before. He looked in wonder at these mushrooms. He could see all the detail of these glowing mushrooms and yet they seemed somewhat transparent. They reminded Jake of something he had seen before but couldn't quite put his finger on.

There was a small field of mushrooms covering the floor. Jake looked around the space he was now in. It was much larger than the first cavern he was in, but not huge. If he had to guess, the ceiling in this cavern was about one-and-a-half stories high in the middle, about 15-yards wide, and maybe twice as long. The opening Jake had come through was one of the long sides of the cavern close to the back of the space and there was another at the far end of the cavern to his right. A small footpath made of the same hard packed dirt he had been walking on went winding down the center with the glowing blue mushrooms growing on either side of it. The air in this part of the cave was still cool, but more humid than the first cavern he was in. There was even a slight mist hanging in the air. Jake looked back at the mushrooms. What did they remind him of? Jake had to think for a minute before the answer came. They reminded him of jellyfish. Just like seeing jellyfish in an aquarium where they swam and you could see such minute detail, yet they were transparent enough to see things through them. That was how these mushrooms looked. All clustered together like a sea of jellyfish.

Jake took a deep breath, the cool humid air filled his lungs. The air didn't smell musty like Jake imagined dark, damp places smelled. Instead, it had a light sweet smell to it. In fact, it smelled just like the tea he had drank at Tobias' house! So these were the mushrooms the old man had mentioned.

Jake walked a short way down the path that lead through the mushrooms. The ground on either side of the path gradually rose to meet the walls of the cave on either side. Jake stared around at the cavern and looked at the blue light from the mushrooms casting their glow on the path and the walls, it was beautiful. He knelt down for a closer look at the mushrooms. Some were very small growing under and around the larger mushrooms. The larger ones were about the height of a wine glass and as large around on the top as a soft ball. Jake smelled one and knew he'd been right; the sweet smell was definitely coming from the mushrooms. He reached out and picked a handful of the small mushrooms nearby. He had expected them to be fragile on account of their transparency, but found they felt pretty much the same as regular mushrooms. He figured they must be safe because he'd already drank tea made from them. He put them in one of his jacket pockets, figuring if he needed to make tea out of them they would probably need to be dried like tea leaves. Jake noticed even after he put them in his pocket, the mushrooms continued to glow.

Jake stood and slowly continued down the path. He was still being cautious because he didn't even really know where he was, not to mention what to expect. As he neared the second opening, he could see this one was much wider and opened up directly into another cavern beyond, this one much larger. The mushroom patch on either side of him ended and the hard packed dirt path widened to meet the opening.

Jake reached the opening and stared out into the large cavern. The dirt floor of this cavern sloped slowly down away from Jake and was riddled with small pebbles, rocks, large stones, and big boulders. In fact, once far enough into the room, you couldn't even see the dirt because of the layers of rock piled on top of one another. Jake also noticed the blue light he had been seeing by was gone, replaced by another, more natural light coming in through a tunnel in the far wall, which was at the lower end of this large cavern. The light coming in the opening seemed brighter than the blue light, which could mean getting out of the cave for good. It came through a small enough opening though that, by the time it reached Jake at the other end of this large cavern, it wasn't much brighter than the blue light. This cavern looked to be the size of two or three football fields. The ceiling was much higher and gave the cavern a more ominous feel.

Jake's pulse quickened. He now wanted to be out of the dark cave and into the light so badly, he almost started running right then. The only thing stopping him was that he couldn't run. He would have to pick his way carefully over the rocks or risk breaking his leg and being stuck in here. Jake studied the floor of the cavern, trying to see a safe way down to the far end. There was no easy path. Whichever way he took would be a winding route, climbing over and around the rocks, stones, and boulders.

While Jake was studying the room, his eyes started to play tricks on him again. He started to feel like the walls in this cavern were slowly moving, shifting, and changing. It was so slight Jake had to blink several times before it stopped. First, the darkness of the storm, then waking up in the dark cave above, and now this cavern. Jake was getting frustrated. He was so tired of looking into darkness he was seeing things that weren't there. Having decided on a course, Jake was just about ready to start his slow climb down to the other opening when he saw the rabbit again. It was sitting about 10 feet away where the rocks became too numerous to see the dirt, staring out at the cavern, alert as if it were trying to spot an unseen danger.

That was strange, Jake thought, but maybe it couldn't figure out a way through all the rocks. Jake stepped through the opening and onto the rocky soil. The ground wasn't covered with rocks here, but there were enough to make a slight sound for the rabbit to hear. It turned its head toward Jake and, upon seeing him, decided its waiting was over. It turned, hopping and scrambling over and around the rocks, trying to get away from Jake. It was doing a pretty good job until it hit an area with smaller rocks that went scattering when the rabbit landed.

The next moment happened in slow motion. The rabbit had just gotten its footing to hop again when a huge dark shadow emerged from Jake's right. It happened fast, but so unexpectedly, that the image froze in Jake's mind. A large, clawed hand reached out and snatched the rabbit as it was in the air and Jake watched as the huge torso the arm was attached to went back into the wall followed by the arm and hand holding the rabbit. Then, the wall was solid stone again. Jake leaped backward through the opening he had just come through and pressed himself up against the wall to hide himself, hoping the thing hadn't seen him.

He was breathing hard. What *was* that thing? He knew whatever it was couldn't be good and could most likely hear him breathing. Now he knew he must be in a place called Under Earth, because what he'd just seen was unlike anything he'd ever seen before. Jake waited there against the cold wall for a few minutes, allowing himself to calm, unwilling to stir just yet.

After another minute, and his breath under control again, Jake leaned out and peered into the large cavern again. Nothing. Just rocks. Jake watched and listened for a few more minutes and still nothing happened. Then his gaze wandered back to the wall were he'd first thought his eyes were playing tricks on him. After a moment, he saw movement. The walls shape didn't change but its texture or color shifted slightly. After seeing the rabbit's demise, Jake knew he wasn't just seeing things. There was really something there. *What had happened to the rabbit?* Jake thought. Whatever happened to it, he knew it couldn't have been good. He was lucky. If the rabbit hadn't been ahead of him, he would have been toast.

Jake glanced around the room a little longer. There were more places around the room where Jake could see the slight shifting, occurring somewhere other than the first place he'd seen it. There were even a few places on the ceiling. He was thinking these areas might be connected to whatever had come out of the wall. Jake decided to test his theory and, without a sound, he carefully reached around the corner and grabbed some small rocks and pebbles. He figured whatever that thing was, it must not be able to see because both he and the rabbit had been inside the room for a few minutes and nothing had happened.

Jake took one of the rocks and threw it out across the room. It landed close to where he'd last seen the rabbit. It bounced, making a small noise when it landed and, before landing a second time, another large shadow, maybe the same one, came out of the wall, grabbed the rock, and went back into the wall so quickly, Jake only had time to see the large arm and clawed hand. The only thing that was different than the first time was, that instead of pulling the rock into the wall, it hit the wall, passed through the shadowed hand, and fell to the floor. Strange.

From the safety of the smaller cavern, Jake threw rocks in different directions around the open room. Each time the same thing happened. A large shadow would emerge and grab the rock, then return to the wall, letting the rock fall to the floor. So, for some reason, the thing had been able to absorb the rabbit into the wall but not the rocks. So far, Jake had only thrown one rock at a time and, in turn, only seen one shadow creature each time in different places. Was there only one, or multiple creatures that came out depending on where the sound came from? He threw a hand-full of rocks all at once, trying to fling them in as many different directions as he could in one throw. They landed across a large area with much clattering noises in different places and Jake had his answer.

If he had to guess, at least 20 different creatures emerged from the rock walls and ceiling of the cavern, each in a different place ready to strike, but this time they held still. This was the first time Jake had seen them stationary. They were either confused or they had figured out it was a trick. Whatever the reason for their stillness, Jake could now see them fairly well. They all had two arms with a single head and torso. They were huge! They looked like giants. The only thing different was that none of them appeared to have legs. Their torsos apparently connected to the place in the wall or ceiling they had come out of as if they were a part of the cavern. Jake could see more detail on the creature closest to his hiding spot in the smaller cavern. A small amount of light reflected off its surface and it looked exactly like the texture of the rock. It was moving slightly as if breathing and Jake could see its texture and color were the same as the wall, only alive. Its hand flexed every now and then and Jake could make out large muscles on its arms and back. They were like living rock creatures. It turned its head a few times, but Jake couldn't discern a face, just more rock where a face should have been.

Slowly, the creatures went back into the walls and ceiling. Great! Even if they couldn't come completely out of the walls and walk around the room there were enough of them to reach everywhere in the cavern. How was he going to get past them? Jake knew he couldn't stay in the cave, but hated the idea of trying to cross the cavern. He'd be doomed for sure.

After a few minutes he had a plan but he had to be sure the creatures couldn't see first. He threw a hand full of rocks out into the middle of the room. When the creatures came back out, Jake threw a single rock and hit one of them in its back with a loud crack, like stone hitting stone. It twisted as if it were looking toward Jake. Suddenly, Jake realized how foolish he'd been. If the creature could see and leave its spot, the small cavern he was in wouldn't be any safer and he was doomed. After a moment, the creature still hadn't moved and relaxed a little. It was time for the second test. He lobbed a small rock just past the creature's head, but the creature continued searching the room for whatever had hit it and didn't notice the rock until it landed behind it. It then turned and, with one quick movement, grabbed the rock and returned to the wall.

So, they couldn't see in the normal sense, but they must be able to hear or see sound, which is how they were able to find the rocks and the bunny. They most likely couldn't leave their spot either because only the creature or creatures nearest the noise appeared to come out. Since multiple sounds confused them Jake's plan was to grab a handful of pebbles or rocks and toss them away as far as he could, wait for their sound to cover his steps, and then get as far as he could before the sound of the rocks' echoes stopped. Then, once the creatures had come out and retreated again, Jake could repeat the process. It wasn't an exact science, but as long as they couldn't see, it might just work. The only trick would be not getting grabbed or hit by accident when they came out.

With a deep breath to steady himself, Jake tried it. His first throw was long and hard. When the rocks started clattering, Jake took as many steps as he could before the sound died away. He was now out in the open of the large room and he felt much more exposed here, but the creatures had emerged and once again looked confused so, after a short while they returned to hiding. Okay, thought Jake, so far so good. His heart was racing and he could feel sweat starting to form from his nervousness, but he would force himself to stay calm and get this done.

Jake's plan was to cross through the middle of the cavern. He would feel more exposed, but then he should only have to worry about the creatures in the ceiling above him and not the ones in the walls. He continued the process. It was a time consuming task, but as long as he was safe and getting closer to freedom he didn't care. Jake had reached the middle of the room when he slipped while trying to jump from one large rock onto another. The sound of him sliding continued a half second after the rock clatter had ended. All of the stone heads turned Jake's direction. The creature nearest Jake, which hung from the ceiling, leaned in Jake's direction. He froze. He knew if he ran now he'd be a goner. He had to hope the creature didn't know his exact location.

Jake could see the creature very clearly now, its rocky form hanging from the ceiling with muscles flexing and head searching. If Jake had not been completely terrified at this moment it would have been an amazing sight. The creature started reaching with his arm in his direction. Without moving from his spot, Jake got as low as he possibly could and quietly flattened himself against the rock he'd fallen on. The creature swung his clawed hand right through the position Jake's head had just been a moment before and it hit a few rocks to Jake's right, sending them crashing around the room. Jake could barely breathe.

The creature continued to swing its arms and knock some rocks around in a few different places. It must know Jake was close by and it was trying to scare him into moving. He stayed frozen in his spot watching, listening, with his heart pounding loudly in his ears. It took longer than usual, but slowly, one by one, the creatures went back into hiding, the last being the one that almost caught him. Jake breathed a silent sigh of relief and waited again a few moments for his heart to calm down.

It was then he realized his biggest mistake. Up until then he had been grabbing handfuls of small rocks and pebbles from the ground near his feet, but now he was standing on larger rocks with no little ones nearby for him to use. At the most, he could only pick up one rock and it was too big to throw very far and it wouldn't cause enough confusion to cover his steps. He had no choice but to do his best to be silent. Jake figured he'd be more silent stepping on the large rocks barefoot so he quietly took off his shoes and socks. He stuffed his socks into his shoes and then tied their strings together and wrapped them around his neck so his shoes hung down his back. It wasn't comfortable, but this way he still had his hands free. The rocks were cool on his feet and thankfully dry so he wouldn't slip easily. The only benefit he had now was that these large rocks were packed tightly together and didn't shift or move under his weight.

It must have taken over an hour to cross the middle of the cavern this way, but he finally made it silently to the other side of the large rocks and boulders and could, once again, use the small rocks for cover. He repeated the same procedure of throwing the small rocks. After what seemed like an eternity, Jake reached the other opening, his muscles aching from being so tense for so long.

Before entering the tunnel where the natural light was filtering through much brighter now, Jake looked back. He knew he'd probably have to come back this way again to get home and now that he knew how long it would take he regretted the thought of it. Then Jake's mind went to Isabelle. She was the reason he'd come here and if he found her safe and could get her home it didn't matter what he had to go through. It would be worth it.

Jake turned back to the small tunnel filled with light and entered. It was almost too bright at first, but the short walk through this tunnel allowed his eyes to adjust and it felt great that he could see fully once again. Suddenly, the tunnel took a left turn and Jake was out of the cave. His journey through the caverns hadn't prepared him for what he now saw and it took his breath away.

Chapter 6

Under Earth

Jake stood there just outside the cave and stared. Of all the things running through his mind of what might await him after the cave, what he now saw filling his vision had never entered his wildest dreams. The first thing Jake noticed was the sky, if sky was the correct description. Jake was just outside the cave's mouth on a ledge, staring upward. At least that's what Jake figured it had to be, but it was unlike any sky Jake had ever seen. It wasn't the normal blue or white he was accustomed to seeing, but an orangish-pink color.

The color, however, wasn't the most unusual part. What caught Jake's attention was the light source or lack thereof. Instead of the sun lighting the sky, the whole sky radiated light! Jake turned his head to see as far as he could. He was standing on a ledge on the side of a mountain a few hundred feet up in the air. From one end of his field of vision to the other, the whole sky emanated the orangish-pink light. It was bright enough for daylight, but Jake figured it must not be as bright as the sun, because he had been looking at it a minute and only now were his eyes beginning to water.

Jake closed his eyes to let them rest for a minute. He saw spots. Jake waited until the spots faded and then opened his eyes again. It was almost like staring at a light bulb for too long, you didn't get hurt like staring at the sun but it still made your eyes water and blinded you for a short while.

Jake scanned the horizon one more time. It was definitely the sky because he now saw low hanging white clouds here and there. He thought he must be pretty high up because the clouds didn't look much higher than him.

The next thing Jake noticed were the trees. He was standing on a ledge a few hundred feet up the side of the mountain looking at a beautifully colored landscape below. The whole valley before him was filled with trees of every color imaginable. It was kind of like fall when all the trees started turning, except even more colorful. There were, of course, the bright yellows, oranges, and reds like fall, but that is where the similarities ended. As Jake continued to look, he could see blue leaves, purple leaves, pink leaves, turquoise leaves, and even black leaves. While he looked at the forest, it appeared to Jake that the whole color spectrum was right in front of him. He saw so many different colors and tints and shades of those colors he felt like he must be dreaming though he knew he wasn't.

As Jake looked, he could see birds flying here and there throughout the sky; some soaring high while others seem to be playing a game of chase, flying up out of the canopy of trees, veering into steep inclines and sharp twists, and then quickly diving back below the leaves only to shoot up again in a different spot. Jake glanced around him and tried to get his bearings. It looked like there was a river or stream out in the distance because he could see a small silver line weaving in and out through some of the trees. It was only then Jake realized how hungry and thirsty he was.

Jake took off his backpack and set it down. Taking out his lunch, he ate it. His apple was now bruised in a few places because of his climb through the cavern, but still refreshing. This would help, but he had to find some water soon or he wouldn't last very long in this humid air. As Jake ate the apple, he took his socks and shoes off his neck and put them back on. It felt good to have the soft feel of cotton touching his feet again after the rough rocks and sand he'd been walking on.

As he sat there eating, he continued to watch the landscape below him and allowed himself a moment to rest and take in the beauty. He could hear a breeze rustling down again through the forest below, and every now and again he could hear the sound of an animal calling. He hoped it wasn't a dangerous one. Jake could see several other mountains in the distance but couldn't tell how far they were. The warmer air felt good, but it was also much more humid than the caves. Jake took off his jacket and put it in his backpack and then slung his backpack over his arms. Leather jackets were definitely not made for humid air.

Jake stood up and looked around the ledge he was on. To his left the ledge curved around and eventually rose and became part of the mountainside. To the right, however, it curved a little farther out before turning even more and disappearing behind the side of the cave he had just come from. Jake was hoping for a trail because he definitely didn't have any rope to climb down the steep rock. He walked over toward the right and cautiously walked around the bend. Jake was glad to see the start of the trail going down, but suddenly, he stopped short.

There, just where the trail began, was Isabelle's green jacket. Jake's heart started to race. He ran to it and picked it up. It looked like it had been out in the weather a long time because it was sun bleached and dirty and had a small tear near the shoulder, but otherwise it appeared normal. Relief and concern washed over Jake in equal measure. Isabelle was here somewhere and Jake was filled with hope that this bizarre journey he was on would lead him to her, but the concern came right back. He finally had the confirmation that she had been taken. This meant he was on the right trail, but where was she and was she safe, lost, or hurt? There were too many possibilities and, of course, the worst ones vied for top position in Jake's mind.

Jake made himself shut the thoughts out. This was a good sign, but he couldn't let worry creep in or it would cripple him. Jake took the jacket and put it in his backpack with his own. Before he had much time to start worrying again, Jake started down the trail and hoped he would find more clues as to where she was when he got down, otherwise he wouldn't know which way to go. The trail was fairly easy to navigate. It was steep in some places, but mostly just a slowly winding trail down the mountainside. It wasn't dangerously narrow either making the hike down fairly gentle and uneventful, but slow going.

It took Jake a while to get used to seeing the steep wall of mountain on one side and the equally steep drop-off on the other side. Once his eyes adjusted to the sight and his equilibrium steadied, Jake was able to hike faster down the trail.

After a time of hiking, Jake finally got low enough to the tree level that he could see the colorful trees and plant life much better. As he continued to hike, he looked out at the vegetation all around. Beautiful didn't quite say it right; indeed, it was unlike anything Jake ever seen. Even the plants were colorful. Jake could tell as he got lower that the trees varied greatly in not just color, but also size and shape. Some trees reminded Jake of rain forest trees, with large gnarled roots, huge trunks, and high reaching branches. Others were short and wide in shape. There were even some trees that had the appearance of large mushrooms. Jake thought they were huge mushrooms at first until he looked closer and saw the branches went out from the top of the trunk and fanned the leaves out making almost a perfect dome canopy like a mushroom.

Another thing he noticed as he got lower was that many of the leaves were one color on the top but the undersides of the leaves were a different color. One of the trees closest to Jake had bright blue leaves on the top while being deep crimson underneath and the rest of the tree was covered by a medium grey bark. The tree next to that had leaves that were black on top and white on the bottom. As he continued to look around, Jake saw so many different variations of trees and plants he couldn't take it all in.

Jake reached out to the tree with the blue and red leaves, as it was near enough to touch, and felt the leaves. They were thick and smooth to the touch and felt a bit rubbery. The blue and red leaves on this tree reminded Jake of a maple leaf only much larger and thicker.

A couple of minutes later, Jake reached the bottom of the trail and glanced back up at the ledge he'd been standing on to try and gauge which way he needed to go to find the river. He figured if he turned to his left a little and headed out straight he should run into it sooner or later.

Before he set off, Jake took his jacket out and put it back on. He knew he'd be a little miserable in this humidity, but the vegetation was pretty thick in places and he was in a different world now. If any of the plants were poisonous, he'd rather have the extra protection. He started hiking in the direction he figured the water was. Jake realized, as he walked, that he was beginning to feel tired. He didn't know how long he'd been here, but, since waking up in the cave and hiking all the way through the caves and down the mountain, he figured at least four or five hours had passed. He hoped that finding water would rejuvenate him a little, but with all the new sights and sounds, his senses were on an overload and he was starting to get a headache

As Jake hiked through the forest, he took in his new surroundings while trying to keep track of which way he'd come so he could find his way back. Jake glanced back and could still see the mountain he'd come from. He relaxed a little and let his mind wander knowing, as long as he could see the mountain, he'd be able to get back.

Jake wished his friends were with him now. Other than a few birds and maybe a snake he thought he saw quickly slide away, he hadn't seen anything other than the colorful plant life. Even in all the surrounding beauty Jake felt lonely. He knew he would find Isabelle at any cost, but knew if his friends were with him he was sure they would have been able to help him find her much faster.

Ever since Jake had met TJ, Eric, and Patrick, he never had to worry about problems alone. They were basically part of each other's family now and whenever any one of them had a problem they would face it together. TJ and Jake were the founding members of the group as they had met first all the way back in the fourth grade. The first time Jake met TJ was halfway through their fourth grade year. TJ's family had moved into town and he was placed in Jake's class at school. They befriended each other the first day TJ was there during recess and the bond solidified the next Wednesday when Jake went to church for his Wednesday night class and found TJ there because his family had decided to attend. Both of them recognized each other right away and both were equally excited to have a common friend at school and church. They had been best buds ever since.

TJ stood for Timothy Jeremy, both names his mom liked but his dad didn't. Their compromise was to name him Timothy Jeremy but call him TJ. TJ was a few inches taller than Jake with blond hair. Both of them went out for the same sports even though Jake was always better at track and TJ was much better at basketball.

Eric was the third member of their group. Jake and TJ met him in the sixth grade, when all of the sixth-graders combined into the middle school from the various elementary schools in the city. Eric wasn't fat, but was a big kid and seemed intimidating to a lot of the other sixth-graders. Jake and TJ invited him to play Frisbee during gym the first week of school and he fit right in. Eric was a football player. The next year all three went out for the same sports and when they weren't at school or home they were hanging out together. After an invitation from TJ, Eric started coming to church with them on Wednesday nights and his family soon followed.

Patrick was the most recent member of their group, having met them in the eighth grade. Patrick wasn't a typical sports guy like the rest of the group. Although he tried his hand at various school sports, he was pretty average and didn't have a huge interest in them. He did like Frisbee and was actually very good at archery, but the school didn't have either of these as options for team sports. What Patrick did excel in was his studies. He could remember anything he learned with stunning accuracy. Patrick wasn't really a nerd in a stereotypical sense, but, until he became a part of their group, he had kept a low profile and didn't have many friends. One day, during his eighth-grade year, he was getting some books out of his locker after school when a small group of trouble-makers decided he was an easy target and surrounded him.

Patrick was doing pretty well at ignoring them until one of them shoved him into the lockers from behind. Eric, who just turned down the hall could see what was about to happen and started walking toward the group while texting both Jake and TJ to meet him. There were five bullies surrounding Patrick, but before they could start anything else, Eric called out to them. All of them looked his way. "Are you guys bored or something?" Eric asked with a slight smile. He was the biggest kid there, but the bullies weren't on the small side. They held their ground and the leader of the group told Eric to get lost.

Eric didn't flinch but glared right back at them. "I think you're the ones who should get lost, what do you think guys?" As he asked, this Eric shifted his gaze from the bullies to behind them where Jake and TJ now stood.

The group of bullies suddenly realized this and started to become nervous. Jake could still remember TJ stepping forward and saying, "I think you're right Eric, these guys better get moving, I hate for us to have to ruin their weekend."

At that point seeing the confidence practically fly off the bullies' faces almost made Jake laugh out loud but he managed to keep a straight face. The bullies were nervous and tense and wanted no part of the confrontation anymore. They quickly shuffled the long way around Eric and fled for the exit. Just when Jake thought he could contain it no more the group of bullies disappeared out the door at the end of the hall and Jake, TJ, and Eric burst into laughter.

Patrick just stood there unsure of them and still in a little shock. Once the laughter died down, Eric broke the ice by introducing himself along with Jake and TJ and then offered Patrick his hand.

"Thanks guys, I'm not sure what I'd have done if you hadn't come when you did," stammered a very relieved Patrick.

"No sweat," Eric exclaimed smiling. "Hey, we're about to go grab a burger and fries down at Sandy's Malt Shop, do you want to come?"

Patrick didn't even hesitate, "Sure."

From that point on, the group of four had been very tight. Sure, they all had a lot of other friends, but their small group was different, family. Jake felt himself wishing they were here now.

Wait, what was that? Jake was shaken out of his reverie by a small sound. He'd been walking for an hour or more and, other than his footsteps, a few birds, and the breeze flowing through the forest, he hadn't heard anything. Jake stopped and listened, turning to see if anything was hiding in the colorful plants around him. He didn't see anything up or down the trail he was on, but he was sure he'd heard something. Some small steps, maybe a sound that stood out from the nature sounds all around him.

Jake started to walk slowly, more careful this time to see if he could hear the sound again. He glanced behind him from time to time, feeling like he was being watched. He felt tense and his heart pounded while his mind was telling him that anytime something could jump out from its hiding place behind the beautiful foliage just a few feet on either side of him. As the minutes went by and no new noises presented themselves, Jake began relaxing again. Either he hadn't heard anything or whatever had caused the noise had gone on its way. After a few more minutes of walking, Jake began to hear the running water through the trees. He'd made it! Jake picked up his pace and made his way to the water.

The trail Jake was on came to a small clearing next to the water's edge, turned left and followed the water a few yards, and then plunged back into the forest. Jake was so thirsty after his hiking he didn't even consider whether the water was clean enough to drink. He dropped his backpack, got down on his hands and knees, and started cupping the water into his mouth. The cool liquid was refreshing and Jake couldn't drink it fast enough. After a couple of minutes, Jacob sat up to take a breath.

It looked like this must be a small river about 30 feet across at this point. Jake bent back down and was about to reach for another drink when he caught a quick movement in the water to his right. Suddenly, sirens of danger went off in Jake's mind and in a split second he flung himself as far back as he could. It was a good thing too for, at the same time, a huge shape shot out of the water and large jaws snapped shut just where Jake had been kneeling.

The creature had dark blue leathery skin much like an alligator. Only it was slightly taller with stockier legs in a broader body. At the moment, however, Jake only noticed its head. The head of the creature was like nothing Jake had ever seen. It was large and shaped like a hammerhead shark, but the difference was the huge hammer portion of its head was its mouth with rows of razor-sharp teeth showing even when closed. Jake couldn't see any eyes to speak of, but was sure the thing was staring right at him. It opened its massive jaws and let out a loud roar. Jake flinched, he couldn't remember if alligators or crocs could roar, but this thing sure could. The creature suddenly reared back and Jake knew it would leap right on top of him just a few yards away and he didn't have time to escape.

Just when the creature started to leap Jake saw a blue sparkling beam of light come from his left and hit the creature square in its chest. The creature froze, literally froze with its mouth parted, front feet in the air, and back feet still on the ground with its tail still half under the water.

Jake couldn't comprehend what he was seeing, but his body reacted without a second thought. Jake jumped up and turned to run, but his foot caught on a root he hadn't seen in his panicked state. Jake tripped and fell forward, hitting his head on the side of a tree before hitting the ground and rolling onto his back. His head swam and his vision was blurred. The last thing Jake saw before he passed out was a tiny object hovering over him and his last thought was that he wouldn't be able to save Isabelle.

Chapter 7

The Three Sisters

"Is he okay?" A voice asked.

"I don't know, he hit his head pretty good, he's still breathing though. I think he might've just knocked himself out," replied a second voice.

"Good thing we came when we did or he would have been lunch," proclaimed a third voice. "Wait, I think he's waking up."

Jake's head throbbed and he felt very tired, but something in the back of his mind was nagging him to wake up. He could hear voices. He didn't recognize them.

"Is he human?" One of the voices asked.

"Yes, I believe he is," a second one answered.

"What does this mean?" the third voice chimed in, sounding strangely excited.

"I don't know, but stop staring at the young man like that." The second voice instructed. "If this is a big surprise for us, think of how he's going to react!"

Jake heard this, but his mind was still foggy and he was only half listening so he didn't understand what they were saying. Jake tried opening his eyes several times, but his eye lids did not want to cooperate. Finally, he got them to open far enough to see a little light and what appeared to be bugs flying around his head. He couldn't really tell because his vision was blurry, but he thought it must be daytime. But what were bugs doing in his room…

Suddenly everything came back to Jake and he jerked up into a sitting position, hitting one of the large bugs with his head, sending it flying and stared wide-eyed at the creature that was still there, frozen, at the edge of the water. Its bulging eyes still looked down at Jake from the sides of its large head and its jaws were still open, showing rows of razor-sharp teeth. Its thick, leathery, blue hide was still wet from the water and glistened in the sunlight. It was still frozen in mid-jump and a strange blue light silhouetted its form.

Jake didn't know how the creature could be frozen like that, but he didn't really care. He was just glad he was still alive. He didn't know how long his luck would last, but felt that, at any moment, the creature could come back to life just as quickly as it had frozen. He was just about to leap up and run when he heard a voice beside him.

"Hey, watch it now; is that any way to treat someone who rescued you?"

Jake spun his head around in every direction but only saw water and forest.

"Up here." directed the small, pleasant sounding voice.

Jake looked up and saw what at first appeared to be three brightly colored butterflies. But wait! They couldn't be butterflies Jake thought, for, as he looked at them closer, he saw three beautiful young women between the wings. The first woman had shiny silver hair and transparent silver wings. The middle one had electric blue hair with matching wings and the third had bright fuchsia hair and matching wings. Even stranger though, was that all three wore regular khaki cargo pants and T-shirts almost like you would find at any Gap store. But, these couldn't really be what Jake thought they were, could they?

As if in response to Jake's thoughts the blue one laughed with a knowing smile, "Yes young man you're seeing us right. We are, in fact, fairies."

Jake noticed she was dusting herself off and realized she was the bug he'd hit with his head. He felt embarrassed and wanted to apologize, but his words came out in a jumble. "I'm sorry, I… I mean, did I hit you when I sat up? I thought you were a bug." As soon as he'd announced it, Jake wished he could take it back. The blue fairy gave Jake the most incredulous look he'd ever seen and turned around so that her back was facing him.

"A bug! Of all the inconsiderate things to say! I have half a mind to let the creature have you now!" The fairy with the blue hair snapped in a huff.

"Now sis," the silver fairy chimed in, "this is probably the first time he's seen a real fairy, give him a break."

"I think we can forgive his mistake since he did have a bakkara bearing down on him," the fuchsia one laughed.

The blue fairy sighed and, with a graceful twist of her wings, turned back around to face Jake. "Fine, but if you ever call me a bug again you'll be sorry," she vowed with a mischievous scowl.

"Please forgive my sister," begged the silver haired girl, smiling at her sister. "She lets her temper get the better of her from time to time."

Blue hair turned her scowl from Jake to her silver haired sister and stuck out her tongue.

"Oh silly me, where are my manners?" the silver haired one replied. "These are my two sisters. The one with the pink hair is Fieora, the one with the blue hair and short fuse is Sapphire, and I'm Claira. What is your name young man?"

"Jake," he responded, rubbing the back of his head where he could now feel a large welt forming. "Good thing you came when you did," remarked Jake looking back at the bakkara, which was still frozen, but now had long tendrils of drool hanging from its jaws. "Sick, is it supposed to be doing that?" Jake asked. "I thought it was frozen."

Fieora chimed in, "Oh he's frozen alright, but that just keeps him suspended where he is for a while. He's still alive. He can still breathe, think, and, as you can see, drool."

Jake gulped, realizing the reason the creature was drooling was because it was imagining him for lunch!

"Do you think you can walk Jake?" Sapphire asked with a more pleasant tone. "I know we all have questions, but I don't really want to hold this bakkara here all day. The longer he's frozen the angrier he becomes and the harder it is to hold him there."

Jake jumped up at the thought of that thing being able to come at him again. He wavered just a moment, feeling slightly dizzy, but certain he could overcome it. "Yes I'll make it," he remarked, eyeing the bakkara again warily.

"I think he's tired of being reminded he was almost lunch," Fieora giggled.

"You two take him on ahead," advised Sapphire. "I'll stay here until you're far enough away to let the bakkara go and then I'll catch up. "

"Where are we going?" Jake asked, looking at Claira.

"We're taking you back to our home." Claira explained as she and Fieora started into the woods along the trail. "It will be safe there for you to wash up and rest. You look like you could use it and afterwards we need to talk. There hasn't been a human in Under Earth for quite some time. We have some questions for you about why you've come and you need to be warned of the dangers here."

Jake turned and followed, feeling the fatigue set in, but still feeling the urgency of finding Isabelle now that he knew there was a chance to save her. "But I don't have time, I came here looking for my friend and I have to find her."

Claira turned midair and continued to fly gracefully backwards next to Fieora, but facing Jake. "Jake, first of all we might, and I emphasize *might* be able to help you, but first, you need to rest. I think you have a long journey ahead of you and you'll never be able to help your friend if you're too exhausted to walk."

Jake frowned, frustrated. He knew she was right. He could feel his limbs getting heavier and his eyelids wanting to close, but he couldn't help the urgency his heart felt. "So, how did you find me?"

Claira, who had resumed leading them down the trail, let Fieora answer. "We were out gathering fresh fruit when the small elf, Jibber, found us. He was out looking for a friend's son who got lost this morning when he spotted you on the trail. He followed you for a short time, but when he realized the danger of where you were going, he came to find us."

"Why didn't he just warn me himself?" Jake asked confused.

"First, because he didn't know if you were dangerous or not. Second, because small elves never show themselves to anyone but their own kind unless a trust has been earned first."

"So, why did he talk to you?"

"Because fairies, like small elves, like to be invisible, although we aren't as religious about it," Fieora responded smiling. "Besides, our family has a history with theirs that goes way back. We've had their trust for quite some time."

"Follow me," Claira urged from the front as she flew into the forest where a vague trail verged off the main trail.

Jake followed the two sisters quietly through the forest for a while, lost in his own thoughts. Suddenly, a scratch and a sharp pain followed by a numbing sensation flowed through Jake's right hand. "Ouch," he yelled as he looked at the back of his hand.

"What's the matter?" Fieora asked, turning around. "Claira," Fieora called sharply as she saw what had happened.

Claira spun in a blur of silver and spotted Jake standing near a plant with purple leaves, pink budding flowers, and green spines sticking out of the buds. He was staring dumbly at his hand where green spider webs were starting to make their way outwards from the cut. "Quick, find a strong vine we can tie his arm off with to slow the poison." Fieora quickly flew off into the trees.

"Poison!" Jake responded, alarmed.

"Did someone say poison?" A voice asked from behind Jake. Sapphire emerged from a bend in the trail and flew out to meet them. "I was only behind for a short while and you've already found more trouble to get into?" Sapphire joked with a playful grin and sarcasm in her voice.

"It was a nettle leaf Saph," Claira answered.

Upon hearing this Sapphire's smile vanished and her face turned white. "Where?" she asked looking around.

"Right behind you," Claira stated, pointing to the colorfully wicked looking plant.

"I didn't think there were any growing this far south," Sapphire wondered, concerned.

"Nor did I, which is why we took this trail. I was here a week ago and I'm sure it wasn't there then," Claira exclaimed looking very troubled.

Sapphire took a closer look. "The dirt is disturbed and I can see some of the roots. It looks as if someone planted this here recently and in a hurry. By the look of the soil, probably even today."

Just then Fieora came back out of the brush with a small dagger in one hand and a green vine and the other. "Help me get this tight," she directed going to Jake. "Jake, I need you to take off your jacket, lie down, and put your arm up so we can get this done quickly."

Jake complied, already feeling the numbness traveling up his forearm.

"Where is it numb to?" asked Fieora and Jake pointed to his forearm just below his elbow. "Okay, we're going to tie this above your elbow. It will probably hurt."

The three sisters went to work tying off Jake's arm and they were right, it hurt. "It's traveling fast," Fieora added examining their work. "Okay, that should do, now I'll make it cinch itself a bit tighter and freeze in place." Fieora took out her wand and shot a pink jet of light at the vine, which somehow pulled itself even tighter, something which Jake didn't think was possible, and then it froze in place.

"Why can't you just freeze me like you did with that creature back there?" Jake asked.

"Bakkara," Claira corrected, "and because, like we told you before, just your movement would be frozen, the poison would still be free to spread inside you. Now stay lying down, I'll have to float you the rest of the way."

At that, Claira took out her wand and silver light struck him and kept him lying down, but lifted him into the air. "This will keep you from moving too much so the poison doesn't spread as rapidly." Claira responded. "Now, try to remain calm and stay conscious for as long as possible." Claira looked at Fieora with a worried expression. "We need some of those blue mushrooms. How quickly could you make the trip to get some?"

Before Fieora could respond however, Jake mumbled, "I've got some in my jacket pocket."

Claira looked at Jake questioningly.

Jake shrugged, "I thought they were cool so I picked some." He whispered with a sleepy expression on his face.

Some of the worry left Claira's face. "Could you make us invisible for the trip?"

"You think someone is watching?" Fieora asked, worried.

"I think with what's happened we can't be too careful."

Fieora waved her wand in a quick circle and a pink light swirled around the group. "There, that should do the trick. Let's be off, this is going to wear me out."

Any other time Jake would've been exhilarated at the sensation of floating in the air, rushing behind the three sisters as they made their way through the trees as fast as they could without letting Jake hit anything. But at the moment, Jake could only think about his arm. The numbness stopped at his elbow, but he couldn't feel his forearm or hand at all now. Since Fieora and Sapphire were carrying his jacket and backpack, Jake could turn his head and see the green spider webbing reaching up to his elbow and just slightly past the tie.

After a few minutes of floating, Jake knew the poison and probably exhaustion were starting to affect him. He was feeling dizzy and he could barely keep his eyes open now, since he didn't have walking to keep his mind active. Jake's last thought as he drifted off to sleep was of Isabelle. "Lord,"

Jake prayed as hopelessness set in, "please help me, all I want to do is find Isabelle."

Chapter 8

Memory

Jake fell into a restless sleep while the poison and exhaustion wracked his body. The three sisters flew Jake quickly and quietly through the forest to their home where they mixed up the antidote to the nettle leaf poison and administered it to Jake. During this time, dreams and memories flashed quickly through Jake's mind and he was unable to focus on any one thing for long. Once the poison started to lessen and the antidote took effect, Jake's body finally rested and his mind settled on a memory that stood out from the others.

A slight warm breeze rustled through the green grass as many feet ran through.

"Jake," Patrick yelled from across the field.

Jake took a step forward, pivoting right and down under the arms of the blocker, throwing the disc straight to Patrick who caught it and immediately threw it to Eric farther down the field. "We've almost got them," yelled TJ as he sprinted past Jake to get into a good position.

Eric turned and threw the Frisbee to a girl on their team while the other team made up the distance. The girl threw the disc to TJ just before the other team surrounded him. TJ pivoted in place for a few seconds, trying to see an opening he could get the disc through. Then, in between two of his blockers, he saw Patrick running up on the left. TJ feigned right but then jumped straight up and flung the disc as quickly as he could to the left. It was almost clear when it hit the side of a blocker's hand and wobbled in the air turning sideways.

Patrick jumped for it, but fumbled as it came down crooked. Just before it would have fallen out of his hands,

Patrick regained control, took a step, and launched the disc to Eric who was wide open. Eric caught the disc, spun, and threw it to another girl on their team who had made it across the goal line. She jumped, catching the Frisbee with one hand and landed back in the end zone. The red team, which Jake, Eric, Patrick, and TJ were all on during this class, had won. A cheer went up from the red team as they hurried over to shake hands with the black team.

It was a little unfair, thought Jake as he hurried over to the "good game" line. Having Eric, Patrick, TJ, and Jake on the same team stacked it in their favor. It wasn't that they were superior athletes, because there were many good athletes in this class, but because they had been friends so long they could anticipate each other's moves very quickly. It was the last period of the day in gym class on an early out day and the gym teacher Mr. Johnson didn't split the teams by randomly handing people ones and twos like he usually did, but rather let them pick today. Even with their team stacked, the red team had only won by a single point.

Jake liked having gym at the end of the day. It was a good time to unwind and nice not to have to worry about studying or tests right before the school day was out. It also meant you didn't have to get all sweaty right before your next class. The year before he had gym first period and that was a drag because after getting energized and sweaty, it would take him the next two class periods to stop sweating and dry off, not to mention, it was hard to sit still.

Mr. Johnson blew his whistle and told the class to huddle around. "Good job today class. For some reason you always seem more excited and motivated on early out days," Mr. Johnson bellowed, chuckling. "Go get changed and you can leave when you're done. It'll only be a few minutes before the bell anyway. If anyone has a problem with it just refer them to me."

This was another reason Jake enjoyed having PE at the end of the school day. Mr. Johnson was a middle-aged, heavyset, balding man with what looked like a perpetual scowl at first glance. He had a rough voice and didn't like people who were lazy or disobedient. His appearance intimidated almost everyone including many of the teachers, and even the hard cases in school listened to or steered clear of him. He demanded respect. However, if you knew this and chose to obey and could show you were willing to work hard, Mr. Johnson's frown would turn into the largest smile you'd ever seen and, as long as you continue to work hard, you'd receive special privileges like getting out of last period a few minutes early. Needless to say, Jake's class had this figured out and, therefore, was always on Mr. Johnson's good side, something most would say he didn't have.

As the class started jogging back to the locker rooms, TJ caught up with Jake. "Jake, I'm running back to my locker quick for some change and then Eric, Patrick, and I are going to grab a quick ice cream cone from Sandy's before heading home. You coming?"

"Aren't you guys going to change?" Asked Jake.

"Doesn't look like it," TJ indicated, pointing toward the left end of the school where Eric and Patrick were already disappearing behind the side of the school. "They said they needed to wash their gym clothes anyway, so they are wearing them home. If you ask me though, I think they just wanted to take full at advantage of our early, early out," he admitted smiling.

"I would come but I already promised Isabelle I would walk her home today."

"Okay, see you at youth group tonight," TJ answered, jogging off toward the other end of the building.

Jake walked back to the locker room, letting himself air out a bit. It looked like everyone else in class must have had the same idea to flee before the bell because Jake was the only one back in the locker room to change. He put his jeans and shirt back on and threw his gym clothes back into the locker, thinking they could go another week or two and not wanting to carry them home, since he was leaving his backpack at school.

The teachers had made a pact with them this year that if the students would do their best to pay attention on early out days, they would do their best to not give homework. So far, the system was working. There had only been one early out, so far, where homework was given and that was only because the students had standardized testing the week prior and the teachers needed to make up for lost time.

Jake finished tying his shoes and walked out into the back hallway, which separated the locker rooms and athletic offices from the gymnasiums. The hall was a ghost town as it was still two minutes before the bell would ring and all the classrooms were at the other end of the building. He planned to meet Isabelle in the courtyard lobby, but he hadn't counted on getting out extra early.

Jake made his way to the lobby, which was on the side of the school parking lot and overlooked a small courtyard with a little landscaping, a few trees, some benches, and a nicely manicured lawn. In truth, it was probably the nicest looking side of the old school building. Jake went out into the courtyard and picked a bench to wait on. He chose his favorite bench; it sat in the back of the courtyard near the building underneath a Japanese maple, a small ornamental tree with red feathery leaves.

The bell rang just as Jake was sitting down. Isabelle would be out shortly. Jake's heart leapt with thought. As Jake watched some squirrels play on the other side of the courtyard, he could feel the gentle fall breeze flowing around him. This was Jake's favorite time of the year, after the heat of summer, but just before the cold of winter. Fall always seemed to draw out the fresh smells in the air that hadn't been there before and, for Jake, it brought a sense of adventure.

Students started coming out of the building, first a small trickle and then a quickly flowing river of students all eager to make the most of their early out. Jake waited until most of the students were gone and stood when he saw Isabelle come out one of the side doors. She glanced toward

Jake and started walking his way, but looked distant and distracted. As Jake got closer, he could tell she was upset about something.

"Hey, why the long face?" Jake asked, trying to lighten the mood.

"Can we just walk for a bit?" Isabelle asked, reaching for his hand.

"Sure," Jake responded, taking her hand in his and turning to lead her on a meandering route back to her house. His heart did a double twist first, because she was upset and second, because every time he held Isabelle's hand he felt like he was hanging on to the most precious person in the world.

Jake hated seeing Isabelle upset, probably because it was so rare. Most people who saw her from a distance usually thought she was very reserved and shy, but those who knew her well knew she was always joyful and full of life with a fiery sarcastic side that would show itself when most people least expected it. Isabelle was usually very resilient and most things would just roll right off her but every once in a while, something would bother her and it would take her a while to snap out of it. Jake had known her long enough to know it was best to wait until she was ready to talk.

Jake led Isabelle away from school into their neighborhood down one of their favorite tree-lined streets. They were passing Haven Park when Isabelle finally broke the silence. "Jake, do you think I'm pretty?"

This question came up every once in a while, and almost always for the same reason. Isabelle was beautiful with her brown, wavy hair, gorgeous green eyes, and bright smile; but she was always self-conscious about her birthmark that started like a thin spider web just below her left ear, followed her jaw line, and then went down her neck. Jake had never seen a birthmark as unusual as Isabelle's, but he'd never thought it made her any less stunning. Even so, she usually wore shirts with collars or turtlenecks to try and cover it up.

About the only reason anyone ever made fun of Isabelle was because she came from an extremely wealthy family. Because of this, everyone knew who she was. Some, when they found out, assumed she was a stuck up snob, which couldn't have been further from the truth. Anyone who knew her loved her and Jake had never seen her actually be mean or rude to anyone. Others were just jealous because of her family's wealth and couldn't resist giving her a hard time. Usually, Isabelle just ignored them, but somehow they must have gotten to her today.

"Iz, how could you even ask that?" Jake consoled turning to face her with concern and disbelief etched on his face.

She looked him in the eye and Jake noticed a single tear making its way down her cheek before she looked at the ground. "No, seriously Jake, do you think I'm pretty?"

Jake could feel himself getting angry at whoever had made her think she was ugly, but he forced himself to stay calm. He put his finger under her chin and raised her head back up so she could see his eyes. "Isabelle, you're absolutely beautiful and I love you!"

Jake proclaimed it before he even realized what he had said. They had been friends since they were kids and, although they both had felt this way about each other for a long time, it had always been an unspoken truth until now.

Jake continued to look at Isabelle until he realized her tear was gone and her eyes were wide open with her mouth turning into a slight smile. Suddenly his words dawned on him and he blushed. Just as he was about to say something, Isabelle put two fingers over his lips to silence him. She smiled, probably the biggest smile Jake had seen from her, and replied, "I love you too!"

Then she wrapped her arms around him and gave him the best hug he had ever had. They stood there for a long while, neither one caring to let go. They didn't care how long they took, or what other people thought of them. In truth, they had loved each other for a long time now. They, as well as their friends and family, knew it and yet, they had never actually voiced it to each other until now. So they stood, hugging each other in a warm embrace, relishing the moment.

Chapter 9

Messenger

A lone figure walked slowly down the long, dimly lit corridor, his pale yellow skin could be seen briefly in the flickering light of torches spaced too far apart. His thin frame trembled nervously with every step he took as his footfalls echoed off the stone floor and walls of the long hallway. His name was Getchen and his life was a pitiful one. Getchen's first mistake in life was being born to a lowly goblin's family, one neither strong, quick, or crafty. In the goblin world that meant he was a slave, for if you weren't strong enough to take, quick enough to steal, or crafty enough to trick away, everyone else took from you. Getchen had always been lowly, but his station now was the worst he'd ever had.

At first, Getchen thought his new position would be a step up from the tar pits where he'd worked for years under a cruel master who sold the tar to many creatures throughout Under Earth. In the beginning, he was right. He went from the bottom of the totem pole, being picked on by fellow slave to master alike, to the station of messenger under the craftiest goblin who had ever lived. He answered to no one but his master, so he only had one to fear. This, he soon learned, was a small consolation to the price he would pay. The longer he'd served this new master, the more he learned his master was crueler than all the others combined.

In his other stations Getchen at least knew what each grueling day would hold and that he at least had a few hours of rest at the end of the day. Now, Getchen was stretched thin, never given time to rest, not having much to eat, and never able to live up to his master's expectations. Getchen knew he would soon have to figure out a way to get himself some help or he would be doomed. Maybe, after he delivered this message, he would have some time to find a slave of his own. Then he would be able to get more done, which would please his master and hopefully help him move up in the ranks.

Getchen hated being a messenger because he always brought bad news and got in trouble for it, even though it was not his fault. Even the times he brought good news his master barely tolerated him. The news he now carried was such that he feared what his master would do. His dread was so great he couldn't force himself to go any faster than the slow walk he was currently using.

As Getchen neared the end of the corridor, he could hear conversation. His master had company! Getchen knew that was bad news. If he entered now, he would be interrupting, which he knew his master hated; however, Getchen also knew his master hated to be kept waiting for important information even more. He decided he'd better go in.

Getchen reached the end of the passage where it came to a T, one passage went left and the other right. Directly in the center of the T, one lone torch lit up the intersection. Few knew this passage existed and none other than Getchen, his master, and a handful of other trusted servants knew its true purpose. The entrance to the passage was very difficult to find at best and, unless one knew where to look on the outside, they would walk right past without ever noticing the door. If someone did get in, they would find the long, dim, stone passage Getchen had just come through and wind up at this T intersection. Going to the left or the right made no difference because either passage took you gradually up and back around to a cliff above where the passage first began.

The intersection was the real passage. Getchen, having traveled the secret path many times, reached out with his right hand and counted four stones down and three stones right from the stone the torch was mounted to. He pushed the stone and it slid in smoothly and without a sound.

There was a soft click followed by a quiet hissing noise. Then, a small section of the wall below the torch slid noiselessly down to become even with the stone floor.

Getchen quickly stepped through the opening and, as soon as he did, the wall slipped back into place as quietly as it had opened. Now, Getchen stood in his master's throne room in a kitchen area that, at one time, had served as an attendant area where servants would prepare food and drink for their king, queen, and any family or guests who might be with them. The room was designed as a hidden space underneath the large stone platform that held the royal thrones. Now, instead of a brightly lit room with much activity, it was a dark empty space filled with cobwebs, dust, and little else.

Getchen walked over to one of the thick curtains that separated the small space from the rest of the throne room and stood there sweating. He needed to calm his cramping stomach before going out which wasn't very easy because he could tell from the way his master was talking that he was already very upset.

After a few moments, Getchen slipped through the curtain into the main part of the throne room. As he did, he realized there were more than a few guests in the room. With a quick glance, Getchen had to guess at least 50 different creatures were standing before his master's throne. Some goblins, trolls, and turogs were standing in the small circle of light emitted by the two torches placed at the bottom of the stairs leading up to the throne platform, which was now cast in dark shadow. The other creatures of various sizes and shapes stood too far back in the shadows of the large room for Getchen to make out.

"Getchen!" came the shout of his master's high-pitched raspy voice. "You're late!"

Getchen turned, bowing low. "My apologies Master, I was delayed," he replied, hoping his master didn't yet know the news he was about to deliver.

"Well, speak, before I let one of the trolls near you see how easy it is for their axes to cut through your goblin flesh." The raspy voice hissed from the shadowed top of the throne platform.

Getchen cringed as he replied, "A young man entered Under Earth yesterday. I saw him come out of the gateway cavern at about midday and I followed him until he reached the bakkara feeding grounds." An eerie silence settled over Getchen and he started to worry. A human had never made it into Under Earth before. This news should have caused a commotion, but the creatures were silent and still behind him.

"Why did you not come and tell me right away?" the raspy voice spewed with a subtle rage Getchen knew all too well.

Getchen knew he would have to choose his next words carefully or face his master's wrath. "My apologies my master, I would have done exactly that had I not had opportunities to get rid of him before he became a problem."

"Did you get rid of him then?"

Getchen was tempted to lie, but knew if his master ever found out the truth he would kill Getchen. "Unfortunately not master. I was able to stir up a resting bakkara by hitting it with a rock I threw from near the young man's position. The bakkara would have eaten him too if it wasn't for those pesky fairies. They saved him by freezing the bakkara. Once I saw this, I guessed they would travel along the safer forest trail rather than leading the boy along the more exposed River Trail. I quickly found a nettle leaf plant by the river and made haste to a narrow part of the forest trail to plant it so the boy might get stung by the thorns."

"And," the raspy voice growled with impatience.

"It worked, the boy scratched his hand and I saw the poison start to take effect, but the fairies with him must have suspected something because, shortly after this, they became invisible. I could not track them any farther so I left immediately to give you this message."

"You're sure you came right here with all speed?" his master asked accusingly.

"Yes my master, why do you ask?" Getchen whimpered, feeling the knot in his stomach tighten.

"Because Zetchel here brought me news of the boy two hours ago. Tell me Getchen, if you would have come back here with the news right away like I had asked, might we have been able to track him still?"

Getchen didn't like where this conversation was heading. He wanted to run but knew he'd be caught before he made it more than a few steps.

The raspy voice continued, "If you hadn't spooked the fairies with the boy, our spies might know where he is this very moment!"

"I'm sorry master," Getchen cried, "it won't happen again!" Getchen hated to be humiliated, and right now, in front of the many fierce creatures present, Getchen found it all the more humiliating.

Suddenly, the raspy voice changed from angry to pleasant, almost pleased. "Well, don't worry Getchen, I have a plan. You only did what you thought would please me most and I can't blame you for that! Come up the stairs."

If it were possible, Getchen was even more unnerved hearing his master sound forgiving. He'd never heard it before and the dread that came with it was worse than getting yelled at. Having no other choice, Getchen ascended the stairs and stopped a few steps from the top where his master stood in the shadows.

"Reach out your hand Getchen, touch my staff and all will be forgiven."

This was such an unusual gesture from his cruel master that all of his senses at once started screaming, danger, imminent danger! Getchen had no choice, he either obeyed and received an unknown punishment, or he disobeyed and received certain punishment. Getchen reached his hand toward the staff held by the tall cloaked figure of his master concealed in the shadows.

The instant Getchen touched it, a flash of pink light came from the end of the staff briefly illuminating the large crooked nose and fiercely angled cheekbones of his master beneath the hooded cloak. The hooded figure then stepped back a pace, but Getchen didn't stir. He felt a current run through his body when his hand touched the staff. Getchen pulled back, but found he could not move. Instead of flesh, his body was now pink crystal. Once their eyes adjusted after the flash, the other creatures in the room could see Getchen's now pink form shining dully in the flickering light of the torches. Getchen was panicking now and he started to whimper, but no one could hear it.

The raspy voice spoke again, "Getchen, Getchen, you failed to realize your job was not to think for yourself, but to do what I told you to do. Because you failed, I have crystallized your body. Not fully, however. You can still hear me perfectly fine, but I'm sure you have lost some of your sight and, of course, you can't move. The crystallization keeps you in a state of hibernation. You'll soon lose the ability to think clearly, but before you do, I wanted you to know why you have been punished and also serve as an example to everyone else here."

Some of the creatures glanced around at each other not liking what they'd heard while others stayed perfectly still, not wanting to show any sign of fear.

"I wanted you to spy on him only and then report back to me quickly as to his whereabouts. That way I could have sent my experienced trackers to take care of him. All you have done Getchen, is spooked the fairies that were with him. Since they became invisible and took the boy with them, we now have no way of knowing where they are." Getchen's master stated, his voice taking on a hard edge.

The cloaked figure's voice now rose to a shout as he yelled "Now all my planning could be for naught because you failed at your simple mission." The cloaked figure stepped forward and, taking his staff with one hand, proclaimed,

"This is the price of failure!" The figure reached out and touched Getchen lightly on the forehead with the staff.

The instant the staff touched Getchen's head, microscopic cracks started forming all over Getchen's form. Intense pain seared through Getchen's entire body and he started screaming with all his might although no sound was heard.

The creatures in the rest of the room only heard silence followed by a small hum. Light started to emanate out of Getchen's form as now, visible cracks started to form. Then, with the sound of shattering glass, Getchen's body exploded outward from the platform into thousands of tiny crystals. Even the evilest creatures were stunned as they began wiping the small crystals off their clothes and skin.

The voice came from the platform again, "that, my dear friends, is what awaits you should you fail me. Now go and find the boy, track him and retrieve what I seek!"

The creatures, large and small alike, turned and hurried out of the room to search for the young man. Each one was eager to please their master and, most of all, not end up like Getchen.

Once everyone had left, the tall, cloaked figure with staff in hand turned and walked back behind his throne where he opened another secret passage. Walking through the door, he turned right and descended a long flight of stairs to a stone tunnel beneath the ground. He traversed this long tunnel for over a mile and then reached another flight of stairs at the other side. The figure ascended the stairs higher and higher until he was very high up inside a mountain and reached a small passage at the top. This passage emptied out into a gigantic cavern. Inside the cavern no torch could be seen. Only the dim light coming from the stairway illuminated a small spot just inside the door. The rest of the cavern was pitch black.

"Go, see what you can find," the cloaked figure commanded.

Suddenly, it seemed as if the whole cavern started to churn. Small lines of light started filtering into the cavern. Moving sand and loose gravel, as well as something hard grinding upon rock, could be heard. What, at first glance, appeared to be a gigantic cavern completely closed inside a mountain was actually a shallow cave with a large platform and a huge opening blocked by an enormous black shape. Then suddenly, with a rush of wind, the black shape was gone, leaving the gigantic cavern in the side of the mountain with one whole side open to the outside light.

Chapter 10

Tree House Breakfast

Jake woke up to sunlight pouring in through a small round window on the wall across from him. He was groggy and felt like he must have had a very deep restful sleep. He was lying on a comfortable couch in the middle of a quaint little living room. There were three large, cushioned chairs in a neat circle to his left, a large colorful area rug in front of the couch and a large table with a bookshelf on it to his right, up against the wall.

Jake stood up and stretched, taking in the rest of his surroundings. He turned right in a slow circle. Just a little way past the desk and bookshelf behind the couch was a large dome-shaped door with another small window. After that, Jake saw a wooden spiral staircase leading up to a hole in the ceiling. As he continued to turn, the back of the room curved away from him, opening up into a quaint little kitchen. Then, the wall started to bend and disappear behind another wall. In fact, the whole place bent and curved in a natural way. There wasn't a straight wall in the place.

This place looks strange, Jake thought as he walked toward the kitchen. He could see that behind the other living room wall opposite the door it bent around forming a small hallway with the kitchen wall. The wooden walls looked so natural that the walls all blended seamlessly together, which played tricks with his eyes. Something else about the place unnerved Jake. As he looked at his surroundings, he thought they seemed bright and pleasant, but his senses were telling him he was missing something.

Jake entered the kitchen and, to his amazement, everything from the counters, sink, and even the small island in the middle curved right out of the walls and the floor.

Even the faucet spout, made out of wood, seemingly sprouted right out of the wall. On either side of the sink were two more round windows that let light in. Lining the back of the counter all along its length were beautifully painted clay pots. After investigating, Jake found some held spices while others were filled with dried fruit, veggies, and even some held things Jake couldn't identify, but the smells that came from them made his mouth water.

After looking at the kitchen, Jake walked back through the hallway and found two more rooms that curved out from each other, both separated from the hall by curtains. Jake went through the first one on his left and found it to be the bathroom. All of its features were made of wood also, except for a few small crystals, one in the shower, two on the sink, and one on the toilet. Jake's curiosity got the better of him and he reached out and touched the crystal on the top of the toilet. Immediately water flooded the bowl and drained away like normal, although Jake didn't hear any water running afterwards like usual.

Jake went into the next room, it too was lit by one round window in the outside wall. Jake couldn't quite figure out this room's purpose right away. It just had an empty shelf on one wall with two clay pots near it. A large tub sink under the window and the wooden device leaning against it seemed familiar. The wooden device gave Jake the answer. It was a laundry room. The device was an old style washboard much larger than one would normally use by hand.

Jake walked back out to the living room thinking the three sisters must be upstairs sleeping. Well, they must have gotten him the antidote to the plant he was poisoned by because he felt great and only had a small scratch on his hand from the thorn.

I'll just see where I am while I wait for them to get up, he thought as he walked over to the door and opened it up. He quickly regretted his decision. Just outside the door was a drop off of what appeared to be thousands of feet down to the forest floor below. Jake's equilibrium was instantly thrown off. His vision tunneled and he started to fall forward. Jake's pulse quickened and he quickly grabbed the door frame before he completely lost his balance. He waited for the dizziness to go away, took some deep breaths, and tried to make sense of what he was seeing. It appeared that he was inside a huge tree in the forest. He was looking straight out at the branches and leaves of many colorful trees.

"Jake, I wouldn't go that way just yet. You're probably going to need our help to get down," suggested an amused voice from behind. Jake spun back into the room, putting his back to the wall for stability. Fieora was standing at the foot of the stairs in pink pajamas, smiling, and she was as tall as he was! Suddenly it dawned on him what had been bothering him about this home was the fact that everything in it was normal size and not fairy sized. Everything should be tiny. Obviously he was missing something. Jake didn't understand.

"Where am I? How did I recover, and how did you get so big?" Jake asked, wondering if he was ever going to see anything normal again.

"First of all, you're in our home, which we made in this tree, hidden in the forest. We've had several different homes over the last few years, but this one's our favorite so far. As to your second question, we made a tea from a few of the mushrooms that were in your jacket. Lucky you picked them because I don't know if we could have acquired them in time to help you. Lastly, I haven't changed in size, you have. We shrunk you. If you were your normal size we'd only be about a 100ft off the ground and you wouldn't fit in our home. Either way, I doubt you'd want to fall out the door," Fieora laughed.

"Hey, what's going on down there? Hasn't anyone heard of sleeping in?" Sapphire asked from the top of the stairs.

"If we'd slept in, our guest would probably be a pancake at the bottom of the tree right now," Fieora replied, still amused by the petrified look on Jake's face.

"Not funny," Jake gasped, trying to calm his nerves and wipe the scared look off his face.

"Tried going out our front door, did you Jake?" Claira asked, walking down the stairs behind Sapphire. "Sorry, we should have left a note on it warning you. We were all so tired yesterday after getting you back here, we didn't think about it."

Jake looked at the three sisters as if seeing them for the first time. He had thought they were pretty when they were small, but now that he was the same size, he could see they were all very beautiful. Little details he hadn't notice the previous day because they were too small for his eyes to see then. They were all identical except for their color, which even tinted their skin slightly. On closer inspection, it was as if a small amount of glitter the same color as their hair and wings was sprinkled on them so they sparkled in the right light.

Sapphire walked to the door and closed it.

"Well, since we're up, I'm going to start breakfast," Fieora announced, starting for the kitchen.

"I'll help," Sapphire yawned, following her sister.

Claira looked at Jake. "Jake, while we are making breakfast, why don't you get washed up? I'll show you to the washroom. I think our younger brother left some of his clothes here when he came to visit. They're clean, but I'll have to resize them after you're done washing so they'll fit. Once you've cleaned up and we've eaten, we'll discuss why you're here and some things you need to know. Also, it's a good thing you were curious enough to pick some of the blue mushrooms. We needed them for your antidote, but didn't have any. It saved us a lot of time when they fell out of your jacket pocket."

"I was told by someone earlier that they come in handy so I picked a few," Jake replied.

"That was good advice!" With that Claira led Jake back to the room he'd found while exploring. She showed him where the soap was and how to operate the water by touching the crystals and tapping them to get warmer or cooler water. She then laid out some clothes that looked just a size too large. "Wash up and put these on," she directed gesturing to the clothes. "After that, come on out and I'll tailor them to fit you before we eat. You can toss your dirty clothes into the wash room next door and we'll clean them later." With that Claira turned and walked out, shutting the curtain behind her.

Jake stood there for a minute, feeling a little uncomfortable in the strange home. He turned on the water and felt the warm liquid run over his skin. On the other hand, it would feel great to have a hot shower and put on clean clothes.

After taking a longer than normal shower, Jake got out, dried off, and put on the new clothes. The hot water had helped his muscles relax and now he could almost fall asleep again if he wasn't so hungry with the scent of breakfast reaching him from the kitchen. The clothes were a bit loose like they were a size too big, but Claira said she could tailor them and Jake had a feeling she could do it a lot better and quicker than needle and thread.

Jake walked to the kitchen, thinking about Isabelle. He knew he needed something to eat, but he was getting anxious to be on his way to find Isabelle. The more time he wasted, the more harm she could come to and the greater the chance he wouldn't be able to find her. He was glad the fairies had found him, but hoped they knew something that would help.

Jake came out of the hallway to the sight and smell of the three fairies putting the finishing touches on breakfast. Fieora was placing the last of the food on the table while Sapphire was setting the dishes and Claira was putting cooking utensils into the sink. Claira turned to grab a spoon off the counter and caught Jake out of the corner of her eye.

She put the spoon in the sink, and then turned to give Jake her full attention.

"Well, those look pretty good on you. We'll have to adjust them a little bit, but not much."

Jake was wearing green pants, which felt a little like light canvas, and a tan, long sleeve, button down shirt with no collar, which felt like cotton.

Claira walked over to Jake with a mixed expression of joy and sadness. She reached out and touched Jake's sleeve with a thoughtful expression on her face. "I had hoped that our brother would be back soon to retrieve these, but it has been a while since we have heard from him." Her expression softened and then she let her pretty face resume the smile it had before. "Still, it looks very nice on you Jake. Now, let me get this size adjusted."

With a flick of her wrist Claira shot a silvery streak from her wand directly at Jake. Although he had been expecting something like this, it was so quick and foreign to Jake that he flinched a little, which made Claira laugh.

As the silvery light struck the clothes, Jake could feel them shiver and billow around his lean, muscular frame as they quickly and quietly tightened to fit his size. Jake could feel the fabric pulling softly over his skin just as if he was putting the clothes on, yet he still stood with his arms at his sides. It was a strange feeling. Then, just as quickly as it started, the clothes stopped shrinking and Jake moved his arms and legs, feeling the snug fit of the perfectly tailored clothes.

"You know, you could make a killing as a tailor or hair dresser," Jake exclaimed admiring the clothes.

The three laughed as Fieora and Sapphire finished putting breakfast on the table. They all sat down and Jake was surprised when all three sisters grabbed each other's hands and then Fieora and Sapphire, who sat on either side of Jake, extended their hands. Jake reached out and took them and the sisters bowed their heads. Jake did the same and Claira prayed.

"Today we thank our Creator for allowing us to find a new friend in Jake and the perfect timing to help him when he needed it. We pray that you would allow us to continue to help him and that you would give him the strength he needs for the journey ahead. Thank you for this food and let it give us the nourishment we need. We pray this in the name of the Son of Light."

Jake felt the two hands he was holding release and looked up. Fieora smiled at Jake and Sapphire slugged him on the shoulder. "Eat up," she encouraged as she started dishing out food for herself.

Not much was said over the next half hour as the four of them ate. Jake was famished and, once he started eating, he didn't have the desire to talk, just to eat. The fairies didn't seem to mind as they too ate in silence. There were three different types of fruit on the table, or at least Jake assumed they were fruit because none of them looked familiar. Jake tried one of each.

The first was long and thin with a shiny soft purple skin. It was really sweet. The second one Jake tried was a turquoise color and shaped like a teardrop about the size of a peach. It wasn't nearly as sweet as the purple one, but had a very rich flavor. The third fruit was round, hard, and spiky. It was brown, but the small spikes were black. Jake had to watch Fieora cut hers in half and eat it with a spoon before he attempted eat his. It was sour at first and he almost didn't take a second bite, but then the sharp sour taste faded to one of the most pleasant flavors Jake had ever tasted.

After the fruit, he tried a bite of some green fluffy stuff on his plate. It tasted exactly like scrambled eggs though what it really was he didn't know. Jake started to laugh and almost choked as he giggled out loud. "You wouldn't by chance have any ham to go with this would you?" Jake asked nearly falling off his chair with laughter. The three fairies just watched him curiously until he stopped laughing and resumed eating.

Jake finished by polishing off a small loaf of bread and a large glass of water, some type of meat dried into jerky, and a second brown and black fruit.

As he finished, Sapphire looked at Jake questioningly. "So what's so funny about the eggs?"

"One of my favorite stories when I was a kid was called *Green Eggs and Ham*, but I never thought I'd actually eat green eggs."

"What color are the eggs you eat?" Sapphire asked.

"Yellow," Jake replied and was amused when Sapphire scrunched up her nose like that was one of the most disgusting things she had ever heard.

After they had finished eating, Jake waited for the three sisters to clean off the table. Now that he no longer felt hungry and weak, he wanted to go find Isabelle. After a few minutes, the fairies rejoined him at the table, but before he could say anything, Claira spoke in a serious tone. "So Jake, why have you come?"

"I'm looking for my friend."

"What makes you think your friend is here?" Sapphire asked.

"Well, my friend just vanished one night while we were out walking and no one has been able to find her." So, Jake told the fairies about Isabelle's disappearance and what had happened since. Then he told them about the morning he left for school, the storm, Tobias, the caves, and finding Isabelle's Jacket.

"So that's when I made my way down the trail and through the forest to the river where you found me." Jake concluded. There were a few moments of pause and Claira was about to speak when she suddenly froze and concern washed over her face. Fieora and Sapphire turned their heads and looked in the direction of Claira's gaze. Claira whispered so quietly Jake almost couldn't hear her. "A shadow just passed."

Jake looked at Claira and was about to speak, but was cut short by Fieora's hand covering his mouth. Jake froze as he saw the concern on the fairies' faces. They were all holding their breath. Suddenly, for the briefest moment, the light in the living room window near the couch where Jake had slept flickered, as if something had cut off some of the light.

Sapphire looked to Claira who nodded. As quietly as she could, Sapphire got up and snuck over to the doorway. Jake felt a chill crawl down his spine as, one after another, the windows grew dark. With a flick of her, wand Claira put out any candles that were lit and they sat in relative darkness.

Suddenly, the tree house shuddered and shook as if a great weight had perched in the upper branches of the great tree. Jake could feel the tree swaying back and forth slightly as they waited. Time slowed and Jake could hear the tree groaning in protest, sounding like there was a weight on it that it was never meant to bear. Jake was looking out the nearest window where the darkness was almost complete. Then, Jake thought he saw the wall of darkness moving slightly. Silence enveloped the four as they waited breathlessly.

All at once, there was a deep resounding growl, very low and guttural. It was loud enough to hear plainly, but also sounded muted, as if whatever made the noise wasn't being as loud as it could be. After it subsided, the silence returned. A few moments later, there was another lurch that sent Jake and Fieora, who still had her hand over his mouth, tumbling to the floor. The darkness lifted like a curtain, allowing the light to return, and Jake heard the loud and repeating sound of a thunder clap and rushing air. After a few seconds, the sound started to fade and after a minute it was gone entirely. No one stirred until the large tree stopped rocking.

"All clear," Sapphire announced turning from the door.

Both Fieora and Claira breathed a sigh of relief as Sapphire rejoined them.

"That was close," Fieora exclaimed, getting up from the floor and offering Jake a hand.

"What was that about?" Jake asked, wondering what had just happened.

It was Sapphire who answered first. "It was Gargoth the Black Dragon. He is looking for us and now, more importantly, probably you Jake."

Jake almost stopped breathing. Believing in three beautiful fairies that had helped him out of a jam was one thing. Believing in a real dragon, which was large enough to create that kind of darkness and shake the gigantic tree they were in, was something his mind couldn't do. Jake sat down on the couch and the three sisters joined him by pulling the three cushioned chairs near him.

"Okay, it's time to level with you Jake," Claira stated, catching his gaze. "I believe you came here to find Isabelle and that is all you are concerned with. From what you have already told us, I think you are right to assume she is here in Under Earth and we are going to do everything we can to help you find her. That being said Jake, we also believe you are here for another reason as well." Claira paused to let her words sink in.

Jake sat there for a few moments in silence, his mind slow to process. Then Claira's last sentence sunk in. "Wait, what do you mean?" Jake asked, puzzled, looking at the faces in front of him.

Claira resumed her talk as Fieora got up and walked over to the bookshelf. "Jake, I am going to explain things clearly to you, but this story will take a few minutes and it would be best if you wait to ask questions until after I'm done."

Claira stopped and waited for Jake to respond. He thought for a moment before responding. Jake wanted to hear what Claira had to tell him, but he also just wanted to find Isabelle and go home. He knew, however, that he didn't know where to look and he needed help to find her. The possibility of having a dragon on his tail made Jake realize it might not be as simple as he had thought to rescue Isabelle.

"Okay, I'll do my best to not interrupt you as long as this helps me find Isabelle."

Chapter 11

The Prophecy

Claira sat facing Jake, unsure where to start. "Jake, there are a few things we think you need to know before you go to find Isabelle. From what you have told us, we believe we might know where Isabelle is or at least who is responsible for her disappearance."

Jake felt his heart leap when he heard what Claira had said and his urgency to find Isabelle rose up even higher, but before he could say anything Claira cut him off.

"However, if you wish to help her, you must not run to her without fully knowing the situation. The black dragon that was just here is but one example of the things you still don't know about Under Earth, which could get both you and Isabelle killed if you don't act wisely."

Jakes urgency to act quickly was tempered a little by Claira's statement.

When Jake waited, Claira continued, "Under Earth has many different races, creatures, and species. Some of them are good, some are not. As you saw by the river, it is easy to stumble across something that could end your journey to find Isabelle very quickly."

"I understand this will be difficult to hear, but many things you have considered fantasy or mythology are very much real or at least based on very real things. I hope, since you are now in the presence of three fairies this will be a little easier to believe than it would have been a day ago." As if for more emphasis Claira's silvery transparent wings unfolded from her back slightly and then went back to their resting position.

"In Under Earth there are Elves, Dwarves, Trolls, Dragons, Goblins, Giants, and Fairies, just to name a few.

We all came to Under Earth a very long time ago. You see Jake, we used to live on Top Earth just like you, but the Creator sent us here for our protection and yours as well. We don't know exactly when in your history it happened, but because we were seen as strange and not normal, many humans came to envy and despise us."

"Once we came to Under Earth, only a few were given the ability to travel back and forth or grant permission for others to do so. The Creator gave one staff of power to each race to accomplish this. Each staff of power also had unique abilities. Most of those who received these staffs became the rulers of their races. Some used this authority wisely and lead their people to prosperity. Others let that authority consume them with thoughts of greed and power. A few races even lost their privilege to go up top or use their staff because of how they abused their authority." Claira paused, "Are you following so far Jake?"

Jake nodded yes, so Claira continued.

"Goblins are one of the races this happened to. You see Jake, goblins used to be elves and their race has always been a very intelligent and clever one, but some of them chose to use that intelligence and abilities for their own selfish gain. Instead of serving their Creator, they became extremely selfish, evil, and vile creatures that used their abilities for evil things. That is why, if you look closely, they appear similar in size and shape to elves, but instead of looking graceful and elegant, they look vile and evil. So many goblins followed this path that they became a different race entirely. This all happened before we came to Under Earth."

"They came to despise the fact that humans were the ones made in the image of the Creator and envied the fact that the 'Son of Light' was to be born among them, so they started a plot to use their abilities, travel to Top Earth and conquer it, intending to enslave humanity and rule over it."

As Jake listened to Claira talk about the Creator and the Son of Light it sounded a lot like the Bible. He was about to ask Claira about it, but she continued and he lost his train of thought.

"Now, not all goblins felt this way. There were a few who had turned back to their Creator. One of these faithful ones, known as Vishor, was the last heir to the Goblin Throne. He was the one who had the power to use the gateway staff entrusted to his race for travel between Under Earth and Top Earth. The goblins staff, gave the power to control rock. This made the evil goblins want it even more."

"Now, a staff of power can only be used by one bearer. That bearer can choose to pass it on to a successor or it can be taken from them if they are killed. Vishor knew the evil goblins would try to overthrow him, take the staff, and put their plan to conquer earth into action. He also knew there were too few good goblins left to stand against the evil ones and they were led by Agor, his former second in command. Agor was a faithful servant to Vishor, but he always held the desire to try and make their race the supreme one on Earth. Agor tried convincing Vishor over the years that it was what they needed to do, but finally realized Vishor wouldn't change his mind, so Agor left Vishor's service and started gathering followers."

"Vishor knew if he was defeated, Agor would ask for the staff first, but would take it by force if he had to. In knowing that, he asked as many faithful goblins who were able, to stand with him against the evil uprising and sent their families into hiding. Soon after, the goblin underground fortress was besieged by the evil insurgents. The faithful ones held out as long as they could, but were eventually overcome."

"Vishor even used his staff's power to control rocks to make mighty rock Golems to defend him, but there were too many enemies for even them to defeat. Once all the defenses were breached, Agor demanded Vishor give him the staff and make him the staff bearer. Vishor knew he couldn't do this so, in the end, he did the only thing he could have done. Vishor used his authority and spoke to his staff. Just as Agor reached for it the staff cracked and shattered into thousands of pieces."

"Agor was so angry he struck Vishor down on the spot. Once that happened, the goblin race was thrown into a frenzy, questioning who should rule. Agor tried ruling, but only succeeded for a few days because many were angry he had allowed the staff to be destroyed. His generals killed him to appease their army, which was on the verge of revolting against them. Ever since, many have tried taking the throne through strength or craft and only a few have managed to hold it for any length of time."

"Now, because the goblin race is ruled by survival of the fittest, their race is but a shell of what it once was. Treachery and infighting have decimated their numbers so that now there are not many left. Of those that are left, most of them are the most vile, ruthless, and evil creatures you would ever want to meet. There are only a handful of the good ones left and they hide from the rest of their race because they are seen as traitors."

"Now, here is where we start to catch up to the present, Jake." Claira stated, snapping his attention back to her.

Jake nodded that he was paying attention. This was an interesting story, but he didn't see how it helped him rescue Isabelle. He hoped Claira would get to the point soon. Claira looked at her sisters and then back to Jake and he saw a change in their expressions. It looked as if what she was about to tell him was more personal than what she had already told him.

Claira looked at Jake and continued. "Twenty years ago, a cold and vicious goblin, who's rightful name we do not know, came to power; we believe it is he who has kidnapped Isabelle, though we can't guess why."

Jake had listened intently up until this point, but his sense of urgency suddenly overcame his caution. "So, do you know where this goblin is or where he has taken Isabelle?" Jake asked, looking from sister to sister.

The three sisters glanced at each other and Jake could tell what the answer was before they spoke. "Yes Jake, we believe we do." Claira answered with apprehension in her voice.

"Okay, so let's get going. You three can show me the way and, once we get there, we can sneak up on the goblin, one of you can freeze him so we can get away, and I'll get Isabelle!" Jake exclaimed, excitement building with each word.

"Jake, wait."

Jake had jumped up from the couch and started to pace, but stopped when he heard Claira and saw the pained expression on her face.

"It's not that simple," she whispered.

"Why not?" Jake blurted, a little louder than he had intended, as all of his excitement turned to frustration and rushed out in those two words.

"Because, Jake, the goblin has amassed many followers now and we wouldn't be able to get close."

"There has to be a way," Jake remarked, less angry, but no less frustrated. Jake looked to Claira, her head bowed a little now, her eyes looking at the floor.

She spoke just above a whisper as a tear ran down her cheek. "Even if there was a way to get him we can't," her sentence trailed off and she became quiet. Both Sapphire and Fieora got up and went to her, putting their hands on her shoulders.

It was Sapphire who spoke next. Her face was still turned toward her sister, but she appeared to be looking past her, as if remembering something, and her blue wings waved slowly behind her as she spoke. "Twenty years ago, we were six years old. One day, while we were playing with our baby brother as our mom and dad watched, a messenger came for our father. It was a little unusual at the time because our father had a strict rule that he was not to be interrupted when he was with his family, unless it was very urgent. You see

Jake, our father's name was Palinor and he was king of our people."

Jake caught the word 'was' and felt his frustration suddenly fade away. Sapphire continued, "The messenger told our father that an envoy from the goblins had arrived and wanted to speak with him about a permanent end to the strife between our races. The goblins had been kidnapping any fairy they could find and forcing them into servitude, making them do the goblins' bidding. Some escaped and managed to bring us news, others we managed to set free, but some were never seen again. Our father had been looking for a way to stop the kidnappings without having to result to fighting, because our race has little experience in such things and the goblins' history was full of it. He knew we would all be in great danger if a war came about, so he jumped at this chance to find a way to forge a lasting peace."

"Father met with the strange goblin who showed him we had a traitor in our midst who was helping the goblins find and kidnap fairies for a price. An investigation was started the same day and, by evening, the traitor was discovered, imprisoned, and questioned in an effort to find the rest of our missing people. "

"Our father then asked the goblin what he could do to help make peace and repay him for his help. The goblin took a stone ring out of his pocket and asked our father to turn it into crystal, for that is one of the special powers of our staff. He said the ring would be both payment and a sign to his people that there was a trust between us. Trusting the goblin, because of what he helped us do, our father went to a secret vault and took out the staff. While our father was distracted, the goblin took out two knives he had concealed beneath his cloak and threw them, killing our father's guards before they had a chance to respond."

Now, even Sapphire had tears running down her cheeks and her voice wavered and cracked as she tried to finish before emotion overcame her. "Our father turned to see what was going on just in time to see the goblin rush up with another knife. The goblin stabbed him through the heart and took the crystal staff. He became the staff bearer and turned our weapons and wands against us. We had to flee or become enslaved by him and, even now, we dare not go close enough to the goblin or he could use our own abilities against us."

"That's why we live concealed in this tree, Jake." Fieora sniffed, brushing her fuchsia hair off her glittering tearstained cheeks. She turned her head and looked at Jake. "The day our father died trying to help our people, our mother took us and our brother into hiding far away from our old home. We can't even live with the other exiles because, if too many of us are gathered in the same place for too long, the goblin can use the staff to sense where we are. We live hidden in small groups, in many different places around Under Earth. We never use our abilities for too long or for too large of a task, because we don't want to be caught."

"The goblin has some of our people as his slaves, even now. There are some who didn't get away quick enough when he got the staff and others, he was able to find using the staff. There have been a few attempts to free them, but anyone who has gone has never returned. They are most likely either dead or slaves to his will now."

Fieora became silent and Jake looked up to see all three sisters staring at the floor with tears running down their glittering cheeks. Jake waited a few moments before speaking, not wanting to belittle their concern or what they had told him, but sure now, more than ever, that he had to reach Isabelle as soon as possible.

"I think I understand what you are saying," Jake started, "and I realize this must be difficult for you. I can't even imagine what this has been like for you. I realize this is going to be very dangerous, but you must tell me where to find Isabelle because, if what you say is true, then who knows what evil things have happened to her? I have to get to her as soon as possible."

"No!" came Claira's loud reply from the chair across from Jake. She was standing now and, through her tears, Jake saw a determined, fiery expression he'd only ever seen on his mother's face.

"I'll go alone," Jake replied, trying to pry the answer from them before they shut him out. "You don't have to help."

Claira sat and motioned for Jake to do the same. He didn't even realize he was standing again until then and he slowly sat back down. Claira's face softened and she continued, "I don't think it is our help you need Jake. Please, listen a little longer. There is an old prophecy that dates back for generations, long before we lost our home. I would like you to listen to it, Jake and then I'll try to explain the best I can what we think we know."

Claira waited for Jake to nod and then turned to Fieora who opened the book she had taken off the shelf. She carefully took out an old piece of parchment from in between the book's pages. It was worn and yellowed with age and looked like it was torn near the bottom.

Fieora looked at Jake, wanting his full attention. "This prophecy has been handed down for many generations. No one in Under Earth is old enough to remember who wrote it except one, and he will not say. None of our people could make sense of it. We had almost forgotten about it until after we were exiled. Then a historian, who was one of our elders, found the prophecy in some old manuscripts he had managed to save when we fled. He read it to us and it suddenly made sense. It is known as the Prophecy of Tri because when it was written it had three parts; however, shortly after, it was torn apart and we don't know what happened to the other two parts."

"This is the first part and it reads:

'One shall come from the world above to reclaim a stolen treasure
He will seek to find the Sword of Light to break the evil spell
With the help of friends, he will go and fight to win and reclaim her

and break the bonds of the liar's tricks and free the throne that fell.'"

When she finished, Fieora looked up and all three sisters stared at Jake. It was Sapphire who spoke next. "You see Jake, once we were exiled we started to believe, or at least hope, that the throne that fell was our father's. When we found you yesterday, we believed the time had come because we have never seen a human in Under Earth before."

"No," shouted Jake, who had suddenly become very angry and couldn't keep quiet any longer. "I didn't come here for treasure. I came to rescue Isabelle. I'm sorry about what happened to your family, I really am, but it isn't my fight. I wish I could help, but my concern is Isabelle."

Before he could continue, Jake noticed he was suddenly still, but his legs and arms were in mid-stride where he had been pacing in front of the couch. He noticed a silver glow around his skin. He found he could only turn his eyes, so he looked as far to the left as he could and watched as Claira stood with her wand still outstretched and walked over to face him.

"I'm sorry it came to this, Jake, but I need you to listen. I know this is hard for you and I can understand your desire to rush out and help your friend, but you have to be ready or you will go in vain. I believe the treasure the prophecy talks about is referring to Isabelle. That is why it goes on to say you will reclaim '*her*' and not '*it*'. I am also not suggesting you make our desire your highest priority. What I believe the prophecy is saying is that when you free your friend Isabelle, you will also free our people. All you need to do is be prepared before you go to find her, which means you must go to find the Sword of Light."

Jake started to calm down, partly because he couldn't move and partly because of what Claira suggested.

"I'm going to let you go now, Jake, please forgive me for freezing you and try to stay calm." Claira lowered her wand and the silver light on his skin disappeared. Jake stumbled forward, still being in mid-stride when he was unfrozen, but without the momentum to carry him on. Fieora caught him so he didn't fall and helped him regain his balance.

Jake took a step back and looked at the three sisters in turn, each pretty face looking back with apprehension in its gaze. Jake sighed and looked at Claira. "Okay, where can we find this sword?"

Chapter 12

The Forest of Forgetfulness

A few hours had passed since the three sisters had lead Jake away from their hidden tree home. They had returned him to normal size once they reached the ground, so they could fly and he could keep pace. Even then, Jake had to walk quickly to keep up. They were taking the narrowest and most out of the way trail, so as to stay out of sight and not encounter anyone who might pass by and report their whereabouts. They were all still visible because, as Fieora had pointed out, they didn't want to attract any undue magical attention either.

They walked mostly in silence, unless one of the three sisters had something useful to tell Jake about a particular plant or tree or a comment about an area they were passing through. Jake walked along, feeling cooler than he had the day before because of the light clothes he was wearing. He'd left both his jacket and Isabelle's at the sisters' home, as well as his backpack.

After a while, all three sisters stopped suddenly and Jake tensed expecting trouble. Then, relaxed as he realized they were all staring at one of the most beautiful flowers he had ever seen. It had petals that opened to look like a five pointed star. The petals were deep red around the edges and then slowly transformed into deep purple in the center where yellow seeds emerged. It also appeared to glow slightly.

"Wow, that's a pretty unique flower, what is it called?"

"It is called a Shade Star," Fieora explained as she continued to gaze at it thoughtfully. "It's rare to find one so far away from the Forest of Forgetfulness because that is the only place they grow naturally."

"Why do they only grow there?"

"We think it is because of Under Earth's sky. Since our whole sky is a light source there aren't many dark places outside of caves and structures. The Forest of Forgetfulness is the only place in the open air dark enough for them to grow. Our mother used to grow them in her garden before we had to leave the palace. She chanced upon one growing on the outer fringes of the forest when she was on a short walk one day."

At this, Jake noticed Claira shoot a strange glance at Fieora, who momentarily lost her train of thought.

"So how was your mother able to have them grow in her garden?" Jake asked trying to start the conversation back up.

"Our mom had to build a special shaded place with magic to account for the flower's special needs. After some time it seeded and she was able to grow a small garden of them, which she tended daily. I used to sit and watch mom tend to the flowers. It was one of my happiest memories of our old home."

After this statement, she grew quiet and they walked on in silence. After what must have been another hour, the four travelers paused in a small clearing in the large forest. The clearing had a couple of bushes from which grew some of the same fruit Jake had eaten earlier that morning. They all ate a light snack of the fruit and rested for a few minutes before starting on again. Jake pocketed two more pieces of fruit for later, in case he got hungry while they were hiking.

A short while later, Claira brought them to a halt at what looked like an end to the path they were on. Two other paths branched off, one to the left and one to the right. Claira looked a bit frustrated and worried, her silvery wings fluttering quickly as she flew upward to get a better view of the area. When she came back down, Jake asked what was wrong.

"This path should keep going straight, right here where this tree has fallen, but it looks like it has overgrown since I was here last. Sapphire and Fieora, stay here with Jake and I will scout ahead to see if we can get back on it up ahead." At that, Claira disappeared into the colorful trees of the forest ahead. She reappeared a while later, looking fairly disappointed.

Sapphire and Fieora went to her side. They talked in hushed tones and Jake had a hard time making out what they were saying. "What does it look like?" Sapphire asked.

"Not good," replied Claira. "The path ahead is completely overgrown as far as I can see. We could go that way, of course, but Jake wouldn't be able to follow on foot and we dare not use magic here."

"So which path do we take?" Asked Fieora, worry lining her glittering pink eyes.

"From what I remember, the left goes away from danger and would be safer , but it also goes quite a long way off-track of our destination. The right is a much more direct route, but it gets dangerously close to the Forest of Forgetfulness," replied Sapphire. Both sisters looked at Claira.

Claira eyed Jake, who tried to appear as though he was very interested in the orange and yellow bush next to the path and not eavesdropping in on their conversation. Claira thought for a moment longer and then admitted, "I don't think we really have a choice. We would take the safer route if time allowed but, as of yet, time is not on our side; so we must risk taking the more direct route." The three sisters looked at each other, worried but determined, as they hovered in their circle. Then, they broke their meeting and fluttered over to where Jake stood.

"Jake," Claira said, her beautiful silvery eyes looking sternly into his. "We are going to take the trail to the right because it is much quicker; however, it is also very risky because it takes us much closer to danger than we would like to go. If we go this way, you must stay very close to us and follow us exactly. To not do so could have disastrous consequences."

Jake nodded his acceptance and they started off again, Claira in the lead, then Fieora, Sapphire, and Jake. Pretty soon, the path started to curve slowly back to the direction they had been traveling before. Somewhere along the curve in the path, they came to a very small clearing not much wider than the path itself, but slightly less dense with foliage. The three fairies hugged the left side of the trail with quick worried glances to the right. Jake did the same.

As he passed through the clearing, he noticed on the right side it parted for another trail and, just beyond, through the trees he noticed something vastly different than he was used to seeing in the past couple of days. Even though it was just a passing glance, Jake saw a very different looking forest from the one he was in. The trees in it looked gnarled and twisted and drained of all color except for a dull greyish green. It looked dark too, not only for the lack of color, but also it seemed the light from the sky couldn't penetrate it like it did elsewhere. It wasn't as black as night, but inside the forest it looked like the grey of evening just before the sun goes down.

Just as Jake was leaving the clearing, which gave him the view of this dark and foreboding place, he noticed a few of the Shade Stars Fieora had talked about earlier. The image triggered something in Jake's mind and his pulse quickened, though he was unsure why.

The group walked on for another few minutes as Jake puzzled over what he had seen. He knew what he had just glanced at was important, but he couldn't put his finger on it. Obviously the other forest must have been the Forest of Forgetfulness, because the flowers Fieora had talked about grew there in greater numbers. Jake remembered Fieora talking about her mom and getting a strange glance from Claira, but he couldn't figure out what it meant. Then, Jake remembered the story Fieora told him about her mother going for a walk and suddenly it clicked! The realization was so abrupt, Jake stopped walking without even realizing it.

If the fairies' mother was on a short walk, it must mean their childhood home, the palace they were exiled from, was close to the Forest of Forgetfulness! The fairies had to flee that place because the goblin took over and, since it was probably the goblin that had Isabelle, he was very close to finding her. That was why Claira had shot that warning glance to Fieora, she didn't want Jake to piece it together. Suddenly, his urgency overrode his better judgment. The three sisters hadn't yet noticed he wasn't following them anymore. In fact, they were fairly far down the trail, almost out of sight. If he turned and ran, he could get back to the clearing and probably part of the way through the Forest of Forgetfulness before the fairies even realized he was missing.

Then they would have to figure out what happened and where he was, which probably wouldn't take long at all, but Jake wasn't sure what they'd do then. They might chance trying to catch him, but they were very afraid of getting too close to the goblin, so they might not even try to follow him. Either way, the odds of them noticing he was gone grew greater with each second that passed. Jake turned and ran! He knew he was risking a lot, but he was sure if he could just find Isabelle he could find a way to rescue her.

Jake hit the clearing in less than a minute, running as fast as the trail and forest would allow. Without stopping, he turned and darted through the small gap in the trees and onto the trail leading into the Forest of Forgetfulness. When he stepped over the dividing line between the two forests, a shiver ran down his spine, but he was running too hard to notice. As he rushed down the short trail into the Forest of Forgetfulness, he noticed it almost seemed as if the darker forest was slowly trying to overtake the colorful one. In the short space between the two forests, there were some colorful trees and some of the gnarled grey-green ones. However, the closer the colored trees grew to the darker forest, the more wilted, stunted, and less colorful they became.

At first, the gnarled trees were very scattered and far apart, but, as Jake ran, they grew denser until Jake could no longer see out of them. He was now completely immersed in the strange twilight as he ran on. His plan was to run, as straight as possible, until he was through the forest. He knew he would have to slow down so he didn't lose his bearings, but he wanted to be sure the fairies couldn't catch him. He knew they were only trying to help, but he couldn't wait anymore, not when he was this close.

After another minute, Jake stopped to catch his breath and check his bearings. As he breathed heavily and the sweat from running through Under Earth's high humidity poured from him, Jake checked his surroundings. It was actually a bit cooler in this forest and Jake noticed a slight mist just above the ground. It smelled like pine trees and rain, even though none of the trees looked like evergreens and it wasn't raining. He could tell which way he had come from and he guessed which way he had to go, but there was no straight path anymore. Crooked trees, fallen logs, and deadwood covered the forest floor, and vines hung from the trees, trailing everywhere across the ground. He was going to have to walk carefully the rest of the way.

The trees around him were still gnarled and twisted and their greyish-green color cast an eerie light about him. It was strange; none of the trees looked the same. All of the trees were gnarled and twisted and the same grey-green color, but some had rough bark while others were smooth. Some had large leaves and others small, while still others had no leaves at all and looked as if they were dead. He also noticed more Shade Stars, peppered here and there in the darkest shadows of the forest, and realized they did in fact glow. As he continued to walk Jake was greeted with a strange feeling that something wasn't quite right about this forest. His mind felt like the mist he could see in the air was trying to get in and cloud his mind. Jake shook the thought off, knowing he was just a bit fatigued because of his quick sprint through the woods.

Once Jake had caught his breath, he started walking again in the direction he figured he had to go. Jake knew the fairies had fled, and was now sure they lived on the opposite side of the forest from their old home. If he could get through the forest, he was sure it wouldn't be too hard to find their palace. Jake suddenly realized his mistake. What if he couldn't go straight through? What if the forest curved or meandered on a crooked path through the mountains? What if there was more than one way to go in or come out of the forest? No! He couldn't think like that. He would never find Isabelle if he doubted himself now. Jake decided to continue on the route he was on. Then he would…Jakes thoughts momentarily slipped as he looked into the dim light all around him. Isabelle, he would find her and everything would be fine.

As he picked his way through the woods, he felt his urgency lessen. He was sure he would be able to accomplish his task now, so he allowed himself to observe his surroundings again. Not only were the trees' texture and size different, but some were very narrow and twisted while others were thick and burly. The tree to his right had small leaves that looked similar to pine needles, while the tree beside it had larger, thicker needles that curled in different directions. The tree in front of him was short and thick with matted greenery, which almost appeared to be hair, all tangled and falling over it. There were some similar, but so far each tree looked strangely different and unique from those around it. As he continued on, Jake knew he needed to keep going, but now was less sure why. His thoughts became slow and sluggish. He breathed in the damp, cool air, which now had an earthy scent to it. It was certainly a strange forest, strange but beautiful.

Jake knew he was trying not to get caught, but he couldn't remember now who he was trying to evade. He also knew he was looking for a friend, but he couldn't remember her name. He knew these were important details, which should have given him cause for alarm; however, he couldn't seem to force himself to worry about them. He continued to walk deeper and deeper into the thick, dense forest and soon, he realized he no longer remembered where he was going or why he was trying to get there.

As quick as a flash of lightning, an image of a pretty girl with brown, wavy hair whose name was Isabelle flashed through Jake's mind. His mind raced, wondering how he could have forgotten her, even for a moment, and it was then Jake realized something was wrong. His mind screamed at him to get out of the forest and run to Isabelle, but his emotions were as calm as ever. His heart beat a steady, slow cadence and his breathing was regular and calm. Jake knew something had gone dangerously wrong, yet he could not get himself to respond to his thoughts. Then, as quickly as they had appeared, Isabelle's image and his worried thoughts vanished and his mind returned to admiring the forest surrounding him.

As he looked around him, his worry about what he'd forgotten was replaced by an awe of the beauty surrounding him. What, at first, he took to be a dark, strange, twisted forest, now looked like the most beautiful thing he'd ever seen. The trees grew crookedly out of the earth and their branches intermingled until they reached up and formed a canopy of gnarled branches and leaves, almost blotting out the sky. It was as if the twisted trees were reaching out and entangling his mind so he could no longer think about anything else. Jake turned then and started walking in a different direction.

The cooler air here calmed him and the slight grey mist covering the ground flowed between the trees, giving Jake a feeling of comfort and peace. As he was walking through the darkness, Jake saw a tree even stranger than the others in the forest. It almost looked like a small boy with a face and pointed ears, however, he was covered in a light grey bark. Jake walked over and found it smooth to the touch. The tree had a few small sprouts appearing here and there, but otherwise it was just covered in bark. Its face seemed asleep, but it very much resembled a little boy. Jake even saw that the two roots could almost be mistaken as feet.

But no, they couldn't be feet. The roots were too long and crooked and too spread apart to be toes. Also, the tree's neck was a little too long to be natural, as well as the overall look of the tree being slightly crooked. Still, it did almost look like a little boy. Strange, Jake thought, the roots didn't seem to be attached to anything. Curious, Jake reached down and found he could pick the little tree up. It was not quite as heavy as what Jake thought a small tree of this size should be, but it still very much felt like a tree. For some reason though, Jake didn't want to put the tree back down so he started walking again, unsure of where he was going. He would show this tree to someone when he left this forest, though he couldn't think of who right now.

After a while Jake had stopped walking, not remembering what he was trying to do and barely aware of who he was anymore. He also didn't care about what he couldn't remember. A singular thought was trying to invade his mind, he would like to stay and become a part of this beautiful forest so he could admire it and be admired forever. He also felt very tired. His limbs grew heavy along with his eyelids. The grey mist circled around him, lulling him to sleep. Jake sat down on a nearby log, which was decaying back into the forest around him, still holding the small tree in his arms.

Jake was struggling to stay awake. He knew he needed to, even though he couldn't remember why, but he was so tired. He fought his eyelids, but they just kept sinking lower until, finally, they closed altogether. Jacob Cross fell asleep in the Forest of Forgetfulness, a thin bark like substance forming on his skin.

Chapter 13

Father Time

"Jacob Cross, wake up!" thundered an old but commanding voice. In his mind, Jake heard this, but found it very difficult to do. His sleepy mind figured it hadn't really heard anything and was drifting back to its slumber when the voice resounded again.

"Jacob Cross, you will wake up now!"

This time, Jake's mind cleared slightly and he knew he had heard a voice and needed to respond because the voice was addressing him, but he still found it very difficult to open his eyes. When he was finally able to, he found that his eyes, though tired, didn't feel quite as heavy as before. He still couldn't remember much from before because his mind was clouded and he couldn't think clearly. The only thing he knew for sure was the voice was talking to him so he must be this Jacob.

"Jake, you must get up and come with me."

Jake searched for the source of the voice but in the greying mist slowly flowing between the trees it was hard to see. Finally, Jake's gaze fell upon a dark cloaked, figure across from him, standing between two trees. The figure's face was lost in the shadow of his hood, but Jake could clearly see it must be an old man because a silvery beard came out from the hood and spilled down the front of the cloak. One of the figure's arms was at his side and the other was holding a wooden staff of a deep red color, which stood in stark contrast to his dark cloak and the grey of the forest.

"Get up," commanded the old man from under his hood. Jake tried, knowing he needed to get up, but his limbs still felt like lead and were unwilling to budge.

The cloaked man walked toward Jake, causing the grey mist to swirl about his robes. When he reached Jake, he swung the red staff to strike Jake on the head. Jake knew he should be alarmed. He should have tried moving, dodging, or evading the blow, but no emotion of warning or panic came and his body still refused to respond. He watched, only mildly interested, as the red staff struck him straight on his forehead and Jake could tell it had been a hard blow, yet he didn't feel any pain, in fact, he had barely felt anything at all.

Suddenly, he heard a cracking sound that started small, but became noisier and started multiplying. Little pieces of something fell past Jake's eyes. Involuntarily, Jake tried reaching up and brushing his eyes with his hand and, when he did, he found the resistance give way with more sharp cracking noises. He brought his hand up and brushed his forehead and heard more cracking and his skin felt rougher than usual. Jake brought his hand back down and looked at it.

His hand was covered by a thin layer of greyish green bark! Jake suddenly understood where the noise was coming from. Himself! Before he had time to consider what this meant, however, the hooded figure reached out and grabbed Jake's free arm and pulled him to his feet with more loud cracking noises.

As he came to his feet, large pieces of the thin bark fell away from Jake's arms and legs and Jake found he suddenly felt lighter and less lethargic.

"Follow me," the figure responded, turning to walk away from Jake. "And please carry the boy."

At this, Jake looked around, trying to figure out what the old man meant until it dawned on him and a chill ran down his spine. The strange little tree he was still carrying didn't just look like a small boy, it *was* a small boy covered in the same bark that was now falling off Jake. Fear and panic came back to Jake like long forgotten friends. He started off after the hooded man quickly, clutching the boy-tree tighter as he went.

Jake didn't really understand what had just happened, but he knew this old man had just saved him from something terrible and he wanted to stay close and get out of this evil forest.

As Jake followed, he found himself becoming lighter and more clear minded. The bark still flaked off, but most of it was gone now. After a few minutes, Jake found they were coming out of the Forest of Forgetfulness into the light of Under Earth again on the same side he had entered. The air became warmer again and the fresh scent of live plants started to clear away the smell of pine and musty earth he had been breathing in. Jake felt the stale weight fade even more in the light of Under Earth's sky and the warmth got his blood flowing again and reinvigorated him. Weird, he thought as he continued to follow the stranger. It seemed as if he had been walking in the Forest of Forgetfulness for a long time, yet it only felt like it took a few minutes to get back to where he had entered.

Now that they were back in the light again, Jake could see the stranger he was following was wearing a charcoal grey cloak and was fairly tall. Once they had reached the small trail leading back into the colorful forest where the grey trees were few and the colorful ones were scattered but strong and healthy looking, the cloaked figure stopped and turned to face Jake, reaching up and lowering his hood. He was a tall, old man, as Jake had thought, with silvery hair and beard, pronounced cheek bones, and hooked nose, but, when Jake looked into his dark green eyes, he was suddenly unnerved. The old man standing before him seemed like he must be 80 or 90 years old, but his eyes betrayed someone much older. It was as if, by looking into this old man's eyes, Jake was able to gaze back through time. His stature also looked different. Although his wrinkled skin and bony fingers showed age, he stood like he was as strong and as young as Jake, almost like age had no effect on him.

The old man spoke for the first time since leaving the Forest of Forgetfulness and Jake could hear it in his voice too! It was a strong voice, but hinted at the fact that this was no normal old man. "Jake, I'm glad I found you when I did! If you had been in that forest much longer, even I would not have been able to help you. Now, I must introduce myself. My proper name is in a language you would not understand, but you would probably recognize me by the name Father Time."

Jake nodded, but responded nothing so as to allow the old man to finish. He knew he should stop feeling surprised with things in Under Earth, but it seemed the more he learned the more it amazed him.

"If you would be so kind as to follow me, I will show you to my home where you can rest, because I believe you have been up for a full day by your reckoning. You probably don't even realize it yet, as there is no night in under Earth and it never gets dark here except for when the storm comes."

Jake made a mental note about the way Father Time mentioned the storm, like it was an Event and not just an occurrence.

Time continued, "Once you have rested, I will do my best to answer some of your questions, as I'm sure you have a few, and then I will escort you to your next destination." Father Time smiled and then turned, using his red staff as a hiker would a walking stick on a casual walk through the woods.

Jake followed, still carrying the small boy/tree. They got back on the path Jake had been on earlier with the three fairies and started going the way they had gone before. Jake felt guilty now. The fairies had been right in telling him he wasn't ready for this task and he was ashamed he had not trusted them more. He decided there was nothing he could do about it now except to apologize if he saw them again. He hoped they had not endangered themselves in trying to find him.

"Father Time?" Jake asked, wanting to voice his concern quickly now that he had thought of it.

"Yes Jake," he replied from up ahead.

"I was with three fairies before I went into the Forest of Forgetfulness. You don't think they went in to look for me, did they? I didn't mean to put them in danger."

"No Jake, Claira, Sapphire, and Fieora are fine. They came to me when they found you were missing. I sent them to search the trails to make sure you hadn't gotten lost in this forest while I went to see if you had indeed wandered off into the Forest of Forgetfulness as its powers cannot affect me."

Jake was relieved he hadn't caused the sisters to come to harm and let his mind wander a bit as he followed Father Time through the colorful forest. The trees never ceased to amaze him with their variety. The one he just passed on his right, had bright yellow bark and deep red leaves, which almost matched the color of the staff in Father Time's hands. The one just to his left, had leaves which were light pink on top, dark pink on the bottom and dark purple bark.

As he continued to follow and look at his surroundings, he could feel himself begin to fatigue. It wasn't the unnatural tired feeling like in the Forest of Forgetfulness, just the fatigue from a long day of hiking. He was about to ask Father Time how much farther they had to go when, suddenly, the trail they were on spilled out into a clearing.

Jake caught his breath as he saw six menacing figures standing in the center of the clearing, looking like they had been there just waiting to pounce on anyone who happened to be following the trail. Although Jake had never seen these creatures before, he guessed they were trolls. In stories he had heard many different and varied descriptions of trolls, but a troll was all he could think of when he looked at these creatures. They were all taller than him and most matched Father Time for height. They had dark green skin, large, muscled frames, long, pointy ears, and vicious looking eyes.

A couple of them had tall Mohawks for hair, starting at the front of their heads and running down part of their necks. One Mohawk was bright red and the other a bright yellow. Two of the others were bald with short stubbly beards. They appeared as if they were twins. The fifth one had a long, braided, orange ponytail going almost all the way down his back. The sixth one was slightly larger than the rest and had dark purple dreadlocks hanging down past his shoulders. They all had long, crooked noses and their bottom jaws stuck out a little farther than their upper jaw. Two long fangs came out from their bottom jaw and rested on their upper lips.

When Father Time and Jake stepped into view, they all turned toward them and Jake could see they all wore battle armor and they were heavily armed with cross bows, swords, axes, and shields. The largest one, with the purple dreads, stepped forward and growled a low guttural bellow.

Jake was frozen and looked at Father Time to see if he would tell him to run, but the old man seemed unconcerned. Jake was sure the trolls would attack, as they all had their hands on their weapons, but Father Time simply commanded "Come, Jake," and started walking toward the trolls.

The troll with the purple dreads must have been the leader of the group because he growled again and brandished his large battle axes, one in each hand. They gleamed in the sunlight and looked sharper than razors. The troll looked as if he could cut down a tree with one swipe from one of his axes. He strode toward Father Time and spoke with a deep growl of a voice, "Stop where you are. You are now our prisoners and we will take you to Medusa's Heir for questioning. We will take your possessions and escort you to the goblin's fortress. If you refuse or try to trick us, you will pay for it with your lives!"

Father time stopped and turned to face the troll, but still looked unfazed by the threat. "You do not know whom you address. You cannot harm me nor anyone under my care."

In a flash, the troll's countenance went from sneering to furious, and he reached up to swing one of his large axes right at Father Time's neck. Jake was going to shout, but quicker than Jake thought was possible, Father Time spun his staff straight out in front of him and struck the ground.

There was no flash, no sound, and nothing changed except for the fact the trolls were now frozen in place. Jake looked at each of them in turn. The leader was in mid-swing, with his muscles tense, and Jake could see that even the sweat beading on his forehead wasn't moving. The other trolls were in mid-motion also. A couple of them had started to run, while the others were in the middle of drawing their weapons.

Jake thought for a second that Father Time must be able to freeze things just like the fairies, but, as he continued to look around, he saw more things frozen. The trees and leaves still bent as if they were in a slight breeze. The grass was bent from the wind, but there was no more wind and the grass was not moving, and even a few insects in flight were stopped in mid-air.

Jake looked at Father Time. "How did you manage to freeze everything?" he asked, astounded.

Father Time looked at Jake with a curious expression on his face. "I haven't frozen anything Jake, nor could I if I wished to do so. I have simply stopped time for the moment. Right now I am outside of time and I have allowed you to come with. We will get a safe distance away from these creatures and then I will let time resume. Now, follow me."

With that, Father Time turned and continued on walking right past and through the trolls. Jake was astounded again and, even though he was sure the trolls couldn't harm him right now, it made him a little nervous to walk right past these large, fearsome creatures.

Jake followed Father Time along the trail back into the forest, silently, all the while noticing the surreal. Leaves stuck in mid-air as they fell from a tree, a frog in mid-leap from a bush to a tree, and even a bird frozen while in a dive through the air, only moments away from catching an insect for lunch. The whole time the lack of air movement or sounds, other than those he or Father Time created, made for an experience unlike any other. The trail ahead curved and on the right there was a rock cliff about twice Jake's height. A small waterfall cascaded down it and ended in a pool at the bottom, which flowed into a small stream.

As Jake crossed the small wooden bridge that was built right next to the pool spanning the stream, he stopped to look. He had seen the visual effect of water stopped mid-air in movies, but this was better by far. He could actually reach out with his hand and push it through the spray and water droplets, feeling the cool wetness on his skin. He could see the ripples frozen and even the water hitting the bridge where it would spray back up in even finer droplets.

Jake waved his hand through the water again. Some of the water stuck to his hand while the rest came off and hung in the air where his hand left it. The water should have fallen from his hand when he moved it through, but it just stayed suspended in the air. Jake continued to disperse the water with his hand, creating a space to stand in. Once enough of the water droplets were relocated, he stepped forward into the space where the water had been coming down to hit the bridge. He stood looking up and around at the water above him and surrounding him on three sides. The sight was incredible!

Jake looked at Father Time who was stopped a little way ahead looking back. "This is awesome!" Jake hollered looking back at the water.

"If you think that is cool, watch this!" exclaimed Father Time reaching out again with his staff. Suddenly the water, which was quietly frozen a split second before, came down onto Jake, soaking him quicker than he could jump off of the bridge with the small boy in his arms.

"Hey," Jake hollered and looked toward Father Time.

The old man broke out into a large grin and started laughing uncontrollably. Father Time almost doubled over, holding onto his staff for support while he heaved with laughter.

Jake started to laugh too, knowing he had allowed himself to be caught in the perfect trap.

After another minute, Father Time's laughter subsided and he looked back at Jake and smiled. "You wouldn't believe how long I have been waiting to do something like that! I'd say I'm sorry, but you stepped right into that one, no pun intended."

"I sure did, glad I could oblige," Jake sputtered, half smiling while he ran his fingers through his hair, wringing some of the water out.

They started walking again around the bend in the trail, leaving the small waterfall behind. When they arrived at the other side of the rock, Jake noticed the rock here wasn't as steep. They walked a bit farther around and then on the right, just as the trail started turning left, Father Time disappeared. Jake jogged up to where he had seen the old man a moment before and came to an opening in the rock..

If he hadn't seen Father Time go this way he would have missed the opening, cleverly hidden from the trail by rocks and plants. Father Time was waiting on a stone stairway that was cut into the rock, winding up around a bend Jake couldn't see past. Father Time started up and Jake followed. There was no railing, but the stairs weren't very steep and were fairly easy to climb. At first, the stairs were carved shallow in the rock, but they went deeper into the rock as they went on, causing Jake to lose sight of the forest on either side, which was replaced by rock walls. They continued going up, sometimes curving right and other times left. Jake couldn't see very far ahead because the stairway continued to curve and he lost count of how many turns it had been since the bottom.

After another minute of climbing, he could see the rock level out a short way up and, when the stairway ended, Jake found himself in a small clearing. In front of him were a couple of benches around a fire pit. To his right the clearing continued to an overlook where Jake could see quite some distance into the forest. They weren't high enough to see over the trees, but it still provided a wonderful view of the forest. To his left there was a cavern leading back into the rock, which continued upwards.

Outside the cavern door, which was just the right size for Father Time to walk through without stooping, there were two wooden chairs. They were different than the benches though because the benches seemed rough and unfinished where as these seemed very well made with intricate carvings and designs on them. He had never seen something made out of wood this well. Father Time turned and watched Jake. He must have guessed what Jake was thinking for he answered, "I have had a long time to perfect my craft." He then turned and walked into the cavern.

Jake followed, noticing the cave was very well lit. When he entered, Jake found a very comfortable home. It was slightly cooler and less humid than outside, even though there was no door and there were holes carved along the left side of the cavern for windows. These also looked out into the forest and had no coverings. The cave home wasn't tiny, but not huge either. It seemed perfect for one person to live in. Father Time sat down on a chair a little way to the right of the doorway. The first room was almost round, except for a stairway in the back right corner, and the left side opened into another space that looked like storage.

Father Time motioned Jake to come over. He walked over on weary feet. "Let me have the boy and I will tend to him while you get some rest. You did a very good thing by rescuing him from the forest, Jake, even though you may not have realized it at the time. The boy was in there for longer than you were, which is why he looks more like a tree than you did, but you found him in time for me to help him. After Jake handed the boy/tree to Father Time, he stretched his arms, trying to undo the cramps that had developed from carrying the boy. He wandered over to the back wall where a very comfortable looking bench or couch was located covered with soft padding and blankets. Jake sat down and faced Father Time.

"You see, Jake," Father Time continued, "I am able to help those to whom the Creator sends me, but I cannot interfere with things unless I am given permission. Since I already had permission to find you, I was able to help you, but if you had not found this little one before I found you, I would not have been able to help him. He and his family are truly in your debt. Now, lie down and get some rest while I tend to the boy. It will be a while, I think, before the fairies return and you need to sleep.

Jake laid down and watched as Father Time got up and started mixing some herbs and liquids together, presumably to help the boy. Jake fell asleep and, for the first time in a long while, he didn't have any dreams or nightmares. He just slept a very restful sleep.

Chapter 14

The Immortals

Jake woke up feeling very rested and rolled up to a sitting position to stretch his muscles. He yawned and looked around. In the chair that Father Time had sat in, there was a small boy curled up asleep, now looking much more like a boy than a tree. Most of the bark was gone and only a couple of sprouts with leaves remained on him and those looked withered and ready to fall off. Jake watched him for a few moments as the boy's steady breathing rose and fell. Jake noticed the boy's features were angled and he had a pointed nose and ears . He looked like a young elf.

Jake stood up and stretched again, then walked over to the door. Father Time was outside, sitting in one of the intricately carved chairs, smoking a pipe while his staff rested by his side. The old man motioned toward the benches near the fire pit and Jake saw a plate containing some dried meats, fruits, and bread. He walked over and picked it up, popping some of the fruit into his mouth as he walked back to rejoin Father Time. Jake sat down in the other chair. It was very comfortable with a gentle backward slope, so he could sit in a reclined position.

"The sisters came back while you were resting and were glad to see you safe Jake."

"Where are they now?" Jake asked, eating some of the meat, which was quite similar to jerky.

"I sent them to find the boy's family," he replied.

"So, what now?" Jake asked, looking over at Father Time.

"We will wait for the boy's family to come and get him and then, after resting a bit more, we will travel to the Granite Castle where you will find the Sword of Light and train with its keeper. Only after this, will you be able to defeat Medusa's Heir and rescue your friend."

"Who is Medusa's Heir?" Jake asked.

Father Time looked at Jake a moment before speaking, "I assume the sisters already told you what they know?"

Jake nodded.

"Very well, so you already know of a few of the things this goblin has done. The goblin they told you about is the one whom I referred to as Medusa's Heir. He was given that name because of his fondness for turning living things into crystal. He uses the staff he stole from the fairies to do this, which is why he is able to turn things into crystal instead of stone."

Jake interrupted as a new question tugged at the back of his mind. "Are you telling me Medusa was real?"

Father Time smiled, "You spent the past couple of days in the presence of the three fairies, you were just about turned into a tree, and now you're sitting here talking to me after getting past the trolls and seeing time stop and yet you question whether Medusa was real?" Father Time chuckled and waited for Jake to respond.

Jake thought for a few moments. "Well, I guess, it's just that I've spent my whole life hearing about these things, like they were just fictional stories, and it is hard to change that idea in a day."

Father Time took a long draw on his pipe and blew out a few large rings of smoke before letting the rest of his breath out. "Some of the things you grew up hearing are true, Jake. However, as with most, things, the stories have been changed slightly or distorted over time and with many retellings. Some things happened very similar to myth or legend and others happened completely differently. What I am about to tell you may be hard to understand, and only a few know it, but I believe the time has come for you to learn."

Father Time looked at him and Jake nodded his head.

"Many old stories are based in truth, some more than others. You know that many old cultures from Earth, such as Egyptian, Greek, and Roman, had many different gods as well as some current religions such as Hinduism. What I am telling you is that many of these so-called gods did exist at some point or still do exist, except for the fact that they aren't gods at all and never were. You see Jake, there is only one Creator, only one who gives life. When He created the universe and the things in it, He also created stewards to govern certain things. These stewards had the authority to govern or control certain areas or aspects of creation; however, the important thing to remember is that they were also created. They were given their authority by the true Creator and so their authority could also be stripped from them."

"For a long time, these stewards governed their responsibilities wisely and peacefully. However, after a while people started worshiping these stewards in place of their true Creator. After generations of people continued to do this, many of the stewards started to believe this themselves and lost their way. They forgot they were created, just like people, and started to believe themselves worthy of human praise and worship. They allowed themselves to be called gods in many different cultures and they went by many different names. They tried taking the Creator's authority as their own. As a result, they were stripped of their powers and cast down, much like the angels who tried rebelling in heaven."

"There are only a few stewards left who still worship their Creator. You see Jake, I am one of them, a steward of the Creator. That is why I have the authority of time. I have many different names in many different cultures and people have tried worshiping me, but the difference is, I do not accept their worship because I remember I serve a higher authority as well. I am a creation of the true Creator and worship Him alone. I only have my authority because He has given it to me and, if I started to believe myself greater than

Him, I would be lying to myself and become lost as well. Does this all make sense to you Jake?"

It was a lot to understand, but Jake felt he understood the basics and nodded his agreement.

"This problem has been around since the beginning of, well me! Even people throughout history have done this. The Egyptian Pharaoh's believed themselves gods and even some current day religions teach that people themselves are, or can become, gods. Pride and selfishness have a way of blinding anyone who spends too much time giving in to them and they lose sight of who they really are. In essence, this is what Medusa's Heir is trying to do."

"Now, I have been given permission by the Creator to help you get to the Sword of Light and make sure you are trained. After that, however, it will be up to you and I will have to go my own way. The Creator has assigned you the task of rescuing your friend. Even in this, however, you will not be alone, you will still have help."

"Now, Medusa's Heir is a very crafty goblin. He is sure to know of the Prophecy of Tri and, even though he might not fully understand it, he knows enough to try and stop you, whatever the cost. That is why you must find and learn to use the Sword of Light. It is the sword of the Creator and, only by using it, can you defeat Medusa's Heir and save your friend. Even so, things may arise that call for help from friends. Don't refuse those who want to help you in this, for it may mean the difference between victory and defeat. Medusa's Heir does not have an army yet, but he still has many at his disposal."

At the mention of friends, Jake thought about his. He suddenly wished that they were here with him. Although he would not want to put them in danger, they would be a great encouragement. TJ was always up for an adventure, even when Jake wasn't. Eric was always confident and reassuring. It might have something to do with his size, but Jake found his attitude infectious when he himself wasn't feeling very confident. Patrick wasn't known for his adventurous spirit or his confidence, but his archery skills might be very helpful. Jake's attention was brought back to the present as Father Time continued talking.

"His greatest threat, however, is not physical. Medusa's Heir is a very able fighter, but his greatest weapon is his keen intellect. The guardian of the Sword of Light will help train you, not only how to fight with the sword but also how to trust in it and use it to help you see the truth through the trickery and lies of Medusa's Heir."

Jake thought, as he listened to Father Time and finished off the last of the food on the plate. He had never been in many fights and wasn't sure what he could do, but, if it meant he could rescue Isabelle, he would put everything he had into learning.

"Now, I believe the fairies are almost back with the boy's family, so we should go wake him now." With that, Father Time put his pipe down on the arm of his chair, took his staff in hand, and went back into his home.

Jake followed Father Time and put the plate he was carrying on the counter space under the natural cave windows that looked out into the forest. He made it back, into what he considered to be the living room, just in time to see Father Time put a purple pasty substance on the boy in a couple of places where the sprouts had been. Jake figured it must have been something to help with the healing process.

Father Time set the bowl containing the purple paste on a small table nearby and gently shook the boy to wake him. The boy slowly opened his eyes, still pretty groggy from the effects of the Forest of Forgetfulness. Father Time held out a mug of a blue substance, which Jake realized must be the same tea he had drank at Tobias's house, the one made from the glowing blue mushrooms. The boy accepted the mug and sipped some tea then, after a few moments, the boy felt the tea's rejuvenating effects and gulped the rest down quickly.

Jake then heard footsteps hurrying toward the cavern. Through the door flew the three fairies followed closely by the boy's parents. They were tall, with sharp features and pointed ears. The man had dark brown hair, which fell straight down his back, while the woman's hair was slightly lighter brown with a deep red tint to it. They both wore robes of green and, at first glance, Jake knew they were elves. Both were pleasant looking. The man had strong, handsome features while the woman was pretty, with softer features. They carried themselves with a graceful elegance, that was fluid and effortless. It was this elegance, even more than their natural appearance, that made them look so foreign.

When they came into the room, the small boy's eyes widened and all traces of sleep vanished. He jumped from the chair with a cry of joy and ran to his mom who knelt down and received him into a warm embrace. The boy's father knelt beside them and cradled them both as his mother cried tears of joy. Father Time, the three sisters, and Jake just stood there for a few minutes, watching the happy reunion.

Then, the boy's father stood with tears in his eyes and walked over to Jake. "I hear you are the one I have to thank for finding my son in the forest. Thank you! We thought we had lost him forever and I cannot repay what you have done for my family. My name is Gadlonin and this is my wife Gwenn. We are in your debt! If there is anything you need in which I can be of service, just send word and I will come to your aid."

Then the mother stood, still cradling the boy in her arms, and joined her husband in front of Jake. "What my husband says is true, may the Creator bless your journey to save your friend and, if there is anything we can do to aid you, you only need to ask. We will be going home now, but if you do need to reach us, the fairies know where we live. If they are unavailable, send someone to the elves in the North and they will get word to us."

Jake stood there, overwhelmed by the sense of gratitude they showed him, and all he could think to do was bow his head with respect. The family, including the small boy, smiled at Jake and then turned and left.

Jake then turned to his right, where the fairies were resting on a chair, looking weary. "I owe you three an apology. I let my worry lead me to do the exact thing you tried warning me against and I wouldn't have made it if Father Time hadn't found me when he did. I'm sorry for not listening and possibly putting you in more danger!"

Though she was weary, Fieora jumped from the chair, flew over to Jake and hugged his arm. Claira smiled wearily and nodded her head, but Sapphire glared. "Don't let it happen again!" she barked and flew outside. Fieora let go of Jake and floated back over next to Claira. "Don't worry Jake, she isn't as quick to forgive, but she'll come back around soon."

"I hope so, I don't like the thought of her being mad at me," Jake declared, smiling. He was only half joking. Claira seemed like the level headed one. She could be serious, but in a loving, motherly way. Fieora was the joyful one who saw the good in everything. Jake bet it would take a lot to make her angry. Sapphire, however, was the most unpredictable. She could have a good time with the best of them, but if something happened she didn't like, her mood could change quick. Still, Jake got the impression she was angry more because he had been reckless than foolish. She cared, but didn't want to show it, so it came out as anger.

Jake turned to Father Time, "So, what now?"

Father Time sat down in the chair the boy had been sleeping in and looked at Jake. "Now we rest a while longer. The fairies have had a long day of flying and need to recuperate and you will need your strength for the hike and the training you will endure after it. I know you just woke up a little bit ago, but try to get some sleep if you can. Otherwise, just do something restful you can enjoy." With that, Father Time leaned his head back into the tall chair and closed his eyes.

Was he asleep already? Jake couldn't tell, but it looked as if Father Time had instantly fallen asleep. Jake smiled. Even Time slept, from time to time. Jake glanced over at the two sisters still in the room. Fieora had gone over to where Jake had slept on the bench and was already fast asleep. Claira was still in the chair she had been on but was now seated in a reclined position letting her eyes slowly close.

Jake chose to walk outside and watched the forest from Father Time's overlook for a while. He didn't think he could fall asleep right now anyway. Jake walked out across the clearing, past the fire pit, to the small grassy area overlooking the forest. He noticed Sapphire on his way. She was curled up on a soft looking green plant near the brook off to the left, fast asleep as well.

When Jake got to the overlook, he found a place where the ground sloped down and then leveled out, creating a perfect natural recliner. He could sit on the grass and lean back just enough to be comfortable, but still be able to look out at the colorful forest and watch the plants stir in the breeze. He saw birds and insects and even spotted a couple of creatures he didn't recognize. He drifted off to sleep, not because he was tired, but because he was comfortable.

Chapter 15

The Granite Castle

The next day, Jake woke up abruptly after Sapphire had used a little magic to pick up some cold water from the stream and drop it on him. Apparently, he made a pretty good face when he awoke because Sapphire immediately fell to the ground laughing. Jake didn't mind though because she appeared to have forgotten her anger from the day before.

They all ate a quick breakfast and then Father Time led the way to their destination. The three sisters took turns riding on Jake's shoulders and Father Time's. This time Jake enjoyed the trip. The three sisters were relaxed and not worried about anything, unlike the day before. Jake knew they felt safe now that Father Time was in their company. They talked, joked, and laughed. They showed Jake things about the forest and even Father Time would chime in with an interesting piece of information or a story that he remembered.

Gradually, the landscape changed. Jake noticed the trees became thinner and the ground began to slope downhill. They eventually came to the edge of the forest. After a hundred feet of open grassy space, the ground sloped downward into a valley.

When they came to the edge where the ground fell away, Jake could see the valley spread out before them. In the center of the valley, surrounded on three sides by water, was the largest castle Jake had ever seen. Not that he'd actually ever been to a real castle before, but this one had to rival the largest ones topside. The castle was situated on a large peninsula, which jutted out from the shore and rose up out of the large lake. It made the castle look as if it were on a pedestal.

"Jake, that is the Granite Castle where the Sword of Light resides and where you will train," Father Time declared, looking out over the valley.

Jake stood, staring at the beautiful valley before him, squinting slightly now as the full light of Under Earth's sky could be seen without the trees to block some of it. Jake was glad it wasn't as bright as the sun because he would have gone blind pretty quickly. They descended into the valley as a pleasant warm breeze blew over them, making the long colorful grasses around them dip and rise like ocean waves.

They had to cross over the large river using a raft hooked to a rope and pulley system. Father Time showed Jake how to pull the raft across the river by walking the rope down the length of the raft, pulling it across. Jake didn't mind at all. He was learning something new and, after just walking for days, it felt good to use his arms. As he worked, Jake continued to glance at the castle. It was different than any castle he had seen as well. It wasn't square shaped, but curved. From his current position he couldn't see the front, but it didn't look like a complete circle either.

Once they were across the river, they walked around the lake to the front side of the castle. It was the only side of the castle which was connected to land where the peninsula it sat on jutted out into the lake. Once they came to the bottom of the peninsula, it started to rise out of the lake. It took the group a while to walk uphill to get closer. The incline was gradual at first and then became much steeper as they went on. Jake figured this made the castle easier to defend, yet he still hadn't seen anyone or anything near the castle stir. It seemed empty.

As they walked, Jake could see why the castle had looked strange. The back was round, but the front curved back in, similar to the shape of a crescent moon, although it must have been much deeper. Its round side must go back quite a way, from what he saw when he was coming out of the forest. The two sharp corners jutting out from the sides were slightly taller than the middle of the castle where it curved back to where the gate was. The ground leveled out at the top and Jake got a better view.

They were still outside the reach of the outside wings of the castle, but Jake could see more walls the same shape as the outer wall, but reaching higher. There looked to be three different walls, each mirroring the other. They were one inside the other and, in the center, a tower rose high above them and disappeared into a mist, which surrounded it in the sky. Strange, thought Jake, the mist didn't look like a cloud. It appeared more like a light fog hovering around the top of the tower. The mist didn't seem to flow with the air, but stayed centered around the top of the castle, obscuring it from view.

As they drew closer, Jake was even more impressed by the size of the castle. If he thought it was large before, now, walking up to it, the castle seemed immense. It stretched until it was almost touching the lake on both sides and the walls towered above them. True to its name, it appeared to be made of solid granite. As they came in closer, inside the crescent shape in the front of the castle, Father Time held out a hand to stop them. The fairies who were sitting on Jake's shoulders at the moment exchanged curious glances and Jake could tell they were confused too.

Father Time walked about thirty yards ahead and then stopped. Suddenly, a deafening roar split the quiet breeze, sending all types of small animals and birds Jake hadn't seen or heard before fleeing through the tall grass. The fairies clung to Jake tightly as they all kept their eyes on Father Time. He glanced back, seemingly unconcerned, and motioned for them to stay still. Jake knew what the fairies were thinking because he was thinking the same thing. Could the black dragon have found them?

The sound, which appeared to be coming from the castle, died off and, as they watched the dark grey walls of the castle, a glittering red caught their eyes for a moment. It was just a brief glimpse, but something was moving behind the walls. Jake heard a familiar sound. A large red dragon rose above the walls of the castle and came to rest on the outer wall, wings outstretched and ready for a fight. Even with Father Time standing there, the sight was so terrifying, it made Jake want to turn and flee, even though he knew if the dragon attacked he wouldn't get away.

A low, rumbling growl sounded from the dragon and it opened its maw and let out another roar. This one wasn't quite as loud, meant more as a warning, Jake thought. Father Time answered by raising his red staff. The dragon studied him for a moment and then spread its wings and hopped off the wall gliding to the ground. It landed in front of Father Time with a jarring force, sending tremors through the earth at Jake's feet. The red dragon then folded its wings and brought its head down to Father Time, who reached out and patted its scaly nose.

"It's good to see you again too, Crimson." Father Time affirmed. Then, he turned toward Jake and the fairies. "It's good to see you both as well, Ocean and Sunstrike."

Jake suddenly realized Father Time was addressing something behind him. A chill ran down his back as he turned around. Jake jumped backwards, nearly knocking the fairies from his shoulders, as he saw the two other dragons behind him. One was a beautiful blue and the other a magnificent yellow. They were both roughly the same size as the red dragon, yet, somehow, they had managed to sneak up on them without a sound. That sent an even bigger chill down his spine, knowing something so large and ferocious could be so quiet.

"It's alright, Jake," Father Time reassured. "They are friends. Let me introduce you to the three dragons known as the Primes. The yellow dragon's name is Sunstrike, the blue one is called Ocean, and the red one behind me is known as Crimson." As if in response, the three dragons roared into the air and Jake and the sisters had to cover their ears. The sound was so loud, the ground shook.

Jake turned back to face Father Time and Crimson when he heard a strong, clear voice, more in his head than with his ears. It was definitely male and appeared to be coming from the red dragon. "It's good to meet you, Jake, Claira, Sapphire, and Fieora, but we'd better leave the introductions until later. You are safe here, but it is still wise to get you inside before prying eyes see you here. We will stay here for the moment while Father Time takes you into the castle."

Crimson stepped aside to let them pass, causing tremors as he went. Father Time motioned for Jake to follow, but Jake had a hard time doing so because he continued to look back at the dragons. It was the first time he had actually seen a dragon, since he had only heard the black dragon before while in the tree house. They were all magnificent creatures. They looked majestic and fierce at the same time. It looked as if the three were talking amongst themselves. Jake was forced to tear himself away from the sight and follow Father Time more closely once they got near the castle's outer wall.

The castle looked ancient, even though the granite was in pristine condition. They came up to the massive doors in the outer wall. Jake was just wondering how they were going to open them when he saw a smaller set built into the middle of the large ones. Both sets of doors were made of granite also, but instead of the dark grey of the castle walls, they were white with intricate carvings on them. The large doors rose straight up and curved into a dome about two-thirds of the way up the wall. The smaller set matched them identically and were just a few feet taller than Father Time. As they got close, the smaller set of doors slowly and quietly opened, but instead of swinging they slid inward and then, each one slid behind the wall on the inside.

It took them a full minute to walk through the outer wall. Jake didn't know how far it was, but as he looked back he realized the walls were incredibly thick. They came out into a large courtyard in between the outer and middle walls. Jake figured it must follow the walls all the way around. The group continued on through two more walls and two more courtyards until they reached the keep. They followed Father Time in through a small doorway in the right corner and went down a flight of stairs to a room that appeared to be a kitchen area.

Hunger flared up inside Jake as he smelled fresh food and bread. They had stopped several times along the way for a quick rest and a small snack, but Jake suddenly realized the hike had made him very hungry. There was food on a center counter already prepared for them, although they had still seen no one since entering the castle.

Father Time turned to them, "This food was prepared for us, so eat up and we will rest for a while."

Jake walked over and started to prepare a plate for himself while the fairies flew off his shoulders and did the same. Even Father Time took some food and they all sat around a table at the far end of the room. The fairies found there was already a smaller table and chairs sitting on top of the larger table, which was perfectly sized for them. When they were seated, Fieora asked Father Time why it was there.

"The Granite Castle used to be home for many different races and creatures back when Under Earth was first created. Even some fairies called this home." This must have been new information to the three sisters because all of them had surprised expressions on their faces.

"We never knew who lived here," Sapphire muttered, munching on some fruit.

The group spent the rest of the time eating, talking about the dragons, the castle, and joking around with one another. After a while, Father Time stood, "It's time I showed you to your rooms. We have traveled a good deal today and Jake, you especially need your rest, for tomorrow you start your training."

Jake's limbs groaned in protest as he got up from the table. He relished the thought of sleep. His urgency to find Isabelle was still there, but he realized now he would have to see to his training, so he could make sure he could rescue her and not fail in the attempt.

The group followed Father Time out the back of the galley, up some stairs, and down a long hallway. As they continued, they passed many rooms. Many of the doors were closed, but the ones that were open were of varying sizes. They went up a few flights of stairs and down some more corridors until Jake thought they had come to the back of the castle. They had passed some windows along the way, but they were still low enough inside the tower that Jake could only see the inner courtyard and inner castle wall. They came to a wide circular room with tall oval windows that that seemed to rise endlessly. Jake looked up and got dizzy as he realized this room's ceiling must be at the very top of the keep.

"You may want to sit down for this since it is your first time," Father Time announced as he went to the center of the room where there was a pedestal with a crystal imbedded in the top. The pedestal was made of white granite that rose up out of the black granite floor.

"I would suggest sitting here, but face the windows," Father Time instructed, as he gestured to Jake.

Jake went and sat where he was directed and watched while Father Time put his hand over the crystal on the pedestal. Jake felt like the smooth grey walls and immense windows were moving down past the black floor. He watched out the windows as they passed. It suddenly dawned on him that it was actually the floor moving upwards. He saw the walls of the castle pass by as they rose higher and it was disorienting. He could see they were moving, but there was no noise or feeling of movement except for a slight breeze washing over him. He was glad he had sat down because otherwise he would have fallen over. They quickly rose above the castle wall and Jake could see out across to the clear lake that stretched about as far as he could see.

This was better, now that he had some perspective, and the dizziness left. Jake was amazed at how quickly they rose and it was a grand sight to behold. They were up far enough now that Jake could barely discern mountains at the end of the lake a long way off in the distance. One oval window would pass and another would be right above it, giving Jake an almost continuous view out.

The fairies were similarly mesmerized; it was new to them also.

"I never thought I'd be able to see the inside of this place," Claira remarked, sitting next to Jake's left foot.

"This is great!" Fieora squealed in a higher than normal voice.

"Sure, if you like the whole magical ride into the air while looking at a beautiful landscape," Sapphire responded, smiling sarcastically.

Fieora gave her a playful punch on the arm while Claira just rolled her eyes at her sister.

When they stopped, Jake looked up. He could see the ceiling of the chamber now, but it was still quite a way up, so they must not be to the top of the tower yet. The door to the level they were currently on opened and Father Time took his hand off the crystal and walked through. The fairies, who were next to Jake, took off to follow and Jake brought up the rear.

As he followed, he looked at the corridor around him. Although the granite floors were black, the walls were grey and the ceiling a cream color. Jake couldn't see any seams. It reminded him of the fairies' tree home, like the whole castle was made out of one piece of granite. It didn't seem possible, yet Jake had seen plenty of things that were impossible in the last few days, so he wasn't really surprised. Even where the granite changed colors, there were no seams. It just simply changed color.

They came to a hallway in the front part of the castle and there were many rooms on either side. They turned right and Father Time motioned to the first door on the left. "This room will be yours during your training. The fairies will take the next one just down the hall. You can look around for a little bit, but I would suggest you rest soon, Jake, for tomorrow will be a long day for you."

Father Time guided the fairies to their room and then went back down the hall they had come from. "Rest well, Jake," Sapphire called out as she followed her sisters into their room. "I promise not to play any jokes on you tonight," she teased with a playful laugh.

Jake turned to the red wooden door and reached out to the latch. The door was thick, but swung inward very easily. He walked in and closed the door behind him. The room was large for a bedroom. It had a couple of windows and a doorway was centered between them, which led to a balcony that overlooked the front side of the castle. Jake walked out and took a deep breath. It was beautiful here. After a few moments, Jake reentered the room and looked around. There was a large bed to his left and in the center of the room stood a table and two chairs. To his right was a comfortable looking bench and book-shelves lined the walls.

Jake wanted to explore more, but he could feel his weariness catching up. He decided he would call it a night, even though it always looked like day here. Thick, purple curtains framed the doors and windows. Jake took off his shoes and socks and felt the cool touch of the granite under his feet. In the warm air of Under Earth, this was a welcome feeling. Jake didn't even take time to wash up, but drew the curtains, which actually made it fairly dark in the room. He crawled into bed and fell asleep within moments.

Chapter 16

The Keeper of the Sword

When Jake woke up, there was already food on his table for breakfast. Again, he hadn't heard or seen anyone. He got up, ate, and washed up before putting on the new set of clothes he found on the back of one of the chairs. They were much the same as the lightweight ones he was wearing, but freshly cleaned.

When he was ready, Jake left his room to find the sisters and Father Time. He didn't have to look very long. When he came out, he could see them talking together down the hall by the strange elevator room. As he approached, the four of them turned to face him.

Father Time nodded. "Good morning Jake, I trust you rested well?"

Jake nodded.

"Jake, today you will start your training, but there are a few things I must tell you. First, I have been given permission to let you have adequate time to train. Starting with our arrival here, I stopped time. This means everything inside the Granite Castle grounds can still function, but everywhere else, including on Top Earth, is currently stopped, frozen in time. I was allowed to do this for two reasons, to give you adequate time to train, as well as help you not to worry so much about Isabelle. While you are training, nothing outside this castle is happening, so you are not losing any time here. You have as much time as you need to train and rest."

"Second, you must strive to be patient and learn what you are here to learn. If you do not, you cannot hope to rescue Isabelle. I say this because your training will test you, but you must endure to the finish."

"Lastly, I'll be taking my leave after I take you to the sword Guardian. He is the keeper of the sword. He is an immortal like me and it is his duty to watch over the sword until it is needed and train those who are given permission to use it. I'll remain in the castle until you are done, but you will probably not see me again while you are here. I have something else I must attend to. The Guardian and the fairies will help you train. Now Jake, are you ready to begin?"

Jake nodded and followed Father Time onto the mysterious elevator again. It didn't take long for them to reach the top. Jake watched as they rose through the mist. His head and shoulders broke through the mist, followed by his waist and knees. When the elevator finally stopped, the mist was only half way up his shin. Jake watched it swirl as he moved his legs. The mist still hung about a foot over the floor, covering his feet.

The door to the elevator chamber opened and Jake could see out into a large room that resembled a courtyard. As they walked out, Jake looked around at the grass and plants that grew around the room and covered many parts of the granite floor. The ceiling was open in places, revealing the sky. A few clouds had made it inside and floated high against the ceiling.

In the center of the room stood a large granite stand and a sword that looked like it was made entirely of yellow crystal. The hilt of the sword jutted out the top of the stand while the end of the blade came out the side, as if someone had swung it to chop down through the pedestal and then had left it there. Just behind and to the right of the sword stood a tall man with short jet black hair and a full goatee which came to a point. He had sharp angular features and was dressed in purple. He didn't show any emotion, but stood stoic, waiting for them.

As they drew close, the dark man nodded to Father Time. Father Time addressed the group. "Jake, Claira, Sapphire, and Fieora, this is Dreaden, the keeper of the Sword of Light. He will be instructing you on how to use the sword, Jake. Learn well, for there is no one better at using the sword. The only one who could ever defeat him is the person who wields the Sword of Light. Claira, Sapphire, and Fieora, you will help him with Jake's training if he should direct, but otherwise you should not interfere."

Father Time then turned to Jake and the fairies. "I must take my leave now. I will not see you again while you are here, but I'll remember to ask the Creator to help you and keep you safe."

Jake walked over to Father Time.

"Thank you for your help! If you hadn't come along when you did, I wouldn't be here now." Father Time smiled. "While I appreciate your thanks it should truly be given to the Creator, for it was He who led me to you. Goodbye for now, Jacob Cross, may the Creator light your way."

With that, Father Time turned and left.

Jake turned back to Dreaden and waited. He didn't have to wait long. Dreaden spoke to the fairies first. "Claira, Sapphire, and Fieora, thank you for coming and helping our friend get here safely. I haven't had the pleasure of meeting you three until now, though I knew your parents. I am sorry about your father."

The three sisters nodded and then Dreaden continued. "I'll have need of your gifts from time to time while I train Jake, but today you can feel free to explore the castle and relax. I will need to train Jake alone for a while. Come back every morning with Jake and I will let you know if you're needed."

With that Dreaden waited while the sisters flew over and gave Jake hugs and encouragement. As they left, Sapphire called back to Jake. "Listen and learn well, Jake, or you will have me to answer to." Jake rolled his eyes at Sapphire and she stuck out her tongue in response.

Jake shrugged and looked at Dreaden, but the dark man looked as serious as ever.

Dreaden took a few steps forward and stood directly behind the pillar with the sword. Jake was suddenly nervous to be alone with this man. He had a dangerous look. Dreaden was lean and muscular, but it was the way he carried himself that made him imposing. Like someone with an authority that was not to be tested. But it was the man's eyes that really commanded Jake's attention. It was similar to how he'd felt about Father Time when he looked into his eyes. It was like staring into an agelessness and a wisdom of centuries long since gone. But where Father Time's eyes had a gentle authority, Dreaden's eyes had a hardness and fire to them. Jake figured it would be best to let him speak first, so he waited.

After a few more moments of silence, Dreaden spoke. "Jacob Cross, listen carefully to what I have to say to you now, for if you take it lightly you will not succeed. You have been chosen to wield the Sword of Light. It is known by many different names, but this is its true name. To carry this sword is a great privilege and responsibility. During your time to carry the sword, only you will be able to use it properly."

"The first thing you need to know about the sword is it can never be used for evil. You must always be sure you are using it for good or to defend against evil. During your training, I will teach you technique as well as how to use some of the sword's abilities. Having said this, I must tell you that even I do not know everything the sword is capable of. Also, just as Father Time testified, there is no one on Earth or in Under Earth who can match me with the sword, except the person who can properly use this sword. I am not able to use it myself as I could not pick it up if I tried. I am just its guardian."

"You, Jake, are the only one at this moment who can take the sword out of this pedestal, but I must ask you first, are you ready to take this responsibility upon yourself?"

Jake knew this was the only way to rescue Isabelle, yet he waited a few moments before answering to make sure he realized the weight of his decision. After another few moments, Jake stepped forward. "Yes, I am ready to take this responsibility."

Dreaden's expression turned fierce and he put a hand on his own sword strapped at his waist. "Why do you wish to use the Sword of Light?" Dreaden asked with warning in his voice.

Jacob felt his pulse quicken, but answered honestly, "I wish to use it so I may rescue my friend Isabelle from Medusa's Heir." Dreaden's expression softened as his hand came off his sword to rest at his side again. "You have spoken honestly. You may step forward and take the sword."

Jake felt relieved, but wondered what would have happened if he hadn't spoken truthfully. He slowly walked forward until he was in front of the pedestal. A shaft of light came down from the ceiling and illuminated the yellow crystal of the sword. He was directly across from Dreaden who continued to watch with an expressionless face. Jake reached out tentatively, not knowing what to expect. He grasped the handle of the sword with his right hand, but instead of the cool surface he expected, Jake felt warmth coming from the sword. It felt like it was almost vibrating with energy and yet remained motionless in the granite pedestal. He tried pulling but the sword did not budge.

Jake didn't know exactly what he'd been expecting, maybe a flash of light or possibly the pedestal cracking, letting him take the sword, but not this. Even though he could feel the sword's energy it remained fixed in the pedestal. Now he felt dumb, as if he should somehow have known what to do, but couldn't grasp it and now, had failed before he had begun. With his hand still on the sword, he looked to Dreaden.

Dreaden looked back at Jake. "This is your first lesson Jake, this pedestal is the only thing that can hold the Sword of Light, yet even it cannot hold it if the chosen person comes along. You are chosen to wield it, however, even you must learn to use it properly. Some would call this sword magical, but it is not some mystical item one hordes and uses for their own gain. It is a supernatural sword made by the Creator for special times and purposes. If a person who is chosen to carry it decides to use it for his or her own selfish reasons or its purpose is fulfilled, it will return here.

"That isn't to say you can't or won't make mistakes. If they are honest mistakes, the sword will know. It is only when one makes a conscious decision to use it for their own gain that it returns. Now Jake, can you feel the energy of the sword?"

Jacob nodded.

"Good, if you are not chosen, the sword would feel lifeless and cold to you. The sword will listen to your thoughts and obey your commands, however, you also need to learn how to listen to it and trust what it tells you. To listen and trust in the Sword of Light is to listen and trust its Creator. Without belief and trust in the Creator, you'll never be able to fully use the sword. You must learn to hear the sword speak to you. It doesn't speak audibly. It's more like it gives you a sixth sense you must learn to listen to.

"Keep your hand on the sword and try to listen to it. Once you hear it correctly, it will show you how to release it."

Jake tried concentrating on the sword, but still just felt the same pulsing energy that he had before. Pretty soon his right arm got tired, so he switched to his left. Time passed and Jake continued switching hands while Dreaden stood in silence just watching. He was getting frustrated at his lack of progress. How was he ever supposed to learn anything when he couldn't even pass this first test?

Finally, Jake gave it up altogether and sat down with his back to the pedestal. He was so frustrated, he knew he had no chance of hearing the sword now. He took a few deep breaths to calm himself. He could still feel Dreaden's stare from behind, but didn't really care at this point. He knew his motivation was right. All he wanted was to rescue Isabelle, the beautiful brunette with those shining eyes and bright smile he'd fallen in love with. The sword was just a tool he had to use to do it, but he couldn't even pick it up.

Jake sat for a few minutes with his eyes closed, already tired, though he had barely done anything more physical than stand next to the pedestal.

After a few more minutes of silence, Jake noticed something he hadn't before. He was so frustrated when he sat down, he hadn't realized he could still feel the sword's presence and touch, even though he was no longer physically touching it. Jake explored this feeling, not really excited, but he did lose the sense of failure he been feeling just moments before.

The presence he felt was powerful and full of energy, yet gentle and patient. Keeping a hold of the feeling, he stood up and turned, reaching for the sword. Jake kept his eyes closed as he grasped the handle, just letting the calm and peaceful presence wash over him. He then felt the urge to slowly raise his arm and take the sword from the pedestal like he would a knife from butter. His eyes were still closed when he did this and when he opened them, the crystal sword was in his right hand, free and clear of the granite pedestal. Where the sword had been stuck, no seam or hole was visible. It appeared as if the sword had never been embedded in the pedestal in the first place.

Jake looked up to Dreaden who was actually smiling. "Good work Jake," he responded, genuinely proud. "I could tell you were getting frustrated and feeling defeated, but you allowed yourself time to calm down and listen to the sword. It took you a while, but only someone meant to carry the sword could've done what you just did. I assume you felt the sword even when you weren't in contact with it?"

"Yes," Jake answered, lowering his gaze to the yellow crystal sword he held in his hand.

"That would be a good thing to remember as you may need to use the connection with the sword even though you don't have it in your hands. Now it's time for your second lesson."

Jake glanced up just in time to see the smile vanish from Dreaden's face and his hand reach for his sword.

Without any other warning, and quicker than Jake thought was humanly possible, Dreaden drew his sword and delivered three successive blows to Jake.

Jake was suddenly panicked, but managed to cling to the Sword of Light for dear life. Without realizing it, Jake used the sword to bat away the first two deadly swipes and connected with the third where he stopped, both swords crossed in midair between him and Dreaden.

Jake was terrified, but amazed at the same time. Dreaden struck so quickly and savagely, Jake could never have countered quickly or accurately enough on his own. He knew he should not have been strong enough to deflect Dreaden's blows. He was also amazed that, as the swords struck one another, the yellow crystal sword didn't break when striking the other. Jake knew any normal crystal would have shattered upon hitting metal like that.

"Remember that also Jake," Dreaden submitted as he lowered and then sheathed his sword. "I struck quickly so your only recourse was to trust in the sword to survive. I tell you truthfully, no one but the person who carries the Sword of Light could have survived that attack. If you trust the sword, even when you fight someone more skilled than yourself, it will protect you."

"Having explained that, I will not fight you again using a real sword. I'll be using this wooden sword." Dreaden reached out and picked up a wooden sword that was resting near a bench which faced the pedestal. "Because I'll be using this and I will not be trying to seriously harm you but teach you, the Sword of Light will not automatically help you block everything. Even though you need to rely on the sword, you should still have a basic and proper knowledge of swordsmanship. It will help you learn not only how to use any sword, but also teach you respect, humility, and confidence."

"If you would be so kind as to change your sword to a wooden one as well, so that it does not harm me or cut through my wooden sword, we can get started."

"What do you mean?" Jake asked, confused.

"That is another ability of the Sword of Light. It can change to suit your needs. Its crystal form is the one it returns to when it comes back here, but it is not its true form."

Jake looked down at the sword in his hands. It was only about 2 feet in length with a one-handed grip, medium cross guard, and a double-sided blade narrowing to a sharp point at its end. Once again, Jake concentrated on the sword. He looked at Dreaden's wooden sword and thought he might as well try to imitate it. It had a two-handed grip and a round guard. It had no sharp edges, but rather a round blade which tapered to a blunt end. He didn't really know any better way, so Jake looked at the crystal sword and, in his mind, asked it to form a wooden sword like Dreaden's. With that Jake watched, mesmerized, as the yellow crystal started to darken and turn brown while the edges dulled and rounded off. The blade shortened slightly while the handgrip lengthened. The guard shrank in length, but expanded in width and rounded to a perfect circle. Jake could still feel the energy from the sword and it no longer felt like smooth crystal. Instead, it felt like hard polished wood.

"Good job, Jake." Dreaden praised. "Now we will spar and I will teach you the basics of swordplay. You'll have to work on how you handle the sword as well as how you use your body. I will go easy at first, but even so, this will hurt. You will not be seriously injured, but if you are to truly learn swordplay you must experience your failures as well as your successes. Are you ready?"

Jake doubted it, but nodded yes anyway. He had to rescue Isabelle and if this is what he had to do, then so be it. He followed Dreaden over to an open space past the pedestal where he sparred with Dreaden the rest of the day. Dreaden wasn't kidding. It did hurt, a lot! By the end of their dual, Jake felt like a complete failure and he was bruised everywhere. Jake hadn't managed to land a single hit on Dreaden and, though he hadn't expected to, he was disappointed that he had barely even been able to block any of the blows that had come his way.

Jake's arms and legs had taken the brunt of the beating, but he had also been struck on his sides and back several times as well as each hand and his head once.

In spite of how awful he felt, Dreaden still told him he did a good job and told him to eat a lot and get rested. He was to be back up the next day, ready to go again.

Jake turned to leave and set the sword down on a bench near him. Before he had gone a few feet, Dreaden called out.

"Jake, one more thing."

Jake turned slowly, wearily and looked back at Dreaden.

"Make sure to take the sword with you wherever you go from now on. It is yours until you reach the end of your journey."

Jake was too tired to respond so he just turned slowly, picked up the sword, and left in search of food.

Chapter 17

The Creator

The days melded together for Jake as he settled into a routine. It didn't help that Under Earth's sky stayed light all the time, so Jake couldn't really tell how much time had passed. He was starting to think he should have been marking the passing of the days with something.

Each day started off with the fairies waking him up. Usually it was a knock on the door and one of them would call his name to signify it was time for Jake to start his day. Every once in a while, they would find some creative way of waking him up. Usually Sapphire was to blame. Jake was slightly put off by it the first time. They had placed a trumpet-like instrument next to his bed and sounded it loudly. He had woken up so fast, he'd fallen out of bed. However, as they tried ever more inventive ways to wake him, he came to enjoy it because it was one of the only things that broke the routine of tiresome training days.

They must have some way of keeping track of time in Under Earth, even though he knew that right now everything outside the Granite Castle was frozen in time. Jake had been meaning to ask Claira about how to tell the time in Under Earth, but kept forgetting.

Most days after he woke, he would take a shower and then meet the sisters for breakfast in a room down the hall. At first they just used this time to talk, but after his training was in full swing, the sisters started using breakfast as a class. They taught him general knowledge about Under Earth, its creatures and geography, its beauty and dangers. After breakfast, he would go up for his morning training session. Then lunch, which was back down in the same room as breakfast or up where he was training, depending on what

Dreaden was teaching him and how much time they needed to spend on it that day. The fairies were starting to help more and more with his training now. They used their gifts to make obstacles that Jake would have to dodge or move around while he was sparring. They would also throw things at Jake or shine bright lights to try and distract him, which they accomplished more often than not. He now had a few bruises because something whizzed past his head and he adjusted wrong, leaving himself open for Dreaden to strike, not that Dreaden needed the help.

There were some times Jake managed to get the hang of a block or strike, but most of the time he was frustrated. He was trying to learn, but didn't feel like he was making much progress and, even though he knew he had as much time as he needed, he didn't feel like he was ever going to get there.

Jake's one reprieve was when his afternoon training ended. He had an hour or two before dinner and he used the time to walk and explore the castle alone. Dreaden had told him not to use the elevator room when coming to training so that he could work on his endurance, but after training was over, Jake started taking it down and exploring different areas of the castle. Fieora showed him how to use the crystal to raise and lower the elevator through the castle with different types of pressure and to simply let go when he arrived at the floor he wanted. It took a little practice, as the first few times he tried it alone he missed the floor he was trying for by two or three floors, but he eventually got the feel for it.

Many days this exploration time alone helped him calm down and let go of his frustration from training. One day he was exploring a floor, about halfway between the floor his room was on and the top floor where he trained, when he found a staircase in one of the castle's corners. He almost missed it, as it was an end room. Jake had walked in to find a small study with scrolls on tables. He almost turned and left then, not wanting to disturb anything, when he decided to go out onto the small balcony facing the forest side of the castle.

When he went out, he glanced over to his right where he expected to find the lakeside edge of the castle and instead found a spiral staircase leading up.

Jake was pretty tired, but curious enough to make the effort to find out where the stairs went. He wound his way up the stairs, which were enclosed in granite walls with only small round windows too high to see out of, but they provided adequate lighting for the stairs. Jake couldn't tell how high he was climbing.

It took him a while, but he finally managed to get to the staircase's end. The spot he found became his favorite place in the castle to be alone and rest. The stairs ended at a landing built into the corner of the tower. Where the two outside castle walls should have been, was a curved railing open to the sky. Jake figured the landing must be near the top of the tower because the mist floating at the top of the tower started to form here. It clung to the walls, and formed some wispy clouds around in the air. The room wasn't huge, but large enough for Jake to be comfortable.

When he came off the stairs, to his right was a curved bench with the castle wall curving behind it. To his left, a railing curved around outward with a view facing both the colorful forest and the lake stretching out behind the castle. The air was still moist, but cool and refreshing here. It had a fresh rain scent to it, which probably came from the mist. The roof, which must have been the floor above, extended out to the edge and between that and the mist it was actually a somewhat shady area to get away from Under Earth's bright sky, but still be able to take in the view. Purple vines grew along the walls and railing with little white flowers blooming here and there. Jake could sit on the bench and watch Under Earth in solitude.

It was here Jake found himself again today, fighting off the frustration he couldn't quite seem to shake. It had been an alright morning. Sapphire had done her best job yet at waking him as she had managed to use her wand to pick him up without him feeling it. When she had him about a foot over his bed, she proceeded to let him go and Jake had woken with a start as he fell onto the bed. Jake whirled around terrified, looking for danger and all three sisters started laughing hysterically. Jake retaliated by throwing one of his pillows at them, which they narrowly dodged. Upon seeing their faces as they dodged his pillow, Jake laughed as well.

That had been about the only good part of the day; however, because his morning training session had not gone very well and his afternoon session ended up being even worse. In fact, it had been terrible. Even though his endurance had grown and he had grown tougher and didn't bruise nearly as easily anymore, he still only managed to block about half of Dreaden's attacks and still couldn't land a single blow himself. In fact, he couldn't even come close. In order to rescue Isabelle, he had to master the sword well enough to successfully attack Dreaden, and he didn't see how he could ever manage.

Jake could still hear Dreaden's voice in his head, "Jake, your skill is growing, but you will never be able to use the sword the way you must until you journey past belief to trust."

Even with his determination to save Isabelle, Jake's frustration became too much. After getting hit three more times in quick succession, he threw down the sword. "That's it, I'm done! I can't do it! I have been giving everything to this training and, after I don't even know how many days, I'm still no closer to being able to rescue Isabelle. Why can't you just come with me and help me rescue her?" he grumbled accusingly at Dreaden.

Dreaden just stood impassively and watched Jake rant until he stood, out of breath. "Jake, I know this is difficult for you, but you *must* listen to me now. I have known the Creator a long time and I have learned it is best to trust Him. What He tells me doesn't always make sense and many times it is very difficult to trust. You might think it would be easier to go rescue Isabelle with my help, but that task has not been given to me, it has been given to you. I have learned that I don't need to understand it because His ways are higher than mine and I have learned to trust Him, as should you."

"Well, trust goes both ways," Jake retorted and turned to leave.

"Jake," came Dreaden's voice. It wasn't angry, but clear and firm. "Don't forget the sword."

Jake turned and glared at Dreaden, something he wouldn't normally have dared to do, but he was past caring. Still, he bent down and picked up the sword, sheathed it, and stormed out without looking back, leaving Dreaden and the Fairies staring after him.

Jake had gone straight to his secret ledge. Once he was there, he took off the belt which the Sword of Light was sheathed to, threw it and the sword onto the bench and yelled in frustration, disturbing a couple of yellow birds who were resting on the railing. The birds flew off and Jake collapsed to his knees, burying his face in his hands. Tears blurred his vision as he felt raw emotions take hold. It was hopeless. How could he ever hope to rescue Isabelle? Jake sat there and let his emotions come, until he was worn out and couldn't cry anymore. After a long while, his frustration and sorrow were finally spent and Jake felt nothing but empty and tired. His legs were stiff and asleep when he tried getting up and walking to the bench.

Jake struggled for a minute, trying to let the numbness and tingling sensation in his legs abate. When he was sure he could take a step without falling over, he turned and started walking the couple of yards back to the bench. As he did, he noticed movement on the bench. Jake stopped mid-stride as he looked at the Sword of Light. It was vibrating, almost jumping up and down and then, suddenly, it began to change. The sword and sheath started to shorten and grow thick and the belt grew with it.

When it was finished, the Sword of Light, which had looked like a dull wooden sword inside a leather sheath, had transformed into a large, old, leather bound book! Jake knew the sword could change its shape, but didn't realize it could change its form completely. He slowly walked over and sat down next to the book. The belt the sword had been attached to had also changed. It now seemed more like a sling one could carry on their shoulder and it strapped in the book with a top strap securing the book.

Jake reached out and picked up the book. Taking it out of the sling, he opened it. It looked as if it was ancient, yet it was sturdy and didn't feel fragile, like other old books Jake had seen. The words were strange, written in an alphabet and language he didn't think existed on Top Earth. Jake started flipping through the book, trying to find something he could identify with. When he was two thirds of the way through the book, he noticed the words and letters start to blur and bend.

Jake stopped flipping the pages and just stared at the one he was on. Then, the letters and words started to form ones he recognized. The first one caught his attention and he couldn't take his eyes off of it for a long while. It was a name, his name! Jake sat there and stared at his name, not believing it was real. It looked as if the page was written as a letter, but he couldn't take his eyes off his name long enough to read what the rest said.

Of all the unbelievable things that had happened in Under Earth so far, this shocked him the most. It was as if the book or, the sword rather, was speaking directly to Jake. There was no other way he could think of to explain it. Finally, after thinking through the implications of seeing his name appear, he started to read the rest of the page.

-Jake,

I know you. I have known you since before you were born. Your family has been mine for a long time now, however, whereas your parents and your sister have fully put their trust in me, you have always been content to believe I exist, but live off of their faith or the faith of others. It is time, Jacob Cross, time to decide if you believe in me just because your family does and nothing more, or to make your faith your own.

It's your decision. I know the struggle within you. You believe if you trust me with everything, you will lose everything, but I can assure you the opposite is true. If you trust me with everything and not your own knowledge, if you walk in faith, I will not let you stumble.

The last line caught Jake off guard, he'd read this somewhere before, it was very familiar and Jake's mind started to piece it together. He continued to read.

-The Sword of Light is also called The Word for a reason. I may not always choose to speak to you this way, but my words are always in these pages, waiting to give you whatever you need. Spend time in this book and you will learn to know me better and hear my voice.

With my everlasting, unconditional, and unfailing love,
Your Creator.

Just as Jake finished reading the last words in the letter, it faded and disappeared, but was replaced by a text Jake again found familiar. It wasn't in the same format he was used to. There were no titles or chapters to break the text up. There were no author names he could find and the text was in simple paragraph format, but, as Jake started reading at the top of the page, he understood what he was reading. It read:

"At the beginning of time was the Word, and the Word was with the Creator, and the Word was the Creator. He was with the Creator before time. Through him everything was made, without him nothing was made. In him was life, and that life was the light of all mankind. That light shines in the darkness and the darkness has not overcome it."

Jake stopped reading as he realized what he was holding. It was a Bible, quite possibly the original. Jake wondered, if this one didn't have the author names, because the Creator made this before he had given the words to the people who wrote them down. As the realization dawned on him, he gently sat the book on the bench and wept into his hands.

He realized he had been wrong before. Trust did go both ways, but the Creator had already trusted Jake to carry this sword, one of the highest privileges Jake had ever had, and Jake had treated that trust with contempt. Jake wept, because he realized he had been so foolish. He had believed before, but now realized it was true, he had never made that belief his own faith. He had been content to let others around him have faith so he wouldn't have to accept the responsibilities that came with faith.

Now, on this ledge in a foreign land, Jake spent some time talking to his Creator. It was something he had put off for too long. Jake talked with the Creator, asking for forgiveness for being so foolish. He admitted his weaknesses and failings and asked for the strength to move forward from where he was. He also spent some time asking the Creator to keep Isabelle safe and to give him the strength he needed to help her. Jake completely lost track of time as he made a faith that he had learned his own. He now believed and trusted because he wanted to and no one else could sway him from it.

Time passed in the castle grounds, while everything else outside was frozen in time. Jake spent time reading the Word and talking to his Creator until he drifted off into a very deep and peaceful sleep, lying on the bench with his head propped up on the arm and the book laying open on his chest.

The next day, Jake woke feeling more rested and at peace than he had since reaching Under Earth. He got up and, though he had been lying on a hard bench for a long time, he wasn't stiff or sore at all. In fact, he felt energized and stronger than he had felt in a long time. It wasn't just a physical strength though. Before, where he could only find self-doubt, frustration, and hopelessness, he now had hope and confidence. He knew who he was now. Not according to his own definition, but the One who had made him.

Jake reached down and picked up the book. Without thinking, he held one of the corners in his right hand and swung it outward. It immediately transformed back into the wooden practice sword before Jake had even finished his swing. Jake then strapped on the belt, which was now the sword's sheath again, put the sword in it, and went in search of breakfast, ready for the day ahead.

Chapter 18

Training Complete

As Jake walked through the castle, he felt less uncertain and more confident than he had felt in a long time. He knew he still had much to learn about his newfound faith, but that was the key, it was *his* faith. He also realized that now, he trusted in the sword he had sheathed at his waist.

Before, he believed it was special and could do amazing things because he had seen it transform before his eyes. Now, it was different. Jake didn't just believe in the sword, but trusted in his ability to use it, because he trusted the One who had made them both. He knew, even now, he wouldn't be perfect at using it right away. He may still mess up or come up short at times, but he also knew he would be able to learn from his mistakes and use the Sword of Light the way he needed when the time came.

Jake made it back down to where he usually ate breakfast with the sisters. He chose to take the stairs rather than the elevator room because he wanted to enjoy this lingering peace he had been given. He still desired to rescue Isabelle more than anything, but knew the Creator would help him. He was able to let go of his worry!

As he approached the fairies' room, he could hear them up and about, talking while finishing breakfast preparations. Jake stopped short of the doorway and listened.

He could hear Fieora's voice filled with concern. "Well, all I'm saying is that I hope he's alright. With the way he stormed out yesterday, and now, not having seen him around the castle at all, I just don't know. What if he left?"

Sapphire's voice broke in, "He can't leave yet remember, time outside the castle is still frozen. If he tried leaving, we'd find him stuck mid-stride outside the door. He just needs some time to cool off. You know I do the same thing sometimes."

Claira's voice jumped in next, "Sometimes? Try once a day, at least!"

Jake smiled as he imagined the face Sapphire was probably now directing toward her sisters. He figured he had made them wait long enough. He put his hand on the hilt of the sword and walked in carefully, trying to see if the sword would help him dampen his footsteps. It appeared to work, for he couldn't even hear himself walk.

The fairies were across the room near the counter with their backs turned. He walked over and stopped behind them as they continued to talk.

"It's not my fault you two keep annoying me," Sapphire sighed, as she finished putting food on her plate.

"No, it's just because you're a hot head," Jake remarked, announcing his presence and grinning as all three fairies dropped what they were doing and spun around. Claira and Sapphire had their wands out, pointed at Jake. As Claira saw him, she put hers down, but Jake could tell Sapphire didn't like being surprised, or his last remark. She shot a blue streak of light from her wand directly at Jake's chest.

Yesterday this might have made him jump or duck away, but today he knew better. He drew the sword quick enough to intercept the magic and the sword absorbed it, glowing slightly blue for a second and then fading back to its wooden brown color.

Sapphire frowned and fired a second shot. This time, instead of letting the sword absorb the light, Jake had deflected it right back at Sapphire. When she realized what he had done, Sapphire tried diving out of the way of her own shot, but was too late. The blue light hit her and turned into water with a big splash, knocking her back onto the counter and soaking her completely. At this, Claira and Fieora started laughing uncontrollably. They hadn't seen their sister get a dose of her own medicine for a long time.

Sapphire regained her composure, dried herself off using her wand and then put it away. "Impressive, but don't think this means I can't still get you from time to time."

I'm sure you will still be able to find a way," Jake laughed. "I'm just glad I can give you a bit of a challenge now."

"That's good," Sapphire smiled. "It helps me improve my technique. It's good to have you back."

"I see a change in you today, Jake," Claira commented, recovering from her laughing fit.

"Let's just say I had a chat with a good friend and now I understand things a little better."

Claira smiled a knowing smile, "I was hoping you would get to that sooner or later!"

After that, the four sat down and ate a large breakfast. Jake shared with them some of what had transpired the night before and they listened and shared some stories of their own.

When breakfast was done, Jake asked the fairies to give him a few minutes alone with Dreaden before coming up to his training. Then he walked up the stairs at a brisk pace, amazed at how much easier it was now that he was used to the climb.

When Jake entered the high courtyard, he found Dreaden standing in the same place he stood every day, in the practice field, waiting and looking as stern as ever. Today he was wearing crimson red clothes, but his black hair and angled features still made him look dark.

Jake crossed over to stand in front of him and bowed his head slightly. "Dreaden, I'm sorry for getting angry and storming off yesterday as I did. I was frustrated, but I shouldn't have shown you disrespect like that. I hope you can forgive me."

Jake looked back up at Dreaden, who actually smiled a full smile for the first time Jake could remember. It looked so out of place on his stern face, Jake almost laughed, but managed to keep himself in check. "Of course you are forgiven Jake! I'm glad to see you have put your trust in the Creator. Now, if you are ready, we will begin."

Jake nodded yes. In the split second it took Jake to nod, Dreaden had drawn his sword and swung at Jake's throat. Jake responded in kind, drawing the Sword of Light, and blocked the blow which would have decapitated him. Jake was so shocked at the speed with which he had blocked, he almost forgot he was still fighting. Then Dreaden launched into a series of quick blows, trying to throw Jake off balance and create an opening to strike. It wasn't easy, but Jake found that, by using his knowledge and trusting in the Sword of Light, he was able to keep any of Dreaden's blows from landing. This was a task he had never accomplished before.

After this didn't work, Dreaden tried using a complicated attack of dangerous, but unpredictable blows, trying to confuse Jake and cause him to anticipate the wrong attack so he would leave himself open for Dreaden to strike. Again, Jake was able to keep any of Dreaden's blows from landing. Sometime during this bout, the fairies came in and sat down, just watching as the ferocity of the battle played out before them.

By this time, Jake and Dreaden were soaked in sweat and Dreaden was slightly fatigued. Finally, Dreaden stopped attacking and waited as he and Jake circled each other. Jake knew Dreaden was now waiting for Jake to attack. Jake waited a few more moments to catch his breath and then swung out at Dreaden's midsection, knowing Dreaden would try to block it and follow up with an attack of his own. Dreaden stepped back and brought his sword down, batting Jake's blow away, causing Jake's blow to go extra wide.

If he hadn't been prepared for Dreaden's next blow, it would have cut him in half, but as it was, Jake could sense, if not almost see what was about to happen. It was as if everything was in slow motion, even though, in reality, it happened very quickly. Trusting in the Sword of Light, Jake allowed his blow to go wide and ducked into a roll, using the momentum to spin him through his turn quicker. Dreaden's sword passed over Jake's head through the space he had been standing in a moment before.

Just as Dreaden's swing came to its end, but before he could defend, Jake came out of his roll, propelling himself up with his left hand while his right stabbed with his sword right at the lower portion of Dreaden's ribs. The blow connected in an upward motion that would have gone through Dreaden had the Sword of Light not been in its wooden form. As it was, it struck Dreaden with enough force to make him wince and jump back, panting for breath and putting his hand over the spot Jake had just hit.

Jake was still crouched, with the sword extended, in a bit of shock. He had finally been able to not only defend himself, but land a blow. The fairies must have also been in shock because it took them a few long moments to begin clapping, cheering, and congratulating Jake.

Dreaden straightened, sheathed his sword, and walked over to help Jake up. "Great work Jake! You have learned to trust in the Sword of Light and let it help you. Only one with the sword's help could have struck me as quickly as you just did. You have completed your training. You still have much to learn, but my job is done. Now you must learn to listen to the Creator. He will guide you from here. I'm proud of you Jake. Continue to be patient and the Creator will help you rescue your friend Isabelle! Now go and rest, for tomorrow you will be off. I will meet you down by the gate in the morning to see you off. Keep the sword with you at all times." With that, Dreaden turned and walked out of the room, one hand rubbing his ribs.

"Congratulations, Jake," Claira bubbled, beaming.

"Yes, that was great!" Fieora chimed in.

"Ehhh, it could have been better," Sapphire teased, her voice dripping with sarcasm. Growing more serious, she added, "Just don't let it give you a big head."

Jake nodded in agreement. "I'm hungry, let's go get some lunch."

"Lunch, Don't you mean dinner?" Fieora asked.

"Dinner?" Jake asked, disbelieving.

"Yes," Claira answered, "You've been sparring for seven hours."

Jake stood, dumbfounded, he had completely lost track of time. He felt like he'd just come up a couple of hours ago, but the fatigue in his body and hunger in his stomach now told him they were right.

The four of them went back down to the kitchen near their rooms and spent the next few hours eating, talking, joking, telling stories, and playing games. When they were done Jake was tired, but he felt more hope than he had since losing Isabelle. He went back to his room and drew the curtains, blocking out the light from Under Earth's sky, and fell into bed. He thought it might be hard to get to sleep, but his body was exhausted from the day's training and he fell asleep within a few minutes, thinking of Isabelle as he did.

Chapter 19

Turogs

Everything was quiet on the castle grounds the following morning. Jake didn't feel like he'd slept very well after the previous day's activities. He'd fallen asleep quickly and didn't remember waking up much, but he did remember he'd dreamed about Isabelle.

Jake had imagined her walking by his side in the colorful forest, watching her admire the beauty while he watched and admired her. He could sense the warmth of her hand in his, glance over to see her brown wavy hair stir gently in the breeze, and watched as she pointed, seeing something else she had never seen before. All the while, he knew it was a dream. Somewhere in the back of his mind, his anticipation of now being able to rescue her was building. This was probably why he was now out early, exploring the castle grounds.

Jake sensed it was early, even though the sky was always light. His body must have become accustom to telling the time on its own over the past few months he had been here. At least, that was his closest guess. He hadn't actually counted the days, but thinking back, he figured he had been training at the castle at least a few months, give or take a few days. It was nice to know, however, that time wasn't lost since Father Time had promised to stop the flow of time outside the castle grounds.

Jake was still at peace with the knowledge the Creator would help him rescue Isabelle and wasn't frustrated like before, but he knew it was time to continue on. He felt restless, so when he had woken up this morning or afternoon, or whatever time it was now, he had gotten ready quickly, strapped on the Sword of Light, and went down to explore the courtyards in the castle while slowly making his way toward the front gate where he was to meet the fairies and Dreaden. He did have the foresight to leave a note for the sisters, telling them where he had gone, so they wouldn't think he'd run off again. As he left the keep, the full warmth of Under Earth bore down on him and he started to sweat. He didn't mind though. His training had left him fit and he was now very accustomed to being able to work in hot conditions. It was nice to be outside in the fresh air, even if everything was still frozen in time.

The three courtyards were very different from each other. This was really his first time exploring them as the keep was so tall, and there was enough to explore in the castle in the last few months. Once he had found his ledge, he had done far less exploring and had just gone straight there in his free time.

The first and innermost courtyard was his favorite. It was the smallest of the three and it had many groves of colorful trees, walking paths, and even some streams which were ground fed somehow. Jake walked around the entire inner courtyard, walking over bridges, sitting on benches, overlooking small streams or ponds, and admiring all of the beautiful plant arrangements. In one place, he even found a covered gazebo where the flowers Fieora liked grew. Jake wondered who had the time to tend to all of the landscaping.

The middle courtyard was different. It still had some plants, trees, and other landscaping, but looked as if its main purpose was commercial. There were buildings lining the two walls and back to back in the center, providing two large walkways where Jake assumed people had once walked to trade or buy and sell items. It reminded him of a large flea market or farmers market, though the buildings were all empty and deserted and it looked as if they hadn't been used in a long while. Jake didn't walk very far in this courtyard, since he'd spent so much time in the last one and this one was even larger. By the look of it, the empty buildings continued all the way around it.

When he got to the third courtyard it was even larger still, but it didn't have as much in it as the last two. It was mostly open, with some big buildings built next to the gates and along the front of the wall. There were all sorts of staircases and ladders going up. Some of them went to the top of the wall while some went into various rooms or halls in the outer wall. Jake guessed this courtyard was designed for military use, so soldiers had plenty of room to run about transporting whatever weapons, tools, or materials were needed to defend the castle, with plenty of room left for an army to stage in.

As Jake neared the covered walkway to the front gate, he looked ahead, but didn't see anyone there waiting. He decided, with the time he had left, he would take one of the stairs to the top of the wall and look out at the surrounding landscape. He found a stairway on the inside part of the outer wall, which rose to the top. He climbed up and glanced around. Everything outside was still as clear and colorful as ever, but while there was a slight breeze inside the castle, everything outside was still frozen.

Jake was just about to turn and go back down when movement caught his eyes. He glanced over to his right, in the distance, the hill rose away from the lake to meet the colorful forest again and Jake caught a glimpse of a grey-cloaked figure carrying a red staff, walking. The figure stopped and his hood-covered head turned to the side, like he could tell Jake was watching. Father Time raised his red staff and struck the ground and then disappeared into the trees. Jake smiled, knowing Time had kept his promise and stayed until he'd finished his training.

In the next instant, everything outside the castle began moving again. The trees and the grass gently swayed in the breeze and, for the first time, Jake saw birds and other scampering critters outside the castle walls. It was time! Jake turned and hurried back down the way he had come to the gate.

When Jake arrived, he found the fairies and Dreaden seated by the gate at a small table, eating breakfast. Surprised, Jake took a seat when Dreaden motioned to the chair across the table. Jake joined in the small feast as the sisters were already eating sitting cross legged on top of the table. Dreaden began speaking.

"Jake, this is where we part ways. You have the training you need, but you must understand one more thing. Medusa's Heir received his name because he likes turning things into crystal, just like Medusa turned things to stone. This you already know. What I believe you are unaware of is, he is actually a descendant of someone else you may have heard about in fairy tales, Rumpelstiltskin."

Jake choked on his drink, surprised again by something he thought to be a myth. Dreaden continued without missing a beat. "Now, like his ancestor, Medusa's Heir is a gamester. He enjoys his power, but his favorite thing to do is play games with people and trick them into giving him what he wants. He now has enough power to do a great many things without resorting to playing these games, but he still does because he gets an evil pleasure out of doing so."

"You need to know this for three reasons, Jake. First, from what you have told me about Isabelle's parents' reaction to the news, my belief is she is under a spell, which can only be broken within the laws of the magic that wrote it. You will have to find out what game or trick or, more probable, curse he used to ensnare Isabelle, in order to free her."

Jake interrupted, "But I thought that is what the Sword of Light was for."

"Jake, without the Sword of Light, Medusa's Heir would kill you before you had a chance to break the spell. The sword will help you defeat Medusa's Heir and may play a part in breaking the spell, but you must figure out how it was made in order to break it. I don't think it will be as simple as fighting Medusa's Heir and winning. You see, Jake, if Isabelle was affected by a curse Medusa's Heir made, it must mean she has not yet put her trust in the Creator. If she had, a curse could not hold her and this would just be a simple kidnapping from which you could free her. However, if there is evil magic involved, and you defeat Medusa's Heir without breaking the spell, Isabelle could still be trapped by it and you might never discover the means to free her."

"Okay, and what is the second part?" Jake asked, finishing his food.

"The second reason you need to know this, is because Medusa's Heir is very talented at deception. He will try to trick you in all manner of ways. You must not doubt yourself or the trust you have in the Creator. You must rely on the Sword of Light to know the truth from his lies."

"Now, whatever spell she is under, probably happened when she was very young or possibly even before she was born. Medusa's Heir plans a long way ahead. Spur of the moment isn't his style, so he probably has had plans to take Isabelle for a quite some time. Jake, you have known her since you both were young. Has she ever talked about strange things or been scared for no apparent reason?"

Jake looked unsure of what Dreaden was asking.

"Do you think she knew she had a curse on her?" Dreaden asked, seeing the confusion on Jake's face.

Jake shook his head, "No, she never mentioned anything like that to me and she didn't live in fear. She is usually very optimistic about everything."

Dreaden sighed, "Then she was probably unaware of it herself, which means that it was most likely put on her parents and she is affected by it because she is under them. Her parents must know; they would be the ones to ask. This brings me to my third reason. Because Medusa's Heir is so clever and plans so far ahead, it may be that the curse trapping Isabelle may also harm her family, kind of like a built in failsafe so to speak. It would be grievous indeed for you to free Isabelle only to return home to find out something awful had happened to her family because she was freed."

"Jake, you will now have to go to them and get them to tell you about the spell. After this, you must return and confront Medusa's Heir. Now, once you leave here, the fairies will help you get back to the path that will take you to the cave where you first entered Under Earth. Once they get you on the path, however, they will leave with an assignment of their own. You must make it back to Top Earth, talk to Isabelle's parents, and then return and meet the fairies in the clearing below the cave."

"How will I get back to Top Earth through the cavern?" Jake asked.

"The Sword of Light has the same ability to open the gateway as the staffs of power do. Simply touch the tip of the sword to the ceiling in the room and the gateway will open. Here, take this, Jake."

Dreaden handed him a bag with a strap he could sling over his shoulder. "There is water and some food for your trip. It should take you less than a day to get back to the cavern, if you go quickly."

Jake accepted the bag and put it over his head and shoulder as he stood. The fairies, who were also ready to get going, stood as well.

"Thank you for everything," Jake responded, reaching out and shaking Dreaden's hand. "I don't think I can ever repay you for your training or your patience with me."

Dreaden smiled, "I am proud of you, Jacob Cross, remember to trust in the Creator and follow him. That is all the payment I need, for it was He who gave me my abilities. Goodbye for now, Jake."

With that, Dreaden turned and walked back into the castle. Jake looked at the sisters. "Well, let's be on our way." The three fairies took flight and Jake walked after them as they made their way back over the river and up the hill to the forest. They walked along the forest's edge and went past the trail they had come out of to get to the castle. They continued until they came to another path, which led them back into the forest.

After walking for a few minutes, they came to a split where part of the trail went straight and another part veered right. The sisters stopped in the small clearing and turned to Jake. "This is where we leave you," Claira spoke, looking a little concerned.

Fieora picked up where her sister left off. "If you keep going straight, following the trail, it will lead you back to the main cavern. There are more side paths, but you will be able to follow this one easily because it is larger and more clearly defined."

Just be careful so we don't have to come rescue you again," Sapphire instructed.

"Don't worry so much," Jake replied, putting his hand on the sword. "I'm not as defenseless as I once was."

"That may be true, but if I can still get the slip on you, so can others," Sapphire remarked, grinning.

Jake shot her a questioning look before he noticed her gazing upward. Jake glanced up above his head, ready to jump away, but wasn't quick enough and was rewarded with a face full of water. Sapphire must have set the trap before he had walked up and just waited for the right moment to spring it.

Jake shook his head off and smiled at Sapphire. "I'll keep that in mind. See you three in the clearing when I get back. You be careful as well." With that, the fairies went to the right and Jake continued on down the path leading to the cavern.

Jake had been walking for a couple of hours and could tell he was making good progress because he could now see the cavern getting closer through the breaks in the trees. He had only stopped once to relieve himself and get a snack out of his bag before moving on.

A few yards ahead, the trail emptied into a clearing. Jake walked out into the clearing and, suddenly, saw a family of fawns. He recognized them from his lessons with the fairies. Their lower bodies looked similar to a goat's body, but their upper bodies were mostly human, aside from being slightly hairier and the two small horns sticking out of their heads.

They were surrounded by four evil-looking creatures that looked half fish and half toad, but with a human shape. They weren't as large as the trolls Jake had encountered earlier with Father Time, but they were still very muscular and as tall as he was. Their feet and hands were webbed and they had fins running from the center of their foreheads down their backs. They didn't have tails, but Jake could see gills on the sides of what must be their necks, even though their ugly heads sat directly on top of their shoulders. Their eyes looked like those of a Toad, but they looked much too large for their faces. They were hideous creatures.

Jake took this all in right before the warning started sounding in his head. He reached for the sword and took it out, but was then hit from behind and he blacked out for a moment. When he came to, he was on his hands and knees looking at a fifth toad-creature that stood a few yards ahead of him, with the Sword of Light in his glistening webbed hand.

Jake glanced over at the fawns while rubbing the back of his head with his right hand. He could feel a nice bump forming. The father of the small family was lying on the ground, being held down, and looking like he had been ambushed the same way Jake had. The mother and young daughter were kneeling next to the father, crying and pleading with the evil creatures.

Jake must have stumbled onto a robbery taking place, as he could tell the evil creatures had been rifling through bags belonging to the fawns, before they were alerted to his presence. All of the creatures were armed with short swords. Amazingly enough, Jake didn't feel afraid, just slightly annoyed he had let something get the drop on him, especially with the point Sapphire had made a few hours earlier.

The creature who now held his sword spoke with a voice that sounded garbled and wet. "What do you think you were going to accomplish with this wooden toy? Our swords would make quick kindling out of this." He laughed. At least that is what Jake assumed he was doing, although it sounded more like someone with a chest cold coughing.

Jake realized the creature didn't know what he was holding or who he had captured. That was fortunate because, if he had known, Jake would probably be dead instead of nursing the knot on the back of his head. Jake stood slowly, still rubbing his head. The creatures had their swords ready, but must not have felt threatened by Jake because they did not try to contain him. He looked at the creature in front of him. Its eyes were far apart, almost to the point of being on the side of its head, like a toad's eyes would be. When Jake looked into them, all he could see was malice looking back. Jake knew this was not going to end peacefully.

Jake stopped rubbing his head and stood to his full height. "Give me back my sword, let the fawns go and I will let you leave without harm."

The creatures all started laughing now and the sound almost made Jake sick. Two of the others turned to come surround him, their swords shining along with their wet slimy skin. The creature in front of him, who had taken the Sword of Light, suddenly stopped laughing. "You will now die just like these fawns will."

Jake knew he was going to have to act fast and he couldn't let them surround him. From his lessons with Dreaden, he knew he only had one choice if he and the fawns were going to survive. If he tried defending against the first creature, it would allow the rest to get behind him where he couldn't defend. He would have to completely disable or kill one or two of them before that could happen. Seeing the hate in their eyes, he knew they wouldn't stop otherwise.

In the same moment, the lead creature took a step toward him and Jake reached out his right hand for the Sword of Light. Instantly, the sword flew outward to Jake, breaking the first creatures grip and sending him sprawling in front of Jake. The instant the sword touched Jake's hand, it transformed from the wooden practice sword into a long, double-sided, hand-and-a-half sword. It had a bright silver blade, silver cross guard with ends that tapered out and then rounded off, and a handle of black leather with a spiral silver inlay that ended in a round pommel.

In the same motion, Jake caught the sword, spun it around, and drove it straight down through the neck of the creature at his feet. One down, four to go, Jake thought as he turned to engage the other creatures who had slowed, but not stopped, their advance.

The next creature to reach Jake took a wicked swing with his short sword at Jake's stomach. Jake stepped back quickly, easily avoiding the sword and batted it away hard with the Sword of Light, then kicked the creature, sending him sprawling so he could engage the two other creatures that were almost on him. Both creatures swung at once, the one on the right chopped down toward Jake's shoulder and the other on his left lunged straight to stab him in the stomach.

Jake sidestepped to the left, avoiding both blows, and spun, with his right arm extended, and the Sword of Light took off the heads of both creatures in one swipe. He then continued turning and quickly brought his sword up just inches away from the fifth creature's chest. The creature stopped, sword in hand, but in no position to attack. Jake stepped to the left and kept the sword aimed at the creature. He was now in between the fawns and the two remaining creatures, one of which was just now getting off the ground where Jake had sent him sprawling.

The creature at Jake's sword point started backing away. It sheathed its sword and then turned and fled into the woods. The other one, seeing three of its comrades lying dead on the ground, turned and ran after the other.

Jake waited a few long moments, listening to the creatures flee. When he was sure they had left and weren't coming back, he lowered his sword and turned to face the family of fawns. The mom and daughter were helping the dad back to his feet. He was slightly taller than Jake, with a strong, build and a stern face.

The distraught fawn checked on his wife and daughter, who were shaking and weeping, to make sure they were okay and then turned to Jake, rubbing his head. "I cannot begin to thank you for what you have done," he exclaimed in a strong voice. "The creatures knocked me out before I saw them and I woke up just a minute or two before you arrived. They had us surrounded and, even though I'm strong, I knew I wouldn't have been able to get my family out unharmed."

It was at this point, the fawn realized Jake was human. Jake saw a look of surprise come over his face. "I'm sorry, pardon me for asking but, you're human are you not?"

"Yes, my name is Jake. I have come to Under Earth to find a friend of mine who was kidnapped."

"This is very unusual indeed. I have heard of the humans who live topside, but no one has seen any for centuries. Please, pardon my rudeness, my name is Tallin. This is my wife Shereen and my daughter Lilliby."

"It's nice to meet you and I'm glad I was able to help."

The little girl smiled from behind her mother's dress and Tallin spoke again. "I must get my family home safely, but I would also like to return the favor some time. Is there anything I can do for you?"

Jake was thankful for the request but replied, no. "If you take your family home and keep them safe, that is enough."

Tallin bowed his head slightly and responded, "Thank you again, Jake, if ever we cross paths again, remember my help is available. I could never fully repay you, but you can always count me as a friend." Tallin bowed his head again as did his wife. The three fawns turned away and started back through the trees. The little girl paused at the edge of the clearing and turned, giving Jake a huge smile and a little wave goodbye and then dashed into the woods after her parents.

Jake cleaned off the blade of his sword, sheathed it, and started back down the trail he had been on before the ambush. He ate a light snack as he walked and then started off at a slight jog, trying to make up for lost time. He kept his senses on high alert as he ran, trying to make sure he wasn't ambushed again.

After jogging for a distance, Jake slowed to a stop. Curious, he had an idea he wanted to try. Jake took out the Sword of Light and focused on it. He was getting weary of seeing an ambush behind every tree or curve in the path. He looked around. Fairly certain nothing was too close, he shut his eyes and poured his worry into the sword. After about a minute, Jake felt a peace and reassurance in his heart. Then, he knew the sword was letting him know the path ahead was safe. Jake sheathed the sword and imagined it turning into a short sword he could strap to his back. Immediately the sword changed. Although he knew it would happen, it still amazed him every time he saw the sword change.

Jake strapped it to his back so he could still access it at a moment's notice, then took off down the path at a much faster pace than he had been going before. A short while later, Jake came out of the forest panting, but feeling energized. He was at the mountain and could see the cave entrance, which held the gateway, high up on the mountain. He didn't slow, but continued on up the steep trail. It was hard work, but because of his training, he was able to keep up his pace and keep his footing more easily than he would have before.

When Jake reached the ledge outside the cave, he stopped to catch his breath and eat the rest of his fruit and drink the rest of his water. He would have to replenish both up top or when he got back down, but he would be fine for now. Jake checked to make sure the sword and bag over his shoulder was secured and then entered into the darkness of the cave.

—

It took Jake's eyes much longer to adjust to the darkness than it had ever taken before. He figured it must have been because they had gotten used to the constant brightness of Under Earth's sky and now had to relearn how to adjust to the dark. He felt his way along the walls, going slower than he would have liked.

By the time he had reached the large cavern where the guardians lived, his eyes had finally adjusted. There was only a faint blue glow coming from uphill, on the other side of the rock and boulder littered floor where the smaller cavern with blue mushrooms lay. Jake picked up a rock and tossed it into the center of the cavern. Immediately after it hit, three large shadows rose from the floor and ceiling nearby to catch the source of the sound and then fell back into the rock like they were never there.

Jake took out the Sword of Light and held it skyward with one arm. It changed, transforming into an elegant two-handed sword, and started to shine, letting a brilliant white light burst forth. Strangely, Jake didn't have to shield his eyes or even squint. Even though the cavern was now completely filled with the white light, it didn't hurt his eyes. Jake looked around the room and could now clearly see where each of the guardians lived in the stone. The stone in these areas rippled, as if those spots were not solid but liquid, which was strange when looking at them on the ceiling.

Jake could also see many creatures and animal images on the stones, boulders, floors, walls, and ceiling of the cavern. Some were even layered over each other. The pictures looked like they were alive, which Jake knew had been true before they had been taken by the guardians into the stone. These were all of the things the guardians had caught! He knew if he stood here all day, he wouldn't be able to count them all. Jake's head spun just thinking about it.

He started walking into the room. Suddenly, all of the guardians came out and turned to Jake. Like before, they had large frames with strong muscled arms and hands with clawed fingers, large necks and heads, but no actual features.

Jake could see them clearly now and, even though he knew he was safe because the sword would protect him, the sight gave him pause. They looked like solid rock and matched the cavern exactly, except they stretched and turned as easily and noiselessly as if they were made of skin and not stone.

As Jake watched, all of the guardians together bowed at the sight of the sword and made room for Jake to pass. Jake sheathed the sword on his back and, as he did so, it transformed back into the short sword; yet somehow, even when sheathed, it still lit the entire cavern as it had before. He carefully picked his way across the cavern. It went much faster than the first time, but he still had to be careful how to step so he didn't twist his ankle landing on a rock the wrong way.

When he left the cavern of the guardians, the light from the sword went out, leaving him in the dull, blue light of the smaller cavern of glowing mushrooms. He found his eyes could still see well in the dark without the sword's light. This sword continued to amaze him!

Jake walked the short path through the mushrooms and then headed up the tunnel to the gateway room with the Sword of Light in his hand, allowing it to glow once more to light his way.

When he came to the gateway cave, Jake stopped and looked around. Smooth stone walls and ceiling, just like before. "Okay, I'm not sure how this works, but I've done it before and now I have you to guide me," Jake stated, taking out the sword. Jake reached the sword up and touched the tip of it to the ceiling. The light from the sword suddenly winked out and then, Jake felt himself falling upward!

Chapter 20

The Curse

Jake blinked; the first thing he noticed, was that he was standing next to the old tree on Iola. The second thing he noticed, was that he was suddenly very cold. He remembered the wind and the incredible feeling of falling upwards when, suddenly, he was just standing there watching his breath make smoke in the air. Then Jake felt rain washing over him.

An early spring rain was usually refreshing, but with his body being used to Under Earth's hot and humid atmosphere, this was making him shiver. It looked like it was evening, though Jake couldn't be sure because of the clouds. Jake decided it would be a good idea to visit Tobias and get something warm to wear over to Isabelle's parent's house so he wouldn't freeze. He reached back and felt the sword, but couldn't remember sheathing it. Jake ran up to Tobias' door, but before he could knock, the door opened and Tobias ushered him in.

"Jake, I'm glad to see you!" the old white-haired man announced, handing Jake an old, grey coat. Jake put it on and went to stand by the fireplace. "You've only been gone a week and yet, I can see you've changed."

Jake took a moment to realize what Tobias was saying. He'd lost track of time since leaving and, even though he knew time had stopped while he was training, it felt incredibly strange to find it was true.

"Jake, did you find your friend?" Tobias asked with a doubtful look.

"Yes and no," Jake replied, looking back at Tobias. I know where she is being kept, but I need some information from her parents before going to get her. I must go see them."

"You should go now then Jake, but I must warn you, your parents believe you are now missing and the police, along with many in the neighborhood, are looking for you. If you do not wish to be delayed, then you must go without being seen. The rain will help you a little with that, but you must still be careful or you might not get back to Under Earth very soon, if at all."

Jake nodded; he definitely did not want to be delayed again. "How did you know I was back already?"

"I'm the gate keeper, Jake, remember? Even though there are a few from Under Earth with the ability to use the gate, I can always sense when it is used, though I don't always know by whom. Just as I can tell the sword you carry on your back also has the ability to open the gateway, though I would guess that is not the only amazing thing it can do. You must go now, Jake, but before you go back to Under Earth, come back in and see me. I have a surprise for you that may be of great benefit to the rest of your journey."

Jake looked at Tobias questioningly.

"You'll have to wait and see," was all Tobias answered. "Oh, and one more thing Jake, you may want to conceal that sword of yours better under your coat or leave it here. You don't want to attract any undue attention from neighbors who see a teenager running up the street with a sword sticking up out of his coat."

"I have to keep it with me," Jake replied, "but I know what to do." Jake took the sword out and held it for Tobias to see. Suddenly, it started to shine and transformed into the book Jake had read out of. Tobias jumped and his jaw dropped open.

"I am the gate keeper for Under Earth and I am used to seeing the supernatural, yet that is one of the most amazing things I have seen yet. Indeed, I was right, that sword is much more than it appears to be."

Jake smiled; he remembered what it felt like the first time he saw it transform. He put it back in its sheath, which always transformed to fit the sword, whatever its shape, and headed for the front door.

"Jake, use the hood on the coat so you're harder to recognize."

Jake pulled the hood over his head and went out the door. He headed for the sidewalk and had just reached it when a police car turned from 35th onto Iola. The car was heading his direction! It was too late to run back into Tobias' house. They had probably already seen him and it would only look suspicious if he ran back and, most likely, bring the police knocking. Jake did the only thing he could do, he ran forward fast enough to get out of sight and then veered left for a brick house, which had a large evergreen hedge wrapping around the front right side of the house.

Jake ducked into it, crouching next to the corner of the house, and stopped to catch his breath. He could feel the rain water soaking through his pants where he knelt, but it was the least of his worries right now. Hopefully, the car would just keep going and he could make it to Isabelle's house without further incident, but if for some reason the police stopped, the evergreen hedge should be dense enough to conceal him against the brick house.

The headlights of the car came around the bend in the street and Jake could tell they had just passed Tobias' house. This was it, he'd find out soon enough. Jake could barely discern the shape of the squad car as it slowed to a stop near the brick house. The car's spotlight came on, shining right on the bush and Jake almost bolted, but managed to fight the urge to run off. It started to shine up and down the street and Jake let go a sigh of relief. It wasn't night, but because of the rainclouds, it was fairly dark already.

The light switched off and Jake was just thinking he was safe, when the door to the police car opened and an officer stepped out. He was talking to his partner in the passenger seat and Jake could just make out what he was saying over the rain.

"I just want to check something really quick, I'll be right back," the officer remarked, shutting the door and turning toward Jake.

Jake's pulse quickened. The officer was coming toward his hiding spot. Jake peeked around the corner. The hedge went another three or four feet down the side of the house and then it was open space until the backyard. The gate was open! If Jake was quick enough, and the rain helped cover the sound of his footsteps, he could make it.

Jake glanced back and saw the officer pass the sidewalk into the front lawn only 15 or 20 feet from Jake. Without another moment's thought, and as quietly as he could while crouched behind the hedge, Jake stepped around the corner and tried quietly making his way to the back. Unfortunately for Jake, the ground behind the hedge was just dirt and, with the rain, mud. His feet were sticking a little and he feared the noise might be loud enough to give him away. He had to make it to the grass just past the hedge! It was only a second or two, but Jake felt like it still took too long to get to the grass. If the officer came around to check this side of the house now, he would see Jake in the open.

Jake started for the backyard as quietly as he could manage, when movement caught his eye to the right and he froze. He turned his head slightly to see better past his hood and he saw a woman standing at the window inside the house next door. She wasn't looking out the window, but if she gazed up or if he moved, he was sure she'd spot him. Jake wanted to run, but knew he couldn't. His only chance was that she would turn away enough to let Jake get past before the officer came around. Come on, come on, leave, Jake thought as he stood there. He knew any moment the officer would finish looking behind the bush and glance around the side where he was, now in clear view.

Jake was almost sure he was caught, but then the woman abruptly turned away from the window to talk to someone else in the house. Jake bolted! He knew he was probably making more sound than he had been, but he also knew if he didn't get out of there now, he would be seen for sure, so he had to chance it.

Jake made it through the gate and ran behind the house out of the line of sight. He then ran to the back of the yard, his feet splashing and squishing through the grass and mud. He hopped the fence next to the garage, which came off the alley behind the house. Jake found a couple of trash bins on the other side of the garage he could hide behind and see back to the front. The officer had just checked behind the hedge at the side of the house and glanced around. He must not have seen Jake or he would already be chasing him. He had made it just in time! Jake stayed put until he saw the officer disappear around the front of the house again. A minute later he saw the police car pull past the house and continue down the street.

Jake had a funny feeling the patrol car would pull down the alley next, so he had to find a spot to hide, quickly. He could try to make his way back to the street, but if he continued to run through yards, one of the owners would spot him for sure. The alley was the safer bet, because much of it was blocked from view by garages, sheds, and fences. The neighbors would be much less likely to spot him here.

Jake spotted a large pile of bricks with weeds growing around and through them farther down the alley. He made it to them and had just jumped behind them, when his gut feeling proved true. Headlights turned down the alley as the squad car entered. Jake heard it on the gravel and knelt on his hands and knees, the wet grass quickly giving him a fresh soaking through his pants. It was cold, but he ignored it.

If he hadn't been wet, muddy, and scared of being caught, he might have enjoyed a day like today. The rain fell in a steady rhythm and the air had a fresh spring smell to it. As it was though, all he could think about, was how long the car was taking to come down the alley. The wait seemed endless, though it probably wasn't long at all. When the cruiser got close, Jake took a deep breath and held it as best he could on the chance they might be able to see his breath come up from behind the weeds. The car continued slowly past Jake and then stopped. Jake guessed they were just checking behind the house where he had hidden.

They must have been satisfied nothing was amiss because, a few moments later, Jake heard the tires start to roll again. Jake took a chance and laid down on the ground next to a garage and peeked around it with one eye. He was now cold, wet, and muddy all over, but he was able to see the police car pull out of the alley and turn right.

Unless they floored it, it would take them a few minutes to come back around to Kingman. Jake started jogging. He ran across both sides of Kingman and made it to another alleyway. Jake zigzagged through alleys and side streets until he reached Isabelle's house. He made it to their backdoor completely soaked, but without further incident.

Jake knocked on the door and waited. He was about to knock again when he heard the deadbolt unlock. The door opened part way to reveal Isabelle's mom. Normally, she was a very pretty, energetic, and vibrant woman who loved life, but the woman before him now was haggard and tired. Her eyes seemed red from crying and the bloodshot look told Jake she had been doing it a lot. Jake had never seen her this way.

"Mrs. Stevenson, please let me in," Jake pleaded. The last thing he needed was for Isabelle's parents to turn him away.

"I'm sorry Jake, but you need to leave," responded Isabelle's mom, her voice cracking mid-sentence. "I don't know where you have been for the past week, but since your parents reported you missing, the police have been looking for you. They came and questioned us and we had a very difficult time convincing them we didn't know where you were. I know you cared about Isabelle, but since she disappeared you have caused us nothing but heartache and trouble. Please, leave so that I don't have to report you!" Jake knew she was hurting. He also knew he had the look of a wild man, being soaking wet and covered in mud. Mrs. Stevenson didn't realize what he had been through since she had last seen him, but he couldn't take no for an answer or he wouldn't be able to explain himself. She started to close the door, but Jake stuck his foot in first.

"Please Mrs. Stevenson, I know where Isabelle is!" Doubt showed on Isabelle's mother's face, but Jake also saw a little hope flood her eyes. "I can prove it to you, but you have to hear me out."

For a second, Isabelle's mom didn't budge, trying to decide, but then she slowly opened the door and nodded. "Come in," she sighed, too weary to argue.

Jake followed her into the home, glad to get out of the rain and into the warmer house. Isabelle's home was one of the finest in the neighborhood. It wasn't a mansion, though her family could have afforded one, but it was very large and everything in it was immaculate. Jake had been in it many times, hanging out with Isabelle's family. It was usually very clean and everything in its proper place. Even though they could easily afford to hire a maid service, Isabelle's mom stayed home and kept everything neat and tidy herself. Normally, he would have felt terrible about coming into their home in his present condition but Mrs. Stevenson didn't even seem to notice he was all muddy with weeds all tangled in his shoe laces. Jake glanced around and understood why.

Their house now looked as if it had been neglected for weeks. Their backdoor opened into their kitchen, which was now full of dirty dishes, half eaten meals, and empty food delivery containers. Jake looked through the doorway into the dining room where there were piles of papers and other random things.

He was about to ask for a towel, when Isabelle's dad entered the room looking almost as bad as her mom. He was followed closely by Isabelle's younger sister Rachel. She was only four years old and appeared to be the only one who was well taken care of, her clothes were clean and her hair combed. She had the opposite appearance of her parents who were worn and haggard looking.

Forgetting the towel, Jake blurted out, "Mr. and Mrs. Stevenson, I know where Isabelle is and I believe I can rescue her, but I need your help." As he finished saying this, little Rachel ran around her dad with wide eyes. "You've seen Izzy?" she gasped, excitement showing on her face.

Mrs. Stevenson turned to her youngest daughter. "Rachel, I need you to go up to your room and play for a little bit."

"But mom, I want to see Izzy," Rachel whined, looking hurt.

Mr. Stevenson turned to Rachel, put his hand on her head and, with a gentle voice, he replied, "It's okay Rach, I promise you can be the first one to give her a hug, but we need to talk to Jake right now, so go up to your room and I'll come and get you when we're done."

Rachel turned to leave, but gave Jake a sideways look and responded, "Bring Izzy back with you when you come next time Jake, I miss her." With that, she scurried off and Jake could hear her running up the steps to her room.

Mr. Stevenson turned to Jake, "Let's go into the living room, Jake."

Jake followed Isabelle's father through their dining room and into their front living room, followed by Isabelle's mother. Her parents took seats across from Jake and motioned to the chair across from them, but he chose to pace instead of sit.

Mr. Stevenson chose to start the conversation, "Jake, we know you loved our daughter and we have always been glad she chose such a good young man as her friend, but I don't think you can help. I wish I could explain more, but I just can't."

Jake stopped pacing and faced Isabelle's parents. "Mr. and Mrs. Stevenson, I understand now why you didn't want police involved and why you were so mysterious before. If you had told me the truth, I probably wouldn't have believed you, but that has all changed. I know about the curse."

At that both of Isabelle's parents' faces turned from a state of hopelessness to a look of shock and disbelief. Jake let what he had divulged sink in before he continued.

"I have been to Under Earth and found out where Isabelle is being kept, but I can't free her without knowing what spell she is under and how to break it." Jake looked at Isabelle's parents and waited for an explanation.

Mr. Stevenson was the first to speak. "Jake, I don't know what you're talking about, but we've never heard of a place called Under Earth."

Jake could tell neither of Isabelle's parents believed him so he reached back and pulled out the book. "I know it's hard to believe, but I am going to show you something so you will know I speak the truth." Jake took the book and held it by the edge with his right hand. A soft light started to emanate from it and it started to lengthen and narrow right before their eyes. Jake transformed the sword slowly, so the Stevenson's could take it all in. Both of Isabelle's parents jumped to their feet, surprised, and Mrs. Stevenson let loose a small cry before she clapped her hands to her mouth. The book transformed into the elegant two-handed Sword of Light, shining brightly and then fading back to normal.

Jake was slightly more forceful this time as he instructed, "Now, please sit and tell me what type of deal you made that has Isabelle trapped."

Isabelle's mother sat but her father turned and gazed out the side window as he spoke in a slow voice filled with regret. "You have to understand Jake; we didn't know this would happen. If we had known, we never would have done it."

Jake took a seat, resting the sword on his lap. "Mr. Stevenson, I'm not here to judge you I'm here to find the truth so I can get Isabelle back."

Jonathan Stevenson looked at Jake and then sat, tears in his eyes. "Six months before Isabelle was born, we lived on Iola. Sarah was three months pregnant and I had lost my job two months prior, just before we found out we were pregnant. We were so happy we were going to have a baby, but I was devastated that I was unable to provide for my family. I had been working two part-time jobs while looking for something more permanent and stable. We still didn't have health insurance and the doctor bills were coming in on top of our other bills. We were not wealthy then Jake and we were very much in debt."

"We had just come home from a doctor's visit one day and I was at a low point. We had gotten out of the car and we were arguing because we were both stressed and didn't know what to do. That's when a strange looking man approached us. He was tall and thin and wore a long coat. He had very sharp, angular features and his skin seemed very pale. I think he had dark hair, but it was hard to tell because he was wearing a hood, which partially blocked his face. His hands were gloved, but in his right hand he held a staff he was using as a walking stick. The staff was very peculiar because it appeared to be made out of pink glass."

"As Sarah and I were arguing, the man suddenly appeared in our driveway. He appeared to come out of nowhere. I didn't think anyone was coming down the street, but then again, we were fighting so I wasn't paying attention. I have never seen anyone quite like him, but he was very polite when he approached us. He asked us to forgive him for overhearing our conversation, but he might be able to help us. I thought it was strange, but I was desperate. We hadn't made our house payment that month and I was ready to try almost anything, so we heard him out."

"The man was very pleasant and convincing when he told us he could guarantee I would get a job and become very successful in return for something I could give him that he greatly desired. I was skeptical about this abrupt change of events, but desperate for a chance. I thought maybe he was going to offer me a job, so I asked him what he wanted in return. He promised there was no reason worry about it yet because it would be a while before he needed it. If and when I became successful, he would come back and let me know what he wanted. He told me I didn't have what he was looking for now, but I may someday, and when that day came, he would let me know. All I had to do was shake his hand and success would be mine."

"Again, Jake, I was ready to try anything and a handshake, while seeming too easy, didn't strike me as something I would regret later. The man appeared to genuinely want to help. I figured it was worth a shot. If I didn't become successful, I wasn't out anything, and if I did, I could probably afford what he wanted. I never thought..." Mr. Stevenson's voice choked and tears flooded his eyes. He wiped his eyes and cleared his throat before continuing.

"So I shook his hand. As I did his grip tightened like a vise, his face became dark, and his voice sounded ominous as he spoke."

"A gift I give but not for free, a payment I will require
But if you wish to refuse me, the consequence will be dire
Once my prize is taken, at my own time and pleasure
To get it back one will need to give in equal measure"

"At that point, I was suddenly extremely worried I had made a mistake but then, he let go of my hand abruptly and started to walk away. As soon as he let go, the feeling of danger I had felt magically lessened. I was still concerned, but not nearly as much as a moment before. I looked at Sarah and we exchanged a worried look, but when we looked back at the stranger, he was gone! I ran out into the street and looked both ways, but he was nowhere to be seen. It was like he was there one second and gone the next."

"Sarah and I walked into the house and were about to voice our concern over what had just taken place, but no sooner had we walked through the door, then the phone rang. I answered and it was someone calling to say they had gotten a copy of my resume and wanted to offer me a job. I went to an interview later that day and, before I left, I was hired with a salary and benefits package that was more than I had dreamed of. When I got home and told Sarah about the job, we completely forgot about the strange man and our promise. I know we were excited, but that doesn't account for our memory loss. It was almost like a spell was on us, causing us to forget because we didn't remember our encounter with the stranger until he came back. In less than a year, we had paid off all our debts and I had been promoted twice. By the time Isabelle was born, we were able to sell our old home and move into this one."

"Okay," Jake answered, "I think I understand so far, but what does this have to do with Isabelle?"

Mrs. Stevenson spoke up. "We never gave any of this a second thought because we didn't remember the stranger. We hadn't seen or heard from him since the day he made the deal with us. But the afternoon of the day Isabelle disappeared, he knocked on our door." Isabelle's mom's voice constricted, but she went on. "We both felt dread upon seeing him again as the memory came flooding back like it had never left, but we had him come in anyway. Isabelle was still in school and Rachel was up taking a nap. The man looked exactly like we remembered him, like he hadn't aged at all! He told us the time for our payment had come." At this, Isabelle's mother started crying and put her face in her hands.

Mr. Stevenson continued. "I asked him what he wanted. The words he spoke seemed like a death sentence. He told us he required our firstborn, our oldest daughter." Isabelle's father stopped abruptly, barely choking out the last words. He stood shaking with what appeared to be extreme sorrow and fury mingled together. Jake waited, knowing he would continue when he was ready. After another minute, Mr. Stevenson calmed himself some and turned to look directly at Jake.

"I immediately refused and told him I could give him all the money we had, if he would leave our daughters alone.

He simply stated Isabelle was the only payment he would accept and we had no choice in the matter."

Jake could see the sorrow and fury in Isabelle's father's eyes as he continued to speak. "I told him I was going to call the police and he needed to get out of our house and never show his face again, but he just laughed at me. Now, you know me Jake, I'm not a violent man, but when he told me he was taking my daughter and laughed at my refusal, I snapped. There was no way I was going to let that happen, so I charged him. I ran at the stranger, intending to hurt him as badly as I could and then throw him out, but I only made it a few feet.

"What happened next I wouldn't have believed possible. The man held up his hand and started to speak the words that I had almost forgotten and dreaded to hear."

"A gift I give but not for free, a payment I will require
But if you wish to refuse me, the consequence will be dire
Once my prize is taken, at my own time and pleasure
To get it back, one will need to give in equal measure"

The instant he started speaking I felt my feet leave the ground and I was thrown back against our stone fireplace. I had the wind knocked out of me and, once I regained my breath, I found that I was suspended to the wall, a foot off the ground."

Mrs. Stevenson broke in, "It was like nothing I've ever seen, Jake. The only way I can describe it is it was as if he were using magic. When I tried running to help Jonathan, the stranger struck me and I fell onto the couch. When I looked at the stranger, I knew if I moved a muscle he would kill me."

Isabelle's father continued and there was more grief now then anger. "I couldn't fight it Jake. I hung there while the stranger announced he would be back for my oldest daughter. He stated once she was gone, if we tried finding her or attempted to rescue her, he would kill our youngest daughter and anyone who tried helping Isabelle would die before freeing her. He told me that since we had tried to refuse him, he would put a mark on Rachel and, if we ever tried anything to get Isabelle back, the mark would kill her."

Isabelle's mother broke in again, "I tried running for Rachel, Jake, but he froze me to the couch with his staff before I could take a step. We were both struggling for all we were worth, but we could only move our eyes and watch him go as the tears fell down our faces. He was only up there a minute and what he did we don't know, but once he was gone Rachel had a new mark on the back of her neck."

Mr. Stevenson took over again. "He barely looked at us when he came back down. He just told us to remember what he had said and walked out the front door. Once he left, whatever he had held us with left also. I fell to the floor and Sarah came off the couch and ran for Rachel. Once I had gotten to my feet, I ran out the front door and looked around, but the stranger had again disappeared without a trace. When Sarah came back down she was pale and told me Rachel was still asleep, but she had found the mark on her neck."

"Once that happened, Jake, I became a very desperate man again. Even more desperate than when we had no money. We picked Isabelle up from school and told her we were moving. I was still foolish enough to believe we could escape. If we could just get away so the stranger couldn't find us, we would be okay. That is why I told Isabelle she couldn't leave or talk to anyone. I should have known she would try to see you, but I was so busy getting things we would need together, I never noticed she had left. That is why we didn't want the police involved, Jake. Once you had told us Isabelle was gone, we called my sister and convinced her to lie for us. She had our niece speak to the police on the phone, as if she were Isabelle, and my sister was able to convince them she was there visiting her cousin who was sick. That is why they would not look into your claims further Jake."

"We were just so worried something would happen to Rachel too. We know you didn't believe us when you left, Jake, how could you after seeing her disappear? But we couldn't tell you what had actually happened and, after what we saw the stranger do with his staff, we knew the police couldn't help either. You see, Jake, the same night after you left but before the police arrived, Rachel started screaming that her neck burned badly and, when we looked, the spot had swollen to a bump and was bright red. We were afraid we had meddled too much and she was going to die, but after a couple of minutes, it stopped. I think he was warning us of what he could do if we tried anything again."

Isabelle's dad stopped and Jake saw both of Isabelle's parents looked slightly relieved at being able to tell someone else what they had been keeping bottled up inside, yet they also looked completely exhausted and even more worn out from the telling.

Jake sat in the quiet and used the time to think. While he did this, he reached down and gripped the Sword of Light. Finally, he prayed, asking the Creator what he needed to do. His mind went to Isabelle's sister Rachel and he had a thought. He focused the thought to the Sword of Light. In response, he felt the warmth and a slight vibration, which he knew to mean yes.

Jake stood, sword in hand, and looked at Isabelle's parents. "Thank you for telling me this, I know it couldn't have been easy. I am going to do everything I can to help Isabelle and I truly believe I can get her back, but I need to know if you trust me." He glanced at Isabelle's parents. They looked at Jake and then at each other. Something passed between them and when they looked back, Isabelle's mother nodded yes.

"Okay then, first things first," Jake announced, looking directly into their eyes. "Call Rachel down."

Mrs. Stevenson showed the faintest trace of worry around her eyes, but turned and called her youngest daughter. A minute later, Rachel came into the room. She stopped when she saw Jake standing with the sword and looked questioningly at it. Jake knelt down, but still held the sword in his hand.

"Hi Rachel," he whispered in a gentle voice. "Your mom and dad tell me you have a spot on your neck that hurts you sometimes." At this, Rachel nodded apprehensively, looking like she thought Jake was going to use the sword to cut it from her neck. "I think I can help it go away, but I need you to trust me, can you do that?" Jake asked, looking into her worried expression.

Rachel still looked worried, but nodded yes. "Okay, that's good." Jake replied. "Could you go over and stand by your mom?" She did this and Jake continued. "Mrs. Stevenson, if you could keep Rachel still and facing you and Mr. Stevenson, if you could lift up her hair so I can see the spot and her hair is out of the way."

Rachel's mom held her hands and responded, "Look at me sweetheart, it'll be alright, just keep your eyes on me." Mr. Stevenson stood and carefully took Rachel's hair in both hands, lifting it gently clear of her neck.

Now Jake could see the ugly mark, which now looked like a boil in the middle of her neck. It was brown and about a half an inch wide, but it had an angry redness around it. Jake didn't really know what he was supposed to do, but trusted the sword to show him how to help Rachel. An idea popped into his mind and he knew the sword was directing him. Jake walked around the coffee table so that he stood just behind and to the side of Rachel, opposite of her dad. He held the sword of light out in front of him and it immediately started to give off a red light. The blade started changing color from a cold steel grey to a deep blood red.

The edges of the sword started collecting small droplets, like the sword was actually bleeding. Jake spoke as Isabelle and Rachel's parents stared. "Mr. and Mrs. Stevenson and Rachel, this is the Sword of Light. It is the sword of the Creator, older than time and filled with the Creator's power. No curse, spell, magic, or supernatural power can overcome it. The Creator has allowed me to carry it now, so I can free both of your daughters." With that, Jake took the flat of the blade and wiped it across the spot on Rachel's neck.

What appeared to be blood smeared off onto the spot on the back of Rachel's neck. Jake took the sword away and it turned back to its cold steel form. Rachel giggled, "That tickles." As they watched, the blood evaporated in a cloud of red and with it, the spot. After about 30 seconds, nothing was left except for the clean skin of Rachel's neck. Her mother reached around to look and then hugged her daughter, weeping. "Thank you Jake, thank you!" she responded as she rocked her daughter, who was unsure why her mother was acting this way.

Jake allowed the sword to turn back into the book as Rachel watched, wide eyed. "Don't thank me Mr. and Mrs. Stevenson. It wasn't me who healed her, it was the Creator. Put your trust in Him." Jake looked at them and they nodded back, comprehension and understanding coming from their gaze. "I have to go now," Jake announced, "But if you would pray for Isabelle and for me, I would appreciate it greatly!"

"Jake, how can I help you?" Isabelle's father reached out as Jake turned to leave. Jake looked back at Isabelle's dad, knowing it must be hard for Mr. Stevenson to have to stay behind and let someone else rescue his daughter, but Jake also knew the Creator had called him to this task.

"Stay here and look after your wife and Rachel, Mr. Stevenson. The Creator has given me this task and I will get Isabelle back," Jake answered, with more belief in his Creator than confidence he felt himself. He turned to leave, but turned back one more time. "Actually Mr. and Mrs. Stevenson, there is something you could do for me."

"Name it," Isabelle's father responded.

"I've been gone for a little over a week now, and my parents must be worried sick. I would go and try to explain everything to them about where I've been and why, but that would keep me from helping Isabelle and I've already had too many delays. If you could meet with my parents and try to explain the situation, or at least convince them I'm not lost, but helping Isabelle. That would help a lot."

Mr. Stevenson stuck out his hand. Jake reached out and shook it. "We will go talk to your parents and explain everything. Be safe and please, return with Isabelle," Mr. Stevenson choked.

Jake let go of Mr. Stevenson's hand. "Thank you and I will." With that, Jake turned and looked out the window to make sure the street was clear, and then walked out of the front door.

Chapter 21

Tobias' Surprise

Jacob made his way back to Tobias's house through the alleyways again, stopping only at the intersections to make sure the coast was clear. Jake made sure the patrol car wasn't in sight before making his way to Tobias' front door. He knocked twice in quick succession, anxious to get inside and out of view. The door opened and Jake stopped short, surprised to see who had opened it.

Instead of Tobias, his sister's face was smiling back. He was confused. "What are you doing..." but before he could finish she grabbed his sleeve and pulled him inside, closing the door behind him.

"Hey, Jake, glad you could make it," came a familiar voice from Tobias' living room. Jake turned from his sister and saw TJ, Patrick, and Eric sitting in chairs by Tobias' fireplace while the old man himself stood next to it, smiling!

"Surprise, Jake," Tobias responded with a chuckle.

"How, why..." Jake stuttered as he struggled to comprehend how his sister and his friends had come to be there.

"Your sister said she knew where to find you and told us you needed our help, so here we are," TJ spoke from his chair near the fireplace.

Jake turned and looked at Alisha, "How did you know I would be here?"

Alicia rolled her eyes, "Oh please, it really wasn't that hard. When you didn't show up for school, I figured the only reason that would happen was because you still believed Isabelle was missing and had gone looking for her. Since you claim she disappeared on this street, I made my way here after school. Tobias was out and I approached him and asked if he'd seen you. When I mentioned your name, it was obvious he knew something so I refused to leave until he told me what he knew."

Jake looked over at Tobias and he shrugged. "What can I say Jake, your sister has a very stern look and when I tried fibbing she didn't buy it."

Jake looked back at his sister and it was her turn to shrug. "He's not a very good liar and when I threatened to get the authorities, he told me everything."

"Told you everything," Jake asked, questioningly to Tobias.

Tobias just shrugged and responded simply, "I told her I was the gate keeper to a secret supernatural world called Under Earth and I sent you there so you could rescue Isabelle.

"And you believed him!" Jake asked, incredulous.

"I admit it was hard to swallow, but he didn't look like he was lying and then he went and got his flute thing and showed me what he could do and that convinced me."

TJ piped up, "Not to sound ungrateful for the invite, but Eric, Patrick, and I just arrived and have no idea what you guys are talking about. Would you mind filling us in?"

Alisha walked over and sat down in front of the fireplace to wait for Jake. He could see he would have to take a few minutes to explain everything now, so he walked over to the small circle of chairs by the fireplace and took off the coat Tobias had given him, which was all muddy and soggy.

Tobias took the coat back from him, holding it at arm's length and looking at it with a frown. "That's the last time I lend you a coat," he muttered, taking it into another room and returning.

"Whoa Jake, when did you get ripped?" piped Eric from his chair on the right side of the fireplace next to Tobias.

Jake smiled. "You'll have a hard time believing this, but here it goes." So Jake took the next half hour to tell the group what he had been up to after finding Tobias' note and going to search for Isabelle. He told them about meeting the fairies, Father Time, the dragons, his training with Dreaden, and his new faith. Jake tried being as detailed as he could and hit the important parts of the story, while also trying to keep it as brief as possible.

When he had finished, he could tell TJ, Patrick, and Eric still found it hard to swallow, so he took out the Sword of Light and once again transformed it from its book form back into the elegant double-handed sword.

After a few moments of stunned silence, TJ spoke up, "Well, I think that clears it up for me, how about you guys?"

"Yep, I'm good," responded Eric.

"Nah," chuckled Patrick, wiping the look of shock off his face and replacing it with a smirk. "I see books transform into swords all the time, Jake, you got anything more impressive?"

The room erupted in laughter! When it finally died down, TJ looked at Jake and asked, "So how can we help?"

Jake looked at the faces around him. "I can't ask you guys to come with, it's too dangerous."

"That's why you need our help mate," Eric responded from across the room. "Even with that sword, you can't expect to do this on your own, can you?"

"You guys don't understand; this is life or death we're talking about. I've seen trolls larger than tree trunks. I have the sword and I'm willing to risk it, but I can't ask you guys to do the same."

Patrick piped up, "Jake, you said yourself you went searching for Isabelle long before you had the sword and, last time I checked, you are not my parent, so you can't tell me what to do!"

"Isabelle is our friend too, Jake," TJ stated from the chair to Jake's left. "What does it mean if your friends abandon you when you need them most?"

"You have to admit that we've been handy to have around in a scrap or two, mate," Eric grinned.

Jake knew them well enough to see this argument was a lost cause and he knew they were right, but he had to be sure of one more thing. "Okay, but there's one more thing I need to ask you and you have to be truthful because it is very important," Jake waited a second and, when everyone stayed silent, he continued. "Do you all believe in the Creator and his Son who died for us? If you don't, I really think it is a bad idea for you to come. There is a protection only He can give, but you must believe in Him."

"Jake, how long have we been going to youth group together and it has been *us* trying to convince *you* of this? You were the last holdout and it took some supernatural world to knock some sense into you!" TJ responded, smiling.

Patrick shifted in his chair. "We've been praying for you for a while now, Jake, we just didn't realize a trip to the center of the earth was what it was going to take."

Jake looked around the room. He was still slightly apprehensive about them coming, but he couldn't dissuade them and he couldn't deny that part of him would be glad for their help. His eyes drifted over to Alisha who was still sitting by the fire. He knew she probably had the strongest faith of anyone in the room, but he also knew he had to make sure she stayed. He knew she wouldn't like what he was about to say.

Jake opened his mouth, but Alisha must have anticipated this and was ready for it because she held up her hand. "I know what you're going to say Jake, that I'm your little sister, that I'm too young, and that mom and dad wouldn't want me to go. But before you say that, remember, Isabelle is like a sister to me and I want to help her too, so before you say I can't go, why don't you ask the sword and see what it says? You told us you were to trust it and its guidance right?"

Jake thought he had been ready for any argument she could make, but he hadn't come close to seeing this. As much as he hated it, she was right and he couldn't argue. Jake held the Sword of Light and thought about the question. It glowed and gently pulsed, giving Jake gentle warmth in his hand. He knew it was a yes and begrudgingly nodded at his sister.

"Great! So let's get going!" she shouted, brightly smiling and jumping to her feet.

As everyone stood, Tobias walked over and took out the strange flute he had used to send Jake to Under Earth the first time. "Why don't you lead the way, Jake?"

Jake walked over to the window and peeked out as the others followed. The coast looked clear. There didn't seem to be anyone out and about. They filed outside and followed Jake over to the old, gnarled tree and stopped. The rain had almost stopped now, but the sun must be going down behind the rainclouds because it was getting darker by the minute. Tobias came up behind them, his instrument ready. "Okay, for those of you who haven't witnessed this before, it will seem a little strange. I need you to all hold hands. I will start playing a song and when I do, it will get even darker and the weather will change slightly. It is normal for that to happen. After the first note, I will say your names, so you will be able to use the gateway. Only you will be aware of the change once it happens, as only people who are using the gateway can see it."

"Now Eric, TJ, and Patrick, if you three can tell me your last names I will get started." Once they had told him, they all grabbed hands and Jake took the spot next to the tree. Tobias played a low and mournful note which continued ringing after he had taken the instrument away from his mouth. "Jacob and Alisha Cross, TJ Finner, Patrick Scott, Eric Holden!" Tobias boldly stated and put the instrument back to his mouth. As he played the slow and eerie tune, the sky quickly became pitch black. The air became deadly still and a fog started to build across the ground. Jake couldn't even see Alisha, who was standing beside him, but knew she was there because her hand was still in his. The song reached its climax and Jake reached out his free hand to the same spot on the tree he had before.

Suddenly, the swirling vortex of wind sprang out of the hole, engulfing all five of them and then they were falling. Jake felt Alisha's hand tighten its grip tenfold and he realized it had been a mistake not to think about telling them to expect this. He tried shouting, but could still only hear the music ringing in his ears.

After a short while, Jake felt his feet gently touch the ground. He then noticed Alisha's hand had gone slack in his and it was gently pulling Jake down. He had to crouch to keep hold of her. He realized she must have fallen asleep on the journey down, just like he had the first time.

Without letting go of his sister's hand, Jake reached back with his free hand and took out the Sword of Light, changing it into a short sword at the same time. He wasn't going to wait for his eyes to adjust this time. A soft, white glow started to emanate from the sword. As before, it reached all around Jake, not even leaving a shadow where Jake was blocking it, revealing Alisha, TJ, Eric, and Patrick all lying on the ground in the small cavern. It appeared to have grown to accommodate the group because Jake was positive it had been smaller when he had been there alone. They were lying like they had all let go of each other's hands just before they fell asleep. Jake had been the only one who hadn't fallen asleep. Maybe this was due to the fact that this wasn't his first time or maybe it was because he had the sword, Jake wasn't sure.

Jake set Alisha's hand down and let go as he sheathed the sword. The light once again continued to shine everywhere, unhindered by the fact that it was now sheathed on his back. Jake gently shook Alisha awake. As she stirred, he carefully stepped around her and repeated this with TJ, Patrick, and Eric. They were all slightly groggy, rubbing their eyes as if they had been asleep for a while, though Jake knew it had only been a few minutes at most.

Once they looked more alert, Jake instructed, "Follow me." Jake led the way down the tunnel, which ended in the small cavern with the glowing blue mushrooms. He walked out into the middle of the room and stopped. The group came up behind him and looked around. With the light coming from the sword, the glow from the mushrooms couldn't be seen as well, but it still played tricks on their eyes. Alisha noticed this first.

"Jake, what is it with these mushrooms? I've never seen blue before, but there is something else strange about them."

"I'll show you but I have to put out the light." Jake reached back and touched the hilt of the sword and its light went out. There was a collective gasp and then a "wow" from TJ, and a "That's so cool" from Alisha.

"Well, that's different," said Patrick, with his knack for understatement.

"These were all I could see by when I got here the first time. They make a nice tea once they're dried out." Although Jake couldn't see him very clearly in the low, blue light, he could tell Eric had just made a weird face and Jake knew he'd made a mistake.

"Tea? Wow, this place really has changed you, Jake, what's next? Are you going to develop your own fashion line?" Jake could tell Eric was grinning from ear-to-ear.

"No, I was thinking of taking up modeling," Jake answered in the most snobbish voice he could make.

"I always knew there was something wrong with you," TJ replied as they all laughed.

Jake turned and walked to the end of the small cavern and stopped as the others followed. Jake cautioned them with a wave of his hand and they all stopped quietly. "I'm going to turn the light back on, but first, I want you to see something." Jake stooped and picked up a pebble and then threw it out into the larger cavern. It struck a boulder and immediately, a huge form sprang from the floor nearby and grabbed it and then vanished back into the floor. Everyone but Jake had jumped back a step or two.

"Okay," TJ responded in a whisper, "You know I don't scare easy, Jake, but that was freaky. What was that?"

"Those are the guardians. They keep things from entering or leaving Under Earth that don't have permission to do so. I had a very difficult time getting past them without the sword the first time. It was mostly dumb luck and a rabbit that was unfortunate enough to go first. This sword is one of the few things that will allow us to pass unharmed." Jake reached back and touched the hilt of the sword and it sprang to life again, lighting everything around with a brilliant white light and yet none of them had to wait for their eyes to adjust.

As the light hit the large cavern, the hidden guardians slowly came from their hiding places. The group stood open mouthed as they watched the living stone forms turn to search about. Once again the guardians bowed and Jake turned back to the group. "Follow me, and step carefully."

They set off walking and climbing their way through the large cavern, looking all around them as they went. Patrick was the first to ask about all of the images on the rocks, floor, ceiling, and walls. "Are these images things that were caught by the guardians?" he asked, astonished.

"Yes," Jake responded, remembering the fate of the rabbit that had gone ahead of him, sealing its own fate while allowing Jake to see the danger he had almost unknowingly walked into. "The guardians are blind, but they can sense sound somehow. I barely made it past them and, looking back, I think it was only by the Creator's grace I was able to."

The group reached the end of the cavern and walked down the passage, which lead to Under Earth. It went much quicker with the light of the sword helping them. As they reached the last turn, Jake reached back to let the sword go out. "I'm turning off the light, you'll see why in a moment."

Jake led the way out of the tunnel onto the small ledge outside the cave. "Welcome to Under Earth!" TJ, Patrick, Eric, and Alisha came out and stood open mouthed with a variety of exclamations like wow, cool, amazing, sweet! Jake let them linger a moment and then led them around to start the trek down. The hike went quickly, even though the other four were still trying to take everything in. They talked on the way down about the sky, trees, and other details from the unusual world all around them.

As they neared the bottom, Jake could see tents set up in the clearing before the forest. He cautioned the others and reached back for the sword just as he heard a familiar voice behind him.

"You know, if I had been an enemy you'd be too late," Sapphire stated from a bright blue and pink bush behind Jake. Jake turned and, even though he knew she was there, her wings and hair helped her blend in with the bush so well, it took a few moments to see her grinning broadly back from the bush.

Jake put his arm down as he smiled back. "That's true, but most of them aren't as clever and not nearly as mischievous as you."

"Compliments will get you nowhere," she responded as she fluttered out of the bush and onto his shoulder. The expressions of the others, who hadn't known who the voice belonged to and didn't know where to look, changed from confusion to wonder as they saw Sapphire alight on Jake's shoulder. "So, who are your friends?"

"This is Alisha, my sister," Jake answered, pointing, "and these are my three closest friends TJ, Eric, and Patrick." As Jake announced, them they all waved in succession. "They came to help."

"Good, we've managed to gather some help as well. Why don't we go meet them?" Sapphire took flight toward the tents and Jake's group followed. They entered the clearing from between two of the tents and found a small, but sizable group before them. There were, by Jake's quick estimate, between 30 and 50 creatures all assembled and apparently waiting for them.

When Jake's group entered, all heads turned their way. Before anyone could say anything, however, Claira flew up to join Sapphire in front of Jake, her silver wings a flurry of activity. "Hi Jake, I'm glad you made it back!" Claira cried as she joined her sister. "Trouble free trip I hope."

"I'm glad to be back Claira. I did run into a couple of snags, but everything is fine now," Jake responded as Alisha, TJ, Eric, and Patrick came up beside him.

"We heard about your encounter with the turogs from the family you helped rescue." Claira said, quietly.

"I told you one of us should have gone with him," Sapphire added, sarcastically. "Trouble follows him like a bad habit!"

"That's because I can't seem to get away from you, Sapphire," Jake responded, smiling.

Sapphire grinned, "I'll remember that Jake!"

"Oh, I know you will," Jake replied.

Jake reintroduced the group to Claira.

Claira then flew to the front. "Welcome to Under Earth. I wish it were under different circumstances. Well, Jake, I guess we'd better introduce you to the help we've found. Our first volunteer you might recognize."

"Gadlonin!" Jake exclaimed as the tall, dark haired elf approached. "How's your son?"

Gadlonin smiled, "Very well, thanks in large part to you. He is currently driving his mother crazy! The fairies reached me with word you would be in need of assistance. You helped me before you even knew me, so I wish to aid you in any way I can. These are some of my kin and some of the elves of the north where we live." A group of 22 came forward to stand behind Gadlonin.

An elf, slightly taller than Gadlonin with long black hair and fierce features, stepped forward. "My name is Eventine and I am captain of the northern Elvin armies. When I heard what you had done for Gadlonin, and that you needed help, I gathered the soldiers I could contact and headed here with Gadlonin and his kin. We are all masters of the arrow and blade at your service. I'm sorry I could not find more, but the rest of our army is scattered throughout the land right now and it would take more time than we have to reach them."

Jake glanced from Gadlonin to Eventine. "Thank you for your help, it is greatly appreciated!"

Gadlonin, Eventine, and the rest of their group stepped back into the circle as another group approached. This group, though slightly smaller, was comprised of centaurs, dwarves, and fawns. Again, Jake recognized the first person to come forward from this group as Tallin, the fawn he'd helped rescue from the turogs. Jake stepped forward and shook his hand as the fawn offered it.

"Jake, again, I can't thank you enough. When word reached us that you needed help I gathered some of my friends and neighbors to come and help. We are at your service."

That group stepped back and a smaller group came up behind Claira comprised of five fairies. "Jake, these are a few of my kin I was able to reach in time." All of the fairies bowed their heads in greeting while they hovered in midair. "We will help in whatever way we can, but we'll have to be careful because we will be very close to Medusa's Heir and our stolen staff of power and we do not know how the enemy might use it against us. Now that we have made brief introductions, we will show you to your tent."

Jake looked confused for a second before Sapphire chimed in. "I know you probably think you're ready to go now, but you've been up for a day and a half Jake, you need some rest before we go."

Now that she had stated the obvious, Jake did feel tired and he also remembered how hungry he was, since the last time he had eaten was the snack on the way back to the cave before going topside.

"We didn't realize you were bringing friends back with you, but we'll get bedding for them too. We left some food over by the fire. Go, eat whatever you like and we'll get your tent ready." Claira left and Jake led his group to the fire where they found smoked fish along with fruit and bread. They sat down and ate.

As they ate, the group talked about all of the things they'd seen so far. Alisha loved the trees with their colored leaves. "I love the ones with black leaves but bright colored vein's going through them," she mused, munching on some bread.

TJ piped up next. "Well, I've always liked fantasy novels, but I never thought I'd be in one. So, where did you meet all of these people Jake?"

While they finished eating, Jake described the people he'd met and befriended along the way, but Patrick stopped him when Jake told them about Father Time.

"Wait, you mean he actually exists? Did you get to see him stop time or anything cool like that?"

"I did actually." Jake quickly recounted his encounter with the trolls and spent some more time describing his training. All three of the guys were interested to hear about his training. When Jake was finished, Eric asked, "So, do you think this Dreaden would be willing to teach anyone else? That'd be sweet!"

Jake was about to reply when Sapphire came over. "So, you're Jake's sister?" She questioned, looking at Alisha. Alisha nodded. "I've just got one question," Sapphire said, with a grin, "How do you put up with him?"

Alisha smiled, "Well, it's pretty difficult sometimes, but overall he's a pretty good big brother."

Sapphire turned to Jake, "Wow, you must be alright, Jake. Even your sister has something good to say about you. Well, your tent is ready. You'll all be in the same one for tonight. Sorry, it may be slightly cramped."

Sapphire led the way over to a tent on the right side of the circle, closer to the forest. It looked like a plain, square, white tent that would fit about two people comfortably. Jake was about to say something, but Sapphire had already disappeared inside. Jake followed her in with Alisha, TJ, Patrick, and Eric right behind him. When he entered, his question died in his throat. The inside was much larger than it appeared on the outside. There were five places for sleeping with plenty of space in between.

"Cramped huh," Jake said, smirking at Sapphire.

"What, you wanted us to make it bigger?" she questioned in mock exasperation.

"No, I think we'll manage."

Claira came into the tent. "Get as much rest as you can. Once you're settled, we'll cast a darkness charm on the tent so you'll be able to sleep better. We'll have an early breakfast and then we'll be off."

"Thank you Claira," Alisha responded as she walked over and claimed her spot.

"You're very welcome," Claira replied.

With that, Claira and Sapphire left and the rest of the group laid down. They talked for a few minutes until suddenly, the ever present light from Under Earth's sky went out. The fairies must have worked their magic.

Jake tried going to sleep, but tired as he was, he couldn't keep his mind off of Isabelle. The butterflies he felt in his stomach wouldn't go away. He was exhausted, but he was so close to seeing her again his mind wouldn't shut down. He longed to give her a hug and tell her everything was going to be alright now. To let her rest her head on his shoulder and smell her wavy brown hair. To see her smile while they walked hand in hand through the colorful forest, her hair flowing in the breeze.

Jake couldn't imagine what she had been through or what she was still going through. Was she locked in a dark room somewhere away from everything and the only contact she had was some creature bringing her food a few times a day? Was she made to serve her kidnapper or for what purpose was she taken in the first place? Jake knew she was still alive. Everything he had learned about Medusa's Heir pointed to the fact that she was taken for a purpose. If he had wanted her dead, she wouldn't have even made it to

Under Earth. He could have killed her the night she disappeared.

Jake's mind was starting to worry again, like it had before he had found his Creator. It was spiraling down to ever darker thoughts. Jake quieted his thoughts and reached for the Sword of Light. He gripped the pommel in his right hand and squeezed it. "Creator, thank you for bringing me this far. I owe a great deal to you I can never repay. Please help me now. Help my mind not succumb to worry, fear, and doubt or I won't be any help to Isabelle. Help me to trust you for Isabelle's safety, since I can't be there with her now, and help me get enough rest tonight so I will be refreshed and ready tomorrow."

With that, Jake poured all of his worry and fear into the sword, offered it to his Creator, and the most amazing peace Jake had ever known settled over him. Gone were the worries of the moments before, replaced by the knowledge all was safe in his Creator's hands. Jake fell asleep seeing the picture of Isabelle's smiling face in his mind's eye.

Chapter 22

The Quickest Route

Jake awoke the next morning to the sound of clinking and clanging of metal. Light was streaming into the tent, along with the smell of food cooking over a fire. Jake yawned and sat up, looking around him. He was the only one left asleep, the rest of the beds were empty, and he was alone in the tent. Jake stood and stretched again and then bent down, picked up the Sword of Light and strapped it on.

Jake walked out of the tent to find his friends and sister sitting by the fire eating breakfast, wearing different clothes and sporting armor. The rest of the group was packing up and making last minute preparations. All of them, except for the fairies, were wearing armor and carrying various weapons. The dwarves had their battle axes, the elves all carried swords and bows with a quiver of arrows, the centaurs had a mix of bladed weapons and arrows, and the fawns all had double swords on their backs and what appeared to be some type of throwing weapon tied to their waists.

"Welcome to the land of the living!" Patrick greeted, looking up from his food.

Jake walked over to his friends as the rest turned from their eating. He noticed they all had been equipped with short swords and shields. "How long have you guys been up?"

"A few hours or so," Alisha responded. "Like our new armor?" she asked, smiling and standing up to turn in a circle. Jake looked at his sister and then the rest of the group. How had they all gotten armor that fit? Alisha must have seen the question in his eyes because, as she stopped turning, she replied, "That nice elf, Eventine, brought extra and gave us each a set. They woke us a little early so they could teach us the basics of using our swords and shields and to get our armor fitted. It wasn't a lot of training, but it was more than we had before. They let you sleep because you have already done your training and, having been up for almost two days, needed the rest. Come on over, we saved you some," she commanded, pointing to the food.

Jake sat and ate quietly, thinking, as his friends chatted lightly. He knew the direction they were headed and wanted desperately to arrive at their destination today. With the anticipation building inside him, he wasn't really hungry, but ate his food anyway, knowing he would need his strength. As he finished his food, Eventine approached the fire.

"Jake, we are almost finished packing and I need you to come put on your armor."

Jake got up and followed the tall, black haired elf as he chewed on his last bite of fruit. All of the tents were now gone and it looked as if everyone was just about ready to leave. They walked back to the beginning of the trail that led up the mountain to the gateway cave. Claira was there waiting for them, sitting on a rock with her silvery wings draped elegantly over her back. Next to her on the ground was a gleaming set of armor, like the others in Jake's group wore. It looked a little small though. He was about to say this when Claira pointed to a pile of clean clothes on her other side.

"Why don't you change into these first?"

Grateful, Jake took them and went behind a couple of large bushes to change. He hadn't had time to get washed up since leaving the castle the day before and it felt good to have clean clothes on again. He even felt cooler now because the clean clothes breathed better. Jake went back to where the armor lay.

"So, where do I start?" he asked, pointing at the armor.

Eventine picked up a chain mail shirt and handed it to Jake. "I'll give you the pieces and tell you how to put them on or help you do so."

Jake looked at the chain mail. It still looked too small. "I don't know if this will fit me," he responded, looking at Eventine.

Eventine smiled, "That's why it is helpful to have a fairy on your side." He gestured toward Claira who smiled.

Jake felt his face flush, feeling slightly embarrassed.

"Forgot about that already?" Claira grinned.

"Actually, yes I had," Jake admitted. Then, another thought popped into Jake's mind. "Claira, where is Fieora? I haven't seen her yet."

"She is trying to recruit more help; hopefully she will catch up to us soon.

So together, the three of them put on Jake's armor piece by piece, Claira resizing them to fit Jake perfectly. It didn't take very long and, when they were done, they walked back to the head of the camp where everyone was now waiting.

The two sisters, along with the rest of the fairies, went over to Eventine and Gadlonin to confer with them about the best and quickest way to get to their destination. Jake walked over so he could hear what they were saying.

Claira was talking to Eventine, "You know the paths and routes of this forest as well as anyone. What route would you choose as the quickest, but safest?"

Eventine took a long stick and drew in the sand in front of him. "Here is our destination," he said, marking an X. He then proceeded to draw outward from that point to show the main boundaries between where they were and the X. "As you can see, we will have to take the mountain passes on one side of the Forest of Forgetfulness or the other." Eventine marked lines over the squares on the sides closest to the circle. "That will take us a full day and we will arrive sometime late in the day today. Otherwise, we would have to take the dwarfs' tunnels on the right, which would be a good two to three-day journey, or the mountain pass closer to Father Time's home, which would be about the same. If I were to guess, all of these avenues are being watched, though who is watching them and how many there are, I have no idea. The route past Father Time's place would, of course, be the safest, but the two passes over the mountain would be faster."

Jake had already thought about this earlier and knew what he must do. "What if we could go through the Forest of Forgetfulness?" he asked loud and clear.

The whole group stopped what they were doing and looked at Jake. Even those behind him, who had been chatting amongst themselves, were silent. Claira sputtered and responded, "But Jake, you know what happened the last time you tried that. You were almost lost forever!"

Jake didn't look at Claira, but continued looking directly at Eventine. Eventine looked directly at Jake and studied him for a moment and then responded, "If we could do that, we would arrive there in half the time it would take us to go over one of the close passes. Probably a few hours, but unfortunately, we don't have a way to get through."

"I believe I do," Jake stated with more confidence than he felt. He remembered clearly that he had almost forgotten himself completely in the forest and, if Father Time hadn't turned up when he did, Jake would have turned into one of those forgotten trees. However, Jake wasn't willing to sacrifice any more time than he had to in order to rescue Isabelle and he believed the Sword of Light could help them get through.

Jake turned his head to look at the group around him. Fear and doubt lined the faces of everyone except his sister and friends. They just looked confused. Jake reached down and took hold of the sword, drawing it out and holding it high. "This is the Sword of Light, the sword of the Creator." As Jake said this, the sword erupted in a brilliant white. Jake turned so everyone could see it. "I believe it will allow us to get through the forest unharmed. All you need to do is trust the Creator. If anyone doesn't want to risk it, you can go one of the other routes, but I'm going through the forest."

Sapphire grabbed Claira's hand, "It will be alright!" Claira nodded and Sapphire and turned to Jake. "We're coming with you Jake!"

"So am I," responded Gadlonin, stepping forward along with the rest of his kin.

"You can count me in," vowed the fawn, Tallin, coming forward along with the rest of his group who looked uncertain, but determined.

Jake looked back at Eventine who still looked serious. Then, without warning, a large smile spread across his face. "I was hoping to avoid detours, but I wasn't sure if you knew how to use the sword to get through the forest."

Jake let the light fade from the sword and sheathed it then asked, "So you knew the sword is capable of getting us through?"

"It was an educated guess. We all know, or have heard of, the Sword of Light, but no one has seen it for a very long time. It is true, I believed it was possible to use the sword in this way, but I was not going to list it as a possibility because you are the only one capable of wielding the sword. If you did not know you could use the sword in this way, I may have caused more harm than good by telling you to try it before you were ready to do so. Especially, because I have never used the sword myself and could not give you any guidance."

"I believe we will all go with you Jake, though I must warn you, the forest empties into a valley on the other side and we will be more vulnerable at first than if we were to come down from higher ground. Still, our destination is in the lowest and centermost part of the valley, so we will have to risk the open ground at some point anyway. We may also have the element of surprise on our side, as that will probably be the least likely place the enemy will expect us to come from."

Jake was relieved to hear they were all coming. He didn't know exactly how yet, but he was sure he could get them all through.

Claira resumed talking to the whole group, "We will follow Eventine to the Forest of Forgetfulness and then Jake will lead the way."

The elves turned to lead the way. Jake, TJ, Eric, Patrick, and Alisha followed and the other group brought up the rear. The fairies all came over and sat on the shoulders of Jake's group, striking up conversations as they made their way into the colorful forest.

Claira came to sit on Jake's shoulder and he could tell Sapphire had chosen to sit on Alisha's as he could hear the two talking right behind him. The hike was slightly more burdensome with the armor and shield strapped to them while walking, but the clothes the fairies had provided did an amazing job of keeping him cool and mostly dry, even though he was sweating profusely.

Claira whispered in his ear. "Jake, when we get to the valley I don't know how much we will be able to help you. We will try to use our gifts, but it may be that we will be little more than useless if we get too close to Medusa's Heir and our staff of power."

"Depending on how much he has learned about using our staff of power, he may even be able to use our powers against you, which would be dangerous. We may have to pull ourselves away from the fight."

Jake nodded in understanding. The rest of the hike was filled with conversations about the forest around them. The fairies switched shoulders from time to time and, when the trail was wide enough, Jake's group would walk together, talking. Though it took a few hours, Jake was gaining energy as he knew every step he took now was a step toward Isabelle. An anxiousness to see her again, born not out of desperation, but of hope, filled him now.

The group paused briefly at the river while the fairies made a temporary bridge of stepping stones to cross over, while a few elves watched for bakkara with wary eyes. They didn't see any and passed the river without incident. Even though Jake knew a few hours must have passed, it seemed like no time at all when they arrived at a clearing where the colorful trees thinned and here and there grey ghostly trees started to appear. All conversations died away at the sight of the Forest of Forgetfulness and their casual cheer was replaced by faces of anxiety. Jake looked across the clearing to see the grey trees become more numerous and then his eyes landed on the wall of thick, tangled, ghostly trees with a spooky grey mist swirling around them. They had reached the Forest of Forgetfulness!

Chapter 23

Through the Mist

The area where they now entered the Forest of Forgetfulness was not the same way he had taken before, but that place couldn't be too far away. Jake strode to the front of the group and Alisha, TJ, Eric, and Patrick followed. Jake stopped next to Eventine and Gadlonin and took out the Sword of Light in his right hand. He stood for a moment, thinking, and then reached out and took hold of Alisha's hand with his left. He turned and addressed the group.

"Everyone needs to make a single file line and hold each other's hand. Whatever happens, don't let go! If you fall or, for some reason lose your grip, you need to find each other's hands again immediately. The fairies should be able to continue on shoulders as long as they are holding on to the person carrying them."

Then, Gadlonin stepped forward and addressed the group. "Please be sure to follow Jake's instructions and don't let go of anyone. This forest has the power to make you forget everything and lose yourself completely. The group started to form a line. Alisha grabbed TJ's hand, TJ grabbed Patrick, and Patrick took Eric's. After that came Eventine and Gadlonin with the rest of the elves. Next were the fawns, centaurs, and dwarves.

Once they were all assembled, Jake shouted back. "Alright, here we go. I'll take it slow."

Jake started forward, holding the Sword of Light out in front of him. He carefully stepped into the forest, concentrating on his footing, trying to make his way through the twisting trees. Once again, the smell of pine needles came from the air. The silvery grey mist swirled around the members of the group, with sudden spurts of movement it rose up not just around their legs, but tried crawling up their bodies and around their outstretched arms. It was more aggressive the farther in they went. Jake didn't remember the smell or the fog being this aggressive last time.

Jake glanced back. He knew the whole group had to be in the forest now, but he could only see back as far as Eric because of all the twists and turns they had to make to get around the trees. The dark grey/green world of the Forest of Forgetfulness, which blocked out even Under Earth's sky, weighed down on the group. Jake's mind started to drift, thinking about the trees around him when suddenly, something like electricity came from the sword and ran through him and it must have continued on because Jake felt Alisha's hand tighten like his hand had on the sword.

Instantly, Jake's mind was clear and he realized they weren't moving. The mist was still swirling around them and alarm swept through Jake. That had been close! He hadn't even realized the forest had been affecting him. "Creator, keep our minds clear so we don't get lost." A soft glow started to emanate from the sword. Jake felt a warmth flow through his limbs, which he hadn't even realized were cold.

Jake looked back and saw color come back to Alisha's face and knew the warmth was spreading. Jake remembered something he'd read when he was at the Granite Castle and the Sword of Light was in its book form. Jake prayed aloud again, "Make my path straight, be a lamp for my feet and a light to show me the way."

The instant Jake said it, the sword flared brightly and a high, clear note rang out from it. The light and sound acted like a shockwave to the mist and it was thrown back from the sword, rippling outward until the whole group was clear of it. It was a strange feeling seeing the mist pushed back by an invisible force. Jake couldn't even feel a breeze, but the mist fell away like a powerful wind was blowing it. Jake also noticed he couldn't smell the scent of pine anymore.

"Well, that was creepy," Patrick voiced from farther back. "Kind of cool though."

Jake felt a small hand touch his neck and heard Sapphire's voice by his left ear, "As inviting as this forest is, why don't you get us out of here, Jake?"

Jake looked out in front of him and was surprised to see a path. It curved slightly here and there, but was, for the most part, straight and it appeared to Jake that the path was a bit brighter than the dull grey/green trees and landscape around him. Jake wondered if it had been there the whole time, but, because of the mist and the forests confusing and forgetful powers, he hadn't seen it. Since he wasn't actually on it yet, Jake angled slightly to his left and took a couple of steps to get onto the path with the Sword of Light held in front still ringing with the high, but beautiful note and ablaze with light.

Once they were all on the path, the group traveled much quicker. Soon, Jake could see the light from Under Earth's sky up ahead. Once the trees started thinning and becoming sparser, Jake brought the group to a halt just inside the tree line.

A large valley spread out before them. On the left and right, the land rose upward to form the peaks and mountains which hemmed in the Forest of Forgetfulness. Out in front of him, Jake could see the land gently slope downward. In the middle of the valley was a strange rock formation. The rock was brilliant white and rose up out of the earth at strange angles that sloped inward and, where the sides met at the top, it was flat like a table. It almost looked as if it was a pedestal meant to display something. The only other thing Jake could see was what looked like a large cavern that started before the rock formation and burrowed down into the earth.

Jake felt a hand on the armor of his right shoulder and turned to see Eventine. "I think it is safe now to let go of each other's hands. We are on the edge of the Forest of Forgetfulness where its evil is weakest. The sword keeps the evil at bay, but I do not think it is wise to linger here."

Jake let go of Alisha's hand and the rest of the group followed suit and gathered around Jake and Eventine. There was a collective gasp from the fairies. Jake turned to Sapphire, who was still resting on his shoulder. "What's wrong?"

"Our palace is gone!" she cried, sorrow in her voice.

"Where was it?" Jake asked, looking around.

Claira spoke from Alisha's shoulder, her voice sad but strong. "It used to stand on the Brightstone, the white rock in the middle of the valley."

Jake looked at the rock formation again, trying to picture it. Although it was very large, Jake had trouble imagining a palace on it. Then he remembered it would have been fairy sized, and realized it must have been very large indeed.

Claira continued, "When we fled, the Crystal Palace still stood on the Brightstone, catching the light of Under Earths sky and shining like a glittering rainbow. It was like a beacon in the center of the valley. Very few of our kind ventured back this way once Medusa's Heir took over for fear of being enslaved. That cavern in front of the Brightstone was not there when we left either."

"The tunnel entrance was built shortly after you were forced to flee," Eventine responded, striding to the front. "The cavern beneath the Brightstone has always been there, but Medusa's Heir had the opening made for a more direct route into and out of it. That is also where you are headed, Jake."

"Where does it go?" Jake asked, gazing at it intently.

"It goes down under the Brightstone to where the Stone Fortress of the goblins lies. That is where Medusa's Heir resides and it is where he is sure to be keeping your friend."

"The goblins lived that close to us the whole time?" asked one of the fairies from behind Jake.

"Yes, although none but the goblins were aware of exactly where it was, since it is almost impossible for anyone to make sense of their winding tunnels. This opening was created a year or so after Medusa's Heir came to power, your palace, however, disappeared days after your people fled," Eventine said sadly, looking at Claira and Sapphire.

Eventine turned to address the group. "It is about the same distance to the Brightstone from any side of this valley, so we will go straight to the cavern from here. We will split into two groups. Jake will lead his friends from Top Earth and I will lead everyone from Under Earth. My group will surround Jake's. Half of us will cover Jake's group on the left and half on the right. We should try to stay together and hopefully, we will get to the cavern before the enemy even realizes we are here, but if we should get separated, Jake, you take your group straight to the cavern and we'll catch up with you when we can. There are bound to be some traps set for intruders, Jake, so be wary."

"Now, I don't see anyone from here, but there are sure to be sentries watching the valley. Our moment of surprise will only last as long as it takes for the sentries to alert the enemy forces and get them into the valley. Once they come for us, it will be the job of the fairies to try and stop their arrows from reaching us. If they can manage that, then we'll force the enemy to come in close while we can still shoot from afar. Some of us will be in front, to deal with anyone who comes in close, while the rest will continue to fire arrows from the middle. Now, prepare your weapons."

As quietly as they could manage, the whole group took their helmets and shields off their backs and put them on, readying their swords, axes, and arrows as well. Jake still held the Sword of Light, although it had returned to looking like a normal sword again. He took off his shield and Alisha, TJ, Eric, and Patrick did the same beside him. They all looked nervous, but determination was etched on their faces. Jake knew none of them had ever been in a battle before.

The other groups got into position on either side of Jake's group, with the fairies flying overhead. A nod from Eventine and they advanced into the valley. Now they were out of the trees and fully exposed to anyone watching, walking as quickly and quietly as they could through the tall grass and plants covering the valley floor.

They were making good progress and over a quarter of the way to the cavern when Jake heard a strange whistling noise. He looked up just in time to see an arrow flying straight toward him!

Chapter 24

Battle in Brightstone Valley

The arrow came to within 30 feet of the group and then stopped midair, with a slight blue glow surrounding it. The arrow then dropped harmlessly to the ground and Sapphire called to the group, "Heads up, they know we're here!"

Jake looked around and saw more arrows coming from the trees and foliage near the mountain sides surrounding the valley. His allies brought their shields up, making a wall on either side of Jake's group, even as the six fairies started making magical barriers around the whole group. The arrows came in volleys from both sides and, by the number of arrows alone, Jake could tell they were outnumbered.

As the arrows came down, they reached a point about ten feet from the group and hit the magical shields the fairies had placed, stopping like they had hit stone, then dropped harmlessly to the ground. After a couple of volleys had come and the elves saw the fairies' magic was holding, they took out their bows and started firing back into the trees.

Jake still couldn't see their enemies, but the elves must have much better sight than he did because he could tell they weren't just shooting blindly. Jake watched as they sent their arrows through the fairies' magical barriers into the forest surrounding the valley and, after a few minutes, fewer arrows were coming at them.

The whole group Jake was with had come to a standstill while they defended themselves. Jake heard Eventine command everyone to start moving toward the cavern again. Slowly and carefully, their group started to walk. Sensing their attacks were not working and seeing

Jake's group starting to advance again, the enemies changed tactics and started to charge.

The first enemy Jake saw emerge from the trees lining the valley was a huge troll. He held two battle axes with his powerful arms and yelled a loud war cry as he ran, his orange Mohawk and long ponytail flapping from side to side. A couple of elves fired arrows at the troll with unnatural speed. Somehow, the troll deflected the first two arrows with his axes but a third one caught him in the center of his neck. The troll slowed ever so slightly, but continued coming, his war cry garbled by the arrow through his throat.

More creatures emerged from the mountainsides as the troll rushed in. As the other elves worked on attacking the other creatures coming to meet them, the two who were attacking the first troll continued hitting him. The troll was fast, its powerful legs and long stride allowed it to traverse the distance between them quickly. Two arrows buried themselves into each of the troll's legs which slowed it, but didn't stop it completely. A third arrow hit the creature in its stomach and, with a loud grunt, the troll fell to its knees struggling to get up, and continued the last few yards to Jake's defenders. One of the two elves finally shot it through the eye and the troll fell over and moved no more.

Jake and his group of defenders were still moving, but much slower now, having to concentrate on defending themselves. Jake wished he could help somehow, but only the fairies who were still blocking arrows and the elves that were shooting back could reach the enemies.

More creatures poured from the mountain sides surrounding the valley and, even with the elves' speed and accuracy, they couldn't stop them from gaining ground. Jake looked around and saw many different creatures trying to close the gap to attack their group. Among the enemy were goblins, trolls, ogres, turogs, orcs, and a few other creatures Jake didn't recognize from his studies at the castle. Jake glanced at the fairies to yell a warning, but saw they were using every bit of strength and concentration they had to block the arrows coming at them. They were already starting to look fatigued.

The tall, thin, but well-muscled goblins and their shorter orc cousins were content to stay back and fire arrows to keep the fairies busy while the rest of the creatures advanced. The trolls were the most fierce, as they had both size and speed at their disposal and, as they charged, Jake could see a reckless lust for blood in their eyes.

The ogres were larger than the trolls, but also thicker and much slower as well. While Jake knew behind the layers of dense fat covering their bodies they were sure to have very strong muscle, they couldn't move very quickly and more lumbered toward the group of defenders outpaced by the other enemies. The turogs, whom Jake had fought in the clearing, were more Jake's size. While they were strong, they didn't have near the bulk of the trolls or the ogres, but they could run very quickly.

Claira flew overhead, now gathering as many of the arrows being fired at them as she could and getting them to the elves who were running low. Even though every shot the elves fired hit its mark, and in many cases brought down an enemy, more continued to come and there was only 50 feet on either side between the defenders and the enemy. They must have called in reinforcements, Jake thought, as a fresh volley of arrows came at them.

Eventine's group switched tactics slightly as their enemies drew closer. Four of the fairies kept the barriers up to shield the group from the arrows while Claira and Sapphire varied between collecting arrows and shooting at the enemies with their wands, sometimes making them stumble or run into an invisible wall and sometimes freezing them long enough for an Elvin arrow to find them.

From the middle of the group, Eventine suddenly called out "Swords," and half of the elves slung their bows to their backs and unsheathed their swords. Likewise, the dwarves, centaurs, and fawns all readied their swords, axes, and shields as the enemies came in among them. There was a clash of steel as the first wave met the defenders. Though the trolls and turogs were fierce, so too were the dwarves, elves, centaurs, and fawns.

To his left, Jake saw a large troll try to break through the ranks, swinging his ax down upon a dwarf who wasn't even half its height. To his surprise, the dwarf stood his ground and, with a swing of his own axe, deflected the blow, then jumped higher than Jake had expected, lopping off the troll's head before it could swing again. The dwarf then took the troll's axe and threw it, burying it into the torso of a turog that was rushing toward him.

The fawns were quick and agile as they ran and jumped between the enemy, using their dual swords to slice and stab as they went. They ran in a circle around the defenders, never staying in one spot, but always on the move. One would strike at an enemy, then continue to run on, distracting it as another fawn came in behind to finish it off.

Jake saw Tallin, who was leading the group of the fawns, pull an object from his belt and throw the weapon at an oncoming turog. It flew at the creature's neck and, in a graceful arc, went around it and flew back to Tallin. The turog's head sagged to one side then fell off its torso, its body kept running a few feet before it finally stumbled and fell.

As quick as the other creatures were, none could match the elves' speed. With a savage grace, the elves almost looked as if they were dancing with their foes, except their partners always ended up on the ground, moving no more.

Jake looked around at his small group in the center of the fighting. All of them had their shields up just in case the fairies' magical shields had a week spot. Alisha was just behind him with TJ on her right and Patrick on her left followed by Eric in the back. Jake was glad his friends had chosen to keep her hedged in. The defenders were now just over half way to the cavern but their movement towards it had all but stopped as they made more of an effort to defend their position.

Suddenly, there was a loud clang to his right and Jake turned to see an arrow head sticking through one of the dwarves' shields. Claira flew over.

"Jake, our gifts are growing weak. We are too close to Medusa's Heir and the Crystal Staff is working against us. We are going to have to leave before he is able to use our magic against us."

Claira turned to leave. Jake thought quickly. He knew if the fairies left the arrows still coming at them would eventually start to shred them apart. He called back to Claira, "Wait, let me try something first."

She stopped and nodded, "Work quickly!"

As Jake poured his thoughts into the Sword of Light he could hear more clanging as arrows hit shields. It only made sense that if the Sword of Light was more powerful than the staffs of power, it should be able to counter act the effects of the crystal staff. As he tried focusing, one of the fairies yelled because a fawn had just been frozen by one of the fairies' spells gone wrong. The fawn had been in mid jump with swords in the air about to swing them down on an unsuspecting turog. The turog turned and jumped back before realizing the fawn was helplessly frozen in the air.

The turog then stabbed at the fawn and would have succeeded if one of the centaurs hadn't seen the fawn's peril and intervened catching the turog's blade on his own large two handed sword. The centaur deflected the stab and then brought its sword back down upon the turog with such force the turog's sword was broken in two and the turog itself cut in half. A second later, an arrow hit the centaur's left hind leg causing him to stumble backward.

Jake fought to focus his mind on the sword and it started to pulse slightly. Jake felt it and in the same instant the arrows were deflected by the fairies shields once again. The fawn that had been frozen fell free and went on to continue fighting. Jake was thankful none of the defenders had been lost yet but there were many who had been wounded and though the enemies were fewer in number now the ogres had finally reached them and the centaurs were rallying to try to hold them off.

Eventine broke away from the fighting and rushed over to Jake. "You and your friends must go as quickly as you can to the cavern. We'll hold them off but you shouldn't wait." Eventine turned back to the fighting, "My group fan out and don't let them advance behind us!"

Jake watched as the group formed a half circle with the open end facing the cavern. The enemies were now on the other side and Jake's group had a clear shot at the cavern. "Let's go," Jake yelled as he took off toward the cavern. The group followed right on his heels.

They started running through the long grass away from the fighting down the valley towards the cavern. Up ahead, Jake saw rocks and boulders scattered around the opening to the cavern. Some were small and some were very large. Hopefully the defenders could get to this point. It would provide some cover and be a more defensible position than the open field.

"What's that?" Patrick yelled pointing off into the mountains behind the cavern. Jake looked to where Patrick was pointing as he ran and his heart almost stopped. On a ridge high atop the back of the valley perched an enormous black dragon. "Gargoth!" Jake gasped under his breath. He couldn't be sure from this distance but the dragon looked as if he was larger than the red, blue, and yellow dragons combined. Jake and his group slowed. He could tell that Gargoth was watching them but he seemed content to stay where he was.

Sensing a trap, Jake cautiously started to make his way forward again as his group followed. They were getting closer to the rocks and boulders in front of the cavern, the perfect place for another ambush. As if in response, Jake felt a warning come from the Sword of Light. Jake stopped and looked around. "Keep close guys, something isn't right." His sister and friends came up beside him, their shields and swords ready. Sweat coated their features. Jake could tell they were nervous, but determined.

Jake looked back at Eventine's group. They were about a football field length away now and still kept the enemies at bay, but Jake wondered how long that would last. Jake had just turned his focus back on the boulder littered ground between him and the cavern when movement caught his eyes.

Jake tensed and through his peripheral vision, he could tell his friends had done the same on either side. He waited and readied himself, thinking the motion he saw was an archer or swordsman jumping out from behind a boulder to attack, until it dawned on him it was the boulder that was moving. Of all the ways Jake had thought they might be ambushed, none of them prepared him for what he saw next!

Chapter 25

The Rock Golem

Before the group, the large rocks and boulders scattered in front of the cavern started to vibrate and bounce. They shifted in their positions as if they were alive and some of them started to jump up and down. Soon, more joined in until the ground before the group looked as if it were boiling with stones.

Then suddenly, a large rock tore from the ground and rocketed into the space between Jake's group and the cavern. As if in response to this, the rest of the boulders and large rocks started to tear loose from the ground and flew in a tight circle around the first rock. As more rocks joined, they formed a swirling column around the first rocks.

"What is happening?" Alisha called out to Jake, barely making her voice heard above the wind of the rushing stones.

"No idea!" Jake shouted back.

Jake looked back and saw Eventine's group was still engaged with the enemy forces and it was all they could do to hold their ground. Jake's group couldn't count on them doing any more than they already were. They were on their own to deal with this obstacle.

"Can we go around it?" TJ yelled from Jake's right.

"I don't think so," Patrick yelled from the left. "Those rocks are going in and out too fast! If one got close it would crush us, and there isn't much room to get into the cave on the other side."

Jake looked back at the column and saw what Patrick was talking about. Some of the rocks were now weaving in and out of the others, moving into the center of the column and then outside a few yards only to return to the center again, all while continuing to circle the center themselves. The effect was very dizzying when one gazed at it too long.

Then, something changed. The ground started to tremble slightly and there was a loud crack as one of the rocks flew to the center and connected with the first rock. The group watched, stunned, as one after another, rocks and boulders flew to the center and joined together. They still looked like individual rocks, but appeared as if they were being held together like a powerful magnet was at the center. As more rocks collected, a form started to take shape.

"This doesn't look good, Jake," Eric yelled from the other side of Patrick.

That was an understatement in Jake's opinion. As they watched, the column thinned as the rocks continued to join the center. Jake couldn't see the first rock anymore because so many had joined it, but two columns of stacked rocks started to form under a large mass in the center. Then, two more columns sprouted from the top sides of the large center and Jake's heart dropped into his stomach. It was forming a giant person!

Then, something the fairies had told him earlier came rushing back. This must be a rock golem! With a final crack and echo, the only large boulder left flew and landed on the top middle of the formation, finishing the look of a human form, complete with hands and feet. The creature was made of rocks of all sizes packed tightly, giving it a very realistic form and definition. It looked like it was a huge body builder with stones for muscles. The thing must have been over 50 feet tall. Just after the head landed, two glowing blue eyes formed and a low deep growl started emanating from the golem, rising in pitch and strength until it was deafening. As it yelled, the creature flexed its arms and tilted its head back to the sky.

Eventine's group and the enemies farther up the valley even stopped fighting momentarily, either because they were startled or in awe of the huge creature. Then, the enemy forces started fighting even harder, encouraged by their new ally.

Just as quickly as it started, the roar stopped, leaving everyone deaf for a few moments. Then, the creature looked at Jake and its eyes narrowed. It growled again, not nearly as loud as the first, but much more menacing and directed toward Jake.

"Spread out," Jake yelled as the creature took an earthshaking step toward him.

TJ ran to the right along with Alisha as Eric and Patrick went to the left. Jake stayed put a moment longer with his right hand tightly clutching the Sword of Light and his other, his shield. The creature swung its right arm down and Jake jumped at the last second narrowly missing the blow which gouged the earth where he had been standing. Jake rolled back to a standing position, which wasn't easy with the armor he was wearing, and he sliced at the creature's arm before the creature had pulled it back. The Sword of Light hit a large rock in the creature's forearm, cutting into it like it was hot butter. The rock was large enough that Jake had only managed to cut through half of it, but the creature howled in pain and jerked its arm back, swinging with its other arm.

Jake tried jumping clear, but didn't quite make it far enough and the creature's fist glanced off Jake's left side, sending him spinning. Jake landed, sprawled out a few yards from where he had been.

Jake was shaken and dazed, but saw the golem take a step closer and prepare to strike again. Just then, a shout rang out as a rock flew from Jake's left and glanced off the shoulder of the golem. The golem paused and turned its head to look at Eric, who had thrown the rock, seemingly confused as to why someone would try such a foolish thing. Jake was dazed, but didn't wait, he jumped up and ran out of the golem's reach. The golem looked back at Jake, ready to pursue him again, but another rock, coming from the right this time, struck its leg and it turned to look in the direction where TJ and Alisha stood.

Before it could react, two rocks flew from the left, hitting him in the side and the back of his head. This must have finally gotten the creature upset because it let loose a low menacing growl and turned its head to look over at Eric and Patrick who had just thrown two more rocks. They struck the golem in the chest as it turned and took a step toward them. Grabbing a handful of dirt, the golem threw it toward Patrick while stepping toward Eric. Patrick jumped to the side and brought up his shield, bracing for the impact. He managed to miss the center of the clump, but the amount of dirt which hit him and his shield still knocked him off balance.

Meanwhile, Eric was doing the best he could to stay out of the golem's reach. Jake could see it wouldn't take much more of this; his group would be too tired to evade the golem for much longer. The Sword of Light could cut the golem, but Jake knew it would take too long to simply hack away at the creature and the golem certainly wouldn't stand still and make the task easy. They needed a plan and a thought occurred to Jake. He ran over to where TJ and Alisha were.

"Try throwing rocks at it and backing up. See if you can distract it and draw it away from the cavern so we can get past!" TJ and Alisha nodded and began a new assault of rock throwing as Jake ran back to where he had been. The creature started toward TJ and Alisha as Jake sprinted to Patrick and Eric and told them the plan.

Then, Jake went back to his spot. His plan almost worked the first time, but, as the golem got far enough away from the cavern, it sensed something was wrong because it stopped its pursuit of TJ and Alisha who were still backing up and throwing rocks. The creature turned and looked at Eric and Patrick who had snuck closer to the cavern, but not close enough to get inside. With surprising speed for its size, the golem ran with earth shaking steps back to the entrance of the cavern. Patrick and Eric barely had enough time to scramble out of reach. The creature didn't pursue them, choosing instead to stand in front of the cavern and growl again.

It was Patrick and Eric's turn and, as they tried drawing the creature away, they began taunting it, calling it things like *big oaf* and *rock for brains*. Jake wasn't sure it knew exactly what they were saying, but it must have the general idea because the creature's growls grew slightly louder as it went after them. Yet, even as before, when the creature started to feel too far from the cavern, it came back to hover in front of it like a goalie protecting its goal.

They tried this approach several more times with the same effect and Jake started to become discouraged. Then, as he watched TJ and Alisha start another attempt throwing stones at the golem, the creature grew tired of their game, for it held up its rock and pebble made hands toward the oncoming rocks. The golem's hands started to vibrate rapidly, all of the large and small rocks that made its hands were moving outward and inward very fast giving it the illusion that the Golem's hands were dissolving and reforming very quickly. When the rocks reached the air close to the Golem, they stopped in midair. A sound came from the golem then, which was low and deep like its growl, but rose and fell. As it continued and got louder, Jake realized what it was and a chill swept down his back, giving him goose bumps. The creature was laughing at them. Then, with sudden abruptness, the laughing stopped and Jake watched in horror as the creature brought up both hands, balling them into fists, and more rocks started pulling from the earth. Debris fell from the rocks as they rose into the air and, as the sand, dirt, and grass rained down, Jake saw the rocks form a circle around the golem.

Then, the golem started laughing again and threw out its arms and the stones flew outward in all directions at rocket speed. Jake had just managed to duck behind his shield when the wave of rocks struck, glancing off his shield and a few striking the armor that wasn't protected by the shield. The force left dents in his shield, but he managed to stay crouched.

When the rocks stopped coming, Jake glanced first at the creature to make sure it hadn't charged any of them and then at his group. TJ was helping Alisha to her feet, but she looked like she was alright, just knocked over. Eric and Patrick looked fine, but all of them had new dents in their shields and armor.

Jake didn't know what to do. They couldn't get past the creature, but they couldn't get close enough to attack it and, since he was the only one who was able to harm it, that approach wouldn't work either. So, he did the only thing he could do. Keeping his eyes on the golem, Jake prayed. "Creator, we need your help! Please show us how to get past this creature."

Jake felt the Sword of Light hum slightly in his hand and he noticed something different. In the middle of the creature's chest, almost where a heart would be, was a rock that glowed blue. It hadn't been glowing a moment before, but Jake was sure he knew what it meant. That was the first rock which had come up to form the golem to which all the others had joined. It must be the piece holding the creature together! If he could destroy it, the creature would fall apart.

Jake shouted. The creature looked his way, but so did the others. Jake motioned them to join him. They were all farther from the cavern now and Jake didn't think the creature would stray that far. Keeping an eye on the creature, the others made their way to Jake.

They were all panting slightly when they reached him, but the golem was still content that they were far enough away because it watched them, but didn't advance. Jake saw his group all had a few scrapes and bruises, but nothing serious.

"What's up Jake?" TJ asked, slightly breathless.

"The Sword of Light has shown me how to defeat the creature, but I need you guys to distract it." So Jake explained his plan to them while keeping an eye on the golem. When he was done, they all nodded in understanding and Alisha jumped over and hugged him. It was very strange to be hugged while they were both in armor, but he tried returning it as his sister said, "Be careful Jake," with concern in her eyes.

"I will, let's go."

Jake took off to the right and the rest fanned out behind him, TJ and Patrick went to the left and Eric and Alisha stayed more toward the center. When Jake got as far as he dared go, he started shouting at the golem and picked up a few rocks and threw them at the creature. The creature looked at Jake and growled. It held up one cobblestone hand and stopped the stones just as before and immediately sent them flying back at Jake, who had expected this. Jake spun out of their path and, to his great relief, saw two more rocks hit the golem in the back. Jake's hopes had come true; the golem couldn't block rocks he didn't see coming. A new rage settled over the creature and it turned toward TJ and Patrick.

Jake took his chance and darted farther to the right, trying to get out of sight before the golem looked back. Eric and Alisha now threw rocks and the group spread out slightly so the creature had to turn to see them and couldn't keep them all in sight. They continued to alternate, throwing rocks and keeping the creature distracted, as Jake snuck around to the rocks that made up the cavern entrance. He didn't go in, however, but started to climb as quickly and quietly as he could. He was very close to the golem now. If the creature heard him, it could turn and smash him like an ant. The others started to shout and taunt the creature again while throwing rocks. Some of the rocks hit the Golem, but others were stopped midair and sent back to the thrower, who either jumped out of the way or hid behind their shield.

Jake was high enough now and could see the blue rock which was still glowing. Jake had hoped he'd be close enough to stab the golem from the rocks, but now he knew he would have to risk jumping to reach it. This made Jake nervous, but he didn't have any other choice. The one good thing about the creature's ability to supernaturally stop rocks and throw them back midair was it didn't have to change its position much to do it. Jake climbed a little higher, so when he jumped he wouldn't fall below his mark.

As planned, once he had gotten on the rocks behind the creature, his friends started grouping closer together to the center directly opposite Jake, so the golem wouldn't have to turn side to side anymore. They kept up their taunting and rock throwing, hoping to keep the creature distracted to the fact that Jake wasn't with them.

Jake was now directly behind and slightly above the glowing blue heart of the golem. He got his footing secure and turned, bracing himself so he could use his arms as he jumped. Slowly and quietly, Jake drew the Sword of Light. He hesitated a moment, worried he would misjudge the distance and end up falling short or jumping too high. Very briefly he closed his eyes. "Guide me," he prayed. Then, opening his eyes and focusing on the blue rock, he shoved off, leaping toward the back of the creature with the sword held in his hands, pointed out and down to strike. For a moment he was weightless in the air between the top of the cavern and the golem's back and then, he landed with all his force centered onto the sword and drove it deep into the glowing blue heart of the golem.

The reaction was immediate! The creature screamed in agony, which once again stopped the fighting off in the distance. As it screamed it brought its head and shoulders back, trying to reach the spot where Jake clung to the sword. The movement was so sudden, Jake was slammed against its back and searing pain went through the right side of his head. Jake blacked out and lost his grip on the sword as he fell against the stone entrance to the cavern, sliding and rolling to the ground unconscious.

The creature's agony was louder than any of its previous roars. It stumbled forward slightly only to stumble back again. It kept reaching back, trying to get the Sword of Light, but it couldn't. The good thing now, was the Golem wasn't paying any attention to Alisha, TJ, Eric or Patrick. The bad thing was, it was coming dangerously close to stepping on Jake while he lay unconscious on the ground. Just up the valley Eventine's group tried coming to the rescue, but the enemies continued their attacks and prevented them from doing anything but defending. Alisha screamed as the right foot of the golem just missed Jake by inches as it continued to stumble.

TJ and Eric started sprinting forward to try and grab Jake and pull him to safety. They managed to get around the golem, however, just as they neared Jake, the creature stepped back, hitting TJ and causing him to slam into the rocks around the cavern. He recovered quickly, however, and met Eric by Jake's side. "You get his legs and I'll get his arms," Eric yelled at TJ as he grabbed Jake's arms. Normally, Eric could have probably managed to throw Jake over his shoulder, but with their armor on, they had a hard enough time just trying to keep a hold of his arms and legs. As quickly as they could manage, they half carried, half drug Jake away from the golem's stomping feet. This was made all the more difficult because the ground shook with every step the giant creature took.

Then, a new sound reached their ears and they looked up in time to see the blade of the sword sticking out of the rock burst into flames. It must have been doing the same inside because the rock the blade protruded from started to turn orange and then red around the sword and then, slowly moved outward, changing the whole rock, superheating it. At this, there was a dink and then a clank as small rocks started coming loose from the creature, raining down on TJ and Eric. Then, one of the larger rocks from the creature's side came loose and landed next to Eric.

"It's falling apart, we have to get out of here now!" TJ exclaimed, trying to get a grip on Jake's legs.

"Help me get him on my back, so I can hold his arms over my shoulders," Eric commanded, trying to reposition Jake. The two worked furiously as another large boulder fell from the golem's right arm, which they were directly under. They had just gotten Jake in position on Eric's back, when TJ saw it falling toward them. TJ pushed on Jake's back, which in turn pushed Eric forward, before he was completely ready. He stumbled forward onto one knee while TJ jumped back and narrowly missed being crushed by the falling boulder that gouged deeply into the ground where he had stood a moment before.

TJ raced around the boulder to find Eric struggling to his feet. He turned and asked, "What was that... Oh, thanks," as he realized he had almost been crushed by the boulder.

Eric turned and attempted to run with Jake's arms draped over his shoulders, but Jake's feet were still dragging on the ground, which made it difficult. TJ ran up and grabbed Jake's ankles to prevent this and ran behind Eric, which helped them run faster. They ran toward Alisha and Patrick who were standing a safe distance away, with terror on their faces.

As they drew near the other two, TJ and Eric noticed the light from Under Earth's sky had suddenly dimmed slightly. They set Jake down on the ground and turned to see what was keeping Alisha and Patrick's gaze. Their hearts leapt into their throats as they gazed upon the sight that had indeed partially blocked out a section of Under Earth's light.

Above where the golem still thrashed wildly losing rocks, perched atop the Brightstone, stood an enormous black dragon. It was so big the group couldn't see any of the valley behind it and it made the golem look like a mouse. It looked as if its sheer weight could crush the Brightstone flat. The dragon's red eyes narrowed and it opened its huge maw, revealing rows and rows of razor sharp teeth. Craning its head into the air it let out a roar that shook the earth.

Everyone in the valley dropped to the ground, covering their ears in pain. Jake stirred as his ears registered the sound. After this, the creature looked at the golem below it, considering it for a moment. It looked as if the dragon thought this creature was pathetic. The black dragon took in a gulp of air and then, with sudden savagery, let loose a concentrated and continuous stream of white-hot fire down onto what remained of the golem.

Even though the fire did not reach them, the heat was so intense; Alisha, TJ, Eric, Patrick, and even Jake could not shield themselves from the hot air around them. The fire had turned the air into an instant furnace, singeing their exposed skin. It only took a few seconds for the fire to melt the mighty rock golem into a puddle of molten rock. It hurt Jake's group to move because their armor was now hot and burned them anywhere it touched their skin directly. Jake, now awake enough to understand what was going on, though still too dazed to formulate a plan, struggled to his feet.

Alisha ran over to support him as he wavered in place. She held onto him, switching hands when the heat from his armor started to penetrate her gloved hands. Quickly, the rest of the group joined them.

The black dragon then turned his gaze toward them and looked directly at Jake. Then, in a voice filled with malice and hate it spoke. It spoke directly into their minds, seemingly bypassing their ears. They knew it was coming from Gargoth, and what he said made their blood run cold. "Now, it's your turn to die!"

Chapter 26

The Black Dragon

Jake stood, frozen with indecision. There was nowhere to run and nowhere to hide. They were in the middle of the valley and, the only place close enough to escape was the cavern entrance, however, that wasn't exactly an option as the black beast was perched directly over it. His sister and friends were beside Jake and he was sure the same thoughts were racing through their minds. The rock golem had been bad enough, but at least it wasn't very bright. It could have crushed them one by one, but they had been able to distract and defeat it, which was still no easy task. As Jake gazed at the dragon, he knew this enemy was more cunning than he himself was.

Jake glanced back to see if Eventine's group could help. They were still engaged with a few enemies and it looked as if they were still too far off to help. Even if they were now standing by his side, Jake was unsure what the elves, dwarfs, centaurs, fawns and fairies could do against this dragon. Jake glanced around, trying to think of options, but his mind was still too slow and sluggish from being knocked unconscious and he was finding it hard to breath, which didn't help. The Sword! He'd lost it when he had fallen. So, where was it now that the golem was melted?

He started to yell to his group to look for it when another growl emanated from the black dragon. It hopped off the side of the Brightstone and landed amid the still glowing molten rock, seemingly unaffected by its heat and making indentations in it with its feet which splashed the molten puddle in all directions. The impact caused the valley to shake and knocked everyone to the ground. The dragon was now close enough it could easily melt them with its fire, chomp down on them with its enormous jaws and razor teeth, or swipe them with its feet or tail.

Jake knew, in the back of his mind, that he needed to call for the sword, but his breathing was still difficult and it kept him from thinking straight. He looked down and saw his chest plate was crushed inward, keeping him from breathing properly. The growl came again from the throat of Gargoth. It parted its mouth and smoke came boiling out, rising up through its teeth and into the air. Then, suddenly, the smoke stopped and the dragon opened its mouth wider as it slowly inhaled its breath. Jake's body screamed *run*, but his mind continued to ask *where*.

Jake heard Alisha whisper beside him "Creator help us!"

A split second later, they heard a loud, fierce roar. However, it hadn't come from the black dragon in front of them, but from somewhere behind them. The black dragon had heard it also because it had stopped taking in air and jerked its head up to look into the distance. A second after the first roar, came a second and then a third. Each came from behind and each was distinctly different from the others.

The black dragon unfurled its wings and roared a challenge, causing Jake's group to cover their ears. The black dragon crouched and then leapt into the air, flapping its wings to gain height. The force of the wind alone kept Jake's group pinned to the ground. Once the black dragon was high enough, the wind from the dragon's wings grew weaker and Jake's group was able to get up again.

Eric got to his feet first and turned, pointing, "Look!"

Jake and the rest of them turned just in time to see the three Primes fly into view. From over the mountain pass on the right came the blue dragon, Ocean, from the left came the brilliant yellow dragon, Sunstrike, and from the center, high over the Forest of Forgetfulness, came the red dragon, Crimson. Although all three were huge by normal standards, they were each only about a third the size of the black dragon. What they lacked in size, however, they made up in speed and numbers. At the same time, all three pulled in their wings and angled downward into steep dives, gaining speed in the direction of Gargoth who was still trying to gain height, so as not to be at such a disadvantage. Again, four roars came from the dragons, three from the Primes and one of defiance from the black dragon.

Gargoth must have reached the right height because he stopped going up and started straight for Crimson. All three of the Primes leveled off to meet him. It looked as if all four would collide, for a moment. Just as Gargoth sped up to meet Crimson, Crimson flared his wings to slow his speed and then spun to the right, narrowly avoiding Gargoth's snapping jaws. At the same time, Ocean used her speed and weight by pulling her head back and ramming Gargoth with her feet on his right side, knocking him off course, while Sunstrike tried going up over Gargoth.

Unfortunately, though outnumbered, Gargoth wasn't without skills of his own. As he half flew, half fell to his left, knocked off course, he used his momentum to whip his tail into Sunstrike. Sunstrike was able to angle enough to keep the blow from breaking her left wing, but couldn't avoid it entirely. Gargoth's tail hit Sunstrike underneath, clipping her legs in the process. Sunstrike grunted in pain and was sent spinning toward the ground.

As Gargoth regained his balance in the air to avoid falling, Crimson and Ocean swung back around from the right, unable to help Sunstrike or their advantage would be lost. Sunstrike finally managed to right herself and spread her wings to slow her downward fall and started gliding just 100 feet from the ground. She then circled back around, viciously eyeing the black dragon who battled the other two.

Crimson had managed to land a bite on Gargoth's right wing, but because he was so large, Gargoth was only hurt, not disabled. Ocean, likewise, had been able to circle around and shot flame at the black dragon's head seconds after Crimson's bite, allowing the red dragon to get away.

The fire, however, didn't seem to hurt Gargoth and he sent a volley of his own, which Ocean couldn't entirely avoid; part of her right wing was singed. More blows were exchanged before Sunstrike was able to get back and help the others.

The ferocity of the battle overhead became greater as the fighting continued. Jake decided he would never want to face a dragon because even the three Primes who were his allies were so vicious, he knew he had never, and probably would never see another creature capable of such savagery.

All of the dragons now had wounds and it seemed neither the black dragon or the Primes could get the advantage. The Primes were quick and tried coordinating their attacks, but were not always successful as Gargoth anticipated what they would do. More volleys of flame shot out overhead as all four dragons circled in the air far above the valley floor. The flame attacks didn't seem to faze the black dragon, however, and his size and strength continued to be an advantage the Primes could not completely overcome.

The air was filled with the sounds of the dragons' fight: roaring, thundering of wings, the snapping of immense jaws, and shooting flame, which drowned out any other noise. As Jake watched, he started to see red droplets hit the ground here and there and, wherever one landed, it would sizzle and send up a small wisp of smoke as it scorched the place where it fell. At first, it was only a couple of drops, but soon it was sprinkling onto the battlefield in a steady but random pattern.

Then it dawned on Jake that it was the dragon's blood! The four dragons were bleeding as they fought above the valley and the blood drops were acidic. Suddenly, Jake heard screams and he looked over to see the last of the enemies fleeing from the blood rain, as the fairies were frantically trying to put up shields to protect the allies. Jake thought he heard his name being called, but it was so noisy with the dragons fighting he could barely make it out. He glanced over and saw Gadlonin yelling, waving his hands and pointing his direction, but he couldn't make it out. A droplet hit Jake's arm and melted a hole in his armor, then another and then another. There was suddenly a lull in the battle, and Jake heard Gadlonin clearly for a brief moment.

"... Cavern, Jake, run to the cavern!"

Just as he heard this, Jake saw the reason for the lull in the fighting. Gargoth had gone into a steep dive from high overhead and was heading straight for Jake, with Sunstrike and Ocean hot on his heels!

Jake's head cleared instantly and he spun, yelling "*Run*," and started for the cavern, his sister and friends hot on his heels. Their feet pounded the earth as quickly as they could, but Jake was sure it wasn't fast enough. They neared the large puddle of molten rock, but were forced to run around it because the heat was still too intense and Jake was sure, if they tried running straight through, they'd be burned alive. His breath came in gasps as his armor was still restricting his breathing and running only made this problem worse.

Jake's group was almost around the molten rock when they noticed the light flickering around them. They all instinctively rolled to the ground, thinking that the dragon was bearing down on them. A roar of pain split the air and Jake looked up just in time to see that Sunstrike had caught up and sunk her teeth into Gargoth's tail. The black dragon flared its wings and swung around, trying to dislodge Sunstrike. He was successful, but only in part. Sunstrike was forced to let go, but Ocean collided with Gargoth and dug her claws into his neck. She let go just in time to miss Gargoth's huge jaws, which snapped shut in the empty space she had been a split second before.

Just as Gargoth swung around to find Jake, Crimson fell like a rock from straight above. The red dragon hit him with his full weight and drove Gargoth toward the ground. The black dragon tried spinning, so he could get Crimson to hit first, but they were too close to the ground. Just before impact, Crimson leapt off the black dragon, so he wouldn't crash with him.

Jake, his sister, and his friends scrambled off the ground and sprinted toward the cavern entrance as quickly as their legs could carry them. A few moments later, just as they neared the entrance, they were thrown from their feet again by the bone jarring impact of Gargoth hitting the earth. The earth shook and loose rock around the cavern entrance fell. Jake glanced back through the haze of dust billowing up from where Gargoth landed. It was too thick to see, but Jake could hear roars and growls coming from within the dust. It sounded like some of the dragons had landed and were fighting in the cloud.

The cloud of dust started to thin and Jake realized he and his friends shouldn't stay and watch. Gargoth's huge form completely filled the valley between his group and Eventine's. The other group was either crushed or fleeing like Jake's group. Crimson and Ocean were prowling around the black dragon, trying to strike and Sunstrike, who hadn't yet landed, was swooping down to earth from above with quick, striking dives and then was gone the next second, only to swing back and do it again. Gargoth was favoring his front left leg, but otherwise did his best to take on the other three at once. He lashed out with his other foreleg, knocking Ocean back as she tried maneuvering around and then Gargoth sent his tail into Crimson's side as he came in from the opposite direction. Crimson was hit with such force, he was knocked off his feet and landed, dazed. Gargoth would have sunk his jaws into Crimson then had it not been for Sunstrike, who came down at that precise moment. She sank her teeth into Gargoth's right shoulder, causing him to twist away from Crimson.

Jake was beginning to feel light headed, but shouted to his group. "Go, into the cavern quick or we'll be crushed!" His sister and friends ran into the mouth of the dark cavern as Jake followed, taking one last look behind him. Something caught his eye and he stopped. In the center of the cooling molten rock was the glowing handle of Sword of Light! Of course! Jake had completely forgotten about it in the midst of the battle. He started to run toward it before remembering the sword would come if he called.

Jake reached out his right hand and the sword responded, it pulled from the cooling stone, which sent molten rock flying, and headed to Jake. Just as the sword reached Jake, Jake saw Gargoth twist. He had caught part of Ocean in his mouth and, with all his might, he hurled her straight at Jake. Jake ran as fast as he could into the cavern, the sword still glowing and lighting his way. He flew straight past his sister and friends without saying a word, but the look on his face and the speed with which he ran must have told them enough. They followed right on his heels.

Inside the cavern entrance, it widened out, with a low ceiling just above their heads. The back of the cavern was completely open, reaching into the darkness. When Jake reached it, he dove to the ground and covered his head and his friends did the same. A moment later, Ocean collided with the cavern entrance, making the earth tremble yet again, completely crushing the entrance.

Outside the cavern, Ocean howled in pain as she tried righting herself. Gargoth advanced and sent a jet of flame at Ocean. Crimson landed beside Ocean and sent a jet of white-hot flame back at Gargoth. The two flames collided, but Gargoth's flame was stronger. His flame was slowed, but continued to advance toward Crimson and Ocean.

Then, Sunstrike landed and sent her own jet of flame. Gargoth's flame stopped advancing and was now at a standstill with Crimson's and Sunstrike's. A moment later, and with considerable effort, Ocean pulled herself up and roared. Fighting through her pain, she sent a third jet of flame, which joined with those of her siblings. The three united flames were hotter and considerably stronger, forcing Gargoth's flame back, moving it slowly at first and then pushing it rapidly.

Gargoth was caught off guard as the Primes' flames extinguished his own. The three combined flames hit the black dragon's head with full force and Gargoth scrambled back, ducking his head to get it out of the flame. The flames raced down his side and seared through the scales wherever it touched. Gargoth's face was already blistering and scarred. He couldn't withstand the heat and had to get away before he was overcome. Gargoth leapt free of the flames and, with his mighty wings, beat the air with desperation. He gained height quickly and he flew away, this battle, lost.

—

Back inside the cavern, Jake's group picked themselves up, coughing from the dust and hot air. The cavern entrance was completely blocked by rock; their only choice now, was to go forward.

"Well, I suppose I should have had second thoughts before we entered the cave," Patrick said, looking back at the cave-in.

"No, you can have them now, there's just nothing you can do about it anymore," TJ responded, coughing.

"What's that?" Alisha asked as she came up next to Jake and Eric who were standing at the edge of where the cave dropped away into darkness. What appeared to be an even larger cavern opened up before them. They couldn't be sure of the cavern's size because the light from the sword was dim right now. Each one of them could sense that an enormous space stretched out and down before them. The feeling was creepy. Then they noticed light coming from far below. It looked like a castle lit with torches stood down below. After exploring the area, they found a stone walkway that appeared to go downward toward the castle. It was off to their left; in the rest of the darkness there appeared to be a sheer drop off. Eric picked up a rock and threw it out into the darkness. The group stood for a minute and listened, but never heard it hit the bottom.

"Well," Jake mused as he strolled over to the stone walkway, "at least we know one thing."

"What's that?" TJ asked

Jake looked back and smiled, "That we'd better not step off the path. Now, can someone help me get this chest plate off, it's making it hard to breath." After TJ and Patrick helped him take off the piece of armor, Jake could breathe well again. They tried to bend it back, but the metal wouldn't yield, so they left it behind. The group turned to the walkway.

"I love walks through dark and dangerous caverns," Patrick exclaimed.

With that, the group started down into the darkness.

Chapter 27

Ruins of the Past

They walked slowly in near silence, the light from the sword casting a greyish light a few yards in front and behind. Their footsteps echoed off the stone walkway. The only other sound they could hear was a crackling all around them. Jake worried about what it meant and was just about to voice his concern when TJ asked instead.

"Is that the rock ceiling cracking we are hearing because, if it is, I doubt that's a good thing."

"Hey Jake, how about a bit more light?" Alisha asked nervously.

Jake held up the Sword of Light, "Here it goes."

The incredible white light came from the sword again and left not even the slightest shadow. The light reached out into the enormous cavern and the group stood, breathless and had to grab the short wall along the walkway or each other to stay up. A sense of vertigo came on them when they saw the cavern for what it really was. The cavern floor was at least a few hundred feet down and everywhere they looked were the remnants of a lost civilization. The floor and walls of the cavern were covered in buildings, similar to those Jake had seen in pictures of ancient Indian civilizations where they had carved their homes directly into the rock, one on top of the other.

Most of the dwellings on the walls were intact, but the floor looked as if a battle had taken place long ago. Sections of the city, especially the parts close to the fortress were reduced to rubble. Here and there were places which seemed untouched, but for the most part, the city had been destroyed. This must have been where the story Father Time had told him about had taken place. Where the goblin king,

Vishor, had made his last stand against Agor and the ones trying to overthrow him.

The walkway, bridge, or ramp they were on rose in a winding curve from the castle up to the top where they had entered.

At a couple of points, it connected with platforms on either side and, at four different intervals, there were stone structures going up over the walkway. They looked as if they were once used as guard houses to defend the ramp from intruders and Jake thought that they had better be careful when they got close to them. They could also see fine dust falling from the ceiling in many different areas and realized this was the crackling they were hearing. The impact and tremor from the dragon hitting the entrance must have caused it. Hopefully, nothing would break loose until they were out, if they could find their way out.

The group had been looking around for about a minute, but instead of lessening, the vertigo got worse. Jake turned to look at the others. They all looked pale and Alisha and Patrick almost looked a little green. They felt as bad or worse than he did.

"I'm going to dim the light back down so we can't see everything. Remind me that we need to be careful when we get to those structures spanning the walkway though, they'd be the perfect place for an ambush!"

The group nodded in agreement and there was a collective sigh of relief as the light from the sword went back to illuminating only the area around them on the walkway. After a couple of minutes' pause to let the vertigo pass, the group gathered themselves and started slowly into the darkness once again. The darkness now seemed more ominous, since they had seen the enormity of the cavern they were in. Every once in a while, they would see fine dust falling around them from the small fissures in the rock of the ceiling, which continued to get higher and higher as they traveled down the ramp.

Soon, they neared the first structure that spanned over the ramp. It came up suddenly, looming out of the darkness like a large mouth ready to swallow them up. Jake motioned them to stop. If there was an enemy within, it would already know of the group's presence because of the light from the sword, which Jake still held in his right hand. They couldn't do anything about that now, but they didn't need to be reckless either.

Everyone in their group took their shields off their backs and drew their swords, just in case, and held them ready. They clustered together at the right side of the ramp and held their shields up to try to cover each other, in case arrows started to fly. Advancing slowly, Jake at the front and Eric in the rear, they walked toward the structure. It covered only about 30 feet of the walkway, but there was plenty of space for an ambush from above.

They arrived at the structure with no incident. They continued on walking through it, noticing various openings in the walls and ceiling as they passed through. On the other side, TJ pointed to two doorways, one on the right and one on the left going up into the back of the structure. "We should check it out. Better to make sure an enemy isn't behind us, if we can help it."

Jake led the way onto a narrow staircase that went up into the stone structure, with his shield up, guarding the front. The rest of the group followed behind and Eric came at the rear, guarding the doorway with his shield. They made it quickly up to the top where the stairs opened up into one rectangular room which led across the walkway to another staircase on the other side.

Once they had all made it up, they spread out to explore the space. There were narrow windows on either side, looking out onto the walkway in front and behind. There were also narrow slits in the floor large enough to shoot arrows through or pour or drop things onto intruders. Another feature they saw along the front and back of the room, were long, thin, rectangular holes spanning the entire walkway. They were about six inches wide with the remnants of a broken gate in each one and were hooked to a pulley system that was controlled by a wheel on either side. Apart from these, a couple of broken benches, and a large cracked table, there was nothing in the room, but a thick layer of dust.

"It's a good thing these gates are broken or this would be a perfect place for trapping someone and filling them with arrows." TJ muttered, attempting to lighten the mood, but sounding more worried than he had meant to.

We'll have to remember that and plan accordingly for the next one, just in case," Jake responded.

The group headed down the other staircase and back to the walkway, noticing the inside wall facing the walkway had more narrow slots. It would definitely be easy for a defender to shoot at intruders from here and very hard for the intruders to shoot back through such a narrow opening while being attacked from above and both sides.

The group traveled quietly down the walkway with their shields and swords at the ready, just in case. "That's creepy," Alisha whispered, stopping suddenly. The rest of the group stopped and followed her gaze. She was looking back at the looming shadow of the gatehouse behind them and then, she turned and looked at the next one just barely visible in front of them. The group was almost directly between the two and, from this spot, the silhouettes of both structures looked ominous and imposing. Each member of the group couldn't help feel a chill run down their backs. They continued on and they soon came to the second gatehouse.

The group huddled up to the right wall just like before, and Jake called back, "Alright. Just like we did before, only we run through the opening as quickly as we can, just in case there is anyone up there."

They all nodded in agreement and hurried forward at a quick jog. They made it to the other side without incident and checked the second gatehouse just like they did the first. This one was completely empty, except for the wheel and pulley system for the gates. The ropes were ripped and torn and the wheels broken off their mountings and shattered on the floor in pieces. The gates themselves were completely missing.

As they neared the third gatehouse, they could tell it wouldn't be necessary to check it. It had been blown apart by an explosion or torn apart by something very large. The left side of the structure still partially stood. The outer wall and most of the steps went up to meet part of the floor, but the ceiling was gone and nothing else remained of the gatehouse. The right side was completely gone, along with a chunk of the walkway, revealing the darkness beyond. The group had to carefully pick their way through the debris of the shattered gatehouse now lying along the walkway. Pieces of broken gate and large sections of the broken structure were scattered along the ramp.

After they wound their way carefully through the debris, Patrick waved at them to stop. "Is it just me, or is the crackling getting louder?"

They all listened for the sound. They had grown so accustomed to the noise in their journey down and they had almost forgotten about it. The ceiling was now at least a hundred feet or more over them and it was hard to judge the sound over the distance, but it did indeed sound like it was getting louder and more frequent.

"We'd better get moving, just in case," TJ shouted, just as a loud crack could be heard above. The group scrambled forward as a large chunk of ceiling fell into view. It hit with a sickening thud amongst the rubble of the third gatehouse where they had just been. Now the group was running, while bits of fine dust and small gravel started to fall among them. Soon, larger rocks were falling near them. One struck Eric on the shoulder, denting his armor and knocking him over. He recovered quickly and continued running.

Alisha tripped over a rock and fell sideways, hitting the ground hard. The impact knocked the air from her lungs. She rolled onto her back, struggling to breathe, and heard a loud crack directly above her. A large chunk of the ceiling came loose and fell down toward her. She screamed, but still had no air in her lungs to give power to her voice. Just as she realized she wouldn't be able to move in time, she felt someone grab her arm. Her armor scrapped the floor as she was pulled across it and out of the way, just as the rock landed where she had been with a loud crack. Her breath suddenly came back and she gasped and coughed. Patrick came into view standing over her.

"You okay?"

She nodded.

"Well, we'd better get you to your feet. It's not safe here." Patrick helped Alisha up and they ran to catch up to the others.

The group ran as fast as they could toward the fourth gatehouse, now looming up out of the darkness. Large chunks of rock were now raining down among them and it was a miracle none of them had gotten hurt worse than a dent in their armor or a scratch on their skin. There were a couple more stumbles, but they managed to reach the fourth gatehouse before any of them were badly hurt, or worse.

The group ran under the gatehouse, breathing hard, as rocks and dust rained down on both sides of the opening. The sound wasn't deafening, but it was loud enough that no one in the group heard the gates on either side of the gatehouse start to lower into place.

Chapter 28

Ambushed

"Is everyone alright?" Jake shouted and looked around to see everyone nodding, still too out of breath to talk. They were all leaning on the right wall of the gatehouse as they caught their breath. Patrick and Alisha were on Jake's left and TJ and Eric to his right. It was then the sword's light turned red, giving Jake a warning. Jake looked up and saw movement behind TJ and Eric. At first, he thought it was just the falling rocks, but then quickly realized, in the dim red light, that the gates were closing.

All Jake had time to do was point at the gate and yell "Run!" He didn't even consider going out the closer gate where they had entered because he might not be able to reach Isabelle then.

They bolted for the gate, which was now three quarters of the way down. TJ and Eric were closest and dove underneath, just barely getting past as the spiked bottom edge of the gate reached them. Jake, Alisha, and Patrick pulled up short. Jake was about to swing the Sword of Light at the gate when another warning came from it.

Without thinking, Jake yelled "Shields!" as he brought up his own. The first arrow hit his shield and glanced off as more followed.

Jake, Alisha, and Patrick huddled together trying to stay clear of the holes in the wall behind them while covering each other with their shields as the arrows clinked off of them. TJ and Eric were already in motion, each of them running to a separate stair so they could, hopefully, catch the enemy off guard while they were shooting arrows.

Jake saw them go and worried there might be too many for the two of them to handle. They had never been in an actual battle before now and he hoped the limited training they had would be enough. If it wasn't, or if they didn't hurry, one of these arrows would find its way through or around their shield barrier sooner or later. He needed an advantage, but couldn't think of one quick enough. Alisha yelled into his ear, "Jake, the light!"

Jake struggled for a moment, trying to figure out what she meant. Then, the idea formed and he acted. He held up the sword and asked for a light which would blind their enemies but not them. The sword reacted immediately and sent out a piercing white light. Jake found it extremely bright, but once again, it didn't hurt his eyes. He knew it must be having the opposite effect on their enemy, however, because he heard yelps of pain and the clatter of weapons falling as they covered their eyes. The arrows stopped coming and a bow fell through one of the holes in the floor, clattering onto the walkway. Jake, Alisha, and Patrick kept their shields up, just in case.

Up in the gatehouse, Eric and TJ entered from opposite sides. Two guards were stationed by each stair and four enemies were over the center, apparently the ones responsible for the arrows, until they had been blinded a few moments earlier. All of them were covering their eyes and only one of them was still holding a weapon.

Eric reached the room first and used his shield as a battering ram while he rushed them low and then struck the two guards; pushing up with all his strength, in his best football form, he sent them both flying backwards. They clattered to the floor and the last one with a sword dropped it as the wind was knocked out of him. While they were dazed, Eric ran to them and finished them off. The other two guards turned away from their stair when they heard Eric crash into the others, allowing TJ to cut them down with ease as he entered.

The remaining four in the center still couldn't see, but each of them pulled knives from their belts and started whipping them in all directions, unable to tell where TJ and

Eric were. One of the creatures swung around and stabbed his neighbor in the back, causing him to scream before he fell down, never to get up again. Upon hearing this, the other two swung around, thinking their third comrade was an enemy and attacked him. Now there were only two left, and TJ and Eric each advanced on one and took them out.

"We'd better make sure they're dead," TJ responded, looking grim. Eric nodded and they checked all of them again before calling down to their friends below.

"All clear, we'll try to raise the gate." TJ called down. He and Eric started turning the wheel. It was hard to budge at first, but started getting easier after its first turn. Before long, they had it up and locked back into place.

Footsteps echoed up the stairs as Alisha, Patrick, and Jake appeared from the right stairwell. Once inside the gatehouse, Jake let the light from the sword dim slightly and they looked around. Eight bodies lay where they fell. They looked similar to the goblins they had seen earlier, but they were shorter and broader.

"I wonder if these are orcs?" Jake wondered aloud. "Thanks for acting so quickly, guys. We would have been full of holes before long, if you two hadn't gotten under the gate!"

Eric looked at Jake, "Well, we have you to thank for the well-timed light attack or I doubt we could have overcome all eight of them."

"You can thank Alisha for that," Jake responded, nodding toward his sister, "it was her idea."

"Thanks Alisha," TJ said with a smile. "Glad there is someone clever in your family."

Alisha beamed and Jake laughed, "Ouch, that one stung, TJ."

"I'm not worried, I'm sure you'll manage to get me back soon enough," TJ responded, laughing himself.

"Hey Patrick, do you think you could use one of these?" Eric questioned, holding up a bow.

Patrick walked over and took the bow from Eric, looking it over. "Maybe, it's a little different than my compound bow, but I could probably adjust and make it work with some practice. Gather up as many arrows as you can find."

Fortunately, there were plenty of arrows in the guardhouse. Patrick slung the bow and one quiver full of arrows over his shoulder before they left the gatehouse.

Once outside, Jake dimmed the light even further, back down to where it had been to avoid the disorientation they had felt before. Again, they started down the walkway. The rocks had stopped falling and there were no more crackling sounds to be heard. They were much closer to the fortress now and could see it clearer in the light of its torches, which cast a yellow glow over the structure and lit the landscape around it with a dim light. As they drew closer, Eric was the first to spot something strange.

"Hey guys, do you see that?"

They all slowed to a stop and looked down at the castle.

"What do you think it is?" asked Jake following his gaze.

Outside the wall of the castle, it looked as if there was something that reflected the light all around it. They could all see it now, and kept their eyes on it as they continued on their way. As they got lower and closer Alisha gasped, "It's a maze, a maze made out of crystal!"

As soon as she said it, the rest of them realized it was true. Before them, completely encircling the castle, was a maze of crystal walls. "Well, this is right up your alley sis!"

Alisha had always loved mazes and was very good at figuring them out, at least on paper. She did have a pretty good knack for getting through the mirror maze at the amusement park back home too, usually much faster than the rest of her family, unless they followed her closely.

"I'll do my best," she muttered, slightly apprehensive.

"What are you worried about," Jake replied. "You usually love mazes."

"Yes, but the mazes I usually do don't have things lurking in them, waiting to attack me!"

"Good point," replied Jake.

The group continued down and soon found themselves on the ground level, standing before the pink crystal walls of the maze. There was a large opening in front of them, the walls were at least 15 feet high and much too smooth to climb.

"I guess we won't be able to get a bird's eye view very easily," Eric complained.

"It wouldn't do much good anyway," Alisha responded. "I was watching it as we came down the walkway. It circles around the castle so, unless you stood on the center peak of it, you wouldn't be able to see the whole thing at once to make sense of it."

"Well, Alisha, what do you think?" Jake asked, looking at his sister as she gazed up at the walls of the maze. They were thick, but almost transparent and somewhat reflective. The top of the wall was just barely visible in the low light.

"I think it looks challenging. The crystal maze might be worse than the mirror mazes I'm used to because it is not only reflective, but somewhat transparent as well. It plays tricks with your eyes."

"I would like to let the light from the sword go out, since it looks like we can see well enough now with the light from the castle's torches. It might prevent any enemies from seeing which way we go, but if you think light from the sword would get us through faster, we'll use it."

Alisha thought for a moment before answering. "I think letting it go out would be fine. Too much light would be confusing with the way the crystal plays with it."

Jake let the light from the sword go out. They took a few moments to let their eyes adjust to the light from the torches. As they did, they started to observe where they were. They were standing at the bottom of the walkway, which stretched back to the surface. In front of them, the pink crystal walls of the maze were now iridescent and glowed slightly from the torchlight that reached them from the castle. The walls stretched in both directions as far as they could see.

They were in a courtyard of sorts where the now broken and crumbled city, the maze, and the walkway to the surface all connected. On either side of them, the group saw the rubble of the buildings that used to stand next to the courtyard. The air smelled stale and dusty. As they stood taking in their surroundings, not a sound could be heard. Everything looked deserted. Even the fortress that loomed up in front of them, towering at the heart of the maze, looked empty; though someone had to be there to keep the torches lit.

The group started walking up to the maze, warily eyeing every direction. The walkway between the walls of the maze was wide. As they entered, Jake couldn't help but think a semi could probably drive down the center without a problem. They reached out and touched the crystal, its surface cool and smooth. It was truly beautiful to look at, but the possibility of danger around the next corner tempered their appreciation of it.

After about 100 feet, the group came to a T intersection. Now, they had to choose which way to go. Alisha only stopped long enough to make sure the coast was clear and instructed, "This way," and led them down the left passage. After a short distance, the passage turned left back on itself and they followed it around. Then, they came to an opening on their right. They stood in the opening, looking at three different passages.

"The one to the left probably just goes down and dead ends somewhere near the central hall we came through." Alisha pondered, thinking out loud. "That leaves the one going right and the one going straight ahead. Let's take the right hall, we will probably find out where it goes the quickest."

The group continued like this for what seemed like hours, but only twice did they run into dead ends. Sometimes they felt like they were making progress, only to come to a hall that would take them back toward the edge of the maze and away from the castle. Alisha told them that was a good sign they were headed the right way, as the other tunnels they had passed had to have dead ended up against the one they were in.

The group started getting frustrated. There were a few times they thought they had found a new opening only to realize, as they came up against crystal, they were being fooled by the light and shadow playing on the crystal walls. Suddenly, Alisha stopped. They had just gone left, after trying right at a T intersection, and ran into their third dead end. "Something isn't right." She stated, slightly frustrated.

"What's wrong?" Jake asked, coming up next to her.

"Look," she responded, pointing.

There in front of them, just at the end of the light's reach, was another wall.

"I hope this doesn't mean we're now lost and have to find our way back to the beginning and start over," Patrick grumbled, sounding less than enthusiastic.

"No, this should have been the right way," Alisha answered. "I must have missed something." They followed her back to the T intersection. Alisha opened her mouth to address the group when the air, which had been completely still up until this point, moved. It was slight at first, but then grew to a small breeze.

"Well, that's not good." Patrick exclaimed as they all froze and the hair on their necks stood on end. Something was headed their way.

"We're trapped," TJ said, warily.

"No, I don't think so," Alisha responded, gazing intently at the wall in front of her. "There, see that," she exclaimed pointing at a swirl of dust on the floor. It appeared to go through the wall ahead. "Come on quick!" she urged and ran to, and then through the wall.

The group followed her through an opening they hadn't seen before. The intersection wasn't a T after all, but an opening so narrow and leading into such a small passage between the walls you couldn't see it even when you stared right at it. They followed Alisha down the passage to the right, the air still picking up speed.

A short way down the small passage, the group suddenly stopped and stood still. They could hear and feel a pounding coming closer now. It sounded like something large was coming toward them. They all stilled their breathing, crouched down, and stayed quiet as the rumbling continued to get closer. Suddenly, the vague form of a shadow fell across the wall. There was something in the hallway they had just come from! From the look of its shadow it was large, almost as tall as the wall.

Through the quiet that filled their ears came a new sound...breathing. It was a deep, rough breath, like that of a large animal. The shadow turned this way and that while its owner searched on the other side of the wall. Even though the wall was somewhat transparent, in this light they couldn't make out the creature's exact shape. It looked left and then right while standing in the intersection and then, as if it knew they were there, it stared straight ahead. Jake hoped it didn't know about the passage they were in but that was probably too much to hope for. Whether it did or didn't, it wouldn't be able to fit through the narrow opening, however, Jake wasn't sure if it could break through the wall. They all stood in silence for a few very uncomfortable moments, listening to the deep breathing of the shadow. Then, the creature sniffed the air twice, turned, and ran back the way it had come.

When the sound of the creature's footsteps died away, there was a collective gasp as the group started breathing normally again. "Okay, so I know we've seen giant rock golems and huge dragons already and it could be it's just the dark getting to me, but that was freaky," Patrick exclaimed.

"What was it?" Alisha asked.

"No idea," Jake replied. "But I got the feeling it knew we were here, maybe even in this passage. If that's the case, it knows where this passage ends, which means we'd better get moving so we're not trapped in here."

The group started running with Jake in the lead and Alisha right behind him giving him directions, their armor clanking as they ran. Soon, the group found themselves at an opening that led back out into yet another large hall. Jake waved for everyone to wait and he slowly made his way out into the hall.

They were almost right next to the castle now. Jake thought he could see the stone wall of the castle just on the other side of the crystal. If they could find an opening, they'd be in! Jake couldn't see very far in either direction, but it looked clear and no warning came from the sword. He motioned for the others and they came to stand with him. They could now see that they had gone from the left side of the castle to the right and the hall they were in now had to wrap around the castle.

"We should try that way," Alisha said, pointing back toward the center of the castle.

As they started walking, a warning came from the sword and Jake held up his hand, slowing the group. They held for a few moments, but no danger was apparent. They proceeded again slower, the sword still sending out a warning to Jake. About 30 yards ahead and to the left, the wall appeared to have an opening. Jake indicated for the group to wait while he went ahead to look and make sure there was nothing waiting for them around the corner.

He was about 12 yards away when he noticed something strange out of the corner of his right eye. The stone wall on the other side of the crystal seemed different somehow. He only had enough time to turn his head and tense before a huge crash hit the crystal wall, shattering it into large chunks and small pieces. TJ tackled Alisha, covering her as Eric and Patrick threw themselves beside them, covering everyone with their shields. Crystal chunks and shards bounced off of them as they closed their eyes for protection.

Jake was so close, he only had enough time to jump forward away from the shattering wall before he was struck by a large chunk. The piece of wall hit him from the side, sending him flying into the other wall. His head hit hard. Thankfully his helmet protected him, taking most of the blow so Jake wasn't hurt, just slightly disoriented. He recovered quickly, rolling away from the debris as a large form came through the wall.

The light from the torches was bright enough for them to see the creature clearly now. A Minotaur! It was large, muscular, and covered in brown hide, wearing armor on its legs and upper torso. Its head sat on a short, muscular neck and was that of a huge, gruesome bull with two large curved horns on top. Its eyes were bloodshot and yellow, filled with hatred. In its large muscular arms, it held the largest double-sided battle axe Jake had ever seen! The creature saw them all down and decided to go for Patrick, Eric, TJ, and Alisha first.

Jake saw the beast turn its head that way and scrambled to his feet and ran toward it to try and stop it before it fell upon his friends. They were just getting to their feet and seeing this new threat for the first time. They couldn't avoid the blow that was about to come down on them from the Minotaur's huge axe. Luckily, Jake was able to strike first and swung the Sword of Light at the beast as he came in closer. Jake wasn't close enough for the blade to go deep, but the sword curved through the air, slicing cleanly through the Minotaur's armor, the tip catching on the beast's lower right side.

The beast bellowed in pain and changed direction, bringing its axe down and around. Jake ducked under the swing and the axe bit deeply into the crystal wall. Instead of breaking through though, it got stuck and the beast turned its attention to pulling the axe out with one arm while swinging at Jake with the other. TJ, Patrick, Eric, and Alisha took their chance and ran past, ducking under the Minotaur's outstretched arm. TJ grabbed Jake on the way, pulling him out of reach just as the free arm of the beast came down where he had been standing. A moment later, the beast pulled the axe out with both arms and started after the group.

If they were going to have to fight this thing, Jake wanted to get around the corner of the maze wall first, so they could have a small advantage. He glanced back as they approached the corner and saw the Minotaur quickly gaining. He dashed around the corner, but didn't have time to tell the others of his plan. Jake turned and crouched, ready to swing at the beast's left leg as it came around the corner.

Alisha was the first to realize he wasn't following and skidded to a stop, yelling back at Jake. "What are you doing?"

The others turned and looked. Jake was still waiting, but the beast never came around the corner. It surely would have gotten here by now. Jake turned his head right, afraid the beast had seen his plan and might be standing right behind him on the other side of the wall, ready to break through again. Alarm swept through him, he had already forgotten the walls were partially see-through.

Jake looked through the wall, but only saw what he thought was the empty hall they had come from. He wasn't sure if he should feel relieved the beast was gone, or worried the huge creature had just disappeared without a sound. Jake knew he shouldn't be so scared and he needed to trust the Creator, but everything had happened so quickly, Jake could feel the adrenaline coursing through him as he crouched in the hall. He was shaking slightly because of all the pent up energy.

"Where'd it go?" TJ asked, standing farther down the hall with the rest of the group.

Jake prayed then, knowing the creature was trying to scare them and keep them off balance. As he did, his mind started to calm and clear itself and he stood, allowing his limbs to relax slightly. The sword's warning was gone now, so they weren't in immediate danger, but that didn't mean it wasn't around the next corner.

"What are we going to do now, Jake?" TJ asked, walking toward him; the rest of the group followed.

A thought occurred to Jake as he finished praying. "I think we should go back and try going through the hole the minotaur just made. It's trying to scare us and it knows this maze. If we keep fleeing from it, we're bound to run into its trap sooner or later. If we go back, we may even find another opening that will get us into the castle quicker than finishing the maze. Of course, we could run right into the creature this way also. What do you think Alisha?"

"I think you're right. I believe we have been headed the right way, but it is hard to tell how much longer it will take to get through this maze. It could be a couple of corners away, but I don't think we have even gone through half of it yet. It would be just like a good maze to take you close to its heart only to send you back out and around again. We need to get to Isabelle quickly and I think that new hole is the best bet!"

"Okay, follow me carefully," Jake responded, creeping around the corner, sword held ready. The hall was deserted like before and the group made their way back down to the spot where the minotaur had broken through the wall. They entered the new doorway, carefully avoiding the jagged, sharp edges of the broken crystal. On the other side, they found the tall castle wall was not as close as it had appeared. When looking through the crystal, it appeared like it was directly behind the wall, but it was actually about 20 feet away. Between the crystal wall and the castle wall was an open space with hard packed ground for a floor.

The group gathered in the area and carefully looked around. The castle wall went in both directions. To the right, it went around and disappeared, but to the left they could just see a place where the castle wall came out to meet the maze. That might be the way in! Jake saw it, but before he allowed himself to go running toward it he looked around.

Something was bothering him. It wasn't a warning from the sword, but his own feeling something was wrong. There were still too many shadows in this place, sending his imagination spinning. Too many places to hide, too many hidden dangers, and Jake felt a chill go down his back, like they were being watched.

Jake turned to the group. "Now that we are out of the maze, I'm going to light this place up, any objections?" The rest of the group shook their heads.

Jake allowed the sword to brighten up the cavern once again. The size was still frighteningly large, but now that they were on the floor of it, they didn't get disoriented as before. Jake looked around. The light took away the shadows and now Jake could see there were many nooks and crannies, many corners, stairways, and defensive positions along the castle wall, where danger could be lurking even with the darkness gone.

"Jake, that staircase up ahead on the left looks promising." Alisha pointed out

Jake followed her gaze and saw there was indeed a staircase built into the wall, which came out to meet the maze. "Okay everyone, stay behind me.

The group quickly made their way to the stairway, watching warily for hidden dangers. Once at the top of the stairs, they found a landing where two more sets of stairs met theirs. One on the left, which came up from the maze and the other, directly across from them. To the right was a walkway made of hard packed dirt and rock. The group was elated until one by one, their gaze fell upon the other end.

There, where the walkway went into the castle, just inside the open gate, stood the minotaur! It stood, completely still and silent, just waiting and watching, knowing they had no other choice, but to come his way or go back. They could see him clearly now, even more clearly than before. He stood at least 12 feet tall and had broad muscular shoulders, large muscular arms, and thighs the size of tree trunks. The group just stared at him for a few moments, knowing that if they didn't figure out something quick, it would be their end.

"Well, Jake, any bright ideas?" asked TJ.

Jake shook his head no. "If it was a sword fight, I believe I could win. But if I go up against that thing one on one, I'm not so sure. That axe packs a punch and, even with all of its special abilities, the Sword of Light doesn't give me super strength. It could probably swat me away as easily as a fly if I try to do this alone."

"That's why you brought us mate!" Eric responded smiling. "I have an idea. It's risky, but I think it'll work." The group huddled up quickly while Alisha kept her head up to make sure the minotaur didn't decide to charge while their guard was down. Eric quietly told the group his plan.

"You're right, that is risky. But if no one has any better suggestions, I think it's doable," Jake responded, looking around.

"Let's just hope you're not crushed in the process, Eric," TJ chuckled, only half joking.

"Are you kidding, that thing isn't very big to me," Eric stated, staring it down confidently.

"Well, let's get this over with," Patrick said, looking grim.

They started off toward the minotaur, walking at first, then jogging, and then running. Eric was in the lead, TJ, Jake, and Patrick ran side by side a short way behind him, and Alisha followed, bringing up the rear. When they were about halfway to the beast, they all started to yell. Patrick even started yelling insults at it like "*ugly stinking beast*," and "*stupid cow*."

At first, nothing happened and Jake was worried the plan would fail before they had even started, but then the beast must have understood their meaning because it snarled, bellowed in rage, and started forward, charging them as well. It held its axe in its right hand and tilted its head down slightly, so its long curved horns would gore anyone that came within reach.

When they were about 10 feet from it, and just before the beast could reach Eric, Jake made the sword shine and directed a painful light directly at the beast's eyes. The beast pulled its head up in pain and Eric took the opportunity to dive beneath the sharp horns straight for its legs. He grabbed the creature's left leg , hitting it at full tackle speed, , causing its own momentum to send it tumbling forward. It let go of its axe as it fell and the weapon flew over TJ and Alisha, who both ducked to avoid it.

The beast fell headlong onto the ground, its horns sank into the rock and dirt path. It was unable to pull its head free and tried pushing itself up, but was too late; the boys descended on it. TJ went to the left and Patrick to the right, both of them stabbing into the large arms of the minotaur to keep it from getting up. It bellowed in pain just before Jake leapt over its head and brought the Sword of Light down through the base of its neck, ending its misery. With one final shudder, it lay still. The three rushed around to where Eric still lay pinned under its legs.

"You alright Eric?" TJ shouted as they moved the beast's legs off him. They managed to slide one of the creature's legs over and pulled Eric out. He groaned.

"I'm going to feel that tomorrow," he responded, coughing. "I think I've met my match. Remind me to stick with regular football from now on, no more minotaur's."

"Let's get your armor off," Patrick said, seeing it dented and cracked over Eric's right shoulder where he must have hit the leg. "You're bleeding and we need to make sure it isn't serious."

"No complaints here, it's kind of pinching me now." Eric responded, shakily getting to his feet.

"I know we didn't have another choice, but that's disgusting." Alisha groaned, trying not to look at the beast as she made her way around it to join the group. "It's a good thing they don't allow swords in regular football."

Jake, TJ, Patrick, and even Eric, broke out into laughter.

"I can't believe you just said that sis!" Jake responded.

"Sorry, kind of just slipped out," she giggled, grinning sheepishly.

"Quit making me laugh, it hurts," chuckled Eric.

"Big baby," TJ replied.

They made their way to the castle entrance where they took off Eric's armor to look at his shoulder. There was bruising on his shoulder and a scrape along his neck where the cracked armor had scratched him, but it wasn't very deep. Other than that, he appeared to be fine. TJ tore off part of his sleeve and tied it around Eric's neck, covering the scrape, while Jake and Patrick tried bending the armor back into shape so Eric could still use it, but to no avail.

"That was a hard hit," Patrick exclaimed, as they looked at Eric's armor. "I don't think you will be able to put this back on."

"It definitely helped keep my collarbone from being broken. Let's avoid those creatures in the future," Eric replied, as they made their way into the castle. "I'm not going to be able to do that again!"

Chapter 29

Medusa's Heir

The interior of the castle seemed like a maze of rooms and halls, stairways and walkways. Along the way, there were quite a few different statues of creatures made from crystal. They were very lifelike. They passed one on a pedestal to their right. It was a statue of a dwarf. It seemed as if every detail was there. Even the color matched that of a real dwarf, except for the fact it was slightly transparent because it was made out of crystal. If Jake hadn't known any better, it looked like it could have been one of the dwarves who had accompanied them and fought for them in the valley. By his side, stood a tall elf with sword raised, as if attacking. They both looked so life-like, it was incredible.

The castle was lit well enough with torches, so Jake let the sword's light go out. They walked quietly through the deserted castle, staying in the main corridor, wondering if it was really empty or if another attack was just around the corner.

"I wonder where everyone is?" Patrick whispered.

"Maybe they all went out to fight us in the valley," TJ offered.

"Let's hope so," Alisha replied.

Jake's heart hammered. They had to be close to Isabelle now, he could feel it! They followed this hallway, checking rooms as they went. After turning a few times and going up a few levels, they came around to a doorway that opened into a large room; it looked as if it used to be a waiting area of some kind. There were many chairs and a few small tables thrown here and there in disarray, many broken or overturned. The center of the room was largely cleared.

Across from them was a short hall that led into an even larger room. Jake's heart leapt!

"This is it guys, it has to be!" Jake cried, starting across the room. They slowly made their way to the other side. The sword in Jake's hand suddenly hummed. "Get down!" he shouted and they all dropped to the floor just as the familiar whistling sound reached their ears.

An arrow flew through the air above them, hitting the wall right next to the hallway. It had come from behind them. They were close to the hallway now, so Eric got up and quickly grabbed a table near the hall and turned it over as the others covered him with their shields. Another arrow whistled through the air, this time hitting the ceiling over the hallway. Eric lifted the table and took it into the hallway, so the walls were on either side of it and the group could crouch behind and use their shields as additional cover.

"I think I saw him," Patrick whispered as they took cover. "Jake and Alisha, keep watch and cover us from behind. They nodded and turned, being sure to stay behind the table. Another arrow whizzed by overhead. Patrick looked at TJ and Eric. "If you two can keep me covered, I might be able to get him." They nodded back and raised their shields, so Patrick had a narrow place to look and shoot from. Another arrow hit the wall to their left.

"Well, at least he isn't a perfect shot," Patrick muttered, as he tried spotting the enemy archer again.

"No, but he might get lucky," TJ replied as another arrow bit into the table to their left, the point showed through on their side.

"I see him now," Patrick whispered, taking the bow off his back and fitting an arrow. "He's above, on the balcony over the doorway we came through, on the other side of the room."

Jake and Alisha kept watch behind, trying to look through the short hall into the room behind them. It was dimly lit with torches, much of it lost in shadow, but it looked large. It almost seemed like it could be the throne room to this castle, but there were no thrones to be seen. They could be in the dark shadows somewhere though. In the center of the room on a small pedestal stood an object that reflected the dim light from the torches. It almost looked as if it was another crystal statue. Nothing in the room stirred, everything was eerily silent.

"Jake, what is that?" Alisha asked in a curiously worried voice.

"I don't know, but I want to get a better look. Stay here, I'll be right back. I can check to see if the coast is clear behind us while I'm at it," he whispered to Alisha and started to creep forward, trying to stay covered as much as possible.

"Jake, no, we should stay together."

Jake heard Alisha's warning, but he ignored it. The closer he got to the room, the more it looked to Jake like there was something oddly familiar about the crystal's shape, which filled him with anticipation and dread. All of a sudden, he lost the desire to go on, but he also needed to be sure what he was seeing. Alisha was still calling him as he peeked around the corners of the hall into the room. He could just make the room out in the low light. It was wide and tall with a vaulted ceiling. Jake could tell it had been a magnificent room in its prime, but was now filled with dust and cobwebs everywhere he looked. The coast looked clear.

Patrick let loose his first arrow, just after the enemy shot another, this one flew well over their heads. Patrick's shot missed, flying too high and clanking off the stone wall behind the enemy archer. The enemy didn't stop, but he did duck behind the stone railing for cover as he realized they could shoot back. Patrick fitted another arrow and waited for the enemy to shoot again. When he did so, Patrick adjusted his aim and pull from his last shot and let his arrow fly. This time the enemy's arrow glanced off Eric's shield as Patrick's hit the stone railing, just to the left of the archer.

"I think I'm getting a feel for this bow. I should be able to adjust," Patrick said with satisfaction, fitting another arrow. The other archer was now crawling back and forth, so he could come up at different places behind the railing to shoot.

Behind them, Jake ventured out a short way into the throne room, looking carefully around for danger. Alisha was still calling out to Jake from behind, and almost got up to run and follow him, when an arrow flew over her head and skipped across the floor in front of her. She ducked back down and yelled this time, "Jake!"

Jake heard her and saw where the arrow landed, but he couldn't turn back, not now. He was out of range of the enemy archer now and he hoped he was wrong about what he was seeing, but he had to know for sure. A crippling dread was starting to creep in, trying to steal away his hope.

Another arrow clinked off the wall as Patrick fired again. This time, it just missed the enemy, who had to be a short orc, but the way he kept ducking down behind the wall made it hard to tell. This time, there was a longer pause between the next shot and it came from the opposite end of the balcony. This was going to take forever unless… Patrick had an idea. "Guys, follow my lead," he whispered to TJ and Eric. They nodded back.

When the archer took his next shot Patrick fired back, his arrow flew right where the creature's head had been a moment before. Patrick whispered a little too loudly, "Guys, I'm out of arrows, can you reach any?"

TJ and Eric looked back to see Patrick's quiver still half-full on the ground beside him and one already knocked in his bow. TJ whispered back again, much louder than he needed to, "No, not without going out of cover."

"Me either," came Eric's reply.

The enemy archer fired one shot and ducked. He did this several more times and Patrick stayed hidden and waited, watching their enemy. After a few more shots, the enemy stopped ducking and moving, thinking he had easy targets once again. Patrick steadied his breathing as he snuck up again to shoot. The enemy released one final shot and, as he reached back for another arrow, Patrick released his shot, making the most of his surprise attack. It hit the enemy archer square in its chest, causing the creature to double over and fall head first from the balcony. It landed with a sickening crack and didn't get up again.

Jake neared the statue in the middle of the room, his heart pounding. He hoped against hope he wouldn't find what he already knew he would. He made his way around the statue, seeing the all too familiar shape. When he made it to the front he almost cried out. There, on the small platform in the middle of the room, stood Isabelle, perfectly formed out of crystal. Every detail was there. No statue could be this exact. Somehow, some way, Isabelle had been turned into crystal. Father Time had told Jake that Medusa's Heir liked turning things into crystal, but he hadn't really thought about what it meant until now. It broke his heart.

Suddenly, Jake heard the cries of victory from his friends and looked to the hallway. He saw Patrick, Eric, TJ, and Alisha turn toward him and start forward and then, he noticed something else too. Crystals were starting to sprout from the floor, walls, and ceiling at the entrance to the throne room. They grew and fused together rapidly and even Alisha, who had already started running toward Jake, couldn't get through before they had formed a solid wall of clear crystal cutting them off from Jake. He could hear Alisha's muffled cries from the other side and could see TJ, Patrick, and Eric trying to break through with their swords, but it was already too thick and all they managed to do was clink harmlessly off the crystal.

Now Jake knew he was trapped, but not alone. The enemy he'd come to face was here somewhere, ready and waiting. He searched the room, but still saw no movement. His friends looked safe enough, just cut off, so Jake let his gaze fall back on Isabelle. She was wearing the same clothes she wore on the day she disappeared and she had a confused and frightened look on her face. Everything about her retained its normal color and shape, except for the fact she was semitransparent crystal. Even the mark, which came up out of the turtleneck she was wearing and spread over her lower left cheek like a thin spider web, was the same.

Jake's eyes teared up at the sight of her. He reached out to touch her hand and felt its smooth surface. A knot settled in his throat as he thought about her, wondering if he was already too late. Tears wet his cheeks as he tried saying her name, but choked out a sob instead. Just then, a high maniacal laugh filled his ears.

Jake whipped around, wiping tears from his eyes and raising the Sword of Light, looking for the source of the laughter. There was still no movement, but the back end of the room was lost in shadow where the torchlight couldn't reach. Jake was about to light the room using the sword, when a different light flared to life, then another and another and another. The lights continued to come to life in rapid succession, each one slightly higher and farther back, revealing a long staircase leading up to a large circular platform on which stood a throne, seated high against the back wall of the room. There were other, smaller thrones to the sides of the large one on the platform, but it was the tall center throne that held a vile looking goblin with a tall pink staff in his hand. The evil goblin had sharp, angled features, dark hair, and dark eyes. He wore dark armor and a sword hung at his waist. This must be Medusa's Heir!

The goblin was still laughing at Jake as it stood and rose to its full height. "Pathetic boy," came the high raspy voice. "You thought you could just walk in here and take your friend back, one I have gone to great lengths to take. You can stop your crying, she's not dead. There is no reason I would need to go through all this trouble just to kill someone. No, I have other plans for the young woman. Not that it matters much to you. You'll be dead before you can do anything about it."

"Let her go!" Jake yelled through the sob still stuck in his throat, causing his voice to crack. "If you've harmed her I'll..."

"You'll what?" Medusa's Heir shouted, cutting him off. He paused for a moment and then continued, eyeing Jake with contempt. "I'll admit; I'm surprised you have made it this far. One of my servants managed to poison you and I've heard you have run into a few of my other servants in the forest and survived. Of course, you've had help from other mettlesome creatures who will be dealt with soon enough. Tisk, tisk, tisk, came the sound from Medusa's Heir as he shook his head back and forth. "You even had friends come with you to help you get here to this castle!" The goblin spit in anger. "You're so weak you can't do anything yourself, can you? Well, now you're alone. It's just you and me. You'll have to beat me all by yourself."

The goblin paused, eyeing Jake as he stood there trying to be ready for an attack. Why wasn't the goblin attacking and what "*plans*" did he have for Isabelle? Those were the questions going through Jake's mind. Medusa's Heir had had the advantage before showing himself and, even now, Jake would have thought the goblin would just attack quickly, but he seemed content to just sit there and examine him.

The vile creature grinned and then spoke again. "Of course, you have come across a special sword, and now you think that with it you can defeat me." The goblin laughed again. "Don't you know I hold the Crystal Staff in my hand?" He raised it and a pink light came from it. "It has the powers you can't even begin to understand and with it I will take your pathetic sword and destroy you!" Medusa's Heir pointed the staff at Jake and a pink ray shot from it, hitting the sword in Jake's hand.

Jake held tight as the force pushed against the sword. The pink light surrounded the sword for a moment, but then, the Sword of Light turned bright white and the pink ray shot back, causing the goblin to almost lose his grip on the staff. After the goblin had a firm grip on the staff again, he looked amused. "I don't know how it's shielded from my attack. I would have loved to turn it into crystal, but it doesn't matter.

I have heard about the sword you hold and rumors are, you have to learn to use its powers. Since you have only been here a few days, you couldn't possibly know enough to use the sword against me. I'm sure you have probably never even trained with a sword before. People from your world seldom do anymore."

Jake watched the goblin as he talked, grinning venomously, spittle flying from his mouth. A few days, Jake thought? Then he realized Medusa's Heir didn't know Father Time had actually stopped time. That meant the goblin didn't know he had trained with Dreaden, learned to use the Sword of Light, and trust his Creator! Then, with that thought came another and Jake realized what Medusa's Heir was trying to accomplish. Father Time had once told him that Medusa's Heir's strongest ability was to use his cleverness to trap others and bend them to his will. That was how he had trapped Isabelle in the first place, through the deal he'd made with her parents.

Jake understood the goblin was trying to do the same thing now. He was using this monologue to get Jake to doubt himself and it had almost worked. If he were to doubt himself, then he would be unable to use the Sword of Light correctly to defeat the goblin. Jake silently said a quick prayer, asking the Creator to continue to help him, and then he looked Medusa's Heir in the eye. He could play this game too!

"You don't understand why your attack didn't work because you don't understand the true nature of this sword. Its true name is the Sword of Light. I didn't come to fight you. If you let Isabelle go, we will leave in peace."

"Oh, so you think you're bold now. Well, I've heard of that sword also and you might be surprised how much I know about it. The sword will do you no good. I was actually hoping you would have it so that, once I defeat you, I could add it to my collection of power. As for the girl, I already told you I have plans for your friend. I guess no one will be leaving peacefully after all."

With that, Medusa's Heir shot another beam of pink light. Jake felt no warning from the sword and he stood his ground. The beam hit him square in the chest, the pink light wrapped around him. It didn't hurt at all. In fact, a gentle warming sensation flowed over him, as the sword gradually turned the pink glow white before it dissipated. Medusa's Heir looked slightly startled to see Jake hadn't turned to crystal and Jake took this opportunity to speak again.

"This is the sword of the Creator. Its power is infinitely more than the staff you stole from the fairies. I am the one chosen to use the Sword of Light. You cannot harm me with the staff. With this sword, I will free Isabelle and return the Crystal Staff to its rightful owners."

"If I cannot harm you with the staff, then you shall die by the sword!" Medusa's Heir shouted, as he ran down and jumped from the stairs with inhuman speed. He landed near Jake, swinging the sword in his right hand. Jake managed to block the hit with his shield, but the blow was so hard it dented his shield, causing pain to course up his arm. Jake quickly sidestepped away, before the goblin could use his sword again. The goblin was crafty, however, and instead of striking again immediately with his sword, the goblin used the staff, grazing Jake's shield as he maneuvered away.

The shield instantly turned to crystal and got heavier, almost too heavy for Jake to hold. The goblin was counting on this and rushed at Jake, swinging his sword down on Jake's. Jake barely had time to lift his now heavy shield into place. This time, Jake's shield shattered into pieces from the impact. Jake was knocked backwards. He landed on his back, blinking rapidly, trying to keep the tiny crystal shards, which were flying everywhere, from getting in his eyes while still trying to watch the goblin. Fortunately, the goblin must not have counted on all the little shards of crystal, because he appeared to be having the same problem and was trying to clear his eyes as well.

Jake quickly rolled into a crouched position then stood, gripping the Sword of Light in both hands as it transformed into an agile double-handed sword that would be easy to use with one or both of his hands. The goblin stared at Jake for a moment with hatred in his eyes.

"Well, that was a neat trick," he growled, charging at Jake, using both his sword and the staff to strike.

Jake held the sword of light and tried to fend off the first volley of attacks. He was barely able to keep up with the unnatural speed of the goblin. The goblin swung and stabbed at Jake with a furious volley, trying to cut Jake down. Jake faltered slightly, almost getting his arm sliced by the goblin's sword, and received a nasty knock to his right arm as he overcorrected. The goblin then knocked Jake's sword outward and kicked him in the side.

Jake stumbled and retreated toward Isabelle, trying to keep himself between this evil creature and her. Jake glanced sideways and saw his sister and friends watching, but unable to break through the crystal barrier to come and help.

"Relax boy, it's just you and me now. No mettlesome friends to help you. By the way, it's no use trying to protect your little girlfriend from me. I could have destroyed her already, but as I said before, she is serving another purpose."

Jake let go of his side, which had sharp pain shooting through it. He wished now he had put his breast plate back on as it would have lessened the blow. Luckily, he still had some protection with the chainmail he wore. It would keep him safe from a cut, but he would have to avoid hard hits like that one again. Jake kept his eyes on Medusa's Heir and watched the goblin smirk back. "You'll never touch her again!" Jake shouted through his pain.

The goblin laughed. "You don't realize do you? I could shatter her into a million pieces right now, if I wanted to. All I have to do is think it and the staff will obey."

Jake glanced at Isabelle, worried. He looked at the goblin gloating before him. He had to get the Crystal Staff away from him! If he could free Isabelle from her crystal prison, then she would be safe! Jake thought about the bright light he had used before. It was worth a shot. He took a few steps forward, as if to advance upon the goblin, and raised the sword of light, sending out the bright light again. The goblin cried out, trying to block the light with his hands.

Jake took his chance. Instead of running at the goblin, who was farther away, he turned and ran to Isabelle. Now he knew he couldn't risk attacking Medusa's Heir and have the goblin strike out against Isabelle if he became angry. He had to try and free her first and then deal with the goblin. Jake reached her form standing on the pedestal and brought the sword around, touching her and willing her to be free.

Nothing happened and Jake, once again, heard the maniacal laughter behind him. He spun around to see Medusa's Heir grinning as he stood in a bubble of pink light that shielded him from the light of the sword.

"Fool," he spit, still grinning at Jake. "She is trapped by my spell. As you see, even that sword with all its power cannot save her. Think about it. If that is the Creator's sword, you have to believe in the Creator for it to work. Your friend would first need to know and trust her Creator for the Sword to work and I know she doesn't because my spell never would have worked if she had already put her trust in the Creator."

Jake turned quickly to Isabelle and shouted, "Isabelle, trust in the Creator, trust in Him and His Son and you will be free!"

More laughing from Medusa's Heir brought Jake back around. "She doesn't understand what you are saying. Her crystal form keeps her mind foggy, she is only dimly aware of her surroundings."

Jake looked back at Isabelle, feeling hopelessness rising up in his chest. He turned back to Medusa's Heir, realizing he had almost given into the doubt and hopelessness again. The goblin had used the rush attack to distract him and make him forget to trust the Creator again. Jake remembered it wasn't about his strength, but the Creator's strength through him. The Creator wouldn't have brought him this far on a hopeless mission. He whispered a quick prayer and, suddenly, felt more at peace and knew he would be able to match the goblin's speed.

Medusa's Heir put the staff on his back and came rushing up, using both hands to swing his sword at Jake. Jake spun around and, blow by blow, he countered the goblin's attacks. They circled around, each one trying to gain the advantage. Medusa's Heir swung at Jake's stomach. Jake blocked the blow Medusa's Heir had sent, but realized as he blocked it, the goblin was just feigning. It was too late to block the kick that came his way, but he was able to lean back slightly to lessen the blow.

Still, the impact came and threw Jake backwards onto his back and knocked off his helmet. Jake ignored the helmet and used his backwards momentum to roll to his feet and swing his sword up, just in time to meet the goblin's, which was coming down like a hammer to cleave him in two. Jake hit the goblin's sword with the Sword of Light, knocking it right with a loud clang. The goblin hadn't expected Jake to recover so quickly and had put too much strength into his swing. When Jake knocked it to the side, the goblin couldn't stop his own momentum and Jake brought his sword down on the goblin's exposed shoulder. The Sword of Light sliced into the goblin's shoulder and continued down his side a short way.

The goblin screamed in pain and fury as green blood oozed from the wound. Jake readied himself to follow with another blow, thinking Medusa's Heir would retreat, but Jake had underestimated the goblin. Medusa's Heir swung back, knocking the Sword of Light from Jake's hand and smashed into Jake with his good shoulder, knocking Jake to the flat of his back. The Sword of Light went clanging to the ground a few yards away.

"So you're not as much of a novice as I had taken you for," the goblin hissed through gritted teeth, looking at his bleeding shoulder. "I was going to finish you quickly, but now that you have caused me pain, what kind of host would I be if I didn't return the favor." The goblin leapt over to Jake and stood over him, ready to strike.

Jake reached for the Sword of Light and it slid across the floor then flew through the air to Jake's hand, just in time for Jake to deflect the goblin's next blow, taking the creature completely by surprise. Jake immediately bent his legs into a crouched position and kicked the goblin in the stomach with all of his strength, sending Medusa's Heir flying backwards to land on his own back, for once. Jake didn't take any chances and got to his feet quickly, ready for anything.

This time, however, Medusa's Heir didn't recover so quickly. The goblin was trying to get back on its feet, but it was gasping for air like Jake had knocked the wind out of him. As Jake watched the goblin, he could feel pain in his chest, side, and both arms where the goblin had delivered blows. He took a quick stock of himself. The injuries were painful enough to distract him from the fight, but not serious, so he had to ignore them. He kept his eyes on the goblin, who was now standing tall and taking the Crystal Staff in his other hand again.

Suddenly, bursts of pink light erupted from the staff in rapid succession. Jake reacted instinctively, sensing the warning coming from the sword an instant before, and blocked. The sound of crystal hitting the sword echoed around the room. Medusa's Heir was somehow using the staff to shoot sharp crystal like a machine gun. He was able to block the shards, but many of them broke when they hit the sword, causing them to fly in multiple directions. Some of the pieces were starting to cut Jake's hands and arms. He had to do something quick. Then, he remembered how he had sent Sapphire's water back toward her and now, did the same thing with the crystal. Jake focused on the sword and suddenly, the crystal shards stopped hitting the sword and started flying back at the goblin.

Medusa's Heir ducked as he was hit with his own projectiles and he cut off the magic. The goblin screamed at Jake and ran at him, exchanging a fury of blows faster than before. Jake, however, trusted the sword and so he matched and soon surpassed the goblin's speed. The goblin was using both his sword and staff to strike at Jake and was so angry, he was heedless of his own safety. Even though the goblin was striking faster and faster, with his trust in the Sword of Light, Jake now felt like it was almost slow motion. He could see the goblin's attacks almost before the goblin knew them himself. As he parried both the goblin's sword and the staff with ease, Jake saw his opportunity.

The goblin brought his sword around, trying to cut Jake in half and Jake caught the blade on his own, but instead of parrying it, he let its momentum continue while he spun the Sword of Light around it, catching the sword and flipping it out of the goblin's hand. As the goblin realized what had just happened, Jake kicked him, sending him sprawling back to the foot of the stairs, and brought the Sword of Light to within an inch of his neck. The only thing that kept him from ending the miserable creature right then and there was the fact that he hadn't yet figured out how the curse was to be broken.

Medusa's Heir half lay, half sat on the lowest steps that went up to his throne, panting with the Sword of Light ready at his throat. It was then Jake heard it. It was quiet and raspy at first, in between the goblin's panting, but it steadily grew as Medusa's Heir began laughing louder and louder.

Jake hadn't expected this! Anger or perhaps shock, but not laughter! "What's so amusing?" Jake asked looking down on the goblin. "You're beaten, surrender, free Isabelle, and I'll let you live!"

At this, the goblin laughed even harder and then coughed and wheezed before clearing his throat to speak. When he did, his voice changed. It became more powerful and ominous.

"A gift I give but not for free, a payment I will require
But if you wish to refuse me, the consequence will be dire
Once my prize is taken, at my own time and pleasure
To get it back one will need to give in equal measure"

Jake slowly stepped back while keeping the sword leveled at the goblin, struggling to understand.

"You haven't beaten me. Even if you kill me, Isabelle will still be trapped by my spell. The only way to free her permanently from the spell requires a sacrifice. To give in equal measure means a life for a life. Blood must be shed! Even though you have bested me with the sword, you have still lost. To use a human phrase, I never put all my eggs in one basket." Medusa's Heir watched with glee at the look of confusion on Jake's face. "Someone must die for the young woman, but it must be someone not under my curse. Even if her parents tried to help her at the cost of her sister, they are powerless to help. Don't you think they would have come to her rescue otherwise?" the goblin cackled, smiling again.

Could this be true? Jake thought, taking another step back from the goblin, but keeping the Sword of Light ready. The goblin glared back with greedy eyes and Jake understood what he needed to do even before the goblin spoke.

"In order to free your friend, you'll have to surrender the Sword of Light and sacrifice yourself instead." Medusa's Heir instructed, almost gleeful now.

All along, the goblin had a backup plan, or quite possibly, this was his plan from the start. It could be the goblin had wanted the Sword of Light from the beginning, but since he knew he couldn't just take it, this was his plan to get it. Or maybe it had just worked out that way. How this had come to be didn't really matter now, however, because Jake knew what he had to do and there was no sense dwelling on it. He knew there was no other option, but to trust. He sent out a quick prayer, asking the Creator to take care of Isabelle and felt the gentle, peaceful touch of his Maker letting him know everything would be fine.

Jake lowered the Sword of Light and Medusa's Heir rose to his feet, grinning. "Give me the sword, boy," the goblin croaked, mockingly.

Jake turned the sword so the handle faced the goblin. "Here, I surrender to you, take the sword and I'll take Isabelle's place. Let her go."

Medusa's Heir reached out and took the Sword of Light from Jake. "So this is the all-powerful sword." The goblin victoriously held it up, admiring it. "Let's see what it can do!" With that, Medusa's Heir lashed out with the Sword of Light and stabbed Jake directly through his heart.

Jake gasped, unbelieving for a moment, before he looked down to see the sword he had been entrusted with sticking out of him. He heard muffled screams coming from behind him as his sister and friends saw what had happened from the other side of the crystal wall. As he looked at the sword, it suddenly changed form, from the elegant sword he had been using to a one handed, curved, and wicked-looking black blade. His mind was getting foggy now and he struggled to stay aware. He wanted to know Isabelle was safe.

Behind him, Isabelle started to change from her crystalline form. Pink light emanated from her as the hard pink crystal changed to soft skin. The clothes she was wearing turned back to cotton and suddenly, she breathed in, gasping for breath.

Medusa's Heir pulled the sword from Jake and stood admiring it, its curved, black surface glowing violet. "It is said the Sword of Light can never be used for evil, if it is, it will be destroyed. Now, the most powerful sword ever has been corrupted. It is no longer the Creator's sword, but mine. It is no longer the Sword of Light, but a Sword of Darkness and I will use it to conquer everything!"

Jake stumbled to his knees and held his hands over his heart. It was an involuntary gesture; he knew he couldn't stop the flow of blood. There was too much.

Jake was having trouble thinking clearly, but he heard movement behind him. "Where am…What? Jake!" Jake could hear the alarm in Isabelle's voice as she ran to his side. He wished he could speak. He wished he could tell her everything was going to be okay. He wished he could comfort her. Most of all, he wished he could tell her to leave while the goblin was still distracted, but he couldn't. He was barely able to breathe now.

Isabelle reached him and threw herself down and pulled him onto her lap, cradling him and weeping. "Jake, what happened? What can I do? Please stay with me," she choked in between sobs. Jake looked up into Isabelle's eyes, still unable to speak. He was fading quickly now, but could see Isabelle's beautiful, tear stained face leaning over him. It was the last vision he had as everything went black.

"Jake!" Isabelle screamed at the top of her lungs. "Jake no, no, no!"

"Shut up you little whelp!" Medusa's Heir shouted, coming out of his reverie with the sword. "Yes, your friend is dead because he tried to save you! Unfortunately, your naive friend didn't think this through. Now that he's gone, there is no one to stop me from putting you back into your living crystal prison or from destroying you completely. Don't worry, your pain will be short lived."

Isabelle hadn't even seen the monster until he spoke because she had been too focused on Jake. She continued weeping; not knowing who the goblin was, where she was, how she got here, or what she could do. All she knew was that the young man she had loved for years, her best friend, was now lifeless in her arms.

Medusa's Heir smiled and raised the crystal staff in his left hand, ready to strike at Isabelle. She held Jake even tighter, ready for something terrible when suddenly, the goblin yelled as if in pain. He dropped the Crystal Staff and grabbed his right arm as the staff clanged to the ground. He tried shaking the sword like he was trying to let go, but could not. Isabelle watched in confusion, not sure what was happening. Then, a crack that sounded like thunder echoed from the twisted black sword. The violet light, which had been coming from it, turned blood red. The sword started to hum and it swung to point at Jake. Medusa's Heir growled in pain and frustration as he couldn't let go, but also seemed unable to control the sword either. His hand throbbed now and the pain was increasing.

"I don't understand," he shouted. "What's happening!"

Isabelle saw the sword pointing at Jake and covered him, knowing he was beyond protection and yet, she couldn't bear the thought of anything else happening to him. She peeked up, just as a red beam shot from the sword and struck Jake, enveloping him. Isabelle tried holding onto Jake, but was gently pushed away by the red light surrounding him. The beam coming from the sword stopped, but the red light surrounding Jake continued to pulse and swirl. Little by little, the light started to change. The intensity of the red lessened and it faded to pink and then, to a soft white light. For a moment, the soft white light lifted Jake from the ground and then turned blindingly bright. Both Isabelle and Medusa's Heir clenched their eyes shut.

As quickly as the light had come, it lessened and disappeared. Isabelle opened her eyes and stifled a cry with her hand. There, before her, standing beside the puddle of his own blood, was Jacob Cross, completely healed and smiling back. She jumped up and ran to Jake as he stood with open arms and they embraced, holding each other tightly, tears coming from both sets of eyes. From the other side of the crystal wall, Alisha, TJ, Patrick, and Eric were completely silent, staring open mouthed, unable to believe what they had just witnessed.

"No! This can't be happening!" shouted Medusa's Heir, as much from the pain in his arm as from the miracle he had just witnessed. "No," he shouted again. "You're dead! I killed you. The sword is under my control; it must obey me now!" The goblin raged, still unable to tear his grip from the sword.

Jake turned to face the goblin as Isabelle continued to hold him tight. "That sword will never obey you, it was entrusted to me, remember," Jake boldly stated, with authority ringing from his voice.

The goblin sputtered, "No, I used it for evil...to kill you! It should be corrupted now; I should be its new master!"

Jake spoke again, calmly and clearly, yet his voice rang louder and more powerful than ever before, as if the Creator was giving him the words to speak. "You failed because you still don't understand the true power of the Sword of Light. It is the Creator's sword and the Creator alone is its master. It was only entrusted to me; I was never its master. You knew this sword was one of the only powers that could defeat you and you correctly heard it could never be used for evil. However, you mistook the meaning. You thought if the sword was used for evil and corrupted, it would be destroyed or its allegiance would change just like the Crystal Staff's allegiance changed when you killed its last bearer. In fact, after a long while of thinking about it, your greed consumed you and you became sure, if you could just get the sword, you would possess its power. But the sword was protected. At first, you tried having me killed, but once I made it to the granite castle to retrieve the Sword of Light, you thought you could use this to your advantage and you hatched this plan.

"Your mistake was, you never realized the Sword of Light's true nature. The Sword of Light can never be used for evil because it is the Creator's sword and the Creator is incapable of evil. That is why I died, but now I'm healed. You meant my death for evil, but instead it freed Isabelle, which was good, so the sword allowed me to die. But because you intended my death as evil, I was healed and your evil intentions were not allowed to win. And now, you can't let go of the sword because, in your arrogance, you thought yourself above the Creator." Jake paused and let his words sink in. "Now, your arrogance has destroyed you." Jake said, his words ringing with authority that was not his own.

Medusa's Heir screamed and, with all his might, he tried swinging the sword at Jake, but the sword didn't budge.

It stayed suspended in midair, pointing at where Jake had lain and still, the goblin couldn't let go. It was as if an electric current ran through the sword, keeping his muscles clenched around it. He even tried using his other arm to reach out for a weapon, but it to was now stuck where he had grabbed his sword arm. The goblin's vision became fuzzy as the pain increased. Both of his arms felt like they were on fire, burning from the inside out, yet, at the same time, felt as if they were being crushed from the outside, pushing inward on themselves. The feeling continued to spread to his entire body. He tried screaming again, but the pain was so blinding now that he couldn't even summon the breath to do so.

Jake and Isabelle held each other tightly as they watched Medusa's Heir crumple before their eyes. His body broke out in a white-hot fire and yet, Jake and Isabelle felt no heat from just a few feet away. They watched as the goblin turned to grey ash that started falling like fine dust, which burned up and evaporated before it reached the floor. After a few more moments, Medusa's Heir was no more, completely gone from existence. The Sword of Light hung unsupported in the air, still twisted and black.

Jake lifted his arm and held out his hand. The Sword of Light turned so its handle faced him and flew over. Isabelle jumped, but Jake held onto her with his other arm. "It's alright, it won't hurt us." As Jake grabbed hold of it, the sword transformed back into the elegant two-handed version Jake had been fighting with. Jake glanced over at his sister and friends, still stuck behind the crystal, looking dumbstruck over the events of the past few minutes. "Look who came to help me rescue you." Jake laughed, using the sword to point.

Isabelle smiled through her tears and waved at their friends. Alisha was the first to snap out of it and waved back, beaming, though her cheeks were still wet from tears as well.

"How about we let them in?" Jake asked, walking Isabelle over to the Crystal Staff and letting go of her only long enough to sheath the sword and pick up the staff. Jake knew it would respond to him now, without even thinking about it. He held it up and the crystal wall separating their friends melted away and they came running and jumping, hugging and crying. After a few minutes of hugs, hand shaking, back slapping, cheering, and thanks, Isabelle, who was still overwhelmed and not sure of anything, voiced her concern.

"I don't understand. What happened, where are we, and why are we here?"

So as a group they sat down, there in the large empty throne room, and Jake explained everything he knew about her disappearance and his journey to rescue her. It took some time, but Isabelle was patient. After what she had just witnessed, she knew Jake was telling the truth. The others chimed in when Jake recounted their parts and after they were done, Isabelle sat quietly, holding Jake's hand, and crying tears of joy for the friends who had loved her enough to risk everything to rescue her. Jake sat next to her, content to feel the warmth of her hand in his again.

After a while, she dried her tears and looked at the group. "I think it's time I got to know the Creator like you all have."

With her friends circled around her, praying with her, Isabelle put her trust in her Creator, the One who loved her more than any other.

Chapter 30

Reunion

The group was just finishing up their prayer and wondering how they were going to find their way out when they heard a noise behind them from the direction they had entered the castle. As one, they reached for their weapons, wondering if some of Medusa's Heir's servants had come back to take revenge for their master's destruction. Instead of an enemy though, they saw a short form enter the room through the hallway they had used. It was a dwarf, which looked exactly like the statue they had seen when they had walked through the castle. Next came the tall elf who had stood at his side. Soon, more creatures entered. They were all the same statues they had passed while coming through the castle.

Of course! They weren't actually statues, but living beings frozen in crystal form like Isabelle had been, now freed because the goblin was destroyed. Jake understood now why the goblin had been called Medusa's Heir. They walked, unsure of themselves, as if coming out of a daze, not understanding what had happened.

"It's okay," Jake said, sheathing the Sword of Light. "We are friends!"

The group of creatures came to stand before Jake. The dwarf, who had first entered spoke, his voice was gruff, but strong. "How have we come to be free, human?"

"Medusa's Heir has been destroyed. You will never have to fear him again," replied Jake.

"I'm guessing we have you to thank for this?"

Jake nodded, "We helped, however, it was the Creator who truly defeated him."

"Nevertheless, if you had not come, we would still be in our crystal prisons," responded the dwarf, bowing as the creatures behind him followed suit.

When they stood, the dwarf addressed them again with urgency in his voice. "Have you been to the dungeons?"

"No," answered Jake, "why?"

"We were a rescue party who came to rescue the prisoners Medusa's Heir had locked in his dungeon. We were captured along the way, but I managed to locate them in the dungeon before I was caught. Unless the goblin moved them, they may still be there. They are probably still locked in their cells. We need to free them before we go."

"Of course," Isabelle responded, stepping up beside Jake and grabbing his hand. "Show us the way."

Jake smiled and squeezed her hand lovingly. He couldn't put into words how good it felt to have her by his side once again. He was bruised, sore, and had cuts all over, but barely noticed now that Isabelle was safe and holding his hand again.

Jake's group followed the newly freed rescue party out a side door from the throne room, down a staircase, through some winding corridors, and down a spiral stair. The stair ended in a wide room with a low ceiling. There were chains, manacles, and stocks around the room; it seemed as if it were a holding room of sorts. It was otherwise empty. The dwarf in the lead took them through the room to a stairway on the other side, which led them further down into a hallway lined with cells on both sides.

They quickly made their way down, checking the cells. Most were empty, their doors standing open, but near the end, they heard voices. They rushed to the few cells left and Jake used the Sword of Light to cut through the locks and free the prisoners. There was a joyous reunion as the group of rescuers greeted and hugged the prisoners they had come to save before they too had been trapped.

There were dwarves, elves, centaurs, fairies, and even a few creatures Jake didn't recognize, all overjoyed to be free.

One of the fairies, a young man with deep purple hair and wings flew over to Jake. "Thank you for coming for us. My name is Valance and I am Prince of the Fairies. On behalf of all my kin, I thank you!" With that, the fairy bowed while hovering midair.

Jake smiled. "Prince you say?"

Valance looked up, questioningly.

"I know three young women who will be very glad to see you."

"You've seen my sisters?" the prince exclaimed. "How…where are they? Are they alright?"

"They helped me get here. We were separated up in the valley when we were ambushed, but if I know them, they are just fine. I'd bet on them no matter what the odds."

"So would I," Valance responded, chuckling, "they were always smarter and wiser than I."

"Speaking of that, I don't mean to be rude, but you are small enough to have flown out through the bars. How were you trapped?" Jake asked.

"We were turned into crystal statues for that very reason. Actually, everyone imprisoned here was. We were all freed from the crystal a short while ago, but I wasn't about to leave without freeing everyone else. We were just discussing a plan on how to get everyone else out when you came along." Valance responded.

"Well, if that is everyone, does anyone know the way out of this dump? I'm ready for some sunshine…err or whatever lights the sky here." Alisha spoke from the back of the group.

"Can we not go out the way you came in?" asked the dwarf leading the rescue party.

"No, the entrance to the ramp coming down was kind of destroyed after we came in." TJ responded.

"Plus, as much as I like mazes, I'd rather not have to go through the one surrounding the castle again," Alisha stated.

Jake's group laughed as the others just looked at them.

Valance spoke up. "I know Medusa's Heir had several secret entrances he used to come and go. I believe one of them is in the throne room above. It shouldn't take too long to find."

They turned to leave when Isabelle tugged on Jake's arm. "Did we check the last cell?"

Jake looked and saw the cell at the end of the hall was still closed. There had been no sound coming from it, so he hadn't paid attention to it. They walked over and looked into it. There, in the back corner, was one of the largest trolls Jake had ever seen. It sat with its back to them. Jake hesitated.

"What's wrong?" Isabelle whispered.

"All the trolls I have met have tried to kill me," he whispered back.

"I think this one may be different," Isabelle whispered. "I doubt he's in here for being a good servant."

She had a point.

Isabelle stepped forward and spoke to the troll. "Would you like to be free?"

The troll turned slightly and spoke in a strong, but sorrow filled voice. "Just leave me be, I deserve to rot in here," he responded and turned back to stare at the wall.

Jake stepped forward, his eyes drifting around the room. "From what I have learned about the Creator, He's all about second chances." With that, Jake cut the lock. The door swung open. "Now it's your choice, you can stay here or you can come with us."

Jake took Isabelle's hand and they followed the others back up to the throne room, Jake kept an eye out behind them. He didn't see the troll follow. They arrived back in the room to find the others waiting.

"So, where should we start looking?" he asked.

"I can show you the way." Came a voice from behind. Jake and Isabelle turned and the rest of the group tensed and reached for their weapons as the hulking form of the troll came from the side hall.

"It's okay," Isabelle insisted, seeing the group's reaction. "He was a prisoner too."

"I don't expect you to trust me, but I tell the truth when I say I mean you no harm," stated the troll, with his head still downcast. "Please, just let me retrieve one thing before we go."

With that, the troll turned and ran off into the castle. Within a few minutes, he returned with something in his hand.

"Prince Valance, I believe this is yours." The troll opened up his hand and inside it was a miniature palace made out of crystal.

"But how?" Valance questioned, as he flew over and looked at the object. "We thought it had been destroyed."

"No, not destroyed. When Medusa's Heir took control of your staff and you all fled, he used it to shrink your home and kept it in his fortress as a trophy. Only a few of his trusted servants knew where it was. I used to be one of them. I will carry it to the surface for you if you would like. Then, you may be able to put it back to the way it was."

"Thank you," Valance responded with tears in his eyes. "We are in your debt."

"No, it is but a small repayment for the evil I have contributed to."

"So, where was this way out you were talking about?" TJ asked, coming up behind Jake.

"This way." The large troll walked around the rest of the creatures toward the throne. Instead of going to the stairs, however, the troll walked around them and the platform toward the back wall. Jake and Isabelle came next, followed by the rest of the group. When they neared the back wall, Jake realized the structure holding the platform where the thrones stood had a doorway at the bottom, next to the back wall. It was covered by a thick curtain. There must be a room beneath the thrones. They followed the troll into a dark, dusty place, which looked as if it used to be a kitchen of sorts. The space was lit by a single torch on the back wall. The troll went over and stood by the torch and waited for everyone to enter the chamber, which was clearly not made to hold this many people at once.

When they were all assembled, the troll turned and, with his hand, he pressed on a stone four down and three to the left of the torch. A panel of stone in the wall slid noiselessly down to be even with the floor and Jake could see a hallway beyond. "This will take us back to the surface," announced the troll.

When they arrived at the surface, it took everyone a moment to adjust to the light of Under Earth's sky again. Isabelle turned to Jake, "I know you told me about this," she said, turning in all directions, "But this is amazing!" She continued turning, looking at the sky and the trees.

Jake looked around as well. They had come out from behind a group of large boulders, through some bushes and Jake could see they had come up on the opposite side of the valley, behind the Brightstone. They made their way around to the front where they found the group of allies and the three dragons who had helped them. Cheers erupted from both sides as the warriors and prisoners saw each other.

Jake was relieved to see no one appeared to be missing. Many of the warriors were injured, some worse than others, but all of them were in good spirits once they saw Jake's group come into view.

The three fairies were the first to reach Jake. "Jake you made it!" Fieora exclaimed, flying up and landing on his shoulder and trying to hug his neck even though her arms didn't reach all the way around.

"It's about time!" Sapphire exclaimed sarcastically, trying to look exasperated through her beaming smile.

"We are very glad to see you Jake," Claira said. "And this must be Isabelle."

Jake smiled as he introduced her to the fairies. After the introductions, Jake turned to the fairies and saw that

Valance had snuck around behind his sisters before they had seen him. "By the way, I ran into someone else you three might be interested to see."

All three spun as one when Valance spoke, "So, how have my three favorite sisters been?"

The next moment, Jake, Isabelle, Alisha, Patrick, TJ, and Eric all started laughing uncontrollably as the three sisters tackled their brother midair and all four fairies went tumbling into a pile of long, soft grass.

The merriment in the valley lasted a while as old friends were reunited and new friends were made. Jake took Isabelle around to meet all the creatures who had helped with her rescue. She was a bit hesitant at first when Jake led her over to Crimson, Ocean, and Sunstrike, but warmed up to them quickly after speaking with them. They were resting behind the rest of the group, looking better than when Jake had last seen them fighting. Apparently, they could use the fire they breathed not only to destroy, but to heal each other.

Last of all, Jake took Isabelle over to meet Gadlonin, Eventine, and Tallin. After making introductions, Jake pulled Eventine aside and talked with him briefly about the troll who had helped them get back to the surface. "If he is truly repentant and has changed his ways, I will make sure he is welcomed."

Eventine addressed the group and told them about the troll. Valance also let the group know what the troll had done for the fairies by saving their home. Afterward, the troll came from behind the Brightstone, still carrying the small crystal palace.

"I don't deserve forgiveness, but if the Creator is willing, I will serve him from now on." With that he set the Crystal Palace on the ground near Jake, who was still carrying the Crystal Staff in his left hand and holding Isabelle's hand with his right.

Jake then asked Claira to come over and discussed an idea he had with her. She nodded in agreement and went to tell the other fairies. Afterwards, Jake called everyone in the valley over and told them of his plan. The fairies then shrunk everyone, except the dragons, down to their size and floated everyone up to the top of the Brightstone. The dragons, with their keen sense of sight and hearing, were able to take part, even though they stayed where they were.

Jake then presented the Crystal Staff to Valance who, Jake now realized, was about the same age as he was. "I, the bearer of the Sword of Light defeated Medusa's Heir with the Creator's help and so, won the allegiance of the Crystal Staff. However, this staff is not mine to keep. It was wrongfully taken from the fairies. I now give you Valance, Prince of the Fairies, the Crystal Staff to use for the benefit of your people. Its allegiance is now yours."

Valance reached out and took the staff in his hands, a tear rolling down his cheek. "I'm not sure I'm worthy enough to accept this responsibility."

Jake laughed. "Of course you're not! Just like I'm not worthy enough to wield this sword," he responded, holding up the Sword of Light. "Yet, I believe the Creator still entrusts it to you. If you keep that attitude and listen to the wise council of your sisters, I think you will do just fine. Besides," Jake responded, smiling, "I think from the conversations I've had with your sisters, your father would have wanted you to have it."

"Thank you, Jake," Valance responded as fresh tears ran down all the fairies' cheeks now. "Now, let's put our home back where it belongs." With that, Valance pointed the staff at the small palace. A rainbow of light enveloped the palace and Valance used the staff's power to pick it up and shift it to the center of the Brightstone where it grew in size. A few minutes later, it took up almost the entire top of the Brightstone. Everyone in the valley cheered at seeing the fairies' home restored to its rightful place. Even the dragons let loose a roar of triumph, which was so loud everyone else had to cover their ears until they were done.

Now, standing in front of the palace, the building was enormous. If both were measured to the same scale, Jake thought this palace was probably even larger than the goblins' stone fortress they had just come from. Even fairy-sized, it was still large. Jake could also see now, the palace was not made out of just pink crystal, but of many different colors. They were in just the right place to compliment the whole structure and make it look very grand. From yellows and blues to greens and reds and even grey and silver. It seemed the colorful forest and plants around them were all taken into account when the palace was made. Jake didn't know why it had looked pink when it was small, but it wasn't pink anymore.

Jake would have said it resembled a rainbow of colors, except that description wouldn't do it justice. There were so many colors artfully and skillfully placed, that it allowed the palace to shine in Under Earth's sky without blinding the person looking at it.

"Jake."

Jake turned to see Sapphire hovering nearby.

"I know you and your friends need to get going soon, but we were hoping you could all come on a small tour of our home before you left."

Jake looked at the group around him and all were nodding *yes* rather excitedly. He grinned. "We would be honored to be the first guests in your newly restored home."

It took a little over an hour, but felt like only minutes as Claira, Sapphire, Fieora, and Valance showed off their childhood home. The group had an amazing time looking through the castle and seeing some of the most fascinating things made from crystal. They even saw many life-like statues and sculptures, which had never been living things, but were carved from crystal, originally, Claira assured them. They were also able to see where the sisters' family lived, where their favorite places to get away or have fun were, as well as their favorite childhood hiding places and some of the stories of the games or pranks they had used them for.

Afterward, Jake's group stood on the ground in front of the Brightstone, returned to normal size, and said their thanks and goodbyes. Many of their new friends and allies had left for their homes just after the Crystal Staff was presented to Valance. The only ones left were Gadlonin, Eventine, and Tallin, along with the fairies.

"We can never thank you enough for what you have done, Jacob Cross." Claira spoke, smiling gratefully.

"We'll miss you too!" Fieora cried, wiping away a small tear.

"Yeah, don't be a stranger. Come back and visit often," Sapphire said, with a mischievous grin. "We'd like the chance to get to know Alisha and Isabelle better. I'm still dying to know how either of them has been able to put up with you so long."

"Ha," Valance laughed from beside his sisters. "Probably the same way you three have put up with me, by finding unique ways to torture him every chance they get!" he responded, grinning at the three glares that came his way.

"Thanks for the support," Jake laughed.

"Hey, I've got your back! You rescued me from prison, the least I can do is rescue you from my sisters," Valance joked and held up his hands in surrender.

"I think you may have chosen the more dangerous of the two," Jake responded, smiling.

"You can count on some visits, Sapphire," Isabelle said, squeezing Jake's hand. "I haven't seen half of the things Jake has told me about yet."

"Yeah, I need to get my bag and our coats from your tree home and I suppose it would be nice to actually come when I'm not being chased and hunted." Jake replied.

"We'll see about that!" Sapphire fired back.

At that, the group broke out in laughter again.

"Have a safe trip back," Valance said.

"They will," Eventine replied. "Gadlonin, Tallin, and I will accompany them to make sure."

The group left the valley through the Forest of Forgetfulness and Jake led them with the Sword of Light. Once on the other side, Jake let Eventine take the lead. Jake held Isabelle's hand the whole way back, talking to her and Alisha, who walked on Isabelle's other side. TJ and Eric were up front talking to Eventine and Gadlonin trying to explain the concepts of football and basketball. The elves not only missed the concept of the sports, they also kept confusing the two, asking if it was difficult to throw the football through the hoop to get a field goal or why they had to dribble the basketball and not just carry it for a touchdown.

Behind Jake, Patrick and Tallin were talking about some of the different plants and what they could be used for.

The group reached the gateway cavern entrance and said their final goodbyes to Eventine, Gadlonin, and Tallin. Isabelle stood on the small ledge with Alisha for a few long moments, taking in the full view for the first time.

Isabelle turned to Alisha. "I've never told you before, but I'm thankful for your constant encouragement, Alisha. You have always treated me like a sister and made me a part of your family. Without that relationship, and your invitations and encouragement to come to church with you and Jake, I don't think I would have been ready to accept the Creator, even after this experience."

"Hey, what are sisters for?" Alisha responded, hugging Isabelle.

The group made their way through the tunnels and caverns, pausing a few moments for Isabelle to take in the Guardians, which rose before them when Jake used the sword. They reached the small cavern, which again seemed just big enough to fit them all. They all held hands while Jake told them what to expect. He then used the Sword of Light to once again open the gateway that took them back to the surface.

Chapter 31

A Walk

It was a beautiful spring morning as Jacob Cross stepped out of his front door. There was a slight breeze coming from the west. It was a cool morning, but not the kind which sent chills down one's back. Instead, it was a refreshing and energizing cool with the early scents of flowers in the air and the songs of birds just returned from their winter migration.

Jake turned and called back inside the house, "I'm going to Tobias' house, be back in a while."

His mom called back, "Okay, but remember, we're meeting your father and sister for lunch at the Snack Shack near the park. Tell Isabelle to come with if she's available."

Jake turned and heard his mom come to the door. "Wait, Jake," she said, a slightly worried expression on her face. She walked over and hugged him. "Be sure you don't disappear again, alright?"

"I promise," he assured her, squeezing her back and kissing her on the cheek before turning and walking down to the sidewalk. His mother smiled as she watched him go. It was Saturday and two weeks to the day since they had returned from Under Earth. He thought back on that day. They had gone back to Jake and Alisha's house where their parents, Isabelle's family, as well as TJ's, Patrick's, and Eric's families, had been waiting nervously for a day and a half. Thinking back, Jake could see that his parents had been upset, but their relief upon seeing Alisha and him, and the sight of Isabelle's reunion with her family, made them forget their anger. Everyone was hugging each other and happy to have their loved ones back. Rachel was the first to meet Isabelle and give her a giant hug.

The group had all moved inside Jake's house where they crammed into the living room while Jake started at the beginning of the story again. He started with his walk to school, then his experience in the caverns, meeting the fairies, Father Time, his training with Dreaden and the Sword of Light. It took a while, but his parents and the others just sat and listened without interrupting. Jake wasn't sure whether it was because they couldn't refute his story with Alisha and his friends as witnesses or, quite possibly, it was too unbelievable, so they just sat there trying to take in what they couldn't comprehend. It also may have helped that Isabelle's parents, having a little more knowledge about what had been happening, had prepared them.

When Jake finished explaining his training and his new faith in his Creator, he noticed his parents smiling for the first time while he had been talking. Jake brought out the Sword of Light which had curiously changed back into its book form.

"Mom, Dad, believe it or not, this is the Sword of Light entrusted to me by the Creator." Jake handed the book to his dad who opened it and looked at it for a minute and then handed it to Jake's mom. His dad looked up. "It almost looks like it is a type of Bible."

Jake laughed. "Dad, I think it may be *The Bible*, the original."

At that, both of his parents looked up, slightly dumbfounded, as if it was the strangest thing they had heard so far that day.

Jake reached out and took the book from his mother's hands and then went to stand in an open area away from the others where he once again transformed the book back into the elegant hand-and-a-half sword. The Sword of Light glowed with a soft silvery light, illuminating every face in the room.

Afterwards, Jake, with the help of his friends and sister, finished telling the story of how they had rescued Isabelle. When they were done, all of the adults were looking at their children, beaming at them all with tears in their eyes. After the telling was done, TJ, Patrick, and Eric's families took their leave, saying they should be getting home. Isabelle's family stayed for a while longer, talking with Jake's, and then, with their daughters between them, they also left.

Then, Jake's parents called the police and explained that Jake had snuck off to see Isabelle at her aunt's house without telling them. An officer came to their house to take Jake's statement and sternly warned him not to do something so foolish again. Jake had promised he wouldn't and their missing person report on him was closed.

The last two weeks had been fairly boring. Jake, and everyone who had been to Under Earth, had changed. Some things that had seemed important before no longer mattered to them as much. The group also felt slightly alienated, knowing they had experienced something the people around them would probably never believe or understand.

Jake took a deep breath as he walked down the sidewalk on Kingman toward Iola. The air was fresh and pleasant. Jake's favorite season was usually fall, but he was really enjoying this spring since returning from Under Earth. It felt like a new beginning and Jake loved it. Jake glanced up as he neared Iola to see Isabelle waiting, her brown wavy hair fluttering slightly in the breeze. She was just wearing a green turtle neck and jeans, but Jake once again thought she looked extravagant standing there, smiling.

"Hey stranger," she said, as he approached.

"Hey back," he responded with a smile and took her arm in his as they turned down Iola.

"So, did Tobias tell you why he wanted us to meet him?" Jake asked, turning his head to look at Isabelle.

"No," she answered, looking back. "I thought you'd know."

They reached Tobias' house and walked up to the door, knocking once. A few moments later the old, white haired man appeared, opening the door and smiling. He was wearing hiking clothes and had a pack slung over his shoulder.

"Going somewhere?" Jake asked.

Tobias smiled and opened the door wider, ushering them into his living room. "In fact I am, and I'm glad you two have finally arrived!" the old man answered as he closed the door behind them and rushed around the room, grabbing a few last minute items and putting them in his bag.

"The fairies have accorded me a special honor for my part in helping you, which in turn helped them. Valance paid me a visit last night and told me they would be honored if I would come and visit them for a few weeks so they could thank me and show me around Under Earth. You see, I have been its gatekeeper for a long time now, but I could only ever go into the caverns. I have never been past the guardians into Under Earth. Valance will use the Crystal Staff to get me through and I will go stay at the Crystal Palace.

"Congratulations!" Jake cried. "So why did you have us come?"

"Well, since it is my job to be the gatekeeper, I wouldn't be able to go unless someone were here to keep an eye on the gateway. I would like to ask both of you if you would be willing to be confirmed as temporary keepers. You wouldn't have to stay here or anything, but I would teach you how to use the flute and temporarily transfer keeper authority to you, so that if something should go awry you would be alerted.

Isabelle squeezed Jake's hand and he looked into her eyes. They each knew what the other was thinking and Isabelle turned to Tobias, "Of course we will. You go and have a good time."

Tobias smiled. "I'm glad to hear it! Now, if you would come over here." He led them over to the stand with the instrument and took it out, teaching them the song and how to play it. For the next hour, both of them took turns practicing while Tobias watched.

When he was confident they had memorized it, he put the flute away and handed them each a key to his house. "I don't think you will need to use these because, more than likely, the next few weeks while I'm gone will be uneventful, but just in case." He instructed with a small wink. "Now, I must be off."

Jake and Isabelle followed Tobias out the front door, which he locked behind them. Just as they went down the porch steps, they heard a noise and looked up to see a faint spinning motion by the tree and when it stopped, they saw a fairy hovering by the tree.

"Nice to see you again Valance," Jake greeted, walking up. The youthful fairy now wore dark red robes that were richly decorated and held the Crystal Staff.

"It is good to see you as well, Jake and Isabelle. My sisters regret they were unable to come today, but they are with mother helping her prepare the palace for our people who are still returning from hiding. They did tell me, however, to remind you that you need to come visit soon.

"We will." Isabelle responded, "Though we'll have to wait for Tobias to come back now.

Valance turned to Tobias. "Ready?"

"Yes, although it will be strange not being the one to open the gateway."

Valance smiled. "Glad to be of service."

The fairy perched on Tobias' shoulder and turned to Jake and Isabelle. "See you soon."

"Have fun, Tobias!" Isabelle said.

"I'm sure I will," he responded, smiling as a vortex of wind enveloped him and Valance.

Jake looked at Isabelle. "You're invited to lunch if you want to come."

She smiled back. "Of course, how about you take a walk with me until then?"

"As long as you don't disappear on me again," Jake responded, smiling back.

"Not a chance!" she insisted and grabbed his hand.

Jake and Isabelle walked hand in hand down Iola, off into the beautiful day!

Acknowledgements

I have loved writing since I was young. I always wanted to write a book but never thought seriously about it until a few years ago. I was walking through my neighborhood with Mocha, my adorable Chocolate Lab, when I turned down a street named Iola. It was a cool, crisp day with a light dusting of snow on the ground and, as I neared the bend in the street, I got this feeling. A story started forming in my mind and I just had to write it! Thanks, Mocha.

I walked home and excitedly told Andrea, my wife, I wanted to write a novel. She encouraged me. I quickly wrote the first six chapters and then, nothing. I knew how I wanted it to end but didn't know how to get there. I was frustrated and put the project down for a while. Andrea continued to encourage me and I eventually picked it back up. She supported me through the whole process with encouragement, by being my sounding board, my first editor, and allowing me time to work. For all that, thank you.

Thank you to my parents, Jack and Wanda, who have always been a huge support and encouragement. You're the best parents a son could have. Mom, thanks for braving the minefield and helping edit one of my first rough drafts and sharing your thoughts.

Thank you to my in-laws, Dick and Penny, who read through that same rough draft and let me marry their awesome daughter. Thanks Penny, for also helping edit that minefield and sharing your thoughts.

Thank you to Brian Darr, friend and fellow author, who's advice and assistance editing was huge help.

To my sister, Amy, thank you for taking time out of your schedule to edit and share your thoughts.

Thank you to Elizabeth Hunt for helping me finish the editing process. You did a great job.

Thank you to my nephews, Dylan and Zach, who listened to me read one of my rough drafts out loud and waited patiently while I fixed errors along the way.

Lastly but most importantly, I thank the Creator, my Lord and Savior, Jesus Christ, through whom all of this is possible. To you be the glory, always!

About the Author

Nicholas Konz lives in Des Moines, Iowa with his beautiful wife Andrea, his cool nephews Dylan and Zachary, and his lovable lab Mocha. He has always had a passion for great stories and now enjoys writing his own. He is currently working on the next book in the Under Earth series and enjoying the journey along the way.

New International Version. Biblica, 2011. BibleGateway.com, www.biblegateway.com/versions/New International-Version-NIV-Bible/#booklist.